Praise for the Chri~~s~~
of #1 *New York Times* b~~~~
Debbie Macomber

"Another of Macomber's heartwarming winners.… Tender, funny, sweet, and poignant, this final installment in the bestselling Cedar Cove series brings back favorite characters and ties things up in a way that will satisfy longtime fans and make new readers anxious to indulge in the earlier titles."
—*Library Journal* on *1225 Christmas Tree Lane*

"Familiar townspeople, three impulsive brothers on the hunt, and a pair of appealing protagonists bring to life this sweet, humorous romance that, with its many obvious parallels, is a satisfying, almost tongue-in-cheek retelling of the Christmas story."
—*Library Journal* on *A Cedar Cove Christmas*

"A lighthearted, decidedly modern retelling of the Christmas story, this is vintage Macomber. Its charm and humor are balanced by the emotional impact of heroine Mary Jo's situation, and many readers will find it irresistible."
—*RT Book Reviews* on *A Cedar Cove Christmas*

"Macomber's take on *A Christmas Carol*…adds up to another tale of romance in the lives of ordinary people, with a message that life is like a fruitcake: full of unexpected delights."
—*Publishers Weekly* on *There's Something About Christmas*

"It's just not Christmas without a Debbie Macomber story."
—*Armchair Interviews*

"No one pens a Christmas story like Macomber and this is one of her best. Sweet, witty and supremely heartfelt, it's truly special and guaranteed to warm even Scrooge's heart."
—*RT Book Reviews* on *There's Something About Christmas*

DEBBIE MACOMBER

Christmas Comes to Cedar Cove

mira

mira

ISBN-13: 978-0-7783-0878-2

Recycling programs
for this product may
not exist in your area.

Christmas Comes to Cedar Cove

Contents

Some of the Residents
of Cedar Cove, Washington

Olivia Lockhart Griffin: Family Court judge in Cedar Cove. Mother of **Justine** and **James**. Married to **Jack Griffin**, editor of the *Cedar Cove Chronicle*. They live at 16 Lighthouse Road. **Eric** and **Shelly** are Jack's son and daughter-in-law, who live out of state.

Charlotte Jefferson Rhodes: Mother of **Olivia** and of **Will Jefferson**. Now married to widower **Ben Rhodes**. Ben and Charlotte have recently moved to an assisted-living facility in Cedar Cove.

Justine (Lockhart) Gunderson: Daughter of Olivia. Mother of **Leif** and **Livvy**. Married to **Seth Gunderson**. The Gundersons owned The Lighthouse restaurant, which was destroyed by fire. Justine then opened The Victorian Tea Room. The Gundersons live at 6 Rainier Drive.

James Lockhart: Olivia's son and Justine's younger brother. Lives in San Diego with his family.

Will Jefferson: Olivia's brother, Charlotte's son. Formerly of Atlanta. Divorced, retired and back in Cedar Cove, where he has taken over the local gallery and has just moved into his mother's former home on Eagle Crest Avenue.

Grace Sherman Harding: Olivia's best friend. Librarian. Widow of **Dan Sherman**. Mother of **Maryellen Bowman** and **Kelly Jordan**. Married to **Cliff Harding**, a retired engineer who is now a horse breeder living in Olalla, near Cedar Cove. Grace's previous address is 204 Rosewood Lane (now a rental property).

Cecilia Randall: Married to **Ian**, who is in the navy. The family was most recently stationed in San Diego but is returning to Cedar Cove. Two children, **Aaron** and **Mia**.

Zachary Cox: Accountant, married to **Rosie**. Father of **Allison** and **Eddie Cox**. The family lives at 311 Pelican Court. Allison is attending university in Seattle, while her boyfriend, **Anson Butler**, has joined the military.

Rachel Peyton (formerly Pendergast): Previously worked at the Get Nailed salon. Married to widower **Bruce Peyton**, who has a daughter, **Jolene**. The Peytons live at 1105 Yakima Street.

Bob and **Peggy Beldon:** Retired. They own the Thyme and Tide B & B at 44 Cranberry Point.

Roy McAfee: Private investigator, retired from Seattle police force. Three adult children, **Mack**, **Linnette** and **Gloria Ashton**. Married to **Corrie**. They live at 50 Harbor Street.

Linnette McAfee: Daughter of Roy and Corrie. Lived in Cedar Cove and worked as a physician assistant in the new medical clinic. Now living in North Dakota.

Mack McAfee: A fireman and paramedic, who moved to Cedar Cove and subsequently married **Mary Jo Wyse**. They have a daughter, **Noelle**, and live at 1022 Evergreen Place.

Gloria Ashton: Sheriff's deputy in Cedar Cove. Natural child of Roy and Corrie McAfee. Pregnant by **Dr. Chad Timmons**, who previously worked at the Cedar Cove medical clinic. He and Gloria had an on-again, off-again relationship but are now a couple.

Troy Davis: Cedar Cove sheriff. Widower. Father of **Megan**. Now married to **Faith Beckwith**, his high school girlfriend, who was also widowed. They live at 92 Pacific Boulevard.

Bobby Polgar and **Teri Miller Polgar:** He is an international chess champion; she was a hairstylist at Get Nailed. They have triplet infant sons. Their home is at 74 Seaside Avenue.

Christie Levitt: Sister of Teri Polgar. Married to **James Wilbur**, Bobby Polgar's friend and driver.

Pastor Dave Flemming: Local Methodist minister. Married to **Emily**. They live at 8 Sandpiper Way and have two sons, **Matthew** and **Mark**.

Shirley Bliss: Widow and fabric artist, mother of Tannith **(Tanni)** Bliss. Recently married artist **Larry Knight**.

Miranda Sullivan: Friend of Shirley's. Also a widow. Now working as an assistant to Will Jefferson in his gallery.

Linc Wyse: Brother of **Mary Jo (Wyse) McAfee**. Formerly of Seattle. Opened a car-repair business in Cedar Cove. Married to **Lori** (who was formerly Lori Bellamy and is from a wealthy area family).

Beth Morehouse: Dog trainer and Christmas tree farm owner. Moved to Cedar Cove three years ago. Divorced from **Kent Morehouse** and mother of two college-age daughters, **Bailey** and **Sophie**. Beth lives at 1225 Christmas Tree Lane.

Ted Reynolds: Cedar Cove veterinarian.

Shaw Wilson: Friend of Tanni's. Works at Mocha Mama, local coffee shop.

Dear Friends,

Anyone who knows me or has read my books for any length of time has figured out that I'm crazy about Christmas. For more years than my feeble memory can recall, I've written an annual Christmas story. It just seemed to make sense, considering how much I love the holiday season.

Now, I have to tell you that this year's story is downright inspired (if I do say so myself!). For not one reason, but two... First, when you start reading *A Cedar Cove Christmas*, you'll quickly recognize the source—the original Christmas story that took place over two thousand years ago. Second, this book is a response to the question most frequently asked by my readers: How come there's only one Cedar Cove book a year? My answer's usually "I'm writing as fast as I can." So this Christmas story is a bonus for all my readers who want more Cedar Cove. (Pay attention to the new characters here, because they're bound to show up in future books!)

My hope is that *A Cedar Cove Christmas* will put you in the Yuletide spirit...and that you'll join your Cedar Cove friends in celebrating Christmas. (And for any readers new to town, let me assure you that you'll quickly figure out who's who and what's what!)

I always enjoy hearing from my readers. You can connect with me on my website at www.debbiemacomber.com or on Twitter, @debbiemacomber, or Instagram. And you can write me at PO Box 1458, Port Orchard, WA 98366.

Merry Christmas, everyone!

Debbie Macomber

A Cedar Cove Christmas

To our dear friends Rhett Palmer
and Claudia Faye Johnson
plus Beni, the cutest dog in the universe.

1

Even though she was listening to Christmas carols on her iPod, Mary Jo Wyse could hear her brothers arguing. How could she not? Individually, the three of them had voices that were usually described as booming; together they sounded like an entire football stadium full of fans. All three worked as mechanics in the family-owned car repair business and stood well over six feet. Their size alone was intimidating. Add to that their voices, and they'd put the fear of God into the most hardened criminal.

"It's nearly Christmas," Linc was saying. He was the oldest and, if possible, loudest of the bunch.

"Mary Jo said he'd call her before now," Mel said.

Ned, her youngest brother, remained suspiciously quiet. He was the sensitive one. Translated, that meant he'd apologize after he broke David Rhodes's fingers for getting his little sister pregnant and then abandoning her.

"We've got to do *something*," Linc insisted.

The determination in his voice gave her pause. Mary Jo's situation was complicated enough without the involvement of her loving but meddlesome older brothers. However, it wasn't *their* fault that she was about to have a baby and the father was nowhere in sight.

"I say we find David Rhodes and string him up until he agrees to marry our sister."

Mary Jo gasped. She couldn't help it. Knowing Linc, he'd have no qualms about doing exactly that.

"I think we should, too—if only we knew where he was," she heard Mel say.

Unable to sit still any longer, Mary Jo tore off her earphones and burst out of her bedroom. She marched into the living room, where her brothers stood around the Christmas tree, beers in hand, as its lights blinked cheerfully. Ever since their parents had been killed in a car accident six years earlier, her older brothers had considered themselves her guardians. Which was ridiculous, since she was over twenty-one. Twenty-three, to be precise. She hadn't been legally of age at the time of their deaths, but her brothers seemed to forget she was now an adult.

All four of them still lived in the family home. Linc and Ned were currently seeing women, but neither relationship seemed very serious. Mel had recently broken up with someone. Mary Jo was the only one eager to leave, chafing as she did at her brothers' attempts to decree how she should live her life.

Admittedly she'd made a mess of things; she couldn't deny it. But she was trying to deal with the consequences, to act like the adult she was. Yes, she'd made a massive error in judgment, falling for an attractive older man and doing what came all too naturally. And no, she didn't need her brothers' assistance.

"Would you guys mind your own business," she demanded, hands on her hips. At five-three she stared up at her brothers, who towered above her.

She probably looked a sight, although at the moment her

appearance was the least of her problems. She was dressed in her old flannel nightgown, the one with the Christmas angels on it, her belly stretched out so far it looked like she'd swallowed a giant snow globe. Her long dark hair fell in tangles, and her feet were bare.

Linc frowned back at her. "You're our sister and that makes you our business."

"We're worried about you," Ned said, speaking for the first time. "You're gonna have that baby any day."

"I don't know nothin' about birthing no babies," Mel added in a falsetto voice.

If he was trying to add humor to the situation, Mary Jo wasn't amused. She glared at him angrily. "You don't have to worry about delivering my baby. This child is my concern and mine alone."

"No, he isn't."

From the very minute she'd tearfully announced her pregnancy four months ago, her brothers had decided the baby was a boy. For some reason, the alternative never seemed to occur to them, no matter how often she suggested it.

"You're depriving this baby of his father," Linc said stubbornly. It was a lament he'd voiced a hundred times over the past months. "A baby *needs* a father."

"I agree," Mary Jo told him. "However, I haven't seen David in weeks."

Mel stepped forward, his disapproval obvious. "What about Christmas? Didn't he tell you he'd be in touch before Christmas?"

"He did." But then David Rhodes had made a lot of promises, none of which he'd kept. "He said he'd be visiting his family in the area."

"Where?" Ned asked.

"Cedar Cove," she supplied and wondered if she should've told her three hotheaded brothers that much.

"Let's go there and find him," Linc said.

Mary Jo held up both hands. "Don't be crazy!"

"Crazy," Linc echoed with a snort of indignation. "I refuse to let you have this baby alone."

"I'm not alone," Mary Jo said. She gestured toward them. "I have the three of you, don't I?"

Her brothers went pale before her eyes. "You...you want us in the delivery room?" Mel asked in weak tones. He swallowed visibly. "You're joking, right?"

Mary Jo had delayed registering for the birthing classes because David had promised to attend them with her. Only he hadn't managed to show up for the first session or the one after that or the following one, either. Giving up on him, Mary Jo had begun a session that week—a lot later in the pregnancy than she should have. She'd gone by herself and left the class in tears. Although she'd considered asking Ned if he'd be her birthing partner, she hadn't found the courage to do it yet. And she wasn't sure he'd be the best choice, anyway. Her other options were her girlfriends Casey and Chloe; however, Casey was terrified by the idea and Chloe, married last year, was expecting her own baby.

"Right." She struggled to maintain her composure. "That was a joke."

They released a collective sigh.

"You're distracting us from what's important here." Obviously Linc wasn't going to be put off. "I want to talk to David Rhodes, just him and me, man to man." He clenched his hands at his sides.

"And when Linc's finished, I want a turn," Mel said, plowing his fist into his open palm.

Mary Jo rolled her eyes. She'd defended David to her brothers countless times. She'd defended him to Casey and Chloe—the only other people who knew David was her baby's father. Casey worked with her at the insurance company in Seattle, so she'd met David, since he'd come to their office for meetings every few weeks, representing corporate headquarters in California. David had charmed just about everybody—with the possible exception of Casey.

He'd always had such good excuses for missing the birthing classes, and she'd believed him. It was easy to do because she so badly wanted to trust him. He claimed to love her and while the pregnancy certainly hadn't been planned, he'd seemed genuinely pleased when she'd told him. There were a few legal and financial matters that needed to be cleared up, he'd explained, but as soon as they were dealt with, he'd marry her.

For a number of months Mary Jo had convinced her brothers that David's intentions were honorable. Now, though, she had to resign herself to the fact that David wasn't willing or able to marry her. She realized she didn't know as much about him as she should. Granted, he was older by at least twenty years, but her infatuation had led her to dismiss the significance of that. Now Mary Jo had to doubt his sincerity. She hadn't heard from him in more than two weeks and he wasn't answering his cell phone, and even during their last conversation, he'd been preoccupied and abrupt. He'd mentioned that he'd be in Cedar Cove for Christmas with his father and stepmother and would call her then.

"Do you *want* to marry David?" Ned asked. He was the only brother to take her feelings into consideration.

"Of course she wants to marry him," Linc answered, scowling at him. "She's about to have his baby, isn't she?"

"I believe I can answer for myself." Mary Jo calmly turned toward her oldest brother. "Actually—"

"You're getting married," Linc broke in.

"I won't have you holding a gun on David!"

Linc shook his head, expression puzzled. "I don't own a gun."

She sighed; her brothers could be so literal sometimes. "I was speaking figuratively," she said loftily.

"Oh." Linc frowned. "Well, I'm not talking figures, I'm talking facts." He raised one finger. "You're having a baby." He raised a second. "The father of that baby needs to accept his responsibilities."

"He will," Mary Jo murmured, although any hope that David would take care of her and the baby had long since been dashed.

"Yes, he will," Mel said firmly, "because we're going to make sure he does."

"And that includes putting a wedding band on your finger," Linc informed her, giving her a look that said he wouldn't tolerate any argument.

The baby kicked as if in protest and Mary Jo echoed the child's feelings. She no longer knew what she wanted. In the beginning she'd been head over heels in love with David. He was the most exciting man she'd ever met, and without even trying, he'd swept her off her feet. Mary Jo had been thrilled when he paid attention to her, a lowly accounting clerk. Compared to the boyfriends she'd had—as naive and inexperienced as she'd been herself—David was a romantic hero. An older man, confident, witty, indulgent.

"Mary Josephine," Mel said loudly. "Are you listening?"

Blinking to clear her thoughts, Mary Jo focused on her middle brother. "I guess not, sorry."

"Sorry?" Mel stormed. "We're talking about your future here and the future of your son."

Despite the seriousness of the situation, Mary Jo yawned. She couldn't help it. She covered her mouth with one hand

and placed the other on her protruding belly. "I'm going to bed," she declared.

"Mary Jo!" Linc shouted after her as if she were a marine recruit and he was her drill instructor. "We need to decide what to do *here* and *now*."

"Can't we talk about it in the morning?" She was too exhausted to continue this argument with her brothers at—she glanced toward the antique clock—almost midnight.

"No."

"Linc, be reasonable."

"We have to get this settled." Mel joined forces with his older brother.

Again Ned didn't speak. He cast her a look of quiet sympathy but he wasn't taking sides. Mary Jo could see that he felt Linc and Mel were right—not about becoming Mrs. Rhodes but about the need for her to make some kind of decision.

"Okay, okay, but we've already said everything there is to say." She sagged onto the sofa and tried to keep her eyes open.

Linc glanced at the clock, too. "As of about one minute ago, it's officially Christmas Eve. Rhodes promised to be in touch *before* Christmas."

Exhaling a deep sigh, Mary Jo shrugged. "He might've said *on* Christmas. I've forgotten."

"Well, I haven't." Mel's feet were braced wide apart, his arms folded across his massive chest.

"I haven't forgotten, either." Linc, too, crossed his arms. They looked like bouncers at a tough bar, but Mary Jo feared the person they'd toss out on his ear would be David Rhodes.

And he'd deserve it; she knew that. He'd deceived her not once, not twice, but a dozen times or more. Some of the responsibility was hers, though. Even though she was aware that he'd abused her trust, she'd continued to believe him, giving him chance after chance. Now her brothers were trying to save her from him—and from herself.

"David said he'd contact you *before* Christmas," Linc reminded her. "That's less than twenty-four hours."

"Yes, it is." Her agreeing with him was sure to confuse her well-meaning brothers.

Apparently shocked by her unaccustomed meekness, Linc frowned, then checked the clock again. "Yup, less than twenty-four hours. It's time you realized he has no intention of doing the proper thing."

Mary Jo couldn't argue with that. She was just tired of discussing it. "You never know," she said, forcing a note of optimism into her voice.

"Then you're living in a dream world, little sister," Mel said through gritted teeth.

Ned sat down next to Mary Jo and reached for her hand. "Linc and Mel are right," he told her gently.

"About what?" She was so exhausted, her vision had started to blur.

"Someone needs to get in touch with David. If we can't find him, then one of his family members. He has to be held accountable."

Linc snorted again. "David Rhodes needs to make an honest woman of you."

If Mary Jo heard that one more time she was going to scream. "I *am* an honest woman! I don't need David or any man to validate what each of you should already know."

"Yeah, yeah," Linc muttered. "Don't get your knickers in a knot. It's only an expression."

"What we all want," Mel began, as if to clarify their thoughts, "is for you to be happy—*with* the father of your baby."

Mary Jo doubted that was even possible. She'd lost faith in

David and as much as she wanted to believe he loved her and cared about their child, the evidence stated otherwise.

"He's not giving us any choice," Linc said, his dark eyes menacing. "We're going to find him and—"

"Linc, please. Hold off for a few days. Please." She hated to plead but it was Christmas and she didn't want to see the holiday ruined for any of them. She was protecting David— again—and the irony didn't escape her. Despite all these months of intermittent contact and broken promises, Mary Jo still felt the urge to shield him from her brothers.

But her real concern was for Linc, Mel and Ned. She didn't want *them* ending up in jail because of David.

"We're not waiting a minute longer!" Mel boomed. "If David's in Cedar Cove, we're going to track him down."

"No. Please," she said shakily.

"You don't have a say in this anymore."

"Linc, it's my life! Listen to me. I—"

"We've listened to you enough," her brother said matter-of-factly. "Now the three of us have decided to take matters into our own hands."

Mary Jo couldn't let her brothers get involved. She shuddered as she imagined them storming into Cedar Cove on Christmas Eve, bent on forcing David to marry her.

No, she couldn't allow that to happen. Resolute, she stood up and started for her bedroom. "We'll finish discussing this in the morning," she said in as dignified a voice as she could manage.

Linc seemed about to argue, but her fatigue must have shown because he hesitated, then nodded reluctantly. "There'll be no avoiding it, understand?"

"Perfectly."

"Night, sweetie." He threw his arms around her in a quick hug, as did Mel and then Ned.

Mary Jo slept soundly for six hours and woke in a cold sweat. She knew she'd never be able to stop her interfering brothers from invading Cedar Cove, embarrassing her and possibly doing bodily harm to David. The only solution she could think of was to get there first and warn David and/or his family.

With that in mind, Mary Jo left her brothers a note and slipped quietly out of the house.

2

Cedar Cove was a festive little town, Mary Jo thought when she stepped off the ferry. It was a place that took Christmas seriously. Even the small terminal was decorated, with bells hanging from the ceiling and large snowflakes in the windows. She'd never been here before and was pleasantly surprised by its charm. After taking the Washington State ferry from downtown Seattle to Bremerton, she'd caught the foot ferry across Sinclair Inlet to the small town David had mentioned.

He'd only talked about it that one time. She'd had the impression he didn't like it much, but she hadn't understood why.

She looked around.

A lighthouse stood off in the distance, picturesque against the backdrop of fir trees and the green waters of the cove. Waves rhythmically splashed the large rocks that marked the beach. Adjusting her purse strap on her shoulder and getting a tighter grip on her bag, Mary Jo walked down the pier into town.

Large evergreen boughs stretched across the main street of Cedar Cove—Harbor Street, according to the sign—and from the center of each hung a huge ornament. There were alternating wreaths, angels and candles. The lightposts were festooned with holly. The effect of all these decorations was delightful and it raised her spirits—until she remembered why she was in Cedar Cove.

It was ten in the morning on Christmas Eve, and everyone seemed to have places to go and people to see. So did Mary Jo, except that she was in no hurry to get there, and who could blame her? This was likely to be a painful confrontation.

Not sure where to start searching for David's family, desperate to collect her thoughts, Mary Jo stopped at a coffee house called Mocha Mama's about a block from the waterfront. This, too, was decorated and redolent of Christmas scents—fir, cinnamon, peppermint. And the rich, strong aroma of fresh coffee. The place was nearly empty. The only other person there was a young man who stood behind the counter; he was writing or drawing something in a sketchbook and appeared to be immersed in his task, whatever it was.

"Merry Christmas," Mary Jo said cheerfully, wondering if her words sounded as forced as they felt. She pulled off her wool hat and gloves, cramming them in her pockets.

Her presence startled the young man, who wore a name tag that identified him as Shaw. He glanced up, blinked in apparent confusion, then suddenly smiled. "Sorry. Didn't see you come in. What can I get you?"

"I'd like one of your decaf candy cane mochas, Shaw."

"What size?"

"Oh, grande—is that what you call it here? Medium. One of those." She pointed at a stack of cups.

His eyes went to her stomach, which protruded from the opening of her long wool coat. She could no longer fasten more than the top three buttons.

"You're gonna have a baby," Shaw said, as if this information should be a surprise to her.

"Yes, I am." She rested a protective hand on her belly.

Shaw began to prepare her mocha, chatting as he did. "It's been pretty quiet this morning. Maybe 'cause it's Christmas Eve," he commented.

Mary Jo nodded, then took a chair by the window and watched people walk briskly past. The town seemed to be busy and prosperous, with people popping in and out of stores along the street. The bakery had quite a few customers and so did a nearby framing shop.

"I haven't seen you around here before," Shaw said. He added whipped topping and a candy cane to her cup and handed it to her.

"I'm visiting," Mary Jo explained as she got up to pay for her drink. Shaw seemed to be full of information; he might be just the person to ask about David. She poked a folded dollar bill into the tip jar. "Would you know any people named Rhodes in this area?" she asked speculatively, holding her drink with both hands.

"Rhodes, Rhodes," Shaw repeated carefully. He mulled it over for a moment, then shook his head. "The name sounds familiar but I can't put a face to it."

"Oh." She couldn't quite hide her disappointment. Carrying her mocha, she returned to the table by the window and gazed out at the street again. Her biggest fear was that her three brothers would come rolling into town in their huge pickup, looking like vigilantes out of some old western. Or worse, a bunch of hillbillies. Mary Jo decided she *had* to get to David and his family first.

"Just a minute," Shaw said, suddenly excited. "There *is* a Rhodes family in Cedar Cove." He reached behind the counter and pulled out a telephone directory.

Mary Jo wanted to slap her forehead. Of course! How stupid. She should've checked the phone book immediately. That was certainly what her brothers would do.

"Here," Shaw said, flipping the directory around so she could read the listings. As it happened, there was a B. Rhodes, a Kevin Rhodes and three others—and Mary Jo had no way of knowing which of these people were related to David. The only thing to do was to call every one of them and find out.

"Would you mind if I borrowed this for a few minutes?" she asked.

"Sure, go ahead. Tell me if there's anything I can do to help."

"Thanks."

"Consider it a random act of kindness."

"Not so random." Mary Jo smiled as she brought the phone book back to her table. She rummaged for her cell phone; she hadn't remembered to charge it before she left and was relieved to see that she had nearly a full battery. She dialed the number for B. Rhodes and waited through several rings before a greeting came on, telling her that Ben and Charlotte weren't available and inviting her to leave a message. She didn't. She actually spoke to the next Rhodes, who sounded young and didn't know anyone named David. Of the last three, the first had a disconnected phone line and the other two didn't answer.

Mary Jo had assumed it would be easy to find David in a town as small as Cedar Cove. Walking down Harbor Street, she'd seen a sign for Roy McAfee, a private investigator. She hadn't expected to need one, and even if she could afford to pay someone else to track down David Rhodes, it wasn't likely that Mr. McAfee would accept a case this close to Christmas.

"Any luck?" Shaw asked.

"None." Without knowing the name of David's father, she couldn't figure out what her next step should be. There were three, possibly four, potential candidates, since she'd managed to rule out just one. Her only consolation was the fact that if *she* was having trouble, so would her brothers.

"I can think of one person who might be able to help you," Shaw said thoughtfully.

"Who?"

"Grace Harding. She's the head librarian and she knows practically everyone in town. I'm not sure if she's working this morning but it wouldn't do any harm to go there and see."

"The library is where?" Being on foot and pregnant definitely imposed some limitations, especially now that it had started to snow.

"How'd you get here?" Shaw asked.

"Foot ferry."

He grinned. "Then you walked right past it when you got off. It's the concrete building with the large mural on the front. You won't have any trouble finding it."

Mary Jo had noticed two such murals. She supposed it wouldn't be difficult to distinguish which one was the library. Eager to talk to Grace Harding, she left the remainder of her drink behind. She put the wool hat back on her head and pulled on her gloves. It was cold and the few snowflakes that had begun to drift down seemed persistent, like a harbinger of more to come. The Seattle area rarely experienced a white Christmas, and under other circumstances Mary Jo would've been thrilled at the prospect of snow.

As Shaw had predicted, she didn't have a problem locating the library. The mural of a frontier family was striking, and the library doors were decorated with Christmas wreaths. When she stepped inside, she saw dozens of cut-out snowflakes suspended from the ceiling in the children's area, as well as a display of seasonal picture books, some of which—like *A Snowy Day*—she remembered from her own childhood. A large Christmas tree with book-size wrapped gifts underneath stood just inside the small lobby. One look told Mary Jo this was a much-used and much-loved place.

She welcomed the warmth, both emotional and physical. There was a woman at the counter, which held a sign stating that the library would close at noon. Glancing at the clock on the wall, Mary Jo was surprised to see that it was already ten-forty-five.

She approached the front counter. "Excuse me. Are you Grace Harding?" she asked in a pleasant voice.

"Afraid not. Should I get her for you?"

Mary Jo agreed eagerly. "Yes, please."

The woman disappeared into a nearby office. A few minutes later, she reappeared with another middle-aged woman, who greeted Mary Jo with a friendly smile. She wore a bright red turtleneck sweater under a festive holly-green jumper. Her right arm seemed to be thickly bandaged beneath her long sleeve.

"I'm Grace Harding," she announced. "How can I help you?"

Mary Jo offered the woman a strained smile. "Hello, my name is Mary Jo Wyse and—" The baby kicked—hard—and Mary Jo's eyes widened with shock. She placed her hands against her stomach and slowly exhaled.

"Are you okay?" Grace asked, looking concerned.

"I...think so."

"Perhaps you should sit down."

Numbly Mary Jo nodded. This was all so...unseemly. She hated making a fuss, but she suspected the librarian was right and she did need to sit. Thankfully Ms. Harding came around the counter and led her to a chair. She left for a moment and returned with a glass of water.

"Here, drink this."

"Thank you." Mary Jo felt embarrassed, since almost everyone in the whole library was staring at her. No doubt she made quite a spectacle and people probably thought she'd give birth any second. Actually, her due date wasn't for another two weeks; she didn't think there was any danger the baby would arrive early, but this was her first pregnancy and she couldn't really tell. She could only hope…

Grace took the chair beside hers. "How can I help you?" she asked again.

Mary Jo gulped down all the water, then put the glass down beside her.

Taking a deep breath, she clasped her hands together. "I'm looking for a man by the name of David Rhodes."

Right away Mary Jo saw that the other woman stiffened.

"You know him?" she asked excitedly, ignoring any misgivings over Grace's reaction. "Is he here? He said he'd be visiting his father and stepmother in Cedar Cove. It's important that I talk to him as soon as possible."

Grace sagged in her chair. "Oh, dear."

"Oh, dear," Mary Jo repeated. "What does that mean?"

"Well…"

"Is David in town?"

Grace shook her head, but her expression was sympathetic. "I'm afraid not."

Mary Jo's heart sank. She should've known not to trust David. This was obviously another lie.

"What about his father and stepmother? Are they available?" If she didn't tell David's family about the baby, then her brothers surely would. The information would be better coming from her. The image of her brothers barging into these people's home lent a sense of urgency to her question.

"Unfortunately," Grace went on, "Ben and Charlotte have taken a Christmas cruise."

"They're gone, then," Mary Jo said in a flat voice. She recalled the message on their phone; ironically, Ben had been the first Rhodes she'd called. Maybe she should be relieved they were out of town, but she wasn't. Instead, a deep sadness settled over her. The uncertainty would continue. Whatever happened, she accepted the likelihood of being a single mother, but her brothers would never stand for it.

"According to a friend of mine, they're coming back sometime tomorrow," Grace told her.

"On Christmas Day?"

"Yes, that's what I understand, at any rate. I can find out for sure if you'd like."

"Yes, please."

Grace looked tentative. "Before I phone Olivia—she's the friend I mentioned—I should tell you that her mother is married to Ben Rhodes."

"I see."

"Would you mind if I asked you a question?"

"Of course not." Although she already knew what that question would be...

"Is your baby...is David Rhodes—"

Rather than respond, Mary Jo closed her eyes and hung her head.

Grace touched her arm gently. "Don't be upset, dear," she murmured. "None of that matters now."

The answer to Grace's question was obvious. Why else would someone in an advanced state of pregnancy come looking for David and his family—especially on Christmas Eve?

As she opened her eyes, Grace squeezed her hand reassuringly.

"I haven't seen or heard from David in weeks," Mary Jo admitted. "He occasionally calls and the last time he did, he said he was coming here to spend Christmas with his family. My brothers want to make him marry me, but...but that isn't what I want."

"Of course you don't."

At least Grace shared her point of view. "I've got to talk to

Mr. and Mrs. Rhodes as soon as I can and explain that even if David offered to marry me, I don't think it's the right thing for me or my baby."

"I don't, either," Grace said. "David isn't to be trusted."

Mary Jo grinned weakly. "I'm afraid I have to agree with you. But this is their grandchild. Or…or Ben's, anyway. Maybe they'll be interested in knowing the baby. Maybe David'll want some kind of relationship." She turned to Grace and said earnestly, "Shouldn't I give them that choice?"

"Yes, that's exactly what you should do." Grace squeezed her hand again. "I'll go make that call and get right back to you. Olivia will know Charlotte and Ben's travel schedule. However, it does seem to me that they're due home on the twenty-fifth."

"Thank you," Mary Jo murmured. She was feeling light-headed and a bit queasy, so she intended to stay where she was until Grace returned. It didn't take long.

Grace sat down next to her again. "I spoke with Olivia and she confirmed that Charlotte and Ben will indeed be home tomorrow afternoon."

"Oh…good." Still, Mary Jo wasn't sure what she should do next. If she went home, her brothers would be impossible. They'd be angry that she'd left with no warning other than a brief note. In any case, they were probably on their way to Cedar Cove now. And with some effort, they'd uncover the same information Mary Jo had.

"What would you like to do?" Grace asked.

"I think I'd better spend the night here," Mary Jo said. She hadn't packed a bag, but her requirements were simple. All she needed was a decent hotel. "Can you recommend a place to stay?"

"Oh, yes, there are several, including a lovely B-and-B.

I'm just wondering if there'll be a problem getting a room for tonight."

"A problem?" This wasn't something Mary Jo had considered.

"Let's see if there's anything at the Comfort Inn. It's close by and clean."

"That would be great. Thank you so much," Mary Jo said.

Here it was, Christmas Eve, and she felt as if she'd found an angel to help her. An angel fittingly named Grace…

3

Grace Harding studied the young pregnant woman beside her. So David Rhodes was the father of her baby. Not a surprise, she supposed, but it made her think even less of him. Certainly Olivia had told her plenty—about his deceit, his loans that were more like theft, since he never seemed to have any intention of repaying his father, the rumors of women he'd cheated on…and probably just plain cheated. That Ben Rhodes, who was one of the most decent and honorable men she'd ever met, could have a son like David defied explanation. Not only had David fathered this child, which she didn't doubt for a minute, he'd also lied to Mary Jo.

Well, Grace decided, she'd do what she could to give this poor girl a hand. And she knew Charlotte and Ben would, too.

"I'll get that list of places for you," Grace told Mary Jo, getting to her feet. The library had a sheet with phone numbers of the local bed-and-breakfasts, plus all the motels in the area. The best place in town was Thyme and Tide Bed & Breakfast, run by Bob and Peggy Beldon. However, she recalled, the couple was away for the holidays. So staying there wasn't an option. But there were several chain hotels out by the freeway.

"I'll need to be within walking distance of the Rhodes home," Mary Jo explained as Grace handed her the list. "I didn't drive over."

"Don't worry. If there's a vacancy a few miles out of town I'll take you there myself and I can drop you off at Charlotte's tomorrow evening."

Mary Jo glanced up at her, brown eyes wide with astonishment. "You'd do that?"

"Of course. It wouldn't be any problem. I'm going that way myself."

"Thank you."

Grace shrugged lightly. "I'm happy to do it," she said. The offer was a small thing and yet Mary Jo seemed so grateful. "If you'll excuse me, I need to make another phone call."

"Of course." Mary Jo had taken out her cell phone, clearly ready to start her search for a room. Normally, cell phone use in the library was discouraged but in this case Grace couldn't object.

Grace returned to her office. She'd promised to call Olivia back as soon as she could. Although they spoke almost every day, their conversations over the past week had been brief. With so much to do before Christmas, there hadn't been time to chat.

Sitting at her desk, Grace picked up the receiver and punched in Olivia's number. Her dearest friend was at home today, but unfortunately not because it was Christmas Eve. Judge Olivia Griffin had been diagnosed with breast cancer and had undergone surgery; she'd begin chemotherapy and radiation treatments early in the new year. She'd taken a leave of absence from the bench. The last month had been frightening, especially when Olivia developed an infection that had become life-threatening. Grace got chills just thinking about how close they'd all come to losing her.

Olivia answered on the first ring. "It took you forever to call back," she said. "Is the girl still at the library?"

"Yes. She's decided to stay the night and then meet with Ben and Charlotte tomorrow afternoon."

"Oh, no…"

"Should I tell her it might be better to wait?" Grace asked. Like Olivia, she hated the thought of hitting Ben with this news the minute he and Charlotte arrived home.

"I don't know," Olivia said. "I mean, they're going to be tired…" Her voice faded away.

"The thing is," Grace went on to explain, "I really don't think it *should* wait. Mary Jo's obviously due very soon." She hesitated, unsure how much to tell Olivia. She didn't want to burden her friend. Because of her illness, Olivia was uncharacteristically fragile these days.

"I heard that hesitation in your voice, Grace Harding," Olivia scolded. "There's more to this and you're wondering if you should tell me."

There were times Grace swore Olivia could read her mind. She took a breath. "It seems David told Mary Jo he'd be spending the holidays with Ben and Charlotte."

"I knew it! That's a lie. This cruise has been planned for months and David was well aware of it. Why would he do something like this?"

Grace didn't have an answer—although she had her own opinion on David and his motives.

"He probably used the lie as another tactic to put the poor girl off," Olivia said. "The way David manipulates people and then discards them like so much garbage infuriates me." Outrage echoed in every word.

"It appears that's exactly what he did," Grace murmured. She remembered how David had tried to swindle Charlotte out of several thousand dollars a few years ago. The man was without conscience.

"This poor girl! All alone at Christmas. It's appalling. If I could, I'd wring David's neck myself."

"I have the feeling we'd need to stand in line for that," Grace said wryly.

"No kidding," Olivia agreed. "Okay, now that I know what this Mary Jo business is all about, tell me what happened to your arm."

Instinctively Grace's hand moved to her upper right arm. "You're gonna laugh," she said, smiling herself, though at the time it'd been no laughing matter.

"Grace, from what I heard, you were in a lot of pain."

"And who told you that?"

"Justine. She ran into Cliff at the pharmacy when he was picking up your prescription."

"Oh, right." Small towns were like this. Everything was news and nothing was private. That could be beneficial—and it could be embarrassing. Olivia's daughter, Justine, knew, so Olivia's husband—who happened to be the local newspaper editor—did, too. It wouldn't surprise her if Jack wrote a humorous piece on her misadventure.

"So, what happened?" Olivia repeated.

Grace saw no reason to hide the truth. "I got bitten by the camel."

"*What? The camel?* What camel?"

Grace had to smile again. Olivia's reaction was the same as that of Dr. Timmons. According to the young physician, this was the first time he'd ever treated anyone for a camel bite.

"Cliff and I are housing the animals for the live Nativity scene," she explained. "Remember?" The local Methodist church had brought in animals for the display. Grace wasn't sure where the camel had come from but as far as she was concerned it could go back there anytime. And it would. Yesterday had been the final day for the animals' appearances; they'd be returning to their individual homes just after Christmas. True, she'd miss the donkey, since she'd grown fond of him. But the camel? Goodbye, Sleeping Beauty! Grace almost snorted at the animal's unlikely name.

"Of course," Olivia said, "the live Nativity scene. I didn't get a chance to see it. So *that's* how you encountered the camel."

"Yes, I went out to feed the dastardly beast. Cliff warned me that camels can be cantankerous and I *thought* I was being careful."

"Apparently not careful enough," Olivia said, sputtering with laughter.

"Hey, it isn't that funny," Grace said, slightly miffed that her friend hadn't offered her the requisite amount of sympathy. "I'll have you know it *hurt*."

"Did he break the skin?"

"He's a she, and yes, she did." Grace's arm ached at the memory. "Sleeping Beauty—" she said the name sarcastically "—bit me right through two layers of clothing."

"Did you need stitches?" The amusement had left Olivia's voice.

"No, but Dr. Timmons gave me a prescription for antibiotics and then bandaged my arm. You'd think it had been nearly amputated. This morning I had trouble finding a sweater that would go over the dressing."

"Poor Grace."

"That's more like it," she said in a satisfied tone.

"Let Cliff feed the camel from now on."

"You bet I will."

"Good."

"That's not all." Grace figured she might as well go for broke on the sympathy factor.

"What—the donkey bit you, too?"

"No, but the sheep stepped on my foot."

"Poor Grace."

"Thank you."

"A sheep can't weigh *that* much."

"This one did. I've got an unsightly bruise on the top of my foot." She thrust out her leg and gazed down on it. Her panty hose didn't hide the spectacularly colored bruise at all.

"Oh, poor Gracie."

"You don't sound like you mean that."

"Oh, I do, I do."

"Hmph. We haven't had much of a chance to talk in the last few days, so tell me what you're doing for Christmas," Grace said.

"It's pretty low-key," Olivia told her. "Justine, Seth and Leif are coming over tonight for dinner and gifts, then we're going to church at eight. What about you and Cliff?"

"Same. Maryellen, Kelly and all the grandkids are coming for dinner and then we're heading to the Christmas Eve service. Cliff's daughter, Lisa, and her family are here, as well. Tomorrow we're all going over to Maryellen and Jon's for dinner."

"Jack and I are having Christmas dinner alone. He's let on to everyone that he's cooking but between you and me, D.D.'s on the Cove is catering." Olivia laughed, apparently amused by her husband's resourcefulness. "Justine invited us," she added, "but we declined. Next year," Olivia said, and it sounded like a promise.

Everything would be back to normal by this time next year. Olivia would be finished with her treatments this spring. Seeing what her friend had already endured, and her quiet bravery in the face of what was still to come, had given Grace a deeper understanding of Olivia. Her strength and courage impressed Grace and humbled her. Like every woman their age, they'd suffered—and survived—their share of tragedy and grief. And now Olivia was coping with cancer.

Grace stood and looked out the small window that offered a view of the interior of the library. Mary Jo sat with her shoulders hunched forward, cell phone dangling from one hand.

"I have to go."

"Problems?"

"I should get back to Mary Jo."

"You'll keep me updated, won't you?" Olivia said.

"As much as I can."

"Okay, thanks. And listen, Grace, stay away from that camel!" She laughed, and then the line was disconnected.

The next time they met at the Pancake Palace, Grace intended to make Olivia pay for her coconut cream pie.

Grace called her husband quickly, then stepped out of her office and slipped into the chair next to Mary Jo. "How's it going?" she asked.

"Not so well, I'm afraid. I tried to call David. I have his cell phone number and I thought he'd answer. It's Christmas Eve and he *has* to know I'm waiting to hear from him."

Grace took Mary Jo's hand in hers. "He didn't answer?"

"Oh, it's more than that. He…he had his number changed. Last week—" she struggled to speak "—I tried to reach him at his office in California and learned that he's quit his job. We both work—worked—for the same insurance company, which is how we met."

"Oh, dear."

"I don't dare let my brothers know."

Mary Jo had mentioned them earlier.

"How many brothers?"

"Three, all of them older. I'd hoped David would be here with his parents, but I knew the odds that he'd told the truth weren't good."

Grace nodded, encouraging her to continue.

"I think I told you my brothers want to make David marry me—or at least pay for all the lies he's told. They decided they were going to come and confront him, and if not David, then his family."

Grace could only imagine how distressing it would be for Ben and Charlotte to return from the vacation of a lifetime to find Mary Jo's three angry brothers waiting for them. On Christmas Day, yet.

"That's why it's important I talk to Ben and Charlotte first," Mary Jo concluded.

"I think you should," Grace said.

"Except…"

"Yes?" she prompted.

"Except it looks like I'll have to go back to Seattle this afternoon."

"Why?"

"I called all the places on the sheet you gave me and there aren't any vacancies."

"Nowhere? Not in the entire town? What about the Comfort Inn?"

She shook her head. "Nothing."

"You mean everything's already reserved?"

"Yes. There's no room at the Inn."

4

"Linc," Mel shouted from the kitchen. Three Wyse Men Automotive had closed early due to the holiday.

"In a minute," Linc shouted back. "Where's Mary Jo?" He'd already searched half the house and hadn't found her. He knew she'd taken the day off. Had she gone to the store, perhaps? Or to visit her friend Chloe?

"If you come to the kitchen you'll find out!"

Linc followed his brother's voice and with Ned at his heels, entered the kitchen. As soon as Mel saw him, his brother thrust a sheet of paper into his hands. "Here. This was behind the coffeemaker. Must've fallen off."

Before he'd read two words, Linc's face started to heat up. His stubborn, strong-willed, hardheaded, obstinate little sister had gone to Cedar Cove. Without her family, because she felt she knew best. Tossing the note to the ground, Linc clenched both his fists. "Of all the stupid, idiotic things to do."

"What?" Ned asked.

"Mary Jo's decided to go to Cedar Cove on her own," Mel said.

"By herself?"

"Isn't that what I said?" Mel snapped.

"It's true," Linc informed his youngest brother. "I can't believe she'd do anything this crazy."

"We drove her to it." Ned sank into a kitchen chair and splayed his fingers through his thick dark hair.

"What do you mean?" Mel challenged.

"Explain yourself," Linc ordered.

"Don't you see?" Ned gazed up at them. "All that talk about confronting David and forcing him to do the *honorable* thing. The man hasn't got an honorable bone in his body. What were we thinking?"

"What we were thinking," Linc said irritably, "is that David Rhodes is going to pay for what he did to our little sister." He looked his brothers in the eye and made sure they understood.

When their parents were killed, Mary Jo had only been seventeen. Linc, as the oldest, had been made her legal guardian, since there was no other family in the area. At the time, the responsibility had weighed heavily on his shoulders. He'd gone to his two brothers and asked for their help in raising their little sister. Or at least finishing the job their parents had begun.

Both brothers had been equally committed to taking care of Mary Jo. Everything had gone smoothly, too. Mary Jo had graduated from high school the following May, and all three brothers had attended the ceremony. They'd even thrown her a party.

That autumn he'd gone with Mary Jo to the community college and signed her up for classes. She hadn't taken kindly to his accompanying her, but Linc wasn't about to let her walk around campus on her own. Not at first, anyway. Cute little girl like her? With all those lecherous college guys who couldn't keep their hands to themselves? Oh, yeah, he knew what eighteen-year-old boys were like. And he'd insisted she choose solid, practical courses, not that fluffy fun stuff they taught now.

All the brothers were proud of how well Mary Jo had done in her studies. They'd all disapproved when she'd dropped out of school and gone to work at that insurance company. More than once Linc had to bite his tongue. He'd told her no good would come of this job.

The problem with Mary Jo was that she was too eager to move. She no longer wanted to live in the family home. For the last year, she'd talked incessantly about getting her own place.

Linc didn't understand that, either. This was their *home*. Linc saw to it that Mary Jo wasn't stuck with all the cleaning, cooking and laundry. They all did their part of the upkeep— maybe not quite to her standards but well enough. That wasn't the reason she was so determined to live somewhere else.

No, Mary Jo had an intense desire for independence. From them.

Okay, maybe they'd gone overboard when it came to dating. Frankly, Linc didn't think there was a man this side of Mars who was good enough for his little sister. Mary Jo was special.

Then Mary Jo had met David Rhodes. Linc had never found out exactly when that had happened. Not once in the six months that she'd been dating him had she mentioned this guy. What Linc had noticed was how happy Mary Jo seemed all of a sudden—and then, just as suddenly, she'd been depressed. That was when her mood swings started. She'd be happy and then sad and then happy again. It made no sense until he learned there was a man involved.

Even now that Mary Jo was pregnant with this man's baby, Linc still hadn't met him. In retrospect, that was probably for the best because Linc would take real pleasure in ripping his face off.

"What are we going to do now?" Mel asked.

His younger brothers were clearly worried.

Linc's hand was already in his pants pocket, fingering his truck keys. "What can we do other than follow her to Cedar Cove?"

"Let's talk this through," Ned suggested, coming to his feet.

"What's there to talk about?" Mel asked. "Mary Jo's going to have a baby. She's alone and pregnant and we all know Rhodes isn't in Cedar Cove. He's lied to her from the beginning. There's no way he's telling her the truth now."

"Yes, but…"

Linc looked squarely into his youngest brother's eyes. "What do you think Mom and Dad would have us do?" he asked, allowing time between each word to make sure the message sank in.

Ned sighed. "They'd want us to find her."

"Exactly my point." Linc headed for the back door.

"Wait a minute." Ned raised his hand.

"Now what?" Mel cried out impatiently.

"Mary Jo left because she's mad."

"Well, let her be mad. By the time we arrive, she'll be singing a different tune. My guess is she'll be mighty glad to see us."

"Maybe," Ned agreed. "But say she isn't. Then what?"

Linc frowned. "We'll bring her home, anyway."

"She might not want to come."

"She'll come." Linc wasn't about to leave his little sister with strangers over Christmas.

"If we make demands, she'll only be more determined to stay," Ned told them.

"Do you have any other bright ideas?" Mel asked.

Ned ignored the sarcasm. "Bring her gifts," he said.

"Why?" Linc didn't understand what he meant. They all had gifts for her and the baby that she could open Christmas morning, the way she was supposed to.

"She needs to know we love her and welcome the baby."

"Of course we welcome the baby," Linc said. "He's our flesh and blood, our *nephew*."

"Hang on a minute," Mel murmured, looking pensive. "Ned has a point."

It wasn't often that Mel agreed with Ned. "What do you mean?"

"Mary Jo's pregnant, right?"

That question didn't require a response.

"And everyone knows how unreasonable women can get when they're in, uh, a delicate condition."

Linc scratched his head. "Mary Jo was like that long before she got pregnant."

"True, but she's been even more unreasonable lately, don't you think?"

Mel wasn't wrong there.

"Maybe we should bring her a gift just so she'll know how concerned we are about her and the baby. How much we care. We want her with us for Christmas, don't we?"

"What woman doesn't like gifts?" Linc said, thinking out loud.

"Yup," Ned said, smiling at Mel. "It couldn't hurt."

Linc conceded. "Okay, then, we'll each bring her a gift."

They returned to their individual bedrooms, planning to meet in the kitchen five minutes later. Linc had gone online a few weeks ago and ordered a miniature football, basketball and soccer ball for his yet-to-be-born nephew. He couldn't speak for the others, but he suspected they too had chosen gifts that were geared toward sports. At first he figured he'd bring the football, but then he reconsidered. He'd been after Mary Jo to save money and in an effort to encourage her, he'd purchased a gold coin that he planned to present on her birthday in February. Perfect. He pocketed the coin and hurried to the kitchen.

"You ready?" he asked.

"Ready," Mel echoed.

"Me, too," Ned confirmed.

The three brothers hurried out to the four-door pickup Linc drove. Mel automatically climbed into the front passenger seat and Ned sat directly behind him.

"You got your gift?" Linc asked Mel.

"Yeah. I'm bringing her perfume."

"Good idea," Linc said approvingly. "Where'd you get it?"

"I actually bought it for Annie, but since I'm not seeing her anymore…"

"Ned?" Linc asked.

"Incense," his youngest brother mumbled.

"You brought her *what?*"

"Incense. She likes that stuff. It was gonna be part of her Christmas gift, anyway."

"Okay…" Linc shook his head rather than ask any further questions. Whatever his brothers chose to bring Mary Jo was up to them.

He turned his key in the ignition, then rested his arm over the back of the seat and angled his head so he could see behind him as he reversed out of the driveway. He'd reached the stop sign at the end of the block before it occurred to him to ask.

"Which way?"

"North," Mel said.

"Cedar Cove is south," Ned contradicted.

"For crying out loud." Linc pulled over to the curb. Leaning across his brother, he opened the glove box and shuffled through a pile of junk until he found the Washington State map he was looking for. Dropping it on Mel's lap, he said, "Find me Cedar Cove."

Mel immediately tossed it into the backseat. "Here, Ned. You seem to think you know where it is."

"It was just a guess," Ned protested. Nevertheless he started to unfold the map.

"Well, we don't have time for guessing. Look it up." Linc put the truck back in gear and drove toward the freeway on-ramp. He assumed Ned would find Cedar Cove before he had to decide which lane to get into—north or south.

He was nearly at the ramp before Ned cried out triumphantly. "Found it!"

"Great. Which way should I go?"

Linc watched his brother through the rearview mirror as he turned the map around.

No answer.

"Which way?" Linc asked impatiently.

"South," Ned murmured.

"You don't sound too sure."

"South," Ned said again, this time with more conviction.

Linc pulled into the lane that would take him in that direction. "How far is it?" he asked.

Ned stared down at the map again. "A ways."

"That doesn't tell me a darn thing. An hour or what?"

"All right, all right, give me a minute." Ned balanced the map on his knees and studied it intently. After carefully walking his fingers along the edge of the map, Ned had the answer. "I'd say...ninety minutes."

"Ninety minutes." Linc hadn't realized it was that far.

"Maybe longer."

Linc groaned silently. Traffic was heavy, which was to be expected at noon on Christmas Eve. At the rate they were crawling, it would be hours before they got there, which made their mission that much more urgent.

"Should we confront the Rhodes family first thing?" Mel asked.

"Damn straight. They need to know what he's done."

Ned cleared his throat. "Don't you think we should find Mary Jo first?"

Linc nodded slowly. "Yeah, I suppose we should."

They rode in silence for several minutes.

"Hey." Ned leaned forward and thrust his face between the two of them.

"What now?" Linc said, frustrated by the heavy traffic, which was guaranteed to get even worse once they hit Tacoma.

"How did Mary Jo get to Cedar Cove?" Mel asked.

"Good question." Linc hadn't stopped to consider her means of transportation. Mary Jo had a driver's license but didn't need a vehicle of her own, living in the city as they did. Each of the brothers owned a car and she could borrow any one of them whenever she wanted.

Ned sat back and studied the map again and after a few minutes announced, "Cedar Cove is on the Kitsap Peninsula."

"So?" Mel muttered sarcastically. The traffic was apparently making him cranky, too.

"So she took the ferry over."

That explained it. "Which ferry?" Linc asked.

"She probably caught the one from downtown Seattle to Bremerton."

"Or she might have gotten a ride," Mel said.

"Who from?" Ned asked.

"She wouldn't bother a friend on Christmas Eve." Ned seemed confident of that.

"Why not?" Mel demanded.

"Mary Jo isn't the type to call someone at the last minute

and ask that kind of favor," Ned told them. "Not even Chloe or Casey—especially on Christmas Eve."

Linc agreed with his brother.

They drove in silence for another fifteen minutes before anyone spoke.

"Do you think she's okay?" Ned asked tentatively.

"Sure she is. She's a Wyse, isn't she? We're made of stern stuff."

"I mean physically," Ned clarified. "Last night she seemed so…" He didn't finish the sentence.

"Seemed what?" Linc prompted.

Ned shrugged. "Ready."

"For what?" Mel asked.

Mel could be obtuse, which was only one of his character flaws, in Linc's opinion. He was also argumentative.

"To have the baby, of course," Linc explained, casting his brother a dirty look.

"Hey, there's no reason to talk to me like that," Mel said. He shifted his weight and stared out the side window. "I've never been around a pregnant woman before. Besides, what makes *you* such experts on pregnancy and birth?"

"I read a book," Ned told them.

"No way." Linc could hardly believe it.

"I did," Ned insisted. "I figured one of us should. For Mary Jo's sake."

"So one book makes you an expert," Mel teased.

"It makes me smarter than you, anyway."

"No, it doesn't," Mel argued.

"Quit it, you two." Linc spent half his life settling squabbles between his brothers. "You." He gestured over his shoulder. "Call her cell."

Ned did, using his own. "Went right into voice mail," he said. "Must be off."

"Leave her a message, then." Linc wondered if he had to spell *everything* out for them.

"Okay. Who knows if she'll get it, though."

After that they drove in blessed silence for maybe five minutes.

"Hey, I just thought of something." Mel groaned in frustration. "If Mary Jo took the ferry, shouldn't we have done the same thing?"

Good point—except it was too late now. They were caught in the notorious Seattle traffic, going nowhere fast.

5

Mary Jo hated the idea of returning to Seattle having failed in her attempt to find either David or his family. He wasn't in Cedar Cove the way he'd promised; not only that, his parents weren't here, either. Ben and Charlotte Rhodes would show up the next afternoon or evening, but in the meantime…

The thought of her brothers approaching the elderly couple, shocking them with the news and their outrageous demands, made the blood rush to her face. Her situation was uncomfortable enough without her brothers riding to the rescue like the superheroes they weren't.

The fact that Mary Jo had left on Christmas Eve was only going to rile them even more. Linc, Mel and Ned were probably home from the garage by now. Or maybe they'd skipped work when they found her note on the coffeemaker and immediately set out in search of her. Maybe they were already driving up and down the streets of Cedar Cove…

Looking around, Mary Jo could see that the library was about to close. People were putting on coats and checking out their books. She wondered how an hour had disappeared so quickly. Now what? There wasn't a single vacant room in the entire vicinity, which meant the only thing to do was thank Grace Harding for her help and quietly leave.

She waited until the librarian stepped out of her office. The least she could do was let Grace know how much she appreciated her kindness. As she approached, Mary Jo rose from her chair.

All of a sudden the room started to sway. She'd been dizzy before but never anything like this. Her head swam, and for an instant she seemed about to faint. Blindly Mary Jo reached out, hoping to catch herself before she fell.

"Mary Jo!" Grace gasped and rushed to her side.

If the other woman hadn't caught her when she did, Mary Jo was convinced she would've collapsed right onto the floor.

Slowly, Grace eased her into the chair. "Laurie!" she shouted, "call 9-1-1."

"Please…no," Mary Jo protested. "I'm fine. Really, I am."

"No, you're not."

A moment later, the assistant behind the front counter hurried over to join Grace and Mary Jo. "The fire department's on the way."

Mortified beyond words, Mary Jo leaned her head back and closed her eyes. Needless to say, she'd become the library's main attraction, of far greater interest than any of the Christmas displays. Everyone was staring at her.

"Here, drink this," Grace said.

Mary Jo opened her eyes to find someone holding out a glass of water—again. Her mouth had gone completely dry and she accepted it gratefully. Sirens could be heard roaring toward the library, and Mary Jo would've given anything to simply disappear.

A few minutes later, two firefighters entered the library, carrying their emergency medical equipment. Instantly one of the men moved toward her and knelt down.

"Hi, there." The firefighter's voice was calm.

"Hi," Mary Jo returned weakly.

"Can you tell me what happened?"

"I just got a bit light-headed. I wish you hadn't been called. I'm perfectly okay."

He ignored her comment. "You stood up?"

She nodded. "The room began to sway and I thought I was going to faint."

"I think she did faint," Grace added, kneeling down next to the firefighter. "I somehow got her back into the chair. Otherwise I'm sure she would've crumpled to the floor."

The firefighter kept his gaze on Mary Jo. He had kind eyes and, despite everything, she noticed that he was attractive in a craggy, very masculine way. He was about her age, she decided, maybe a few years older.

"My name's Mack McAfee," he said. "And that guy—" he pointed to the other firefighter "—is Brandon Hutton."

"I'm Mary Jo Wyse."

Mack smiled, maintaining eye contact. "When's your baby due?"

"January seventh."

"In about two weeks, then."

"Yes."

"Have you had any other spells like this?"

Mary Jo was reluctant to confess that she had. After a moment she nodded.

"Recently?"

She sighed. "Yes…"

"That's not uncommon, you know. Your body's under a lot of strain because of the baby. Have you been experiencing any additional stress?"

She bit her lip. "A little."

"The holidays?"

"Not really."

"I'm new to town. I guess that's why I haven't seen you around," Mack said. He opened a response kit he'd brought into the library.

"Mary Jo lives in Seattle," Grace said, now standing behind Mack as the other firefighter hovered close by.

"Do you have relatives in the area?" he asked next.

"No..." She shook her head, figuring she might as well admit the truth. "I was hoping to see the father of my baby... only he isn't here."

"Navy?"

"No... I understood his family was from Cedar Cove, but apparently they're out of town, too."

"Ben and Charlotte Rhodes," Grace murmured.

Mack twisted around to look up at Grace. "The judge's mother, right? And her husband. Retired Navy."

"Right."

"David Rhodes is the baby's father," Mary Jo said. "We're not...together anymore." David had told her one too many lies. She knew intuitively that he'd have no desire to be part of the baby's life.

Mack didn't speak as he took out the blood pressure cuff and wrapped it around her upper arm. "How are you feeling now?" he asked.

"You mean other than mortified?"

He grinned up at her. "Other than that."

"Better," she said.

"Good." He took her blood pressure, a look of concentration on his face.

"How high is it?" Grace asked, sounding worried.

"Not bad," Mack told them both. "It's slightly elevated." He turned back to Mary Jo. "It would probably be best if you relaxed for the rest of the day. It wouldn't hurt to stay off your feet, either. Don't do anything strenuous."

"I'll... I'll try."

"Perhaps she should see a physician?" Grace said. "I'd be happy to take her to the clinic."

"No, that isn't necessary!" Mary Jo objected. "I'm so sorry to cause all this fuss. I feel fine."

Mack met her gaze and seemed to read the distress in her eyes. "As long as you rest and stay calm, I don't think you need to see a doctor."

"Thank you," she breathed.

Although the library was closing, the doors suddenly opened and a tall, regal woman walked in. She was bundled up in a wool coat with a red knit scarf around her neck and a matching knit cap and gloves.

"Olivia," Grace said. "What are you doing here?"

"Why's the aid car out front?" the other woman asked. Her gaze immediately rested on Mary Jo. A stricken look came over her. "Are you in labor?"

"No, no, I'm just...a little light-headed," Mary Jo assured her.

The woman smiled. "I already know who this must be. Mary Jo. Are you all right?"

"This is Olivia, Charlotte Rhodes's daughter." Grace gestured at her. "She's the woman I called to get the information about Ben and Charlotte."

"Oh." Mary Jo shrank back in her chair.

"David Rhodes is my stepbrother," Olivia explained. She smiled sympathetically at Mary Jo. "Although so far, he's been nothing but an embarrassment to the family. And I can see that trend's continuing. But don't assume," she said to Mary Jo, "that I'm blaming you. I know David *far* too well."

Mary Jo nodded mutely but couldn't prevent a surge of

guilt that must have reddened her face, judging by her heated cheeks. She *was* to blame, for being naive in falling for a man like David, for being careless enough to get pregnant, for letting the situation ever reach this point.

"What are you doing here?" Grace asked her friend a second time.

"I'm meeting Will at the gallery. We're going to lunch. I saw the aid car outside the library as I drove by." Olivia turned to Mary Jo again. "I was afraid something like this had happened. Thank goodness for young Mack here—" they exchanged a smile "—and his partner over there." Brandon was helping an older couple with their bags of groceries and stack of books.

Mary Jo felt no less mortified. "I should never have come," she moaned.

"I'm glad you did," Olivia said firmly. "Ben would want to know about his grandchild."

Mary Jo hadn't expected everyone to be so…nice. So friendly and willing to accept her—and her dilemma. "It's just that my brothers are upset and determined to defend my honor. I felt I should be the one to tell David's family."

"Of course you should," Olivia said in what appeared to be complete agreement.

Mack finished packing up his supplies. He placed his hand on Mary Jo's knee to gain her attention. When she looked back at him, she was struck by the gentle caring in his gaze.

"You'll do as I suggested and rest? Don't get over-excited."

Mary Jo nodded.

"If you have any other problems, just call 9-1-1. I'm on duty all day."

"I will," she promised. "Thank you so much."

Mack stood. "My pleasure." He hesitated for a moment and stared directly into her eyes. "You're going to be a good mom."

Mary Jo blinked back tears. More than anything, that was what she wanted. To be the best mother she could. Her child was coming into the world with one disadvantage already—the baby's father had no interest in him. Or her. It was all up to Mary Jo.

"Thank you," she whispered.

"Merry Christmas," Mack said before he turned to leave.

"Merry Christmas," she called after him.

"You need to rest," Olivia said with an authority few would question. "When's the last time you ate?"

"I had a mocha at Mocha Mama's before I came to the library."

"You need lunch."

"I'll eat," Mary Jo said, "as soon as I get back to Seattle." There was the issue of her brothers, but she'd just call Linc's cell phone and let them know she was on her way home.

"You drove?" Grace asked.

"No, I took the ferry across."

Grace and Olivia glanced at each other.

"It might be a good idea if you came home with me," Olivia began. "It won't be any inconvenience and we'd enjoy having you."

Mary Jo immediately shook her head. "I...couldn't." Although Olivia was related to David, by marriage, anyway, she didn't want to intrude on their Christmas. Olivia and her family certainly didn't need unexpected company. Olivia had stated that David was an embarrassment to the family, and Mary Jo's presence only made things worse. Bad enough that she'd arrived without any warning, but it was beyond the call of duty for Olivia to take her in, and on Christmas Eve of all nights. Olivia must have plans and Mary Jo refused to ruin them.

"No," Grace said emphatically. "You're coming home with me. It's already arranged."

This invitation was just as endearing and just as unnecessary. "Thank you both." She struggled to her feet, cradling her belly with protective hands. "I can't let either of you do that. I appreciate everything, but I'm going back to Seattle."

"Nonsense," Grace said. "I've spoken to my husband and he agrees with me."

"But—"

Grace cut her off, obviously unwilling to listen. "You won't be intruding, I promise."

Mary Jo was about to argue again, but Grace talked right over her.

"We have my daughter-in-law and her family visiting us, but we've got an apartment above our barn that's completely furnished. It's empty at the moment and you'd be welcome to stay there for the night."

The invitation was tempting. Still, Mary Jo hesitated.

"Didn't you hear what Mack said?" Grace reminded her. "He said it was important for you to remain calm and relaxed."

"Yes, I know, but—"

"Are you sure?" Olivia asked Grace. "Because I can easily make up the sofa bed in the den."

"Of course I'm sure."

"I don't want to interfere with your Christmas," Mary Jo said.

"You wouldn't be," Grace assured her. "You'd have your privacy and we'd have ours. The barn's close to the house, so if you needed anything it would be simple to reach me. There's a phone in the apartment, too, which I believe is still connected. If not, the line in the barn is hooked up."

The idea was gaining momentum in her mind. "Maybe I could," Mary Jo murmured. As soon as she was settled, she'd call her brothers and explain that she'd decided to stay in Cedar Cove overnight. Besides, she was tired and depressed and didn't feel like celebrating. The idea of being by herself held more appeal by the minute.

Another plus was the fact that her brothers needed a break from her and her problems. For the last number of weeks, Mary Jo had been nothing but a burden to them, causing strife within the family. Thanks to her, the three of them were constantly bickering.

Ned was sympathetic to her situation and she loved him for it. But even he couldn't stand up to Linc, who took his responsibilities as head of the family much too seriously.

If her brothers were on their way to Cedar Cove, as she expected, she'd ask them firmly but politely to turn around. She'd tell them she was spending Christmas with David's family, which was, in fact, true. Sort of. By tomorrow evening, she would've met with Ben and Charlotte and maybe Olivia and the rest of David's Cedar Cove relatives. They'd resolve this difficult situation *without* her brothers' so-called help.

"One thing," Grace said, her voice falling as she glanced over at Olivia.

"Yes?" Mary Jo asked.

"There's a slight complication."

Mary Jo should've known this was too good to be true.

"The barn's currently home to a...variety of animals," Grace went on to explain.

Mary Jo didn't understand why this should be a problem, nor did she understand Olivia's smug grin.

"There's an ox and several sheep, a donkey and—" she paused "—a camel."

"A *camel?*" Mary Jo repeated.

"A rather bad-tempered camel," Olivia put in.

Nodding, Grace pointed to her obviously bandaged arm. "You'd be well advised to keep your distance."

"That's, um, quite a menagerie you have living in your barn."

"Oh, they don't belong to us," Grace said. "They're for the live Nativity scene, which ended last evening. We're housing them for the church."

"The animals won't bother me." Mary Jo smiled. "And I won't bother them."

Her smile grew wider as it occurred to her that she'd be spending Christmas Eve in a stable—something another Mary had done before her.

6

Olivia reluctantly left the library by herself. Weak as she was these days, it made more sense for Mary Jo to go home with Grace. Nevertheless, Olivia felt a certain obligation toward this vulnerable young woman.

Olivia had never had positive feelings toward her stepbrother, and this situation definitely hadn't improved her impression of him. Ben's son could be deceptive and cruel. She knew very well that David had lied to Mary Jo Wyse. Sure, it took two to tango, as that old cliché had it—and two to get Mary Jo into her present state. But Olivia also knew that David would have misrepresented himself and, even worse, abdicated all responsibility for Mary Jo *and* his child. No wonder her family was in an uproar. Olivia didn't blame them; she would be, too.

The drive from the library to Harbor Street Gallery took less than two minutes. Olivia hated driving such a short distance when at any other time in her life she would've walked those few blocks. The problem was that those blocks were a steep uphill climb and she didn't have the energy. The surgery and subsequent infection had sapped her of strength and energy. Today, however, wasn't a day to dwell on the cancer that had struck her so unexpectedly, like a viper hiding in the garden. Today, Christmas Eve, was a day for gratitude and hope.

She parked outside the art gallery her brother had purchased and was renovating. Olivia had been the one to suggest he buy the gallery; he'd done so, and it seemed to be a good decision for him.

Will was waiting for her at the door. "Liv!" he said, bounding toward her in his larger-than-life way. He extended his arms for a hug. "Merry Christmas."

"The same to you," she said, smiling up at him. Her brother, although over sixty, remained a strikingly handsome man. Now divorced and retired, he'd come home to reinvent himself, leaving behind his former life in Atlanta. In the beginning Olivia had doubted his motives, but slowly he'd begun to prove himself, becoming an active member of the town—and his family—once again.

"I wanted to give you a tour of the gallery," Will told her, as he led her inside.

The last time Olivia had visited the town's art gallery had been while Maryellen Bowman, Grace's daughter, was the manager. Maryellen had been forced to resign during a difficult pregnancy. The business had rapidly declined once she'd left, and eventually the gallery had gone up for sale.

Gazing around, Olivia could hardly believe the changes. "You did all *this* in less than a month?" The place barely resembled the old Harbor Street Gallery. Before Will had taken over, artwork had been arranged in a simple, straightforward manner—paintings and photographs on the walls, sculpture on tables.

Will had built distinctive multi-level glass cases and brought in other inventive means of displaying a variety of mediums, including a carefully designed lighting system. One entire wall was taken up with a huge quilt, unlike any she'd seen before. At first glance she had the impression of fire.

Close up, it looked abstract, with vivid clashing colors and surreal, swirling shapes. But, stepping back, Olivia identified an image that suddenly emerged—a dragon. It was fierce, angry, *red,* shooting out flames in gold, purple and orange satin against a background that incorporated trees, water and winding roads.

"That's by Shirley Bliss," Will said, following her gaze. "It took me weeks to convince her to let me put that up. I only have it until New Year's."

"It's magnificent." Olivia was in awe of the piece and couldn't tear her eyes from it.

"It isn't for sale, however."

"That's a shame."

Will nodded. "She calls it *Death.* She created it shortly after her husband was killed in a motorcycle accident." He slipped an arm through Olivia's. "Can't you just feel her anger and her grief?"

The quilt seemed to vibrate with emotions Olivia recognized from her own life—the time her 13-year-old son had drowned, more than twenty years ago. And the time, only weeks ago, that she'd been diagnosed with cancer. When she initially heard the physician say the word, she'd had a nearly irrepressible urge to argue with him. This *couldn't* be happening to her. Clearly there'd been some mistake.

That disbelief had been replaced by a hot anger at the unfairness of it. Then came numbness, then grief and finally resignation. With Jordan's death and with her own cancer, she'd experienced a tremendous loss that had brought with it fears of further loss.

Now, fighting her cancer—and that was how she thought of it, *her* cancer—she'd found a shaky serenity, even a sort of peace. That kind of acceptance was something she'd acquired with the love and assistance of her husband, Jack, her family and, as much as anyone, Grace, the woman who'd been her best friend her entire life.

"My living quarters are livable now, too," Will was telling her. "I've moved in upstairs but I'm still sorting through boxes. Isn't it great how things turned out? Because of Mack," he added when Olivia looked at him quizzically.

"Getting the job here in town, you mean?"

"Yeah, since that meant he needed an apartment. At the same time, I needed out of the sublet, so it worked out perfectly."

After a quick turn around the gallery to admire the other pieces on display, Will steered her toward the door. "Where would you like to go for lunch?" he asked. "Anyplace in town. Your big brother's treating."

"Well, seeing you've got all that money burning a hole in your pocket, how about the Pancake Palace?"

Will arched his brows. "You're joking, aren't you?"

"No, I'm serious." The Pancake Palace had long been a favorite of hers and in the past month or two, she'd missed it. For years, Grace and Olivia would head over to their favorite high school hangout after aerobics class on Wednesday night. The coconut cream pie and coffee was like a reward for their exertions, and the Palace was where they always caught up with each other's news.

Goldie, their favorite waitress, had served them salty French fries and iced sodas back when neither of them worried about calories. These days their once-a-week splurge reminded them of their youth, and the nostalgic appeal of the place never faded.

Some of the most defining moments of their teenage years had occurred at the Pancake Palace. It was there that eighteen-year-old Grace admitted she was pregnant, shortly before graduation.

And years later, it'd been over coffee and tears that Olivia confessed Stan had asked for a divorce after Jordan's death. And later, it was where Olivia told her she'd been appointed to the bench. The Pancake Palace was a place of memories for them, good as well as bad.

"The Pancake Palace? You're really serious?" Will said again. "I can afford a lot better, you know."

"You asked and that's my choice."

Will nodded. "Then off to the Palace we go."

Her brother insisted on driving and Olivia couldn't fault his manners. He was the consummate gentleman, opening the passenger door for her and helping her inside. The snow that had fallen earlier dusted the buildings and trees but had melted on the sidewalks and roads, leaving them slick. The slate-gray skies promised more snow, however.

Olivia had been out with her brother plenty of times and he'd never bothered with her car door. She was his sister and manners were reserved for others.

She wondered if Will's solicitude was linked to her illness. Although he might've been reluctant to admit it, Will had been frightened. His caring comforted her, particularly since they'd been at odds during the past few years.

He assisted her out of the car and opened the door to the Pancake Palace. They'd hardly entered the restaurant when Goldie appeared.

"Well, as I live and breathe, it's Olivia!" Goldie cried. Then she shocked Olivia by throwing both sinewy arms around her. "My goodness, you're a sight for sore eyes."

"Merry Christmas, Goldie," Olivia murmured.

The waitress had to be close to seventy and could only be described as "crusty." To Olivia's utter astonishment, Goldie pulled a hankie from her pink uniform pocket and dabbed at her eyes.

"I wasn't sure if I'd ever see you again," she said with a sniffle.

"Oh, Goldie..." Olivia had no idea what to say at this uncharacteristic display of affection.

"I just don't know what Grace and I would've done without you," Goldie said, sniffling even more. She wiped her nose and stuffed the hankie back in her pocket. Reaching for the coffeepot behind the counter, she motioned with her free hand. "Sit anyplace you want."

"Thank you, Goldie." Olivia was genuinely touched, since Goldie maintained strict control of who sat where.

Although Goldie had given her free rein, Olivia chose the booth where she'd sat with Grace every Wednesday night until recently. It felt good to slide across the cracked red vinyl cushion again. Olivia resisted the urge to close her eyes and breathe in the scent of this familiar restaurant. The coffee had always been strong and a hint of maple syrup lingered, although it was long past the breakfast hour.

Goldie automatically righted their coffee mugs and filled them. "We've got a turkey dinner with all the trimmings if you're interested," she announced.

Olivia still struggled with her appetite. "What's the soup of the day?"

Goldie frowned. "You aren't having just soup."

"But..."

"Look at you," the waitress chastised. "You're as thin as a flagpole. If you don't want a big meal, then I suggest chicken pot pie."

"Sounds good to me," Will said.

Goldie ignored him. She whipped the pencil from behind her ear and yanked out the pad in her apron pocket. From sheer force of habit, or so Olivia suspected, she licked the lead. "Okay, what's it gonna be? And make up your mind, 'cause the lunch crowd's coming in a few minutes and we're gonna be real busy."

It was all Olivia could do to hide her amusement. "Okay, I'll take the chicken pot pie."

"Good choice." Goldie made a notation on her pad.

"I'm glad you approve."

"You're getting pie à la mode, too."

"Goldie!"

One hand on her hip, Goldie glared at her. "After all these years, you should know better than to argue with me." She turned to Will. "And that goes for you, too, young man."

Will raised his hands in acquiescence as Olivia sputtered. "I stand corrected," she said, grinning despite her efforts to keep a straight face.

Goldie left to place their order and Will grinned, too. "I guess *you* were told."

"I guess I was," she agreed. It was nice to know she'd been missed.

Grace would get a real kick out of hearing about this. Olivia would make a point of telling her when they met at the Christmas Eve service later that evening.

Looking out the window, Olivia studied the hand-painted snowman, surrounded by falling snow. The glass next to Will was adorned with a big-eyed reindeer. A small poinsettia sat on every table, and the sights and sounds of Christmas filled the room as "O, Little Town of Bethlehem" played softly in the background.

"Are you sure I can't convince you to join us for Christmas dinner?" Olivia asked her brother.

He shook his head. "I appreciate the offer, but you're not up for company yet."

"We're seeing Justine and her family tonight. It's just going to be Jack and me for Christmas Day."

"Exactly. The two of you don't need a third wheel."

"It wouldn't be like that," Olivia protested. "I hate the idea of you spending Christmas alone."

Will sat back. "What makes you think I'll be alone?"

Olivia raised her eyebrows. "You mean you won't?"

He gave a small noncommittal shrug.

"Will." She breathed his name slowly. She didn't want to bring up past history, but in her view, Will wasn't to be trusted with women. "You're seeing someone, aren't you?"

The fact that Will was being secretive didn't bode well. "Come on," she urged him. "Tell me."

He smiled. "It isn't what you think."

"She isn't married, is she?"

"No."

That, at least, was a relief.

"I'm starting over, Liv. My slate's clean now and I want to keep it that way."

Olivia certainly hoped so. "Tell me who it is," she said again.

Her brother relaxed and folded his hands on the table. "I've seen Shirley Bliss a few times."

Shirley Bliss. She was the artist who'd created the dragon, breathing fire and pain and anger.

"Shirley," she whispered. "The dragon lady." Olivia hadn't even met the woman but sensed they could easily be friends.

"She's the one," Will said. "We're only getting to know each other but I'm impressed with her. She's someone I'd definitely like to know better."

"She invited you for Christmas?"

Will shifted his weight and looked out the window. "Well, not exactly."

Olivia frowned. "Either she did or she didn't."

"Let's put it like this. She hasn't invited me *yet*."

"Good grief, Will! It's Christmas Eve. If she was going to invite you, it would've been before now."

"Perhaps." He grinned boyishly. "Actually, I thought I'd stop by her place around dinnertime tomorrow with a small gift."

"Will!"

"Hey, you can't blame a man for trying."

"Will she be by herself?"

He shook his head. "She has two teenagers, a daughter who's a talented artist, too, and a son who's in college. I haven't met him yet."

Before Will could say anything else, Goldie arrived at their booth, carrying two chicken pot pies. She set them down and came back with two huge pieces of coconut cream pie. "Make sure you save room for this," she told them.

"I'd like to remind you I didn't order any pie," Olivia said, pretending to disapprove.

"I know," Goldie returned gruffly. "It's on the house. Think of me as your very own elf. Merry Christmas."

"Merry Christmas to you, Goldie the Elf."

Will reached for his fork and smiled over at Olivia. "I have the feeling it's going to be a merry Christmas for us all."

Olivia had the very same feeling, despite—or maybe even because of—their unexpected visitor.

7

Linc gritted his teeth. It was after two, and the traffic through Tacoma was bumper to bumper. "You'd think it was a holiday or something," he muttered sarcastically.

Mel's eyebrows shot up and he turned to look at Ned in the backseat.

"What?" Linc barked.

"It *is* a holiday," Ned reminded him.

"Don't you think I *know* that? I'm joking!"

"Okay, okay."

"You're going to exit up here," Mel said, pointing to the exit ramp for Highway 16.

Linc sighed in relief. They were getting closer, and once they found Mary Jo he intended to give her a piece of his mind. She had no business taking off like this, not when her baby was due in two weeks. It just wasn't safe.

His jaw tightened as he realized it wasn't Mary Jo who annoyed him as much as David Rhodes. If Linc could just have five minutes alone with that jerk...

"I'll bet he's married," Linc said to himself. That would explain a lot. A married man would do anything he could to hide the fact that he had a wife. He'd strung Mary Jo along, fed her a bunch of lies and then left her to deal with the consequences all on her own. Well, that wasn't going to happen. No, sir. Not while Linc was alive. David Rhodes was going to acknowledge his responsibilities and live up to them.

"Who's married?" Mel asked, staring at him curiously.

"David Rhodes," he said. "Who else?"

The exit was fast approaching and, while they still had twenty miles to go, traffic would thin out once he was off the Interstate.

"He's not," Ned said blithely from the backseat.

"Isn't what?" Linc demanded.

"David Rhodes isn't married."

Linc glanced over his shoulder. "How do you know?"

"Mary Jo told me."

Ned and Mary Jo were close, and he was more apt to take a statement like that at face value.

"He probably lied about that along with everything else," Mel said, voicing Linc's own thoughts.

"He didn't," Ned insisted.

"How can you be so sure?"

"I checked him out on the Internet," Ned continued with the same certainty. "It's a matter of public record. David Rhodes lives in California and he's been married and divorced twice. Both his marriages and divorces are listed with California's Department of Records."

Funny Ned had only mentioned this now. Maybe he had other information that would be helpful.

"You mean to say he's been married more than once?" Mel asked.

Ned nodded. "Yeah, according to what I read, he's been married twice. I doubt Mary Jo knows about the second time, though."

That was interesting and Linc wished he'd heard it earlier. "Did you find out anything else while you were doing this background search?" he asked. He eased onto the off ramp; as he'd expected, the highway was far less crowded.

"His first ex-wife, who now lives in Florida, has had problems collecting child support."

Linc shook his head. "Does that surprise anyone?"

"Nope," Mel said.

"How many children does he have?" Linc asked next.

"Just one. A girl."

"Does Mary Jo know this?" Mel asked. "About him being a deadbeat?"

"I didn't tell her," Ned admitted, adding, "I couldn't see any reason to upset her more than she already is."

"Good idea," Mel said. He leaned forward and looked up at the darkening sky. "Snow's starting again. The radio said there's going to be at least three inches."

"Snow," Linc muttered.

"Snow," Ned repeated excitedly. "That'll make a lot of little kids happy."

Mel agreed quickly. "Yeah, we'll have a white Christmas."

"Are either of *you* little kids?" Linc snapped. His nerves were frayed and he'd appreciate it if his brothers took a more mature outlook.

"I guess I'm still a kid at heart," Ned said, exhaling a sigh.

Considering Linc's current frame of mind, it was a brave admission. With a slow breath, Linc made a concerted effort to relax. He was worried about Mary Jo; he couldn't help it. He'd wanted the best for her and felt that he'd failed both his sister and his parents.

To some extent he blamed himself for what had happened. Maybe he'd been too strict with her after she turned eighteen.

But to his way of thinking, she was under his protection as long as she lived in the family home.

Not once had she introduced him to David Rhodes. Linc was convinced that if he'd met the other man, it would've taken him all of two seconds to peg David for a phony.

"What are you gonna say when we find her?" Ned asked.

Linc hadn't worked out the specifics. "Let's not worry about that now. Main thing is, we're going to put her in the truck and bring her home."

"What if she doesn't want to come with us?"

Linc hadn't considered this. "Why wouldn't she? We're her family and it's Christmas Eve. Mary Jo belongs with us. Anyway, that baby could show up anytime."

Mel seemed distinctly queasy at the prospect.

Thinking back, Linc realized he should have recognized the signs a lot earlier than he had. In fact, he hadn't recognized them at all; she'd *told* him and after that, of course, the signs were easy to see.

Not until the day Mary Jo rushed past him in the hallway and practically shoved him into the wall so she could get to the toilet in time to throw up did he have the slightest suspicion that anything was wrong. Even then he'd assumed she had a bad case of the flu.

Boy, had he been wrong. She had the flu, all right, only it was the nine-month variety.

It just hadn't occurred to him that she'd do something so dumb. An affair with the guy was bad enough, but to take that kind of chance…

Frowning, Linc glanced in his rearview mirror at his youngest brother. He was beginning to wonder about Ned. He'd never seemed as shocked as he or Mel had, and Mary Jo had always confided in him.

"How long have you known?" he casually asked.

Ned met Linc's gaze in the rearview mirror, his expression trapped. "Known what?"

"That Mary Jo was going to have a baby."

Ned looked away quickly and shrugged.

"She told you as soon as she found out, didn't she?"

Ned cleared his throat. "She might have."

"How early was that?" Linc asked, unwilling to let his brother sidestep the question.

"Early," Ned admitted. "I knew before David."

"You knew *that* early?" Mel shouted. "Why'd she tell you and not me?"

"Because you'd tell Linc," Ned told him. "She wanted to keep the baby a secret as long as she could."

Linc couldn't figure that one out. It wasn't like she'd be able to hide the pregnancy forever. And why hadn't she trusted him the way she did Ned? Although he prided himself on being stoic, that hurt.

Mel tapped his fingertips against the console. "Did she tell you how David Rhodes reacted to the news?"

Ned nodded. "She said he seemed pleased."

"Sure, why not?" Linc said, rolling his eyes. "The pregnancy wasn't going to inconvenience *him* any."

"I think that's why he could string Mary Jo along all this time," Ned suggested.

"You're probably right."

"I warned her, you know." Ned's look was thoughtful.

"When?"

"When she first started seeing him."

"You knew about David even before Mary Jo got pregnant?" Linc couldn't believe his ears. Apparently Mary Jo had shared all this information with Ned, who'd remained tight-lipped about most of it. If he wasn't so curious to uncover what his brother had learned, Linc might've been downright angry.

"So?" Mel said. "How'd she meet him?"

Ned leaned toward the front seat. "Rhodes works for the same insurance company. He's at corporate headquarters in San Francisco. Something to do with finances."

His sister worked in the accounting department, so that explained it, he supposed. "She should've come to work at our office the way I wanted," Linc said, and not for the first time. That was what he'd suggested when, against his wishes, Mary Jo had dropped out of college.

From her reaction, one would think he'd proposed slave labor. He never had understood her objections. He'd been willing to pay her top wages, as well as vacation and sick leave, and the work wasn't exactly strenuous.

She'd turned him down flat. Mary Jo wouldn't even consider working for Three Wyse Men Automotive. Linc regretted not being more forceful in light of what had happened. She might be almost twenty-four, but she needed his protection.

As they approached the Narrows Bridge, Linc's mood began to lighten somewhat. Yeah, Mary Jo needed him, and he assumed she'd be willing to admit that now. Not just him, either. She depended on all three of her brothers.

Ned's idea that they bring gifts had been smart, a good way to placate her and prove how much she meant to them. Women, in his experience, anyway, responded well to gifts.

Except that was probably the same technique David Rhodes had used.

"Did he buy her gifts?" Linc asked, frowning.

Ned understood his question, because he answered right away. "If you mean Rhodes, then yes, he got her a few."

"Such as?"

"Flowers a couple of times."

"Flowers!" Mel said.

"In the beginning, at any rate, and then after she was pregnant he bought her earrings."

Linc sat up straighter. "What kind?"

Ned snickered. "He said they were diamonds but one of them came loose so I dropped it off at Fred's for her. While he had it, I asked him to check it out."

Fred's was a local jewelry store the Wyse family had used for years. "Fake, right?"

"As phony as David Rhodes himself."

Mel twisted around and looked at Ned. "You didn't tell Mary Jo, did you?"

Ned shook his head. "I didn't want to add to her heartache."

"Maybe she already knows." His sister might be gullible but she wasn't stupid.

"I think she considered pawning it," Ned muttered, lowering his voice. "She didn't, so she might've guessed…"

The mere thought of his sister walking into a pawnshop with her pathetic bauble produced a stab of actual pain. "If she needed money, why didn't she come to me?" Linc demanded.

"You'll have to ask her that yourself."

"I plan to." Linc wasn't about to let this slide. "What does she need money for, anyway?"

"She wants her own place, you know."

No one needed to remind Linc of that. Mary Jo did a fine job of informing him at every opportunity. But it wasn't going to happen now. With a baby on the way, she wouldn't be leaving the family home anytime soon.

Linc liked that idea. He could keep an eye on her and on the baby, too. Even if he married Jillian, which was by no means a sure thing, the house was big enough for all of them. His nephew would need a strong male influence, and he fully intended to provide that influence.

"How much farther?" Mel asked.

His brother was like a kid squirming in the front seat, asking "Are we there yet?" every five minutes.

"Hey, look," Ned said, pointing at the sky. "It's really coming down now."

"Did you think I hadn't noticed?" Linc didn't have much trouble driving in bad weather; it was all the *other* drivers who caused the problem. Snow in the Seattle area was infrequent and a lot of folks didn't know how to handle it.

"Hey," Mel said as they approached the first exit for Cedar Cove. "We're here."

"Right." Not having any more specific indication of where they should go, Linc took the exit.

"Where to now?" Mel asked.

Linc could've said, "Your guess is as good as mine." But he figured his guess was actually better. "We'll do what Mary Jo did," he said. "We'll chase down David's family. That's where she's going to be."

Mel nodded. "Whoever said the Wyse Men needed a star to guide them obviously never met the three of us."

8

Olivia couldn't wait to see her husband. For one thing, she wanted to tell him about her stepbrother, get his advice.

David Rhodes...that...that—she couldn't think of a word that adequately described how loathsome he was. She wanted him exposed. Humiliated, embarrassed, *punished*. Only the fact that Ben would be humiliated and embarrassed, too, gave her pause.

When Olivia pulled into her driveway on Lighthouse Road she was delighted to see that Jack was already home from the newspaper office. Impatiently, she grabbed the grocery bag of last-minute items and made her way into the house, using the entrance off the kitchen.

"Jack!" she called out as soon as she was inside.

"What's wrong?" Her husband met her in the kitchen and stopped short. "Someone's made *you* mad."

Olivia finished unwinding the muffler from around her neck. "Why do you say that?" she asked, not realizing she'd been so obvious.

"Your eyes are shooting sparks. So, what'd I do this time?"

"It's not you, silly." She hung her coat on the hook along

with the bright red scarf her mother had knit for her. She stuffed the matching hat and gloves in the pockets, then kissed Jack's cheek.

As she filled the electric teakettle and turned it on, Jack began to put the groceries away.

"Are you ready to talk about it?" he asked cautiously.

"It's David."

"Rhodes?"

"The very one. The man is lower than pond scum."

"That's not news."

Early in her mother's marriage to Ben, his son had tried to bilk Charlotte out of several thousand dollars. He'd used a ruse about needing some surgery his medical insurance wouldn't cover, and if not for Justine's intervention, Charlotte would have given him the money. David Rhodes was shameless, and he'd dishonored his father's name.

"Is he in town?" Jack asked. He took two mugs from the cupboard and set them on the counter; Olivia tossed a couple of Earl Grey tea bags in the pot.

"No, or at least not as far as I'm aware. And frankly it's a good thing he isn't."

Jack chuckled. "I couldn't agree with you more, and I haven't got a clue what he's done to upset you now."

"He got a young girl pregnant."

Jack's eyebrows rose toward his hairline. "And you know this how?"

"I met her."

"Today?"

"Not more than two hours ago. She's young, probably twenty years younger than he is, and innocent. Or she was until David got hold of her. I swear that man should be shot!"

"Olivia!" He seemed shocked by her words. "That doesn't sound like you."

"Okay, that might be drastic. I'm just so furious I can hardly stand it."

Jack grinned.

With her hands on her hips, Olivia glared at her husband. "You find this amusing, do you?"

"Well, not about this young lady but I will admit it's a pleasant change to see color in your cheeks and your eyes sparkling, even if it's with outrage." He reached for her and brought her close enough to kiss her lips, allowing his own to linger. When he released her, he pressed his forehead to hers and whispered, "It's an even greater pleasure to know all this indignation isn't directed at me."

"I've never been anywhere near this upset with you, Jack Griffin."

"I beg to differ."

"When?"

"I remember one time," Jack said, "when I thought you were going to kick me out."

"I would *never* have done that." Her arms circled his waist. They'd found ways to make their marriage work, ways to compromise between his nature—he was a slob, not to put too fine a point on it—and hers.

Olivia liked order. Their bathroom dilemma was a perfect example. She'd been driven to the brink of fury by the piles of damp towels, the spattered mirror, the uncapped toothpaste. The solution? They had their own bathrooms now. She kept the one off the master bedroom and he had the guest bath. Jack could be as sloppy as he wanted, as long as he closed the door and Olivia didn't have to see his mess.

"You're lucky I love you so much," Jack whispered.

"And why's that?" she asked, leaning back to look him in the eye.

"Because you'd be lost without me."

"Jack…"

The kettle started to boil, its piercing whistle enough to set the dogs in the next block howling. She tried to break free, but Jack held her fast. "Admit it," he insisted. "You're crazy about me."

"All right, all right, I'm crazy about you."

"And you'd be lost without me. Wouldn't you?"

"Jack!"

Grinning like a schoolboy, he let her go and she grabbed the kettle, relieved by the sudden cessation of that high-pitched shrieking.

Pouring the boiling water into the teapot, she covered it with a cozy and left the tea to steep. Then she opened the cookie jar and chose two of the decorated sugar cookies she'd baked a few days earlier with her grandson—a tree shape and a star. The afternoon had worn her out physically but she treasured every moment she'd spent in the kitchen with Leif.

Just as she was about to pour their tea, the phone rang.

"Want me to get that?" Jack called from the other room.

A glance at Caller ID told her it was Grace.

"I will," she told him. "Merry Christmas," she said into the receiver.

"Merry Christmas to you, too," her friend said in return. "I thought I'd check in and let you know how everything's going."

"So what's the update?"

"Everything's fine," Grace assured her.

"Mary Jo's resting?"

"She was asleep the last time I looked, which was about five minutes ago. The girl must be exhausted. She told me she didn't get much sleep last night."

"She's in the apartment then, or at the house?"

"The apartment. Cliff's daughter and her family are already here, so…"

Olivia wasn't entirely comfortable with the idea of leaving Mary Jo alone, but it was probably for the best. This way she could rest undisturbed.

"There's something strange…"

"What?" Olivia asked.

"Well, for no reason I can understand, I decided to do a bit of housekeeping in the apartment yesterday. Cal's been gone a few weeks now, and I put clean sheets on the bed and fresh towels in the bathroom. It's as if…as if I was waiting for Mary Jo."

That was a little too mystical for Olivia. "I'm so glad this is working out," she murmured.

"She's an animal-lover, too."

That didn't surprise Olivia. She sensed that Mary Jo had a gentleness about her, a soft heart, an interest in others.

"The minute I brought her into the barn, she wanted to see all the Nativity animals."

"You kept her away from that camel, didn't you?"

"I kept us both away," Grace was quick to tell her. "That beast is going to have to chew on someone else's arm."

"Yeah, David's would be ideal," Olivia muttered.

Grace laughed, but sobered almost immediately. "Listen, Mary Jo has a concern I'd like to talk to you about."

"Sure."

"She's got three older brothers who are probably on their way into town, looking for her, as we speak."

"Does she *want* to be found?" Olivia asked.

"I think she does, only she wants to talk to Ben and Charlotte before her brothers do."

"She's not trying to protect David, is she?"

"I doubt it. What she's afraid of is that her brothers might insist David marry her and she doesn't want to. At this point, she's accepted that she's better off without him."

"Smart decision."

"Yes, but it came at quite a price, didn't it?"

"True. A lesson with lifelong consequences."

"We all seem to learn our lessons the hard way," Grace said.

"I know I did." Her children, too, Olivia mused. Justine and James. As always, especially around the holidays, her mind wandered to Jordan, the son she'd lost that summer day all those years ago. Justine's twin.

"What time are Maryellen and Kelly coming by?" she asked, changing the subject. Although Mary Jo would be staying in the barn, perhaps she should bring her over for dinner. Give her a chance to feel welcomed by Ben's second family. Cliff's daughter, Lisa, her husband and their little girl, April, were out doing some last-minute shopping, apparently, and not due back until late afternoon.

"My girls should be here around six."

"You're going straight to church after dinner?"

"That's the plan," Grace told her. "I was going to invite Mary Jo to join us."

"For dinner or Christmas Eve service?"

"Both, actually, but I'm having second thoughts." Grace hesitated.

"Why? And about what?"

"Oh, about inviting Mary Jo to dinner. I'm afraid it might be too much for her. We'll have five grandkids running around. You know how much racket children can make, and double that for Christmas Eve."

"Is there anything I can do for her?" Olivia asked. "Should I ask her to have dinner here?"

"I'm not sure. I'll talk to her when she wakes up and then I'll phone you."

"Thanks. And tell her not to worry about her brothers."

"I'll do that."

"See you tonight."

"Tonight."

After setting down the phone, Olivia poured the tea and placed both mugs on the table, followed by the plate of cookies, and called Jack into the kitchen again.

His eyes widened in overstated surprise. "Cookies? For me? You shouldn't have."

"I can still put them back."

"Oh, no, you don't." He grabbed the star-shaped cookie and bit off one point. "What's this in honor of?"

"I had pie with lunch. So I'm trying to be fair."

Knowing her disciplined eating habits, Jack did a double-take. "You ate pie? At *lunch?*"

"Goldie made me do it."

"Goldie," he repeated. "You mean Will took you to the Pancake Palace?"

"It's where I wanted to go."

Jack sat down, grabbed the tree cookie and bit into that, too. "You're a cheap date."

"Not necessarily."

He ignored that remark. "Did you enjoy lunch with Will?" he asked, then sipped his tea. Jack was familiar with their sometimes tumultuous relationship.

"I did, although I'm a little worried." Olivia crossed her legs and held the mug in the palm of her hand. "He's interested in Shirley Bliss, a local artist."

"She's not married, is she?"

Olivia shook her head. "A widow."

Jack shrugged. "Then it's okay if he wants to see her."

"I agree. It's just that I don't know if I can trust my brother. It pains me to admit that, but still…" She left the rest unsaid.

Jack knew her brother and his flaws as well as she did. "I want him to be successful here," she said earnestly. "He's starting over, and at this stage of his life that can't be easy."

"I don't imagine it will be," Jack agreed. "By the way, who was that on the phone?"

"Grace. She called to update me on Mary Jo."

"Problems?"

"Not really, but she said we need to keep an eye out for three irate brothers who might show up looking for her."

"A vigilante posse?"

"Not exactly." But now that Olivia thought about it, it might not be so bad if Mary Jo's brothers stumbled onto David Rhodes instead. "If her brothers find anyone, it should be David."

"There'd certainly be justice in that, but David's not going to let himself be found. And I think we should be focusing on the young woman, don't you?"

His tone was gentle, but Olivia felt chastened. "Yes—and her baby."

9

Mary Jo woke feeling confused. She sat up in bed and gazed around at the sparsely decorated room before she remembered where she was. Grace Harding had brought her home and was letting her spend the night in this apartment above the barn. It was such a kind thing to do. She was a stranger, after all, a stranger with problems who'd appeared out of nowhere on Christmas Eve.

Stretching her arms high above her head, Mary Jo yawned loudly. She was still tired, despite her nap. Her watch told her she'd been asleep for the better part of two hours. Two hours!

Other than in her first trimester, she hadn't required a lot of extra rest during her pregnancy, but that had changed in the past few weeks. Of course some of it could be attributed to David and his lies. Wondering what she should believe and whether he'd meant *any* of what he'd said had kept her awake many a night. Consequently she was tired during the day; while she was still working she'd nap during her lunch break.

Forcing her eyes shut, Mary Jo made an effort to cast David from her mind. She quickly gave up. Tossing aside the covers, Mary Jo climbed out of bed, put on her shoes and left the apartment. The stairway led to the interior of the barn.

As soon as she stepped into the barn, several animals stuck their heads out of the stalls to study her curiously. The first she saw was a lovely horse. Grace had introduced her as Funny Face.

"Hello there, girl." Mary Jo walked slowly toward the stall door. "Remember me?" The mare nodded in what seemed to be an encouraging manner, and Mary Jo ran her hand down the horse's unusually marked face. The mare had a white ring around one eye and it was easy to see why the Hardings had named her Funny Face. Her dark, intelligent eyes made Mary Jo think of an old story she recalled from childhood—that animals can talk for a few hours after midnight on Christmas Eve—and she wondered what Funny Face would say. Probably something very wise.

The camel seemed curious, too, and thrust her long curved neck out of the stall, peering at Mary Jo through wide eyes, fringed with lush, curling lashes. Mary Jo had been warned to keep her distance. "Oh, no, you don't," she muttered, waving her index finger. "You're not going to lure me over there with those big brown eyes. Don't give me that innocent look, either. I've heard all about you."

After visiting a few placid sheep, another couple of horses and a donkey with a sweet disposition, Mary Jo walked out of the barn. She hurried toward the house through a light snowfall, wishing she'd remembered her coat. Even before she arrived, the front door opened and an attractive older gentleman held open the screen.

"You must be Mary Jo," he said and thrust out his hand in greeting. "Cliff Harding."

"Hello, Mr. Harding," she said with a smile. She was about to thank him for his hospitality when he interrupted.

"Call me Cliff, okay? And come in, come in."

"All right, Cliff."

Mary Jo entered the house and was greeted by the smell of roasting turkey and sage and apple pie.

"You're awake!" Grace declared as she stepped out of the kitchen. She wore an apron and had smudges of flour on her cheeks.

"I'm shocked I slept for so long."

"You obviously needed the rest," Grace commented, leading her into the kitchen. "I see you've met my husband."

"Yes." Mary Jo smiled again. Rubbing her palms nervously together, she looked from one to the other. "I really can't thank you enough for everything you've done for me."

"Oh, nonsense. It's the least we could do."

"I'm a stranger and you took me in without question and, well… I didn't think that kind of thing happened in this day and age."

That observation made Grace frown. "Really? It does here in Cedar Cove. I guess it's just how people act in small towns. We tend to be more trusting."

"I had a similar experience when I first moved here," Cliff said. "I wasn't accustomed to people going out of their way for someone they didn't know. Charlotte Jefferson—now Charlotte Rhodes—quickly disabused me of that notion."

Despite everything, Mary Jo looked forward to meeting David's stepmother. The conversation would be difficult, but knowing that Charlotte was as kind as everyone else she'd met so far made all the difference.

"Really, Mary Jo," Grace continued. "All you needed was a friend and a helping hand. Anyone here would've done the same. Olivia wanted you to stay with her, too."

"Everyone's been so wonderful." Thinking about the willingness of this family to take her in brought a lump to her throat. She bent, with some effort, to stroke the smooth head of a golden retriever who lay on a rug near the stove.

"That's Buttercup," Grace said fondly as the dog thumped her tail but didn't get up. "She's getting old, like the rest of us."

"Coffee?" Cliff walked over to the coffeemaker. "It's decaf. Are you interested?" he asked, motioning in Mary Jo's direction with the pot. "Or would you prefer tea? Maybe some chamomile or peppermint tea."

"Tea, please. If it isn't any trouble."

"None whatsoever. I'm having a cup myself." Grace began the preparations, then suddenly asked, "You didn't eat any lunch, did you?"

"No, but I'm not hungry."

"You might not be, but that baby of yours is," Grace announced as if she had a direct line of communication to the unborn child. Without asking further, she walked to the refrigerator and stuck her head inside. Adjusting various containers and bottles and packages, she took out a plastic-covered bowl.

"I don't want to cause you any extra work," Mary Jo protested.

"The work's already done. Cliff made the most delicious clam chowder," Grace said. "I'll heat you up some."

Now that Grace mentioned it, Mary Jo realized she really could use something to eat; she was getting light-headed again. "Cliff cooks?" Her brothers were practically helpless around the kitchen and it always surprised her to find a man who enjoyed cooking.

"I am a man of many talents," Grace's husband was quick to answer. "I was a bachelor for years before I met Grace."

"If I didn't prepare meals, my brothers would survive on fast food and frozen entrées," she said, grinning. Thankfully her mother had taught her quite a bit before her death. The brothers had relied on Mary Jo for meals ever since.

The thought of Linc, Mel and Ned made her anxious. She'd meant to call, but then she'd fallen asleep and now…they could be anywhere. They'd be furious and frightened. She felt a blast of guilt; her brothers might be misguided but they loved her.

"If you'll excuse me a moment," she said urgently. "I need to make a phone call."

"Of course," Grace told her. "Would you like to use the house phone?"

She shook her head. "No, I have my cell up in the apartment. It'll only take a few minutes."

"You might have a problem with coverage. Try it and see. By the time you return, the tea and soup will be ready."

Mary Jo went back to the barn and up the stairs to the small apartment. She was breathless when she reached the top and paused to gulp in some air. Her pulse was racing. This had never happened before. Trying to stay calm, she walked into the bedroom where she'd left her purse.

Sitting on the bed, she got out her cell. She tried the family home first. But the call didn't connect, and when Mary Jo glanced at the screen, she saw there wasn't any coverage in this area. Well, that settled that.

She did feel bad but there was no help for it. She'd ask to make a long-distance call on the Hardings' phone, and she'd try Linc's cell, as well as the house. She collected her coat and gloves and hurried back to the house.

A few minutes later, she was in the kitchen. As Grace had promised, the tea and a bowl of soup were waiting for her on the table.

Mary Jo hesitated. She really hated to ask, hated to feel even more beholden. "If you don't mind, I'd appreciate using your phone."

"Of course."

"It's long distance, I'm afraid. I'd be happy to pay the charges. You could let me know—"

"Nonsense," Grace countered. "One phone call isn't going to make a bit of difference to our bill."

"Thank you." Still wearing her coat, Mary Jo went over to the wall phone, then remembered that Linc's number was programmed into her cell. Speed dial made it unnecessary to memorize numbers these days, she thought ruefully.

She'd have to go back to the apartment a second time. Well, there was no help for that, either. "I'll need to get my cell phone," she said.

"I can have Cliff get it for you," Grace offered. "I'm not sure you should be climbing those stairs too often."

"Oh, no, I'm fine," Mary Jo assured her. She walked across the yard, grateful the snow had tapered off, and back up the steep flight of stairs, pausing as she had before to inhale deeply and calm her racing heart. Taking another breath, she went in search of her cell.

On the off chance the phone might work in a different location, Mary Jo stood on the Hardings' porch and tried again. And again she received the same message. No coverage.

Cell phone in hand, she returned to the kitchen.

"I'll make the call as quickly as I can," she told Grace, lifting the receiver off the hook.

"You talk as long as you need," Grace told her. "And here, let me take your coat."

She found Linc's contact information in her cell phone's directory and dialed his number. After a few seconds, the call connected and went straight to voice mail. Linc, it appeared, had decided to turn off his cell. Mary Jo wasn't sure what to make of that. Maybe he didn't *want* her to contact him, she thought with sudden panic. Maybe he was so angry he never wanted to hear from her again. When she tried to leave a message, she discovered that his voice mail was full. She sighed. It was just like Linc not to listen to his messages. He probably had no idea how many he'd accumulated.

"My brother has his cell off," Mary Jo said with a defeated shrug.

"He might be in a no coverage zone," Grace explained. "We don't get good reception here at the ranch, although I do almost everywhere else in Kitsap County. Is it worth trying his house?"

Mary Jo doubted it, but she punched in the numbers. As she'd expected, no answer there, either. Her oldest brother's deep voice came on, reciting the phone number. Then, in his usual peremptory fashion, he said, "We're not here. Leave a message." Mary Jo closed her eyes.

"It's me," she said shakily, half afraid Linc would break in and start yelling at her. Grace had stepped out of the kitchen to give her privacy, a courtesy she appreciated.

"I'm in Cedar Cove," she continued. "I'll be home sometime Christmas Day after I speak to David's parents. Probably later in the evening. Please don't try to find me. I'm with… friends. Don't worry about me. I know what I'm doing." With that she replaced the receiver.

She saw that Grace had moved into the dining room, setting the table. "Thank you," Mary Jo told her.

"You're very welcome. Is your soup still hot?"

Mary Jo had forgotten about that. "I'll check."

"If not, let me know and I'll reheat it in the microwave."

"I'm sure it'll be fine," she murmured. Even if it was stone-cold, she wouldn't have said so, not after everything Grace had done for her.

But as Mary Jo tried her first spoonful, she realized the temperature was perfect. She finished the entire bowl, then ate all the crackers and drank her tea. As she brought her dishes to the sink, Grace returned to the kitchen. "My daughters will be here at six," she said, glancing at the clock. "And my daughter-in-law and her family should be back soon. We're having dinner together and then we're leaving for the Christmas Eve service at our church."

"How nice." Mary Jo had missed attending church. She and her brothers just seemed to stop going after her parents' funeral. She still went occasionally but hadn't in quite a while, and her brothers didn't go at all.

"Would you like to join us?"

The invitation was so genuine that for a moment Mary Jo seriously considered it. "Thank you for the offer, but I don't think I should."

"Why not?" Grace pressed. "We'd love to have you."

"Thank you," Mary Jo said again, "but I should probably stay quiet and rest, like the EMT suggested."

Grace nodded. "Yes, you should take his advice, although we'd love it if you'd at least join us for dinner."

The invitation moved her so much that Mary Jo felt tears spring to her eyes. Not only had Grace and her husband taken her into their home, they wanted to include her in their holiday celebration.

"I can't believe you'd want me here with your family," she said, struggling to get the words out.

"Why wouldn't we?" Grace asked. She seemed astonished by the comment. "You're our guest."

"But it's Christmas and you'll have your...your family here." She found it difficult to speak.

"Yes, and they'll be delighted to meet you."

"But this isn't a time for strangers."

"Now, just a minute," Grace said. "Don't you remember the original Christmas story?"

"Of course I do." Mary Jo had heard it all her life.

"Mary and Joseph didn't have anywhere to stay, either, and strangers offered them a place," Grace reminded her. "A stable," she added with a smile.

"But I doubt those generous folks asked them to join the family for dinner," Mary Jo teased.

"That part we don't know because the Bible doesn't say, but I have to believe that anyone who'd lend their stable to those young travelers would see to their other needs, as well." Grace's warm smile wrapped its way around Mary Jo's heart. "Join us for part of the evening, okay? I'd love it if you met the girls, and I know they'd enjoy meeting you."

Mary Jo didn't immediately respond. Although she would've liked to meet Grace's family, she wasn't feeling quite right. "May I think about it?"

"Of course," Grace said. "You do whatever you need to do."

Leaning forward in the chair, Mary Jo supported her lower back with both hands, trying to ease the persistent ache. Sitting had become difficult in the last few weeks. It was as if the baby had latched his or her foot around one of her ribs and intended to hang on. Mary Jo was beginning to wonder if she'd ever find a comfortable position again.

"Can I help you with anything?" she asked.

Grace surveyed the kitchen. "No, I've got everything under control. I thought I'd sit down for a few minutes and have a cup of tea with you."

Mary Jo nodded. "Yes, please. I'd like that."

"So would I," the other woman said. "Here, let me make some fresh tea. And what about some Christmas shortbread to go with it?"

10

At the fire station, Mack McAfee sat by himself in the kitchen, downing yet another cup of coffee. The only call so far that day had been for the young pregnant woman who'd had the dizzy spell at the library. For some reason, she'd stayed in his mind ever since.

Because he wasn't married, Mack had volunteered to work Christmas Eve and part of Christmas Day, allowing one of the other firefighters to spend the time with family. Unfortunately his mother was none too happy that he'd agreed to work over the holidays.

Mack's parents lived in Cedar Cove and his sister had, too, until she'd left several months ago, her heart broken by that cowpoke who used to work for Cliff Harding. Linnette had taken off with no plan or destination and ended up in some podunk town in North Dakota. She seemed to love her new home out there in the middle of nowhere. Mack didn't understand it, but then it wasn't his life.

He was happy for Linnette, knowing she'd found her niche. She'd always said she wanted to live and work in a small rural town. As an experienced physician assistant, Linnette had a lot to offer a community like Buffalo Valley, North Dakota.

Gloria, Mack's oldest sister, had been given up for adoption as an infant; their relationship had only come to light in the past few years. Mack was just beginning to know her and so far he'd discovered that they had a surprising amount in common, despite their very different upbringings. She'd promised to stop by the house and spend part of Christmas with their parents, but she, too, was on the duty roster for tonight.

When Gloria had first moved into the area—with the goal of reconnecting with her birth family—she'd worked for the Bremerton police. However, she'd recently taken a job with the sheriff's department in Cedar Cove.

Mack's cell phone, attached to his waistband, chirped. He reached for it, not bothering to look at the screen. He already knew who was calling.

"Hi, Mom."

"Merry Christmas." Her cheerful greeting was strained and not entirely convincing.

"Thanks. Same to you and Dad."

"How's everything?"

His mother was at loose ends. Not having any of her children with her during the holidays was hard for her. "It's been pretty quiet here this afternoon," he said.

Corrie allowed an audible sigh to escape. "I wish you hadn't volunteered to work on Christmas."

This wasn't the first time his mother had brought it up. But as the firefighter most recently hired, he would've been assigned this shift, anyway.

"It'll be lonely with just your father and me." Her voice fell and Mack sighed, wishing he could tell her what she wanted to hear.

"It'll be a wonderful Christmas," he said, sounding as positive as he could.

"I'm sure it'll be fine," she agreed in a listless voice. "I decided to cook a ham this year instead of turkey. It's far less work and we had a turkey at Thanksgiving. Of course, I'm going to bake your father's favorite potato casserole and that green bean dish everyone likes."

Mack didn't understand why his mother felt she had to review her dinner menu with him, but he let her chatter on, knowing it made her feel better.

"I was thinking," she said, abruptly changing the subject.

"Yes, Mom?"

"You should get married."

If Mack had been swallowing a drink at the time he would've choked. "I beg your pardon?"

"You're settling down here in Cedar Cove?"

He noticed that she'd made it a question. "Well, I wouldn't go that far."

"I would," she said. "You have a steady job." She didn't add that this was perhaps his tenth career change in the last six years. Mack was easily bored and tended to jump from job to job. He'd worked part-time for the post office, done construction, delivered for UPS and held half a dozen other short-term jobs since dropping out of college. He'd also renovated a run-down house and sold it for a tidy profit.

Mack's restlessness had contributed to the often acrimonious relationship he'd had with his father. Roy McAfee hadn't approved of Mack's need for change. He felt Mack was irresponsible and hadn't taken his life seriously enough. In some ways Mack supposed his father was right. Still, his new job with the fire department seemed to suit him perfectly, giving him the variety, the excitement and the camaraderie he craved. It also gave him a greater sense of purpose than anything else he'd done.

He and his dad got along better these days. Roy had actually apologized for his attitude toward Mack, which had come as a real shock. It had made a big difference in their relationship, though, and for that Mack was grateful.

"You think I should be *married*," he repeated, as though it was a foreign word whose meaning eluded him.

"You're twenty-eight."

"I know how old I am, Mom."

"It's time," she said simply.

"Really?" He found his mother's decree almost humorous.

"Have you met anyone special?" she asked.

"Mom!" he protested. Yet the picture of Mary Jo Wyse shot instantly into his mind. He knew from the conversation he'd overheard at the library that she was pregnant and single and that David Rhodes was her baby's father. He'd also heard a reference to Charlotte and Ben Rhodes. He was familiar with them, but completely in the dark about David.

"I'm not trying to pressure you," his mother continued. "It's just that it would be nice to have grandchildren one day."

Mack chuckled. "If you want, I'll get to work on that first thing."

"Mack," she chastised, "you know what I mean."

He did but still enjoyed teasing her. While she was on the phone, he decided to take the opportunity to find out what he could about the father of Mary Jo's baby. "Can you tell me anything about David Rhodes?" he asked.

"David Rhodes," his mother said slowly. "Is he related to Ben Rhodes?"

"His son, I believe."

"Let me go ask your father."

"That's okay, Mom, don't bother. It's no big deal."

"Why'd you ask, then?"

"Oh, someone mentioned him, that's all." Mack was reluctant to bring up Mary Jo; for one thing, it'd been a chance encounter and he wasn't likely to see her again. Clearly she wasn't from here.

"Mack. Tell me."

"I treated a young woman at the library this morning."

"The pregnant girl?" Her voice rose excitedly.

Word sure spread fast in a small town, something Mack wasn't accustomed to yet. "How do you know about Mary Jo?" he asked.

"Mary Jo," his mother said wistfully. "What a nice name."

She had a nice face to go with it, too, Mack mused and then caught himself. He had no business thinking about her. None whatsoever.

"I met Shirley Bliss in the grocery store earlier," his mother went on to say. "The last thing I wanted to do was make a dash to the store. You know how busy they get the day before a big holiday."

Actually, he didn't, not from experience, but it seemed logical enough.

"Anyway, I ran out of evaporated milk. I needed it for that green Jell-O salad I make every Christmas."

Mack remembered that salad well; it was one of his favorites. His mother had insisted on making it, he noted, even though Mack wouldn't be joining the family for dinner.

"I could've used regular milk, I guess, but I was afraid it wouldn't taste the same. I don't like to use substitutes if it can be avoided."

"Shirley Bliss, Mom," he reminded her.

"Oh, yes. Shirley. I saw her at the store. She was with her daughter, Tanni."

"O-k-a-y." Mack dragged out the word, hoping she'd get to the point.

"That's a lovely name, isn't it?" his mother asked. "Her given name is Tannith."

"Tanni's the one who told you about Mary Jo?" he asked, bringing her back to the discussion.

"No, Shirley did." She hesitated. "Well, on second thought, it was Tanni's boyfriend, Shaw, who told her, so I guess in a manner of speaking it *was* her daughter."

"And how did Shaw hear?" he pressed, losing track of all these names.

"Apparently Mary Jo came into Mocha Mama's this morning and was asking him a lot of questions."

"Oh."

"And he suggested she ask Grace Harding about David Rhodes."

"I see." Well, he was beginning to, anyway.

"Shirley said Shaw told her that Mary Jo looked like she was about to deliver that baby any minute."

"She's due in two weeks."

"My goodness! Do you think David Rhodes is the baby's father?" his mother breathed, as if suddenly making the connection. "It makes sense, doesn't it?"

He already knew as much but preferred not to contribute to the gossip obviously making the rounds. Regardless, Mack couldn't get Mary Jo out of his mind. "Did Shirley happen to say where Mary Jo is right now?" Maybe someone should check up on her. Mack had recommended she rest for the remainder of the day but he didn't like the idea of her being alone.

"No," his mother said. "She'll be fine, won't she?"

"I assume so…"

"Good."

"Where's Dad?" Mack asked.

His mother laughed softly. "Where do you think he is?"

It didn't take a private eye—which his father was—to know the answer to that. "Shopping," Mack said with a grin.

"Right. Your father's so efficient about everything else, yet he leaves gift-buying until the last possible minute."

"I remember that one year when the only store open was the pharmacy," he recalled. "He brought you a jigsaw puzzle of the Tower of London, two romance novels and some nail polish remover."

"And he was so proud of himself," Corrie said fondly.

"We all had a good time putting that puzzle together, didn't we?" It'd been one of their better Christmases, and the family still did jigsaw puzzles every holiday. A small family tradition had come about as a result of that particular Christmas and his father's last-minute gift.

"You'll call in the morning?" his mother asked.

"I will," Mack promised. "And I'll stop by the house as soon as I'm relieved. It'll be late tomorrow afternoon. Save me some leftovers, okay?"

"Of course," his mother murmured. "Gloria's schedule is the reverse of yours, so she's coming over in the morning." Corrie sounded slightly more cheerful as she said, "At least we'll see you both for a little while."

After a few words of farewell, Mack snapped his cell phone shut and clipped it back on his waistband.

He'd no sooner started getting everything ready for that night's dinner than Brandon Hutton sauntered into the kitchen. "You got company."

"Me?" Mack couldn't imagine who'd come looking for him. He was new in town and didn't know many people yet.

"Some guy and a woman," Brandon elaborated.

"Did they give you a name?" Mack asked.

"Sorry, no."

Mack walked toward the front of the building and as he neared he heard voices—one of them unmistakably his sister's.

"Linnette!" he said, bursting into the room.

"Mack." She threw herself into his arms for a fierce hug.

"What are you doing here?" he asked. The last he'd heard she was in Buffalo Valley and intended to stay there for the holidays.

She slipped one arm around his waist. "It's a surprise. Pete suggested it and offered to drive me, so here I am."

Mack turned to the other man. In a phone conversation the month before, Linnette had told him she'd met a farmer and that they were seeing each other. "Mack McAfee," he said, offering his hand.

Pete's handshake was firm. "Pleased to meet you, Mack."

"Happy to meet you, too." He turned back to his sister. "Mom doesn't know?"

Linnette giggled. "She doesn't have a clue. Dad, either. It's going to be a total shock to both of them."

"When did you arrive?"

"About five minutes ago. We decided to come and see you first, then we're going to the house."

"Dad's out doing his Christmas shopping."

Linnette laughed and looked at Pete. "What did I tell you?"

"That he'd be shopping," Pete said laconically.

"Mom's busy cooking, I'll bet." This comment was directed at Mack.

"My favorite salad," he informed her. "Even though I won't be there, she's making it for me. I'm already looking forward to the leftovers. Oh, and she decided on ham this year."

Linnette laughed again. "She discussed her Christmas menu with you?"

"In minute detail."

"Poor Mom," Linnette murmured.

"I wish I could see the expression on her face when you walk in the door."

"I love that we're going to surprise her." Linnette's wide grin was perhaps the best Christmas gift he could have received. His sister, happy again.

Mack hadn't seen her smile like this in…well, a year, anyway.

"Call me later and let me know how long it takes Mom to stop crying."

"I will," Linnette said.

His sister and Pete left for the house, and Mack returned to the firehouse kitchen, where he was assigned cooking duty that evening. He resumed chopping onions for the vat of chili he planned to make—how was that for Christmas Eve dinner? He caught himself wishing he could be at his parents' place tonight, after all. Although he'd just met Pete, Mack sensed that he was a solid, hard-working, no-nonsense man. Exactly what Linnette needed, and someone Mack wanted to know better.

It seemed that Linnette had found the kind of person *she* needed, but had he? Mack shook his head.

And yet, he couldn't forget Mary Jo Wyse.

Which wasn't remotely logical, considering that their relationship consisted mostly of him taking her blood pressure.

And yet…

11

Linc drove down Harbor Street, peering out at both sides of the street. Fortunately the snow had let up—Ned was probably disappointed by that. He wasn't sure what he was searching for, other than some clue as to where he might locate his runaway sister. He'd give anything to see that long brown coat, that colorful striped scarf…

"Nice town," Ned commented, looking around.

Linc hadn't noticed. His mind was on Mary Jo.

"They seem to go all out with the Christmas decorations," Mel added.

Ned poked his head between the two of them and braced his arms against the back of the seats. "Lots of lights, too."

"There's only one that I can see," Linc mumbled, concentrating on the road ahead. His brothers were so easily distracted, he thought irritably.

They exchanged knowing glances.

"What?" Linc barked. He recognized that look. In fact, he'd already seen it several times today.

"In case you weren't aware of it, there are lights on every lamppost all through town," Ned pointed out slowly, as if he was speaking to a child. "The street is decorated with Christmas lights. And that clock tower, too, with the Christmas tree in front of it."

"I was talking about traffic signals," Linc snapped.

"Oh, signals. Yeah, you're right about that." As Linc drove through the downtown area, there'd been just that one traffic light. Actually, he was going back to it. He made a sharp U-turn.

"Where are you going?" Mel asked, clutching the handle above the passenger window.

"Back to the light—the traffic light, I mean."

"Why?" Ned ventured with some hesitation.

Linc's mood had improved since they'd arrived in Cedar Cove. The traffic was almost nonexistent and his sister was here. Somewhere.

He tried to think like Mary Jo. Where could she be? It had started to get dark, although it was barely four in the afternoon. Twilight had already settled over the snowy landscape.

"Practically everything in town is closed for the day," Mel said, pressing his face against the passenger window like an anxious child.

"Stands to reason. It's Christmas Eve." Ned sounded as if he was stating something neither Linc nor Mel had discovered yet.

Linc waited for the light before making a sharp left-hand turn. The road ended at a small traffic circle that went around a totem pole. The building to the right with the large mural was the library, and there was a large, mostly vacant parking lot situated to his left. Directly in front of him was a marina and a large docked boat.

The sign read Passenger Ferry.

Linc immediately went through the traffic circle and pulled into the parking lot.

"Why are we stopping here?" Mel asked in surprise. "Not that I'm complaining. I could use a pit stop."

"Yeah, me too," Ned chimed in. "Let's go, okay?"

"Come on," Mel said. "I wanna hit the men's room."

"How did Mary Jo get to Cedar Cove?" he asked them both, ignoring their entreaties. "The ferry, right? Isn't that what we figured?"

"Yeah, she must've taken it to Bremerton," Mel agreed. "And then she rode the foot ferry across from Bremerton to Cedar Cove." He pointed to the boat docked at the end of the pier.

Linc playfully ruffled his brother's hair. "Give the man a cigar."

Mel jerked his head aside. "Hey, cut it out." He combed his fingers through his hair to restore it to order.

Linc swung open the truck door and climbed out.

"Where you goin' now?" Mel asked, opening his own door.

"It's not for us to question why," Ned intoned and clambered out, too.

Linc sighed. "I'm going to ask if anyone saw a pregnant girl on the dock this morning."

"Good idea," Ned said enthusiastically. "Meanwhile, we'll visit that men's room over there."

"Fine," Linc grumbled, scanning the street as he waited for them. Unfortunately he hadn't found anyone to question in the vicinity of the dock. The only nearby place that seemed to be doing business was a pub—imaginatively called the Cedar Cove Tavern.

"I Saw Mommy Kissing Santa Claus" blasted out the door the instant Linc opened it. A pool table dominated one side of the establishment; one man was leaning over it, pool cue in hand, while another stood by watching. They looked over their shoulders when the three brothers came inside.

Linc walked up to the bar.

The bartender, who had a full head of white hair and was wearing a Santa hat, ambled over to him. "What can I get you boys?"

"Coke for me." Linc was driving, so he wasn't interested in anything alcoholic. Besides, he'd need a clear head once he tracked down his obstinate younger sister.

"I'll have a beer," Mel said. He propped his elbows on the bar as though settling in for a long winter's night.

"Coke," Ned ordered, sliding onto the stool on Linc's other side.

The bartender served them speedily.

Linc slapped a twenty-dollar bill on the scarred wooden bar. "You seen a pregnant woman around today?" he asked. "Someone from out of town?"

The man frowned. "Can't say I have."

"She's *real* pregnant." For emphasis Mel held both hands in front of his stomach.

"Then I definitely didn't," Santa informed them.

"She arrived by foot ferry," Ned told him. "Probably sometime midmorning."

"Sorry," Santa murmured. "I didn't start my shift until three." He rested his bulk against the counter and called out, "Anyone here see a pregnant gal come off the foot ferry this morning?"

The two men playing pool shook their heads. The other patrons stopped their conversation, glanced at Linc and his brothers, then went back to whatever they were discussing.

"Doesn't look like anyone else did, either," the bartender said.

The brothers huddled over their drinks. "What we gotta do," Mel suggested, "is figure out what her agenda would be."

"She came to find David's parents," Ned reminded them. "*That's* her agenda."

"True." Okay, they both had a point. Turning back to the bartender, Linc caught his attention. "You know any people named Rhodes in the area?"

Santa nodded as he wiped a beer mug. "Several."

"This is an older couple. They have a son named David."

The bartender frowned. "Oh, I know David. He stiffed me on a sixty-dollar tab."

Yeah, they were talking about the same guy, all right. "What about his parents?"

"Ben and Charlotte," Santa told them. "Really decent people. I don't have anything good to say about their son, though."

"Where do they live?"

"I'm not sure."

Looking around, Linc saw a pay phone near the restrooms. "I'll check if Ben Rhodes is in the phone book," he said, leaving his stool.

"Sounds like a plan," Santa muttered.

Linc removed the phone book from a small shelf. The entire directory was only half an inch thick. The Seattle phone book had a bigger section just of government agencies than the entire Cedar Cove White *and* Yellow Pages. He quickly found the listing for Ben and Charlotte Rhodes, then copied down the phone number and address.

"Got it," he announced triumphantly.

"Should we call?"

"Nope."

"Why not?" Mel asked. He walked back to the bar and downed the last of his beer.

"I don't want to give Mary Jo a heads-up that we're in town. I think the best thing to do is take her by surprise."

Ned nodded, although he seemed a bit uncertain.

Linc thanked the bartender, got some general directions and collected his change. He left a generous tip; it was Christmas Eve, after all. Then he marched toward the door, his brothers scrambling after him.

In the parking lot again, Linc climbed into the truck and started the engine. He'd noticed that Harbor Street angled up the hill. He guessed David's parents' street wasn't far from this main thoroughfare. Trusting his instincts, he returned to the traffic signal, took a left and followed the road until it intersected with Pelican Court.

Within five minutes of leaving the tavern, Linc was parked outside Ben and Charlotte Rhodes's house.

The porch light was on, which boded well, and there appeared to be a light on inside, too. The house was a solid two-story dwelling, about the same age as the one he shared with his brothers in Seattle. White Christmas lights were strung along the roofline and the bushes were lighted, too. There was a manger scene on the front lawn.

"This is a neat town," Mel said. "Did you see they have an art gallery? We passed it a couple of minutes ago."

"When did you get so interested in art?" Linc asked.

"I like art," Mel muttered.

"Since when?"

"Since now. You want to make something of it?"

"No," Linc said, puzzled by his brother's defensiveness.

Linc walked up the steps leading to the front door while his brothers stood out on the lawn. Mel amused himself by rearranging the large plastic figures in the Nativity scene.

Linc felt smug. If Mary Jo thought she'd outsmarted him, she had a lesson to learn. He didn't want to be self-righteous, but he was going to teach his little sister that she wasn't nearly as clever as she seemed to think. He also wanted Mary Jo to understand that he had her best interests at heart—now and always.

Leaning hard against the doorbell, he waited several minutes and when nothing happened, he pressed the bell a second time.

"Want me to check out the backyard?" Ned called from the lawn.

"Sure."

His youngest brother took off and disappeared around the side of the house.

Mel trailed after Ned, while Linc stood guard on the porch. Since no one was bothering to answer—although there seemed to be people home—Linc stepped over to the picture window and glanced inside through the half-closed blinds.

A cat hissed at him from the windowsill on the other side. Or at least he assumed it was hissing, since its teeth were bared and its ears laid back. Startled, he took a deep breath and stepped away. Although there was a window between them, the cat glared at him maliciously, its intentions clear.

"Nice kitty, nice kitty," Linc remarked, although he knew the animal couldn't hear his attempt to be friendly. This cat was anything but. Linc didn't doubt for a moment that if he were to get inside the house, "nice kitty" would dig all his claws into him within seconds.

Linc hurried to the other side of the porch and leaned over the side, but that didn't provide him with any further information.

A minute or two later, his brothers were back. "The house is locked up. Door wouldn't budge."

This wasn't going the way Linc had planned. "Okay, so maybe they aren't home."

"Then where *are* they?" Mel demanded.

"How am I supposed to know?" Linc asked, growing irritated.

"You're the one with all the answers, remember?"

"Hey, hey," Ned said, coming to stand between his brothers. "Let's skip the sarcasm. We're looking for Mary Jo, remember?"

"Where is she?" Mel asked.

"I haven't got a clue," Ned returned calmly. "But someone must."

"Maybe we should ask a neighbor," Mel said.

"Be my guest." Linc motioned widely with his arm.

"Okay, I will. I'll try...that one." Mel marched down the steps, strode across the street and walked up to the front door. He pounded on it. Even from this distance Linc could hear his knock.

An older woman with pink rollers in her hair pulled aside the drape and peeked out.

"I just saw someone," Ned yelled. "There's someone inside."

Linc had seen her, too.

"Why isn't she answering the door?" Mel asked loudly, as if the two of them had some secret insight into this stranger.

"Would *you* answer if King Kong was trying to get in *your* front door?" Linc asked. Apparently Mel hadn't figured out that most people responded better to more sensitive treatment.

"Okay, fine," Mel shouted after several long minutes. "Be that way, lady."

"She just doesn't want to answer the door," Ned shouted back.

Mel ignored that and proceeded to the next house.

"Knock more quietly this time," Linc instructed.

Mel ignored that, too. Walking to the door, he pushed the buzzer, then turned and glanced over his shoulder. This house seemed friendlier, Linc thought. A large evergreen wreath hung on the door and lights sparkled from the porch columns.

Again no one answered.

Losing patience, Mel looked in the front window, framing his face with both hands. After peering inside for several seconds, he straightened and called out, "No one's home here."

"You want me to try?" Ned asked Linc. Mel wasn't exactly making friends in the neighborhood.

"Do you think it'll do any good?"

"Not really," Ned admitted.

A piercing blare of sirens sounded in the distance, disrupting the tranquility of the night.

Mel hurried back across the street. "Everyone in the neighborhood seems to be gone. Except for the lady with those pink things in her hair."

Despite their efforts, they obviously weren't getting anywhere. "Now what?" Ned muttered.

"You got any ideas?" Linc asked his two brothers, yelling to be heard over the sirens.

"Nope," Mel said with a shrug.

"Me, neither," Linc said, not hiding his discouragement.

They sauntered back to the truck and climbed inside. Linc started the engine and was about to drive away from the curb when two sheriff's vehicles shot into the street and boxed him in.

The officers leaped out of their cars and pulled their weapons. "Get out of the truck with your hands up!"

12

Mary Jo hadn't intended to spill her heart to Grace, but the older woman was so warm, so sympathetic. Before long, she'd related the whole sorry tale of how she'd met and fallen in love with David Rhodes. By the time Mary Jo finished, there was a pile of used tissues on the table.

"You aren't the only one who's ever loved unwisely, my dear," Grace assured her.

"I just feel really stupid."

"Because you trusted a man unworthy of your love?" Grace asked, shaking her head. "The one who needs to be ashamed is David Rhodes."

"He isn't, though."

"No," Grace agreed. "But let me repeat a wise old saying that has served me well through the years."

"What's that?" Mary Jo asked. She dabbed tears from the corners of her eyes and blew her nose.

"Time wounds all heels," Grace said with a knowing smile. "It will with David, too."

Mary Jo laughed. "I guess the reverse is true, as well. I'll get over David and his lies..." Her voice trailed off. "Is everyone in Cedar Cove as nice as you and Cliff?" she asked a moment later.

The question seemed to surprise Grace. "I'd like to think so."

"Olivia—Ms. Griffin—certainly is." Mary Jo sighed and looked down at her hands. "That firefighter—what's his name again?"

"Mack McAfee. He's new to town."

What Mary Jo particularly remembered was that he had the gentlest touch and the most reassuring voice. She could still hear it if she closed her eyes. The way he'd knelt at her side and the protectiveness of his manner had calmed her, physically and emotionally.

"His parents live in town," Grace was explaining. "Roy McAfee is a retired Seattle detective turned private investigator, and his wife, Corrie, works in his office."

"Really." She recalled seeing Mr. McAfee's sign on Harbor Street. What a fascinating profession. She suspected Mack's father got some really interesting cases. Maybe not, though, especially in such a small town. Maybe she was just influenced by the mystery novels she loved and the shows she watched on television.

"I suppose I should change clothes before dinner," Grace said, rising from her chair with seeming reluctance. "I've enjoyed sitting here chatting with you."

"Me, too," Mary Jo told her. It'd been the most relaxing part of her day—except, of course, for her nap.

"I'll be back in a few minutes."

Mary Jo figured this was her signal to leave. "I'll go to the apartment."

"Are you sure? I know Mack said you should rest, but Cliff and I would really like it if you joined our family for dinner."

"Where is Cliff?" she asked, glancing over one shoulder, assuming he must be somewhere within sight.

"He's out with his horses. They're his first love." Grace smiled as she said it.

Mary Jo had noticed the way Cliff regarded his wife. He plainly adored Grace and it was equally obvious that she felt the same about him. Mary Jo gathered they'd only been married a year or two. The wedding picture on the piano looked recent, and it was clear that their adult children were from earlier marriages.

Then, without allowing herself to consider the appropriateness of her question, Mary Jo said, "About what you said a few minutes ago… Have *you* ever loved unwisely?"

Grace sat down again. She didn't speak for a moment. "I did," she finally said. "I married young and then, after many years together, I was widowed. I'd just started dating again. It was a whole new world to me."

"Were you seeing Cliff?"

"Yes. He'd been divorced for years and dating was a new experience for him, too. I'd been married to Dan for over thirty years, and when another man—besides Cliff—paid attention to me, I was flattered. It was someone I'd had a crush on in high school."

"Did Cliff know about him?"

"Not at first. You see, this other man lived in another city and we e-mailed back and forth, and he became my obsession." Grace's mouth tightened. "I knew all along that he was married and yet I allowed our Internet romance to continue. He said he was getting a divorce."

"It was a lie?"

"Oh, yes, but I believed him because I wanted to. And then I learned the truth."

"Did Cliff find out about this other man?"

Regret flashed in her eyes. "Yes—and as soon as he did, he broke off our relationship."

"Oh, no! You nearly lost Cliff?"

"As I said, I'd learned the truth about Will by then and was crushed to lose Cliff over him. I was angry with myself for being so gullible and naive. I'd lost a wonderful man because of my foolishness. For a long time I could hardly look at my own face in the mirror."

"That's how I feel now," she murmured. *Will,* she thought. She'd heard that name before…

"It does get better, Mary Jo, I promise you that. Will, the man I was…involved with, did eventually lose his wife. She divorced him and, while I believe he had genuine feelings for me, it was too late. I wanted nothing more to do with him. So you see, he really was the one who lost out in all this."

"Cliff forgave you?"

"Yes, but it took time. I was determined never to give him cause to doubt me again. We were married soon after that and I can honestly say I've never been happier."

"It shows."

"Cliff is everything I could want in a husband."

The door off the kitchen opened and Cliff came in, brushing snow from his jacket. He hung it on a peg by the door, then removed his boots. "When I left, you two were sitting right where you are now, talking away."

Grace smiled at him. "I was about to change my clothes," she said. "Keep Mary Jo entertained until I get back, will you?"

"Sure thing."

Grace hurried out, and Cliff claimed the chair next to Mary Jo. As he did, he eyed the crumpled tissues. "Looks like you two had a good heart-to-heart."

"We did," she admitted and then with a sigh told him, "I've been very foolish."

"I'm sure Grace told you we've all made mistakes in our

lives. The challenge is to learn from those mistakes so we don't repeat them."

"I don't intend to get myself into this predicament ever again," Mary Jo said fervently. "It's just that…" She hesitated, uncertain how much to tell him about her brothers. "I feel like my family's smothering me. I have three older brothers and they all seem to think they know what's best for me and my baby."

"They love you," he said simply.

She nodded. "That's what makes it so difficult. With my parents gone, they feel *they* should be the ones directing my life."

"And naturally you take exception to that."

"Well, yes. But when I tried to live my life my *own* way and prove how adult I was, look what happened." She pressed both hands over her stomach, staring down at it. "I made a mistake, a lot of mistakes, but I discovered something…interesting after I found out I was pregnant."

"What's that?" Cliff asked. He stretched his long legs out in front of him and leaned back, holding his coffee mug. She noticed that his hand-knit socks had a whimsical pattern of Christmas bells, at odds with his no-nonsense jeans and shirt.

"Well, at first," she began, "as you can imagine, I was terribly upset. I was scared, didn't know what to do, but after a while I started to feel really excited. There was a new life inside me. A whole, separate human being with his or her own personality. This tiny person's going to be part David, part me—and all himself. Or herself," she added, refusing to accept her brothers' certainty that the baby was a boy.

Cliff smiled. "Pregnancy is amazing, isn't it? I can't pretend to know what a woman experiences, but as a man I can tell you that we feel utter astonishment and pride—and a kind of humbling, too."

"I think David might've felt like that in the beginning," Mary Jo whispered. He really had seemed happy. Very quickly, however, that happiness seemed to be compromised. By fear, perhaps, or resentment. She wanted to believe he'd loved her as much as he was capable of loving anyone. She now realized that his capacity for feeling, for empathy, was limited. Severely limited. Barely a month after she learned she was pregnant with his baby, David had become emotionally absent. He continued to call and to see her when he was in town but those calls and visits came less and less frequently, and the instant she started asking questions about their future, he closed himself off.

"It's not all that different with my horses," Cliff was saying.

His words broke into her reverie. "I beg your pardon?" What did he mean? They hadn't been talking about horses, had they?

"I've bred a number of horses through the years and with every pregnancy I feel such a sense of hopefulness. Which is foolish, perhaps, since even the best breeding prospects don't always turn out the way you expect. Still…"

"I met Funny Face today."

Cliff's eyes brightened when she mentioned the mare. "She's my sweetheart," he said.

"She seems very special." Mary Jo remembered the moment of connection she'd felt with this horse.

"She is," Cliff agreed. "She's gentle and affectionate—a dream with the grandchildren. But as far as breeding prospects go, she was a disappointment."

"No." Mary Jo found that hard to believe.

"She's smaller than we thought she'd be and she doesn't have the heart of a show horse."

"But you kept her."

"I wouldn't dream of selling Funny Face. Even though she

didn't turn out like Cal and I expected, we still considered her a gift."

Mary Jo released a long sigh. "That's how I feel about my baby. I didn't plan to get pregnant and I know David certainly didn't want it, yet despite all the problems and the heartache, I've come to see this child as a gift."

"He definitely is."

"He?" She grinned. "Now you're beginning to sound like my brothers. They're convinced the baby's a boy."

"I was using *he* in a generic way," Cliff said. "I imagine you'd prefer a girl?"

"I… I don't know." She shrugged lightly. "There's nothing I can do about it, so I'll just leave it up to God." She was somewhat surprised by her own response. It wasn't something she would've said as little as six months ago.

During her pregnancy, she'd begun to reconsider her relationship with God. When she was involved with David, she'd avoided thinking about anything spiritual. In fact, she'd avoided thinking, period. The spiritual dimension of her life had shrunk, become almost nonexistent after her parents' death.

That had changed in the past few months. She thought often of the night she'd knelt by her bed, weeping and desperate, and poured out her despair, her fears and her hopes. It was nothing less than a conversation with God. That was probably as good a definition of prayer as any, she mused. Afterward, she'd experienced a feeling of peace. She liked to imagine her mother had been in the room that night, too.

"You've got everything you need?"

She realized Cliff had spoken. "I'm sorry, what did you say?" She hated to keep asking Cliff to repeat himself, but her mind refused to stay focused.

"I was asking if you have everything you need for the baby."

"Oh, yes... Thanks to my friends and my brothers." Mary Jo was grateful for her brothers' generosity to her and the baby. Their excitement at the idea of a nephew—or niece, as she kept telling them—had heartened her, even as their overzealous interference dismayed her.

Linc, who tended to be the practical one, had immediately gone up to the attic and brought down the crib that had once belonged to Mary Jo. He'd decided it wasn't good enough for her baby and purchased a new one.

Mary Jo had been overwhelmed by his thoughtfulness. She'd tried to thank him but Linc had brushed aside her gratitude as though it embarrassed him.

Mel was looking forward to having a young boy around—or a girl, as she'd reminded him, too—to coach in sports. She'd returned from work one day recently to find a tiny pair of running shoes and knew instantly they'd come from Mel.

And Ned. Her wonderful brother Ned had insisted on getting her a car seat and high chair.

Mary Jo had knitted various blankets and booties, and her friends from the office had seen to her layette in what might have been one of the largest baby showers ever organized at the insurance company. Other than her best friend, Casey, no one had any inkling who the father was, and if they speculated, they certainly never asked. Regardless, their affection for Mary Jo was obvious and it made a difference in her life.

Grace returned just then and Mary Jo heard the sound of a car door closing. The front door opened a moment later and a girl of about five ran inside. "Grandma! Grandma!" she cried. "I'm an angel tonight! I'm an angel tonight!"

Grace knelt down, clasping the child's hands. "You're going to be an angel in the Christmas pageant?"

The little girl's head bobbed up and down. "In church tonight."

Grace hugged her granddaughter. "Oh, Katie, you'll be the best angel ever."

The girl beamed with pride. Noticing Mary Jo, she immediately walked over. "Hi, I'm Katie."

"Hi, Katie. I'm Mary Jo."

"You're going to have a baby, aren't you?"

"Yes, I am."

The door opened again and a young couple came in. The man carried a toddler, while the woman held a large, quilted diaper bag.

"Merry Christmas, Mom," Grace's daughter said, kissing her mother's cheek. She turned to Mary Jo. "Hello, I'm Maryellen. And I'm so glad you're going to be joining us," she said, smiling broadly.

Mary Jo smiled back. She'd never expected this kind of welcome, this genuine acceptance. Tonight would be one of the most memorable Christmas Eves of her life.

Now, if only her back would stop aching...

13

"Officer, let me explain," Linc said, doing his best to stay calm. His brothers stood on either side of him, arms raised high in the air. The deputy, whose badge identified him as Deputy Pierpont, appeared to have a nervous trigger finger.

The second officer was in his car, talking into the radio.

"Step away from the vehicle," Pierpont instructed, keeping his weapon trained on them.

The three brothers could've been playing the children's game, *Mother, May I* as they each moved forward one giant step.

"What were you doing on private property?" Pierpont bellowed as if he'd caught them red-handed inside the bank vault at Fort Knox.

"We're looking for our sister," Mel blurted out. "She ran away this morning. We've got to find her."

"She's about to have a baby," Linc said, feeling some clarification was required.

"Then why are you *here?*" the deputy asked, his tone none too friendly.

"Because," Linc said, fast losing patience, "this is where we *thought* she'd be."

The second officer approached them. His badge said he was Deputy Rogers. "We had two separate phone calls from neighbors who claimed three men were breaking into this house."

"We weren't breaking in," Mel insisted, turning to his brothers to confirm the truth.

"I looked in the window," Linc confessed, shaking his head. "I didn't realize that was a crime."

Pierpont snickered. "So we got a Peeping Tom on our hands."

"There's no one at home!" Linc shouted. "There was nothing to peep at except a crazed cat."

"I tried to open the back door," Mel said in a low voice.

"Why'd you do that?" Rogers asked.

"Well, because..." Mel glanced at Linc.

As far as Linc was concerned, Mel was the one who'd opened his big mouth; he could talk his own way out of this.

"Go on," Rogers prodded. "I'd be interested to know why you tried to get into this house when your brother just told us you were searching for your sister *and* that you knew there was no one here."

"Okay, okay," Mel said hurriedly. "I probably shouldn't have tried the door, but I suspected Mary Jo was inside and I wanted to see if that elderly couple was at home or just hiding from us."

"*I'd* hide if the three of you came pounding on my door." Again this was from Deputy Rogers.

"What did I tell you, Jim?" Pierpont said. Mel's comment seemed to verify everything the officers already believed. "Why don't we all go down to the sheriff's office so we can sort this out?"

"Not without my attorney," Linc said in a firm voice. He wasn't going to let some deputy fresh out of the academy railroad him. "We didn't break any law. We came to the Rhodes residence in good faith. All we want...all we care about is locating our little sister, who's pregnant and alone and in a strange town."

Just then another car pulled up to the curb, and a middle-aged man stepped out, dressed in street clothes.

"Now you're really in for it," Pierpont announced. "This is Sheriff Troy Davis."

As soon as Sheriff Davis approached, Linc felt relieved. Troy Davis was obviously a seasoned officer and looked like a man he could reason with.

The sheriff frowned at the young deputies. "What's the problem here?"

They both started talking at once.

"We got a call from dispatch," Pierpont began.

"Two calls," Rogers amended.

"From neighbors, reporting suspicious behavior," Pierpont continued.

"The middle one here admits he was trying to open the back door."

Mel leaned forward. "Just checking to see if it was locked."

Linc groaned and turned to his brother. "Why don't you keep your trap shut before we end up spending Christmas in jail."

To his credit, Mel did seem chagrined. "Sorry, Linc. I wanted to help."

Linc appealed directly to the sheriff. "I understand we might have looked suspicious, peeking in windows, Sheriff Davis, but I assure you we were merely trying to figure out if the Rhodes family was at home."

"Are you family or friends of Ben and Charlotte's?" the man asked, studying them through narrowed eyes.

"Not exactly friends."

"Our sister knows Ben's son," Ned told them.

Mel nodded emphatically. "Knows him in the Biblical sense, if you catch my drift."

Linc wanted to kick Mel but, with all the law enforcement surrounding them, he didn't dare. They'd probably arrest him for assault. "Our sister's having David Rhodes's baby," he felt obliged to explain.

"Any day now," Mel threw in.

"And she disappeared," Ned added.

"If we're guilty of anything," Linc said, gesturing with his hands, "it's being so anxious to locate our sister. Like I said, she's alone in a strange town and without family or friends."

"Did you check their identification?" the sheriff asked.

"We hadn't gotten around to that yet," Deputy Rogers replied.

"You'll see we're telling the truth," Linc asserted. "None of us have police records."

With the sheriff and his deputies watching carefully, Linc, Mel and Ned handed over their identification.

The sheriff glanced at all three pieces, then passed them to Pierpont. The young man swaggered over to his patrol car, apparently to check for any warrants or arrest records. He was back a couple of minutes later and returned their ID.

"They don't have records." He seemed almost disappointed, Linc thought.

The sheriff nodded. "What's your sister's name?"

"Mary Jo Wyse," Linc answered. "Can you tell us where we might find the Rhodes family? All we want to do is talk to them."

"Unfortunately Ben and Charlotte are out of the country," the sheriff said.

"You mean they aren't even in town?" Mel asked, sounding outraged. He turned to Linc. "What are we going to do *now?*"

"I don't know." Mary Jo must have discovered this information about the Rhodes family on her own. The only thing left for her to do was head back to Seattle. She wouldn't have any other options, which meant this entire venture through dismal traffic, falling snow and wretched conditions had been a complete waste of time.

"She's probably home by now and wondering where the three of us are," Linc muttered.

"Maybe." Ned shook his head. "But I doubt it."

"What do you mean, you doubt it?" Linc challenged.

"Mary Jo can be stubborn, you know, and she was pretty upset last night."

"We should phone the house and find out if she's there," Linc said, although he had a sneaking suspicion that Ned was right. Mary Jo wouldn't give up that easily.

"Sounds like a good idea to me," Sheriff Davis inserted.

Linc reached for his cell phone and called home. Five long rings later, voice mail kicked in. If his sister *had* gone back to Seattle, she apparently wasn't at the house.

"She's not there," Linc informed his brothers.

"What did I tell you?" Ned sighed. "I know Mary Jo, and she isn't going to turn tail after one setback."

This was more than a simple setback, in Linc's opinion. This was major.

"Have you tried her cell phone?" the sheriff suggested next.

"Yeah, we did. A few times. No answer," Linc said tersely.

"Try again."

"I'll do that now," Linc murmured. He reached for his phone again and realized he didn't know her number nor had he programmed it into his directory.

He cleared his throat. "Ah, Ned, could you give me the number for her cell?"

His youngest brother grabbed the phone from him and punched in Mary Jo's number, then handed it back.

Linc waited impatiently for the call to connect. After what seemed like minutes, the phone automatically went to voice mail. "She's not answering that, either."

"Maybe her cell battery's dead," the sheriff said. "It could be she's out of range, too."

Actually, Linc was curious as to why the sheriff himself had responded to dispatch. One would think the man had better things to do—like dealing with *real* crime or spending the evening with his family. "Listen, Sheriff, is Cedar Cove so hard up for crime that the sheriff responds personally to a possible break-in?"

Troy Davis grinned. "I was on my way to my daughter's house for dinner when I heard the call."

"So you decided to check us out."

"Something like that."

Linc liked the sheriff. He seemed a levelheaded guy, whereas his deputies were a pair of overzealous newbies, hoping for a bit of excitement. He'd bet they were bored out of their minds in a quiet little town like Cedar Cove. The call about this supposed break-in had sent these two into a giddy state of importance.

"The only essential thing here is finding our sister," Linc reiterated to the sheriff.

"The problem is, we don't know *where* to find her," Ned put in.

The sheriff rubbed the side of his face. "Did you ask around town?"

No one at the pub had been able to help. "Not really. We asked the guys at some tavern, but they didn't seem aware of much except how full their glasses were."

The sheriff grinned and seemed to appreciate Linc's wry sense of humor.

"She's *very* pregnant," Ned felt obliged to remind everyone. "It isn't like someone wouldn't notice her."

"Yeah." Mel once more thrust his arms out in front of him and bloated his cheeks for emphasis.

Linc rolled his eyes.

"Wait," Deputy Pierpont said thoughtfully. "Seems to me I heard something about a pregnant woman earlier."

That got Linc's attention. "Where?" he asked urgently. "When?"

"I got a friend who's a firefighter and he mentioned it."

"What did he say?"

Deputy Pierpont shrugged. "Don't remember. His name's Hutton. You could go to the fire station and ask."

"Will do." Linc stepped forward and shook hands with the sheriff and then, for good measure and goodwill, with each of the deputies. "Thanks for all your help."

Troy Davis nodded. "You tell your sister she shouldn't have worried you like this."

"Oh, I'll tell her," Linc promised. He had quite a few other things he intended to say to her, too.

After receiving directions to the fire station, they jumped back in the truck. Finally they were getting somewhere, Linc told himself with a feeling of satisfaction. It was just a matter of time before they caught up with her.

It didn't take them long to locate the fire station.

Rather than repeat their earlier mistakes—or what Linc considered mistakes—he said, "Let me do the talking, understand?"

"Okay," Ned agreed quickly enough.

"Mel?"

"Oh, all right."

They walked into the station house and asked to speak to the duty chief. The man eyed them cautiously.

Linc got immediately to the point. "I understand that earlier today you responded to an incident involving a young pregnant woman. A firefighter named Hutton was mentioned in connection with this call. Is that correct?"

When the chief didn't reply, Linc added, "If so, we believe that's our sister."

The man raised his eyebrows, as if determined not to give out any information.

"She needs her family, chief."

There must've been some emotion in Linc's voice, some emotion he didn't even know he'd revealed, because the man hesitated, then excused himself. He returned a few minutes later, followed by a second man.

"This is Mack McAfee. He's the EMT who responded to the call."

"You saw Mary Jo?" Linc asked. He extended his hand, and Mack shook it in a friendly fashion.

"I did."

Linc's relief was so great he nearly collapsed into a nearby chair. "That's great!"

"She's okay, isn't she?" Ned blurted out. "She hasn't gone into labor or anything?"

"No, no, she had a dizzy spell."

"Dizzy?" Linc repeated slowly and cast a startled look at his brothers.

"Does that mean what I think it means?" Mel asked.

Linc felt sick to his stomach. "I was twelve when Mary Jo was born and I remember it like it was yesterday. Mom got real dizzy that morning and by noon Mary Jo had arrived."

"That's not generally a sign of oncoming labor," Mack reassured him.

"It is in our family. Dad told me it was that way with each and every pregnancy. According to him, Mom had very quick deliveries and they all started with a dizzy spell. He barely made it to the hospital in time with Mary Jo. In fact—"

"She was born while Dad parked the car," Mel said. "He dropped Mom off at the emergency door and then he went to look for a parking space."

That tale had been told around the kitchen table for years. Once their father had parked the car and made his way back to the hospital, he was met by the doctor, who congratulated him on the birth of his baby girl.

"Do you know where she is?" Linc asked with renewed urgency.

"You might talk to Grace Harding," Mack said.

"Who's Grace Harding?"

"The librarian." Mack paused for a moment. "Mary Jo was at the library when I treated her."

"The library?" That didn't make any sense to Linc. Why had Mary Jo gone to the library?

"What was she doing there?" Mel asked.

"That isn't as important as where she is now," Linc said. "Mack, do you have any idea where she might've gone after she left the library?" He remembered seeing it earlier. The building with the mural.

Mack shook his head. "She didn't say, although I told her to put her feet up and rest for a few hours."

"She must've gotten a hotel room." They should have realized that earlier. Of course! If Mr. and Mrs. Rhodes were out of town, that was exactly what Mary Jo would have done.

"I don't think so," Mack said. "I thought I'd check on her myself and discovered she isn't at any of the motels in town."

"Why not?"

"No rooms available."

"Where would she go?"

"My guess," Mack said slowly, "is to Grace Harding's house."

"Why her place?"

"Because it seems like the kind of thing Mrs. Harding would do. I have the Hardings' phone number. I could call if you'd like."

Linc couldn't believe their good fortune. "Please."

The firefighter was gone for what seemed like a long time. He returned wearing a grin. "You can talk to her yourself if you want."

Linc bolted to his feet, eager to hear the sound of his sister's voice. He'd been upset earlier—angry, worried, close to panic—but all he felt now was relief.

"She's at the Harding ranch in Olalla."

The three brothers exchanged smiling glances. "Is she all right?"

"She said she's feeling great, but she also said she's ready to go home if you're willing to come and get her."

"Wonderful." Linc couldn't have wished for anything more.

"I'll give you directions to the Harding place. She's on the phone now if you'd like to chat."

Linc grinned, following Mack to the office, his brothers on his heels.

This was finally working out. They'd get Mary Jo home where she belonged before Christmas.

14

"No, please," Mary Jo said, looking at Grace and her family. "I want you to go on to the Christmas Eve service, just like you planned."

"Are you positive?" Grace seemed uncertain about leaving her behind.

Mary Jo had bowed to their entreaties and been their guest for a truly wonderful dinner, but she had no intention of imposing on them any further that evening.

"I am." There was no reason for them to stay home because of her, either. This crazy adventure of hers was over; she'd admitted defeat. Her brothers were on their way and she'd be back in Seattle in a couple of hours.

"I'd like to meet those young men," Grace said. "But it sounds as if they'll get here while we're at church."

"You will meet them," Mary Jo promised. "Sometime after Christmas." In one short afternoon, she'd become strongly attached to both Grace Harding and Cliff. Her two daughters, her daughter-in-law, their husbands and the grandchildren had made Mary Jo feel like part of the family. They'd welcomed her without question, opened their hearts and their home to her, given her a place to sleep, a meal, the comfort of their company. In this day and age, Mary Jo knew that kind of unconditional friendship wasn't the norm. This was a special family and she planned to keep in touch with them.

While the fathers loaded up the kids and Cliff brought his car around, Grace lingered.

"You have our phone number?" she asked as they stood by the front door.

"Oh, yes. Cell numbers, too." Mary Jo patted her pants pocket. Grace had carefully written out all the numbers for her.

"You'll call us soon."

Mary Jo nodded. Grace was like the mother she'd lost—loving, protective, accepting. And now that she was becoming a mother herself, she valued her memory even more profoundly. It was Grace who'd reminded Mary Jo of everything her mother had been to her, of everything *she* wanted to be to her own child. Even though her baby wasn't born yet, she felt blessed. Because of her pregnancy she'd met Grace, and she was grateful for everything it had brought her. A new maturity, the knowledge that she could rise to the occasion, that she had the strength to cope. This brand-new friendship. And, of course, the baby to come.

"If your brothers are hungry when they get here, there are plenty of leftovers," Grace was saying. "Tell them to help themselves."

"Thank you."

Cliff brought the car closer to the house and got out to open the passenger door. Still Grace lingered. "Don't hesitate to phone if you need *anything,* understand?"

"I won't—and thank you." Wearing her coat like a cloak, Mary Jo walked outside with her into the softly falling snow.

"Wait in the house," Grace said.

"I'll be fine in the apartment. It's comfortable there."

The two women hugged and Grace slid into the car seat next to her husband. Maryellen, Kelly and Lisa, with their families, had already left for the church.

Grace lowered the window. "Thank you for being so patient with Tyler," she said, giving her an apologetic look.

Mary Jo smiled, completely enchanted with the six-year-old who'd received a drum for Christmas and felt obliged to pound away on it incessantly.

"He's a talented little boy." In fact, she loved all of Grace and Cliff's grandchildren.

"Now go inside before you get cold," Grace scolded.

But Mary Jo remained in the yard until the car lights faded out of sight. Then, pulling her coat more snugly around her, she strolled toward the barn. Several of the participants in the live Nativity scene were inside a corral attached to the barn and she went there first.

"Hello there, donkey," she said. "Merry Christmas to you."

As if he understood that she was talking to him, the donkey walked toward her until he was within petting range. Mary Jo stroked his velvety nose, then walked back inside the barn.

"Hello, everyone."

At the sound of her voice, Funny Face stuck her head over the stall door.

"Hi, there," Mary Jo greeted the mare. "I understand you're very special to Cliff," she said. Funny Face nickered loudly in response.

Apparently curious as to what was causing all the commotion, the camel poked her head out, too. "Sorry, Camel," Mary Jo called, "but your reputation has preceded you and I'm not giving you a chance to bite *my* arm."

After several minutes of chatting with the other horses, Mary Jo washed her hands at a sink in the barn and headed up the stairs to the apartment. About halfway up, her back started to ache again. She pressed one hand against it and continued climbing, holding onto the railing with the other.

When she reached the apartment, she paused in the middle of removing her coat as she felt a powerful tightening across her stomach.

Was this labor?

She suspected it must be, but everything she'd heard and read stated that contractions began gradually. What she'd just experienced was intense and had lasted several long, painful seconds. Another contraction came almost right away.

Mary Jo checked her watch this time. Three minutes later there was a third contraction of equal severity.

Only three minutes.

At the class she'd attended, she'd heard that it wasn't uncommon for labor pains to start at fifteen-minute intervals. Perhaps hers had started earlier and she hadn't noticed. That didn't seem possible, though. How could she be in labor and not know it?

The next pain caught her unawares and she grabbed her stomach and doubled over.

"*That* got my attention," she announced to the empty room.

Not sure what to do next, Mary Jo paced, deliberating on the best course of action. Her brothers were due any moment. If she told them she was in labor the second they arrived, they'd panic. One thing Mary Jo knew: she did *not* want her three brothers delivering this baby.

None of them had any experience or even the slightest idea of what to do. Linc would probably order the baby to wait until they could get to a hospital. Knowing Mel and his queasy stomach, he'd fall in a dead faint, while Ned would walk around declaring that this was just perfect. He was going to be an uncle to a baby born on Christmas Eve—or Christmas Day, depending on how long this labor business was going to take.

Another pain struck and again Mary Jo bent double with the strength of it. She exhaled slowly and timed it, staring at her watch. This one lasted thirty seconds. Half a minute. It wasn't supposed to happen this fast! Labor was supposed to last for hours and hours.

Mary Jo didn't know what to do or who to call. Her mind was spinning, her thoughts scrambling in a dozen different directions at once. She considered phoning Grace. If she was going to give birth here, at the ranch, she wanted a woman with her—and she couldn't think of anyone she'd rather have than Grace Harding. But Grace had left just a few minutes before and the only way to reach her was by cell phone. Unfortunately, as she'd learned earlier, coverage in this area was sporadic at best. And she hated to interfere with the Hardings' Christmas plans.

The second person she thought of was Mack McAfee. He'd been so kind, and he was a trained medical technician. He was calm and logical, which was exactly what she needed. He'd called—when was it? Half an hour ago—and urged her to go home with her brothers. There'd be plenty of time to talk to Ben and Charlotte Rhodes after the baby's birth. Her brothers wouldn't have the opportunity to confront David or his father now, anyway, and she'd manage, somehow or other, to prevent it in the future, too. While she was speaking with Linc, she'd realized how desperate her brothers had been to find her. Mary Jo hadn't meant to worry them like this.

If Linc or Mel or even Ned had reasoned with her like Mack had, she would've listened. Too late to worry about any of that now...

Mary Jo went slowly back down the stairs to the barn. She didn't want to dial 9-1-1 and cause alarm the way she had with her dizzy spell at the library earlier, so she decided to call the fire station directly.

Sure enough, when she picked up the receiver she saw that Caller ID displayed the last number that had been received—the firehouse. Mary Jo pushed the redial button.

On the second ring, someone picked up. "Kitsap County Fire District."

Relief washed over her at the sound of Mack's voice. "Mack?"

There was a slight hesitation. "Mary Jo? Is that you?"

"Ye-es."

"What's wrong?"

"I… Grace and her family left for Christmas Eve service at the church about ten minutes ago. I didn't go because my brothers are on their way here."

"They haven't arrived yet?" He seemed surprised.

"Not yet."

Mack groaned. "I'll bet they're lost."

Mary Jo didn't doubt that for an instant.

"I'm sure they'll be there anytime," he said.

"I hate to bother you," she whispered and gasped at the severity of the next contraction.

"Mary Jo!"

Closing her eyes, she mentally counted until the pain subsided.

"What's wrong?" he asked urgently.

"I'm afraid I've gone into labor."

Mack didn't miss a beat. "Then I should get out there so I can transport you to the birthing center."

At the rate this was progressing, he'd better not lose any time. "Thank you," she said simply.

He must have sensed her fear, because he asked, "How far apart are the contractions?"

"Three minutes. I've been timing them."

"That's good."

"I didn't take all the birthing classes… I wish I had, but David said he'd take them with me and it never happened. I went once but that was just last week and—"

"You'll do fine. If you want, I'll stay with you."

"You?"

"I'm not such a bad coach."

"You'd be a wonderful coach, but you have to remember I've only had the one class."

"Listen, instead of talking about it over the phone, why don't I hop in the aid car and drive over."

"Ri–ight." At the strength of the last contraction, Mary Jo was beginning to think this was an excellent idea.

"Where are you?"

"In the barn at the moment." She gave a small laugh.

"Why is that funny?"

"I'm with the animals from the live Nativity scene."

Mack laughed then, too. "That seems appropriate under the circumstances, but I want you to go to the house and wait for me there."

"I'd rather go back to the apartment if you don't mind." It was hard to explain but the place felt like home to her now, at least for this one night.

"Fine. Just don't lock the door. I'll be there soon, so hold on, okay?"

She didn't have any choice but to hold on. "Okay. But Mack?"

"Yes?"

"Please hurry."

"You got it. I'm leaving now."

"No sirens, please," she begged, and Mack chuckled as if she'd made some mildly amusing joke.

Walking seemed to help, and instead of following Mack's instructions, she paced the length of the barn once, twice, three times.

She noticed that the camel was watching her every move. "Don't be such a know-it-all," she muttered. She'd swear the creature was laughing at her. "This isn't supposed to be happening yet."

A sheep walked up to the gate, bleating loudly, and Mary Jo wagged her index finger. "I don't want to hear from you, either."

All the horses in their stalls studied her with interest, but the only one who looked at her with anything that resembled compassion was Funny Face.

"Wish me well, Funny Face," Mary Jo whispered as she started back up the stairs. "I need all the good wishes I can get."

Absorbed in the cycle of pain and then relief, followed by pain again, Mary Jo lost track of time. Finally she heard a vehicle pull into the yard. A moment later, Mack entered the apartment, a second man behind him. They were both breathless; they must have run up the stairs.

Mary Jo was so grateful to see him she nearly burst into tears. Clutching her belly, she walked over to Mack and said hoarsely, "I'm so glad you came."

"How's it going?"

"Not...good."

"Any sign of your brothers?"

She shook her head.

Mack glanced over his shoulder at the second EMT. "This is Brandon Hutton. Remember him from this morning?"

"Hi." Mary Jo raised her hand and wiggled her fingers.

"How far apart are the pains now?"

"Still three minutes, but they're lasting much longer."

Mack turned to the other man. "I think we'd better check her before we transport."

"I agree."

This was all so embarrassing, but Mary Jo would rather be dealing with Mack than any of her brothers. Mack would be impersonal about it, professional. And, most important of all, he knew what he was doing.

Taking her by the hand, Mack led her into the bedroom. He pulled back the sheets, then covered the bed with towels. Mary Jo lay down on the mattress and closed her eyes.

"Okay," Mack announced when he'd finished. "You're fully dilated. You're about to enter the second phase of labor."

"What does that mean?"

"Basically, it means we don't have time to take you to the hospital."

"Then who's going to deliver my baby?" she asked, fighting her tears.

"It looks like that'll be me," he said calmly.

Mary Jo held out her hand to him and Mack grabbed it in both of his.

"Everything's going to be fine," he said with such confidence she couldn't help believing him. "You can do this. And I'll be with you every step of the way."

15

"Admit it," Mel taunted, "we're lost."

"I said as much thirty minutes ago," Linc said sharply. He didn't need his brother to tell him what he already knew.

"We should've gotten the Hardings' phone number," Ned commented from the backseat.

That was obvious. "You might've mentioned it at the time," Linc snapped. They'd been driving around for almost an hour and he had no idea where they were. Mack McAfee had drawn them a map but it hadn't helped; somehow they'd gone in the wrong direction and were now completely and utterly lost.

To further complicate matters, a fog had settled in over the area. It seemed they'd run the gamut of Pacific Northwest winter weather, and all within the last eight hours. There'd been sleet and snow, rain and cold. Currently they were driving through a fog so thick he could hardly see the road.

"Read me the directions again," he said.

Mel flipped on the interior light, which nearly blinded Linc. "Hey, turn that off!"

"I thought you wanted me to read these notes."

"You don't need the light," Ned told him. "I've got them memorized."

"So where are we?" Mel asked.

"You're asking *me?*" Linc muttered in frustration.

"Okay, okay." Mel sighed deeply. "Fighting isn't going to help us find Mary Jo."

"You're right." Linc pulled over to the side of the road and shifted to face his brothers. "Either of you have any other ideas?"

"We could go to the firehouse and start over," Mel said.

"Once we're there, we could get the Hardings' phone number," Ned added. "We could call and let Mary Jo know we're on our way."

Linc gritted his teeth. "Fine. But have either of you geniuses figured out how to get *back* to the firehouse?"

"Ah…" Mel glanced at Ned, who shrugged his shoulders.

"I guess we can't do that because we're lost."

"Exactly," Linc said. "Any other ideas?" He was feeling more helpless and frustrated by the second.

"We could always ask someone," Ned suggested next.

"*Who* are we supposed to ask?" Mel cried. "We haven't seen another car in over half an hour."

"There was a place down this road," Ned said in a tentative voice.

Linc stared at him. "Where?"

"You're sure about that?" Mel didn't seem to believe him, and Linc wasn't convinced, either.

"It's there, trust me." Ned's expression, however, did little to inspire Linc's confidence.

"I remember the name," his youngest brother said indignantly. "It was called King's."

"What kind of place was it?"

Ned apparently needed time to consider this.

"A tavern?" Linc asked.

Ned shook his head.

"A gas-and-go?" Mel offered.

"Could've been. There were a bunch of broken-down cars out front."

Linc didn't recall any such place. "How come I didn't see it?" he asked.

"'Cause you were driving."

That actually made sense. Concentrating on maneuvering down these back roads in the fog, it was all he could do to make sure his truck didn't end up in a ditch.

"I think I saw it, too," Mel said a moment later. "The building's set off the road, isn't it?"

Ned perked up. "Yes!"

"With tires edging the driveway?"

"That's the one!"

"Do we have a prayer of finding it again?" Linc asked his brothers.

Ned and Mel exchanged looks. "I think so," Ned told him.

"Good." Linc put the pickup back in gear. "Which way?"

"Turn around," Ned told him.

Linc started down the road, then thought to ask, "Are you sure this King's place is open?"

"Looked like it to me."

"Yeah," Mel concurred. "There were plenty of lights. Not Christmas lights, though. Regular lights."

Linc drove in silence for several minutes. Both his brothers were focused on finding this joint. Just when the entire trip seemed futile, Linc crested a hill and emerged out of the fog, which made a tremendous difference in visibility. Instantly he breathed easier.

"There!" Ned shouted, pointing down the roadway.

Linc squinted and, sure enough, he saw the business his

brothers had been yapping about. Maybe there was some hope, after all.

Linc had no idea how his sister had ended up in the boon-docks. He wished she'd stayed in town, but, oh, no, not Mary Jo.

As they neared the building, Linc noticed a sign that said King's. Linc could see his brother's point; it was hard to tell exactly what type of business this was. The sign certainly didn't give any indication. True, there were beat-up old cars out front, so one might assume it was some sort of junk or salvage yard. The building itself was in ill repair; at the very least, it needed a fresh coat of paint. There wasn't a single Christmas decoration in sight.

However, the Open sign in the window was lit.

Linc walked up to the door, peered in and saw a small res-taurant, basically a counter with a few stools, and a conve-nience store. He went inside and strolled up to the counter, taking a seat. Mel and Ned joined him.

A large overweight man wearing a stained white T-shirt and a white apron waddled over to their end of the counter as if he'd been sitting there all day, waiting for them.

"Merry Christmas," Linc murmured, reaching for the menu.

"Yeah, whatever."

This guy was in a charming mood.

"Whaddaya want?" the cook asked.

"Coffee for me," Linc said.

"What's the special?" Mel asked, looking at a sign on the wall that said, *Ask About Our Daily Special*.

"Meat loaf, mashed potatoes, corn."

"If you want to order food, it's gotta be takeout," Linc told his brothers, although now that the subject had come up, Linc realized he was hungry, too. Famished, in fact.

"We do takeout," the cook said, filling Linc's mug with

coffee that had obviously been in the pot far too long. It was black and thick and resembled liquid tar more than coffee.

"Is that fresh?" Linc risked asking.

"Sure is. Made it yesterday."

Linc pushed the mug away. "We'll take three meat loaf sandwiches to go," he said, making a snap decision.

"You want the mashed potatoes with that?"

"Can I have potato chips instead?" Ned inquired.

"I guess."

"Say," Linc said, leaning back on the stool. "Do you happen to know where the Harding ranch is?"

The cook scowled at him. "Who's askin'?"

Linc didn't want to get into long explanations. "A friend."

Cook nodded. "Cliff's a...neighbor."

"He is?" Maybe they were closer than Linc had thought.

"Raises the best horses around these parts." The cook sounded somewhat grudging as he said this.

Linc knew car engines inside out but didn't have a clue about horses, and he had no idea how to respond.

Fortunately he didn't have to. "You fellows interested in buying one of Cliff's horses?" the old curmudgeon asked.

"Not really." Linc hoped that wasn't disappointing news. "We're, uh, supposed to be meeting our sister, who's staying at the Harding place."

"We *had* directions," Mel explained.

"But we sort of got turned around."

"In other words, we're lost," Linc said.

"Lemme make you those sandwiches."

"What about giving us directions?"

King, or whatever his name was, sighed as if this was asking too much. "I could—for a price."

Linc slapped a ten-dollar bill on the counter.

The grouch eyed the money and shrugged. "That might get you there. Then again, it might not."

Linc threw in another ten. "This is all you're getting."

"Fine." He pocketed the money and slouched off toward the kitchen. "I'll be back with your order."

Ten minutes later, he returned with a large white bag packed with sandwiches, potato chips and canned sodas. Linc decided not to ask how old the meat loaf was. He paid the tab and didn't complain at the price, which seemed seriously inflated.

"About those directions?" Linc asked.

Ned took out the map the firefighter had drawn and spread it on the linoleum counter. The route from Cedar Cove to the Harding place looked pretty direct, and Linc didn't know how he'd managed to get so confused.

"The King's gonna set you straight," the grouch told them.

"Good, because we are *lost,*" Mel said, dragging out the last word.

"Big-time lost," Ned added.

This was a point that did not need further emphasis. Linc would've preferred his brothers keep their mouths shut, but that wasn't likely to happen.

"Okay, you're here," King informed them, drawing a circle around their current location. He highlighted the street names at the closest intersection. "You're near the corner of Burley and Glenwood."

"Got it," Linc said.

"You need to head east."

"East," Linc repeated.

"Go down about two miles and you cross the highway via the overpass."

"Okay, got that."

The grouch turned the directions around and circled the Harding ranch. "This is where Cliff and Grace Harding live."

"Okay."

"So, all you do after you cross the highway is go east. Keep going until you see the water, then turn left. The Harding place will be about three-quarters of a mile down the road on the left-hand side."

"Thanks," Linc said. Those directions seemed easy enough for anyone to follow. Even the three of them.

The grouch frowned at him, and Linc assumed he was hinting for more money, which he wasn't about to get. Grabbing their sandwiches, Linc handed the bag to his youngest brother and they piled out the door.

"Merry Christmas," Ned called over his shoulder. Apparently he hadn't grasped yet that this man wasn't doing any kind of celebrating.

The grouch's frown darkened. "Yeah, whatever."

Linc waited until they were back in the vehicle before he commented. "Miserable old guy."

"A regular Scrooge," Mel said.

Ned tore open the sack and passed one sandwich to Linc and another to Mel. Linc bit into his. The old grouch made a good meat loaf sandwich, surprisingly enough, and right now that compensated for a lot.

The three of them wolfed down the food and nearly missed the sign for the highway overpass.

"Hey, you two, I'm driving," Linc said, swallowing the last bite. "Pay attention, will you?"

"Sorry." Ned stared out at the road.

"He said to drive until we can see the water," Linc reminded them.

"It's dark," Mel protested. "How are we supposed to see water?"

"We'll know when we find it," Ned put in.

Linc rolled his eyes. "I hope you're right, that's all I can say."

Linc couldn't tell how far they'd driven, but the water never came into view. "Did we miss something?" he asked his brothers.

"Keep going," Mel insisted. "He didn't say when we'd see the water."

"He didn't," Linc agreed, but he had a bad feeling about this. The road wasn't straight ahead the way the grouch had drawn it on the map. It twisted and turned until Linc was, once again, so confused he no longer knew if he was going east or west.

"You don't think that King guy would've intentionally given us the wrong directions, do you?"

"Why would he do that?" Mel asked. "You paid him twenty bucks."

Linc remembered the look on the other man's face. He'd wanted more. "Maybe it wasn't enough."

"Maybe Mr. Scrooge back there needs three visitors to-night," Ned suggested. "If you know what I mean."

"He had three visitors—us."

"Yeah, and I think he was trying to con us," Linc muttered.

"I guess he succeeded," Mel said, just as Ned asked, "But why? What's the point?"

"The point is that he's trying to make us miserable," Linc said. "As miserable as he is, the old coot."

The three of them fell into a glum silence. It sure didn't feel like any Christmas Eve they'd ever had before.

16

By the time Grace and Cliff arrived at church for the Christmas Eve service, both her daughters and their husbands were already seated. So were Lisa, Rich and April. Maryellen held Drake, who slept peacefully in his mother's arms. Katie, as well as Tyler, were with the other local children getting ready for the big Christmas pageant.

Katie was excited about being an angel, although Tyler, who'd been assigned the role of a shepherd, didn't show much enthusiasm for his stage debut. If he displayed any emotion at all, it was disappointment that he couldn't bring his drum. Kelly had explained to him that the shepherds of the day played the flute, not drums, because drums would frighten the sheep. The explanation satisfied Tyler, who was of a logical disposition, but it didn't please him.

Grace and Cliff located a pew directly behind her daughters and Lisa. As they slipped in, Grace whispered that she'd prefer to sit closest to the aisle, craving the best possible view of her grandchildren's performances. Once they were seated, Cliff reached for her hand, entwining their fingers.

Maryellen turned around and whispered, "Is everything all right with Mary Jo?"

"I think so." Grace still didn't feel comfortable about leaving her alone. But Mary Jo had been adamant that Grace join her family, so she had. Now, however, she wished she'd stayed behind.

Cliff squeezed her hand as the white-robed choir sang Christmas hymns, accompanied by the organist. "O, Come All Ye Faithful" had never sounded more beautiful.

Olivia and Jack, carrying his Santa hat, came down the aisle and slid into the pew across from Grace and Cliff. Justine and Seth accompanied them. From a conversation with Justine earlier in the week, Grace knew Leif had gotten the coveted role of one of the three Wise Men.

As soon as Olivia saw Grace, she edged out of her pew and went to see her friend. Olivia had wrapped a red silk scarf around her shoulders, over her black wool coat. Despite everything she'd endured, she remained the picture of dignity and elegance.

She leaned toward Grace. "How's Mary Jo?" she asked in a whisper.

Grace shrugged. "I left her at the house by herself, and now I wish I hadn't. Oh," she added, "apparently her brothers are in town…"

"Problems?"

Grace quickly shook her head. "Mary Jo actually seemed relieved to hear from them."

"Is she going home to Seattle with her family, then?" Olivia stepped sideways in the aisle to make room for a group of people trying to get past.

Grace nodded.

"How did they find out she was with you?" Olivia asked.

"They tracked her down through Mack McAfee. He

phoned the house and talked to her directly. Then Mary Jo spoke with her oldest brother and decided it would be best to go back to Seattle." Grace had been with her at the time and was astonished by the way Mary Jo's spirits had lifted. Whether that was because of her brothers or because of Mack... Grace tended to think it was the latter.

"Mack appeared to have a calming effect on her when I saw them at the library," Olivia said, echoing Grace's thoughts.

"He does," she agreed. "I noticed it after she got off the phone, too. Apparently he suggested she should return home with her brothers."

"I'm glad," Olivia said. "For her own sake and theirs. And for Mom and Ben's..." She paused, shaking her head. "As necessary as it is for them to know about this baby, I'd rather it didn't happen the second they got home."

"Her real fear was that her brothers were going to burst onto the scene and demand that David do the so-called honorable thing."

"David and the word *honor* don't belong in the same sentence," Olivia said wryly.

"Mary Jo's brothers were arriving any minute. I'd like to have met them. Or at least talked to them." Grace would've phoned the house, but by now Mary Jo should be well on her way to Seattle.

Olivia straightened. "We'll catch up after the service," she said and slid into the opposite pew, beside Jack.

No sooner had Olivia sat down than Pastor Flemming stepped up to the podium. He seemed to be...at peace. Relaxed, yet full of energy and optimism. The worry lines were gone from his face. Grace knew this had been a difficult year for the pastor and his wife, and she was glad their problems had been resolved.

"Merry Christmas," he said, his voice booming across the church.

"Merry Christmas," the congregation chanted.

"Before the children come out for the pageant, I'd like us all to look at the Christmas story again. For those of us who've grown up in the church, it's become a familiar part of our lives. This evening, however, I want you to forget that you're sitting on this side of history. Go back to the day the angel came to tell Mary she was about to conceive a child."

He opened his Bible and read the well-known passages from the Book of Luke. "I want us to fully appreciate Mary's faith," he said, looking up. "The angel came to her and said she'd conceive a child by the Holy Spirit and she was to name him Jesus, which in those days was a common name." He paused and gazed out at his congregation.

"Can you understand Mary's confusion? What the angel told her was the equivalent of saying to a young woman in our times that she's going to give birth to God's son and she should name him Bob."

The congregation smiled and a few people laughed outright.

"Remember, too," Pastor Flemming continued, "that although Mary was engaged to Joseph, she remained with her family. This meant she had to tell her parents she was with child. That couldn't have been easy.

"What do you think her mother and father thought? What if one of our daughters came to us and said she was pregnant? What if she claimed an angel had told her that the child had been conceived by the work of the Holy Spirit?" Again he paused, as if inviting everyone to join him in contemplating this scenario.

Pastor Flemming grinned. "Although I have two sons and no daughters, I know what *I'd* think. I'd assume that a teenage girl—or her boyfriend—would say anything to explain how this had happened."

Most people in the congregation smiled and agreed with nodding heads. Grace cringed a little, remembering as vividly as ever the day she'd told her parents she was pregnant. She remembered their disappointment, their anger and, ultimately, their support. Then she thought of Mary Jo and turned to exchange a quick glance with Olivia.

"And yet," the pastor went on, "this child, the very son of God, was growing inside her womb. Mary revealed remarkable faith, but then so did her family and Joseph, the young man to whom she was engaged."

Something briefly distracted the pastor and he looked to his left. "I can see the children are ready and eager to begin their performance, so I won't take up any more time. I do want to say this one thing, however. As a boy, I was given the role of a shepherd standing guard over his sheep when the angel came to announce the birth of the Christ Child. When I grew up, I chose, in a sense, the very same job—that of a shepherd. Every one of you is a member of my flock and I care for you deeply. Merry Christmas."

"Merry Christmas," the congregation echoed.

As he stepped down from the podium, the children took their positions on the makeshift stage. Grace moved right to the end of her pew to get a better view of the proceedings. Katie stood proudly in place, her gold wings jutting out from her small shoulders and her halo sitting crookedly atop her head. She couldn't have looked more angelic if she'd tried.

Tyler had borrowed one of Cliff's walking sticks to use as a staff. He was obviously still annoyed to be without his precious drum, glaring at the congregation as if to inform them that he was doing this under protest. Grace had to smother a laugh.

Oh, how Dan would've loved seeing his grandchildren

tonight. Their grandson was like his grandfather in so many ways. A momentary sadness came over her and not wanting anyone to sense her thoughts, Grace looked away. She didn't often think about Dan anymore. She'd loved her first husband, had two daughters with him, and through the years they'd achieved a comfortable life together.

But Dan had never been the same after Vietnam. For a lot of years, Grace had blamed herself and her own failings for his unhappiness. Dan knew that and had done his best to make things right in the letter he wrote her before his death.

Christmas Eve, however, wasn't a night for troubled memories. The grandchildren Dan would never know were onstage, giving the performances of their young lives.

Out of the corner of her eye, Grace noticed Angel, the church secretary, rushing down the side aisle and toward the front. She went to the first pew, where Pastor Flemming sat with his wife, Emily.

Angel whispered something in his ear and the pastor nodded. He left with her. Apparently there was some sort of emergency.

"Look, there's a star in the East," Leif Gunderson, Olivia's grandson, shouted. As one of the three Wise Men, he pointed at the church ceiling.

"Let us follow the star," the second of the Wise Men called out.

It wasn't until Cliff tapped her arm that she realized Angel was trying to get her attention. She stood in the side aisle and motioned with her finger for Grace to come out.

"What's that about?" Cliff asked as she picked up her purse.

"I don't know. I'll tell you as soon as I find out."

He nodded.

Grace hurried down the center aisle to the foyer, reaching it just as Angel did. "What's going on?" she asked.

"It's a miracle I was even in the office," Angel said.

This confused Grace. "What do you mean?"

"For the phone call," she explained. "I went to get a pair of scissors. Mrs. Murphy, the first-grade Sunday School teacher, needed scissors and I thought there was a pair in my desk."

"The phone call," Grace reminded her.

"Oh, yes, sorry. It was from some young firefighter."

"Mack McAfee?" Grace blurted out.

"No, no, Brandon Hutton. At any rate, he wanted to speak to the pastor."

"Has there been an accident?"

"No... I don't know. I think it would be best if you talked to Pastor Flemming yourself. He asked me to get you."

Dave Flemming was on the phone, a worried expression on his face. When he saw Grace, he held out the receiver. "You'd better take this."

Grace dismissed her first fear, that there'd been an accident. Everyone she loved, everyone who was important to her here in Cedar Cove, was inside the church.

"This is Grace Harding," she said into the receiver, her voice quavering slightly.

"Ms. Harding, this is EMT Hutton from the Kitsap County Fire District. We received a distress call from a young woman who's currently at your home."

Grace gasped. "Mary Jo? She's still at the house? Is she all right?"

"I believe so, ma'am. However, she's in labor and asking for you."

"Won't you be transporting her to the hospital? Shouldn't I meet you there?" Grace would notify Cliff and they could leave together.

From the moment she'd left the house, some instinct had told her she should've stayed with Mary Jo. Some inner knowledge that said Mary Jo would be having her baby not in two weeks but *now*. Tonight.

"We won't be transporting her, Ms. Harding."

"Good heavens, why not?" Grace demanded, wondering if it was a jurisdictional matter. If so, she'd get Olivia involved.

"It appears Ms. Wyse is going to give birth imminently. We don't have time to transport her."

"She's not alone, is she?"

"No, ma'am. EMT McAfee is with her."

Mack. Thank goodness. "What about her brothers?" she asked. Surely they'd arrived by now.

"There's no one else here, ma'am."

Grace's heart started to pound. "I'll get there as quickly as possible."

"One last thing," Officer Hutton added. "Do you normally keep camels in your barn?"

"No. But be warned. She bites."

"She's already attempted to take a piece out of me. I managed to avoid it, though."

"Good."

She set down the receiver and turned to Pastor Flemming. "A young woman who's staying with us has gone into labor."

"So I understand."

"I'll collect my husband and get going." Grace hated to miss the pageant but there was nothing she could do about it.

Returning to the pew, she explained to Cliff what was happening. Maryellen twisted around and Grace told her, too.

"She doesn't have anything for the baby, does she?" Maryellen asked.

Grace hadn't even thought of that. She had blankets and a few other supplies for her grandchildren, but the disposable diapers would be far too big.

"Jon and I will stop by the house and get some things for

Mary Jo and the baby and drop them off. I'm sure I still have a package of newborn-size diapers, too."

Grace touched her daughter's shoulder, grateful for Maryellen's quick thinking.

"We'll bring Lisa, Rich and April back to the house," Kelly whispered. "I wouldn't miss this for the world."

"Me, neither," Lisa said. "There couldn't be a more ideal way to celebrate Christmas!"

17

"You're doing great," Mack assured Mary Jo.

"No, I'm not," she cried, exhaling a harsh breath. Giving birth was hard, harder than she'd ever envisioned and the pain…the pain was indescribable.

The second EMT came back into the bedroom. "I talked to your friend and she's on her way."

"Thank God." It was difficult for Mary Jo to speak in the middle of a contraction. The pain was so intense and she panted, imitating Mack who'd shown her a breathing exercise to help deal with it.

Mack held her hand and she squeezed as tight as she could, so tight she was afraid she might be hurting him. If that was the case, he didn't let on.

"Get a cool damp washcloth," Mack instructed the other man.

"Got it." As though thankful for something to do, Brandon Hutton shot out of the room and down the hallway to the bathroom.

"I'm going to check you again," Mack told her.

"No!" She clung to his hand, gripping it even tighter. "I need you here. Beside me."

"Mary Jo, I have to see what position the baby's in."

"Okay, okay." She closed her eyes. Sweat poured off her forehead. Now she knew why giving birth was called labor. This was the hardest thing she'd ever done. Unfortunately there wasn't time to go to any more classes, or to finish reading the books she'd started... She'd thought she had two more weeks. If only she hadn't waited for David, or believed him when he'd said he wanted to attend the birthing classes with her. *This* was what she got for trusting him.

Suddenly liquid gushed from between her legs. "What was that?" she cried.

"Your water just broke."

"Oh." She'd forgotten about that. She had a vague recollection of other women's stories about their water breaking.

"That's good, isn't it?" she asked. What she hoped was that it meant her baby was almost ready to be born and this agony would come to an end.

"It's good," he told her.

"It'll be better now, right?"

Mack hesitated.

"What's wrong?" she demanded. "Tell me."

"Your labor may intensify."

This had to be a cruel joke. "Intensify." She couldn't imagine how the pains could get any stronger than they were now. "What do you mean...intensify?"

"The contractions will probably last longer..."

"Oh, no," she moaned.

Although she'd discovered this was Mack's first birth, he knew so much more than she did. He'd at least studied it and obviously paid attention during class. Mack had joked that he was getting on-the-job training—and so was she, but that part didn't seem so amusing anymore.

"The baby's fully in the birth canal. It won't be long now, Mary Jo. Just a few more pains and you'll have your baby."

"Thank God." Mary Jo didn't know how much more of this she could take.

"Rest between contractions," Mack advised.

Brandon Hutton returned with a damp washcloth. Mack took it from him and wiped her face. The cool cloth against her heated skin felt wonderfully refreshing.

At the approach of another pain, she screamed, "Mack! Mack!"

Instantly he was at her side, his hand holding hers. Her fingers tightened around his.

"Count," she begged.

"One, two, three…"

The numbers droned on and she concentrated on listening to the even cadence of Mack's voice, knowing that by the time he reached fifty, the contraction would ease.

Halfway through, she started to pant. And then felt the instinctive urge to bear down. Arching her back, Mary Jo pushed with every ounce of her strength.

When the pain passed, she was too exhausted to speak.

Mack wiped her forehead again and brushed the damp hair from her face.

"Water," she mumbled.

"Got it!" Brandon Hutton tore out of the room, like a man on a quest.

Recovering from the pain, she breathed deeply, her chest heaving. She opened her eyes and looked up at Mack. His gaze was tender.

"How much longer?" she asked, her voice barely a whisper.

"Soon."

"I can't stand much more of this… I just can't." Tears welled in her eyes and rolled down the sides of her face.

Mack dabbed at her cheeks. As their eyes met, he gave her an encouraging smile. "You can do it," he said. "You're almost there."

"I'm glad you're with me."

"I wouldn't want to be anywhere else," he told her. They continued to hold hands.

Brandon came back with the water. "Here," he said.

Mack took the glass and held it for Mary Jo, supporting her head. "Just a sip or two," he cautioned.

She nodded and savored each tiny sip.

The sound of a car door slamming echoed in the distance.

"Grace," Mary Jo said, grateful the other woman had finally arrived.

"I'll bring her up." Brandon quickly disappeared from the room.

Another pain approached. "No…no…" she whimpered, gathering her resolve to get through this next contraction. She closed her eyes and clung to Mack, thanking God once more that she wasn't alone. That Mack was with her…

Mack automatically began to count. Again she felt the urge to push. Gritting her teeth, she bore down, grunting loudly for the first time, straining her entire body.

"Mary Jo." Grace's serene voice broke through the haze of pain. "I came as soon as I heard."

The contraction eased and Mary Jo collapsed onto the mattress, sweat blinding her eyes.

"The baby's in the birth canal," Mack told her friend.

"What would you like me to do?" Grace asked.

"Hold on to her hand and count off the seconds when the contractions come."

"No…don't leave me." Mary Jo couldn't do this without Mack at her side.

"I need to deliver the baby," he explained, his words so gentle they felt like a warm caress. "Grace will help you."

"I'm here," Grace said.

"Okay." Reluctantly Mary Jo freed Mack's hand.

Grace slipped into his spot. "I don't want to hurt you," Mary Jo said.

"How would you do that?" Grace asked, clasping her hand.

Somehow she found the strength to smile. "I squeeze hard."

"You aren't going to hurt me," Grace said reassuringly. "You squeeze as hard as you need to and don't worry about me." She reached for the damp cloth and wiped Mary Jo's flushed and heated face.

"I…don't have anything for the baby," she whispered. That thought suddenly struck Mary Jo and nearly devastated her. Her baby wasn't even born yet, and already she was a terrible mother. Already she'd failed her child.

"That's all been taken care of."

"But…I don't even have a blanket."

"Maryellen and Jon are stopping at their house for diapers and baby blankets and clothes for a newborn."

"But…"

"Maryellen still has all of Drake's clothes, so that should be the least of your worries, okay?"

"Okay." A weight lifted from her heart.

Another pain approached. Mary Jo could feel herself pushing the infant from the womb. She gritted her teeth, bearing down with all her strength.

Grace, her voice strong and confident, counted off the seconds. Again, when the pain was over, Mary Jo collapsed on the bed.

In the silence that followed, Mary Jo could hear the sound

of her own harsh breathing. Then in the distance she heard the laughter of children.

"The kids…"

"The grandchildren are outside with Cliff," Grace said.

"Laughing?"

"Do you want me to tell Cliff to keep them quiet?"

"No…no. It's…joyful." This was the way it should be on Christmas Eve. Hearing their happiness gave her hope. Her baby, no matter what the future held, would be born surrounded by people who were kind and encouraging.

Giving birth in a barn, the stalls below filled with beasts, children running and laughing outside, celebrating the season, hadn't been part of Mary Jo's plan. And yet—it was perfect.

So perfect.

This was a thousand times better than being alone with strangers in a hospital. None of her brothers would've been comfortable staying with her through labor. Maybe Ned, but even her youngest brother, as much as he loved her, wouldn't have done well seeing her in all this pain.

Mack had been with her from the first, and now Grace.

"Thank you," she whispered to them both.

"No, Mary Jo, thank *you*," Grace whispered back. "We're so honored to be helping you."

"I'm glad you're with me." She smiled tremulously at Grace, then Mack. How she wished she'd fallen in love with him instead of David. Mack was everything a man should be…

Another pain came, and she locked her eyes with his for as long as she could until the contraction became too strong. She surrendered to it, whimpering softly.

"The head's almost there," Mack said when the pain finally released her. "Your baby has lots of brown hair."

"Oh…"

"Another pain or two and this will be over," Grace promised.

"Thank God, thank God," Mary Jo said fervently.

"You're going to be a good mother," Grace told her.

Mary Jo wanted to believe that. Needed to believe it. All night, she'd been tortured with doubts and, worse, with guilt about arriving at this moment totally unprepared.

"I *want* to be a good mother."

"You already are," Mack said.

"I love my baby."

"I know." Grace whisked the damp hair from her brow.

Mary Jo was drenched in sweat, her face streaked with tears. "I'm never going through this again," she gasped, looking at Grace. "I can't believe my mother gave birth four times."

"All women think that," Grace said. "I know I did. While I was in labor with Maryellen, I told Dan that if this baby wasn't the son he wanted, he was out of luck because I wasn't having another one."

"You did, though."

"As soon as you hold your baby in your arms, nothing else matters. You forget the pain."

Footsteps clattered up the stairs. "Mom?"

It was Maryellen, Grace's daughter.

"In here," Grace called out.

Maryellen hurried into the room, then paused when she saw Mary Jo and smiled tearfully. Her arms were filled with baby clothes.

A pain overtook Mary Jo. Again it was Mack she looked to, Mack who held her gaze, lending her his strength.

She was grateful that Grace was at her side, but most of the time it had been Mack who'd guided and encouraged her. He had a way of comforting her that no one else seemed to have, not even Grace.

"You're doing so well," Mack told her. "We have a shoulder..."

Mary Jo sobbed quietly. It was almost over. The baby was

leaving her body. She could feel it now, feel the child slipping free and then the loud, fierce cry that resounded in the room.

Her relief was instantaneous.

She'd done it! Despite everything, she'd done it.

With her last reserve of strength, Mary Jo rose up on one elbow.

Mack held the child in his arms and Brandon had a towel ready. Mack turned to her and she saw, to her astonishment, that there were tears in his eyes.

"You have a daughter, Mary Jo."

"A daughter," she whispered.

"A beautiful baby girl."

Her own tears came then, streaming from her eyes with an intensity of emotion that surprised her. She hadn't given much thought to the sex of this child, hadn't really cared. Her brothers were the ones who'd insisted she'd have a son.

They'd been wrong.

"A daughter," she whispered. "I have a daughter."

18

"The natives are getting restless," Jon Bowman reported to Grace when she came down from the apartment. After watching the birth of Mary Jo's baby, Grace felt ecstatic. She couldn't describe all the emotions tumbling through her. Joy. Excitement. Awe. Each one held fast to her heart.

Katie, April and Tyler raced around the yard, screaming at the top of their lungs, chasing one another, gleeful and happy. Jon went to quiet them, but Grace stopped him.

"Let them play," she told her son-in-law. "They aren't hurting anything out here."

"Kelly and Lisa are inside making hot cocoa," Cliff said, joining Grace. "And Paul's looking after Emma." He slid his arm around her waist. "Everything all right up there?" He nodded toward the barn.

"Everything's wonderful. Mary Jo had a baby girl."

"That's marvelous!" Cliff kissed her cheek. "I bet you never guessed you'd be delivering a baby on Christmas Eve."

Grace had to agree; it was the last thing she'd expected. She was thankful Mary Jo hadn't been stuck in some hotel room alone. These might not have been the best of circumstances, but she'd ended up with people who genuinely cared for her and her baby.

Grace didn't know Roy and Corrie McAfee's son well, but Mack had proved himself ten times over. He was a capable, compassionate young man, and he'd been an immeasurable help to Mary Jo. In fact, Grace doubted *anyone* could have done more.

After he'd delivered that baby girl, Mack had cradled the infant in his arms and gazed down on her with tears shining in his eyes. An onlooker might have thought he was the child's father.

The other EMT actually had to ask him to let go of the baby so he could wash her. After that, Grace had wrapped the crying baby in a swaddling blanket and handed her to Mary Jo.

The two EMTs were finishing up with Mary Jo and would be transporting her and the baby to the closest birthing center. Maryellen had stayed to discuss breastfeeding and to encourage and, if need be, assist the new mother.

Grace had felt it was time to check on the rest of her family.

"It's certainly been a full and busy night," Cliff said.

"Fuller than either of us could've imagined," Grace murmured.

A car pulled into the yard. "Isn't that Jack's?" Cliff asked, squinting into the lights.

"Yes—it's Olivia and Jack." Grace should've known Olivia wouldn't just go home after Christmas Eve services. She'd briefly told Olivia what was happening before she'd hurried out of the church, fearing she'd caused enough of a distraction as it was.

Jack parked next to Cliff's vehicle. Before he'd even turned off the engine, Olivia had opened her door. "How's everything?" she asked anxiously as she stepped out of the car.

"We have a baby girl."

Olivia brought her hands together and pressed them to her heart. "I'm so *pleased*. And Mary Jo?"

"Was incredible."

"You delivered the baby?"

"Not exactly. But I was there."

Being with Mary Jo had brought back so many memories of her own children's births. Memories that were clear and vivid. The wonder of seeing that beautiful, perfectly formed child. The elation. The feeling of womanly power. She remembered it all.

"If not you, then who?" Olivia asked.

"Mack McAfee. The other EMT, Brandon, was there, too, but it was Mack who stayed with Mary Jo, who helped her through the worst of it. By the time I arrived, the baby was ready to be born."

"I'm sure she was happy to see you."

Mary Jo had been, but she hadn't really needed Grace; she and Mack had worked together with a sense of ease and mutual trust.

Grace almost felt as if she'd intruded on something very private. The communication between Mack and Mary Jo had been—she hesitated to use this word—*spiritual*. It was focused entirely on the birth, on what each needed to do to get that baby born. Grace felt moved to tears, even now, as she thought about it.

"Grandma, listen!" Tyler shouted. He pounded on his drum, making an excruciating racket.

Grace covered her ears. "Gently, Tyler, gently."

Tyler frowned as he looked up at her. "I was playing my best for you."

"Remember the song about the little drummer boy?" Olivia asked him.

Tyler nodded eagerly. "It's my favorite."

"It says in the song that he went pa-rum-pum-pum-pum, right?"

Tyler nodded again.

"It doesn't say he beat the drum like crazy until baby Jesus's mother put her hands over her ears and asked him to go next door and play."

Tyler laughed. "No."

"Okay, try it more slowly now," Grace said.

Tyler did, tapping on the drum in a soft rhythm that was pleasing to the ear.

"Lovely," Grace told her grandson.

"Can I play for the ox and the lamb?" he asked.

"In the song they kept time, remember?"

Grinning, Tyler raced away to show his cousins what he'd learned and to serenade the animals.

"Come in for a cup of coffee," Cliff suggested to Olivia and Jack.

"We should head home," Jack said. His arm rested protectively on Olivia's shoulders.

"I just wanted to make sure everything turned out well," Olivia explained. "Do you think I could see Mary Jo and the baby for a few minutes?"

"I don't see why not," Grace said with a smile.

The two women left the men outside to chat while Grace led the way up to the small apartment. Brandon Hutton sat on the top step with his medical equipment, filling out paperwork. He shifted aside and they skirted around him.

"Mary Jo?" Grace asked, standing in the doorway to the bedroom. "Would it be okay if Olivia came in to see the baby?"

"Of course. That would be fine," Mary Jo said.

When they walked into the bedroom, they found Mary Jo sitting up, holding her baby in her arms.

"Oh, my," Olivia whispered as she reached the bed. "She's so tiny."

"She didn't feel so tiny a little while ago." Mary Jo looked up with a comical expression. "I felt like I was giving birth to an elephant."

"It was worth it, though," Olivia said and tenderly ran her finger over the baby's head. "She's just gorgeous."

"I never would've believed how much you can love such a tiny baby." Mary Jo's voice was filled with wonder. "I thought my heart would burst with love when Mack put her in my arms."

"Do you have a name for her?" Grace asked.

"Not yet. I had one picked out, but now I'm not sure."

"She's a special baby born on a special night."

"I was thinking the same thing," Mary Jo said, kissing the newborn's forehead. Her gaze fell lovingly on the child. "When I was first pregnant… I was so embarrassed and afraid, I prayed God would just let me die. And now…now I see her as an incredible gift."

Grace had felt that way when she discovered she was pregnant with Maryellen all those years ago. It was shortly before her high school graduation; she'd been dating Dan Sherman and their relationship had always been on-again, off-again. She'd dreaded telling him she was pregnant, even more than she'd dreaded telling her parents.

For weeks she'd kept her secret, embarrassed and ashamed. But like Mary Jo, she'd learned to see the pregnancy as an unexpected gift, and the moment Maryellen was placed in her arms, Grace had experienced an overwhelming surge of love. The birth hadn't been easy, they never really were, but as soon as she saw her daughter, Grace had recognized that every minute of that pain had been worth the outcome.

"If you need anything," Olivia was saying to Mary Jo, "please don't hesitate to call."

"Thank you. That's so kind."

Olivia turned to Mack, who hovered in the background. "Are you taking her to the birthing center in Silverdale?"

He nodded. "We'll be leaving in about ten minutes."

"Then I won't keep you," Olivia said. "I'll stop by sometime tomorrow afternoon," she promised Mary Jo.

"Oh, please don't," Mary Jo said quickly. "It's Christmas—spend that time with your family. I'll get in touch soon. Anyway, I'll be with my own family." She looked up, her eyes widening.

"Mary Jo?" Grace asked in alarm. "What's wrong?"

"Oh, my goodness!"

"What is it?" Mack's voice was equally worried.

"My brothers," Mary Jo said. "They never showed up."

"That's true." The entire matter had slipped Grace's mind. "Mary Jo's brothers were due here—" she checked her watch "—three hours ago."

"Where could they be?" Mary Jo wailed.

Grace tried to reassure her. "They're probably lost. It's easy enough with all these back roads. They've never been in this area before, have they?"

Mary Jo shook her head.

"Don't worry. As soon as they arrive, I'll tell them what happened and where to find you."

Mary Jo smiled down at the infant cradled in her arms. "They'll hardly believe I had the baby," she murmured. "But then it's hard for me to believe, too."

"I'll call you tomorrow," Olivia said.

"Thank you, but please…"

"Yes?"

"Don't tell your parents about the baby yet. Give them a

chance to settle back into their routine before you let them know about David and me—and the baby."

"I won't say a word until you and I agree the time is right." Mary Jo nodded.

Grace was impressed that Mary Jo wanted to spare Ben and Charlotte the unsavory news of David's betrayal until they were more prepared to accept it.

"I'll leave you now," Olivia told her. "But like I said, if you need *anything,* anytime, please call. You're practically family, you know."

Mary Jo thanked her softly. "You all feel like family to me… Everyone's been so wonderful."

Grace walked down the stairs with Olivia. She was surprised to see Jack and Cliff still outside, huddled with the children.

"What's Cliff up to now?" Grace wondered aloud.

Jack glanced over then. "You gotta see this!" he said, waving at Olivia. He sounded like a giddy child.

As soon as Grace saw the huge carton of fireworks Cliff had dragged out, she groaned. "Cliff!"

"I was saving them for New Year's Eve, but I can't think of a better night for celebrating, can you?"

"What about the horses?"

"They're all safe in their stalls. Don't worry about them."

"And Buttercup? She hates that kind of noise."

"She's locked in the house."

"Can we, Grandpa, can we?"

The children were jumping up and down, clapping their hands with enthusiasm.

"Why right now?" Grace asked.

Cliff sent her a look of pure innocence. "I was just casting about for a way to keep the grandkids entertained."

"Oh, all right." She sighed loudly, holding back a grin.

"Okay if we stay and watch?" Jack said.

Grace and Olivia exchanged looks. As they'd often had occasion to observe, most men were little boys at heart.

"If you must," Olivia murmured.

The front door opened and Kelly stepped out with Paul, who still held the baby. Grace's daughter balanced a large tray filled with mugs and Lisa followed with a tin of Christmas cookies.

"Anyone for hot chocolate?" Kelly asked.

"I'd love a cup," Olivia said.

"Me, too," Grace added.

Paul glanced over at the kids. "What's going on?"

"Fireworks in a few minutes," Grace told him.

"Wow! Great idea."

"Men," Olivia whispered under her breath, and then both Olivia and Grace broke into giggles, just like they had when they were schoolgirls.

19

"How did we get so lost—twice?" Linc groaned. The only thing left to do was return to Cedar Cove and start over. That *sounded* easy enough, except that he no longer knew how to find the town.

"That King did us wrong," Mel muttered.

"You think?" Linc said sarcastically. He was past frustration, past impatience and past losing his cool. All he wanted was to track down his pregnant sister and bring her home. That shouldn't be such an impossible task, and yet...

"I'm never going back to King's," Ned said in disgust.

"Me, neither," Mel spat. "If I ever go back to Cedar Cove, which is unlikely."

Frankly, Linc was of the same mind, at least as far as King went. The man had blackmailed him into paying for directions and then completely misled him. True, the sandwiches weren't bad, but he'd overcharged them. The old coot had an evil streak a mile wide. If he thought it was fun to misdirect them, then he had a perverse sense of humor, too. Perverse? Downright twisted!

"Let's find a phone that works," Ned suggested, not for

the first time. His brother had harped on that for the last half hour. Their cell phones were useless out here. But it wasn't as if there was a phone booth sitting on the side of the road just waiting for them to appear.

"Okay, you find one, Ned, and I'll be more than happy to pay for the call."

Ned didn't respond, which was definitely for the best.

"What we need is a sign," Mel said.

Linc bit off a sarcastic comment. They needed a sign, all right, and it had better be one from heaven. He could only imagine what Mary Jo must be thinking. By now his sister probably figured they'd abandoned her, yet nothing could be further from the truth.

"What's that?" Ned suddenly cried, pointing into the distance.

"What's what?" Linc demanded.

"There," Mel said, leaning forward and gazing toward the sky.

Linc saw a flash of light. He pulled over to the side of the road and climbed out of the truck. He needed to stretch his legs, anyway, and the cold air would revive him. Sure enough, someone was setting off fireworks. The sky burst with a spectacular display of lights.

"Wow, that was a big one," Mel said, like a kid at a Fourth of July display.

His brothers didn't seem to appreciate the gravity of their situation. "Okay, it's nice, but how's that going to help us?"

"You said I should find a phone," Ned reminded him. "Whoever's setting off those fireworks must have a phone, don't you think?"

"Yeah, I guess," Linc agreed. He leaped back into the truck, his brothers with him. "Guide me," he shouted and jerked the transmission into drive.

"Turn right," Ned ordered.

"I can't!"

"Why not?"

"I'd be driving across someone's pasture, that's why." Obviously Linc was the only one with his eye on the road.

"Then turn as soon as you reach an intersection," Mel told him.

Linc had never liked taking instructions from his younger brothers and he gritted his teeth. As the oldest, he'd always shouldered responsibility for the others. He had no choice now, however—not that things had worked out all that well with *him* in charge.

At the first opportunity, Linc made a sharp right-hand turn, going around the corner so fast the truck teetered on two wheels. It came down with a bounce that made all three of them hit their heads on the ceiling. "Now what?"

"Pull over for a minute."

"Okay." Linc eased to a stop by the side of the road.

"There!" Mel had apparently seen another display in the heavens. "That star!"

"Which way now?" Linc asked with a sigh.

"Go straight."

Linc shook his head. The road in front of him was anything but straight. It twisted and curved this way and that.

"Linc," Mel said, glaring at him. "Go!"

"I'm doing the best I can." He came to a straight patch in the road and floored the accelerator. If anyone had told him he'd be chasing around a series of dark roads, desperately seeking guidance from a fireworks display, he would've laughed scornfully. Him, Mr. Great Sense of Direction? Lost? He sighed again.

"We're getting close," Mel said.

"Okay, stop!" Ned yelled.

Linc slammed on the brakes. The three of them jerked forward and just as abruptly were hurled back. If not for the seat belts, they would've been thrown headfirst into the windshield.

"Hey!" Mel roared.

"Maybe don't stop *quite* so suddenly," Ned added in a voice that was considerably less hostile.

"Sorry."

"Wait, wait, wait." Mel cocked his head toward the sky. "Okay, continue down this road." Mercifully it was flat and straight.

"Here," Ned said a minute later.

Once more Linc slammed on the brakes, only this time his brothers were prepared and had braced themselves.

"Look!" Ned shouted. "This is it. We're here!"

Linc didn't know what he was talking about. "We're where?"

"The Harding ranch," Mel answered.

Then Linc saw. There, painted on the rural route box, was the name Cliff Harding. To his left was a pasture and a large barn.

"I think I see a camel," Linc said. He'd heard about people raising llamas before but not camels.

"Are you sure?" Ned mumbled. "Maybe it's just an ugly horse."

"A camel? No way," Mel insisted.

"I say it's a camel." Linc wondered if his brother's argumentative nature had something to do with being a middle child. Ned, as the youngest, was usually the reasonable one, the conciliator. Whereas he—

"A *camel?*" Mel repeated in an aggressive tone. "What would a camel be doing here?"

"Does it matter?" Ned broke in. "This is where Mary Jo's waiting for us."

"Right." Linc turned into the long driveway that led to the house and barn. The fireworks had stopped, but some kind of party seemed to be taking place, because the yard was filled with people. There was a bunch of little kids running around and the atmosphere was festive and excited.

"There's an aid car here." Ned gestured urgently in its direction.

"Do you think someone's hurt?" Mel asked.

"No," Linc said slowly, thoughtfully. This was what he'd feared from the first. The minute he'd heard about Mary Jo's dizzy spell he'd suspected she was about to give birth. "I think Mary Jo might have had her baby."

"But she isn't due for another two weeks," Mel declared.

Ned opened the truck door. "Instead of discussing it, let's go find out."

A middle-aged woman approached as Linc got out of the truck. "You must be Mary Jo's brothers," she said. "I'm Grace Harding. Merry Christmas!"

The woman looked friendly, and Linc appreciated the pleasant greeting. "Merry Christmas to you, too. Sorry for the delay…"

"We got lost."

How helpful of Mel to point out the obvious.

"Some guy named King gave us the wrong directions."

"King's Gas and Grocery?" A man came up to them, extending his hand. "Cliff Harding."

"That's the one," Ned answered.

Cliff pinched his lips together, but didn't speak.

Linc shook hands with Grace's husband. "Linc Wyse," he said, introducing himself. "My brothers, Ned and Mel."

Hands were shaken and greetings exchanged all around.

"We were wondering if you were ever going to find the place," Cliff told them.

"If it hadn't been for the fireworks, we probably wouldn't have," Mel admitted.

Linc ignored him and glanced at the aid car. "Mary Jo?" He couldn't bring himself to finish the question.

Grace nodded. "She had the baby."

"A boy," Mel said confidently. "Right?" His eyes lit up with expectation.

"A girl."

"A girl?" Linc was shocked. "Mary Jo had a girl?"

"You sound disappointed," Grace said, studying him closely.

"Not…disappointed. Surprised."

Ned felt obliged to explain. "For some reason, we were all sure she was having a boy."

"Well, she didn't. You have a niece."

"We have a niece," Linc said to his brothers. Mel gave him a congratulatory slap on the back that nearly sent him reeling. He suddenly realized what this all meant. He was an *uncle*. He hadn't thought of himself in those terms until that very moment.

"The EMTs are bringing Mary Jo and the baby down now," Grace was saying.

"Can we see the baby?" Linc asked.

"And talk to Mary Jo?" Mel added.

Grace warmed them with a smile. "I'm sure you can."

A little boy raced up to her. "Grandma, Grandma, can I play my drum for the baby and Mary Jo?"

Grace crouched down so she was eye level with her grandson. "Of course, Tyler, but remember you have to play quietly so you won't disturb the baby."

"Okay!"

Two EMTs rolled Mary Jo toward the aid car on a gurney.

As soon as she saw her brothers, Mary Jo—holding the sleeping newborn in one arm—stretched out the other. "Linc, Mel, Ned…oh, my goodness, you're here!"

They hurried over to her side.

"You had a girl," Mel said, staring down at the bundle in her arms.

"She looks just like you," Ned commented.

"No, she doesn't," Linc chimed in. "She looks like the Wyse family—like all of us."

"And like herself," Mary Jo said.

"I'm sorry we were so late," Ned apologized.

"Yeah, we got lost."

If Mel announced that to one more person, Linc might be tempted to slug him.

"Where are they taking you?" he asked.

"To the birthing center in Silverdale," one of the EMTs answered.

"You won't have any trouble finding it," Cliff assured them. "I'll draw you a map."

"No, thanks." Mel shuddered noticeably.

"We'd better follow the aid car," Linc said.

"Mary Jo, we brought you gifts."

"Thank you, Ned." Her face softened as she looked at the three of them. "That's so sweet."

"We're sorry about the things we said." Again this came from Ned, who was more willing to acknowledge he was wrong than either Mel or Linc.

"Yeah," Mel agreed.

Linc muttered something under his breath, hoping it would pass for an apology. He did feel bad about the way everything had gone and the pressure they'd put on Mary Jo. They hadn't meant to. Their intentions had been the best, although he could see now that they'd gone too far. Still, he wasn't letting

David Rhodes off the hook. The man had responsibilities and Linc was as determined as ever to see that he lived up to them.

"Linc, Mel, Ned, I want you to meet Mack McAfee," his sister said, her arm out to the EMT. "Oh, I forgot," she added. "You guys met earlier."

Linc nodded at the other man. So did Mel and Ned.

"Good to see you again," Mack said. "And congratulations on your brand-new niece. Oh, and this is my partner, Brandon Hutton."

Once more the brothers nodded.

"I couldn't have managed without them," Mary Jo said fervently.

Linc thanked them both. "Our family's much obliged to you for everything you've done."

"Just part of the job," Brandon said.

"It was an honor," Mack told them. "I have to tell you this was the best Christmas Eve of my life."

"And mine," Mary Jo said. She looked at Mack, and the two of them seemed to maintain eye contact for an extra-long moment.

"Now, Grandma?" Tyler stepped up to Grace, a small drum strapped over his shoulders.

"Now, Tyler."

The youngster set his sticks in motion. Pa-rum-pum-pum-pum, pa-rum-pum-pum-pum.

Linc glanced over at the barn and saw the ox and the lamb in the paddock. They seemed to be keeping time to the drum, bowing their heads with each slow beat.

Mary Jo was right. This was the best Christmas Eve of his life. Of *all* their lives.

20

Mary Jo woke to find Mack McAfee standing in the doorway of her private hospital room. "Mack," she whispered. Her heart reacted to the sight of him, pounding extraordinarily hard. She hadn't been certain she'd ever see him again.

"How are you feeling?" he asked, walking into the room.

"Fine." Actually, she was sore and tired and eager to get home, to be with her family.

"I brought you something."

"You did?" She sat up in bed and selfconsciously brushed her fingers through her hair.

Mack produced a bouquet of roses, which he'd been hiding behind his back. "For you, Mary Jo." He bowed ever so slightly.

"My goodness, where'd you get these on Christmas Day?"

He raised his eyebrows. "I have my ways."

"Mack."

"Oh, all right, I got them in the hospital gift shop."

"They're open?"

"Sort of… I saw someone I knew who had a key and she let me in."

Mary Jo brought the fragrant flowers to her nose and breathed in their fresh scent. The vase was lovely, too. "You shouldn't have, but I'm thrilled you did."

"I wasn't sure your brothers would remember to send flowers."

Her brothers. Just thinking about the three of them, all bumbling and excited, made her want to laugh. They'd practically shoved each other out of the way last night, fussing over her and the baby. They'd been full of tales about their misadventures in Cedar Cove and the people they'd met and their near-arrest. Mel had a few comments about a meat loaf sandwich, too—and then they'd all decided they were hungry again. Their gifts of the gold coin, the perfume and the incense were on the bedside table.

When they'd arrived at the hospital, her brothers wouldn't let her out of their sight—until the physician came into the room to examine her and then they couldn't leave fast enough.

They'd returned for a few minutes an hour later—apparently well-fed—to wish her a final good-night and promise to come back Christmas Day. Then they'd all trooped out again.

"I stopped at the nursery to see…" Mack paused. "Do you have a name for her yet?"

Mary Jo nodded. "Noelle Grace."

"Noelle for the season and Grace after Grace Harding?"

Mary Jo smiled, nodding again.

"I like it," Mack told her. "The name's just right. Elegant and appropriate."

His approval pleased her. She didn't want to think too closely about how much his opinion meant to her—or why. She understood that they'd shared something very special, something intimate, while she was in labor. But that didn't mean the bond they'd experienced would last, no matter how much she wanted it to. She had to accept that Mack had come into her life for a brief period. Soon she'd go back to Seattle with her family, and he'd go on living here, in Cedar Cove. It was unlikely that she'd see him again; there was no real reason to. The thought was a painful one.

"Noelle Grace was a joy to behold," Mack said with a grin.

"Was she asleep?"

"Nope, she was screaming her head off."

Mary Jo instantly felt guilty. "Oh, the staff should've woken me. It's probably her feeding time."

Mack pulled up a chair and sat down beside the bed. "Nope, she just needed her diaper changed and to be held a little."

"Did someone hold her?" The nursery was crowded with newborns and there were only a couple of nurses on duty.

"I did," Mack admitted, somewhat embarrassed.

"You?"

"I hope you don't mind."

"Of course I don't! I—I'm just surprised they'd let you."

"Yes, well…" Mack looked away and cleared his throat. "I might've led the nurse to believe that Noelle and I are… related."

Mary Jo burst out laughing. "Mack, you didn't!"

"I did. And I have to say that as soon as I settled her in my arms, Noelle calmed down, stopped crying and looked straight up at me."

"You brought her into the world, after all." She probably didn't need to remind Mack of that; nevertheless, she wanted him to know she hadn't forgotten what he'd done for her.

The night before, she'd told her brothers that she would never have managed if not for Mack, and that was true. He'd been her salvation. She wanted to tell him all this, but the right words escaped her. Besides, she wasn't sure she could say what was in her heart without getting teary-eyed and emotional.

"I'm so glad you stopped by... I was going to write you and Brandon and thank you for everything."

"It's our job." Those had been Brandon's words, too, and in his case, she assumed they were true. But Mack... Dismissing her appreciation like that—it hurt. Not wanting him to see how his offhand comment had upset her, she stared down at the sheet, twisting it nervously.

Mack stood and reached for her hand, entwining their fingers.

"Let me explain," he said. "It *is* part of what we agreed to do when we accepted the job with the fire department." He paused for a moment. "But the call from you wasn't an ordinary one."

"How so?" she asked and looked up, meeting his eyes.

"I've never delivered a baby before."

"I know. Me, neither," she said and they smiled at each other.

"It was one of the highlights of my life, being there with you and Noelle."

"Mine, too—I mean, you being there."

"Thank you." His words were low and filled with intent. He leaned forward and braced his forehead against hers. "If it's okay with you..."

"What?" she prodded.

"I'd like to see Noelle sometime."

"See her?"

"See both of you."

"Both of us," she repeated, afraid she was beginning to sound like an echo.

"As long as it's okay with you," he said again.

She nodded, trying not to act too excited. "If you want."

"I want to very much."

"I'll be back in Seattle," she said.

"I don't mind the drive."

"Or you could take the ferry."

"Yes." Mack seemed just as eager to visit as she was to have him come by. "When?"

She wanted him there as soon as possible. "The doctor said he'd release Noelle and me this afternoon. My brothers are picking us up at three."

"Is tomorrow too soon?" he asked.

Mary Jo was convinced the happiness that flowed through her must have shone from her eyes. She didn't think she could hide it if she tried. "That would be good," she said shyly.

"Merry Christmas, Mary Jo."

"Merry Christmas, Mack."

Just then the nurse showed up carrying Noelle. "It's lunchtime," she said cheerfully.

Mary Jo held out her arms for her baby, born on Christmas Eve in Cedar Cove, the town that had taken her in. A town whose people had sheltered her and accepted her. The town that, one day, she'd love to call home.

Home for her and Noelle.

★ ★ ★ ★ ★

1225 Christmas Tree Lane

★ ★ ★

To Paula Eykelhof, my wonderful editor
for more than 25 years.

Dear Friends,

Well, this is it. The last installment of the Cedar Cove series. It's been quite a run, hasn't it? You, my readers, were the ones who inspired the idea in the first place, and I'm most appreciative of that. You taught me how important it is to listen to what you have to say. It's a lesson I won't forget.

Not once did I dream this series would be the success it has become. The Cedar Cove books are responsible for making me #1 on the *New York Times* list for the first time and several times since. You said you loved the stories and the characters, and you told your friends and neighbors, too.

It's fitting that the Cedar Cove series should end with a Christmas story. The holidays have always been my favorite time of the year. Just like my family and yours, the families of Cedar Cove will be gathering, remembering Christmases past and looking toward the future. You'll get one last glimpse of all your friends here in town…

It's never easy to say goodbye. I know Grace and Olivia will always be close; eventually they'll both retire and enjoy traveling with their husbands. Maybe the four of them will even take a road trip together! Charlotte and Ben will live out the rest of their lives in the assisted living complex. Peggy and Bob's B and B, Thyme & Tide, will thrive, and Roy and Corrie McAfee will settle comfortably into life as doting grandparents (with Roy still taking on a few cases—but only those that interest him). The Flemmings and the Coxes and everyone else will do well… And in the meantime, please join them all for Christmas in Cedar Cove.

And speaking of Christmas, look for *Debbie Macomber's Christmas Cookbook*. It's full of wonderful recipes, decorating hints and more, all inspired by holidays at my home and in my stories. If you liked the Cedar Cove cookbook, you'll love this one, too.

Again, thank you for the support you've given these books. I hope the stories will continue to live in your mind as they will in mine.

Debbie Macomber

1

"Mom!"

The front door slammed and Beth Morehouse hurried out of the kitchen. Three days before Christmas, and her daughters were home from college—at last! Her foreman, Jeff, had been kind enough to pick them up at the airport while Beth dealt with last-minute chores. She'd been looking forward to seeing them for weeks. Throwing her arms wide, she ran toward Bailey and Sophie. "Merry Christmas, girls."

Squealing with delight, they dropped their bags and rushed into her embrace.

"I can't believe it's snowing. It's so beautiful," Bailey said, holding Beth in a tight hug. At twenty-one, she was the oldest by fourteen months. She resembled her father in so many ways. She was tall like Kent and had his dark brown hair, which she'd tucked under a knitted cap. Her eyes shone with a quiet joy. She was the thoughtful one and that, too, reminded Beth of her ex-husband. Three years after the divorce, she still missed him, although pride would never allow her to admit that. Even her budding relationship with Ted Reynolds, the local veterinarian, paled when she thought about her life with Kent and their history together.

"My turn." Displacing Bailey, Sophie snuggled into Beth's embrace. "The house looks fabulous, Mom. Really Christmassy." This child was more like Beth. A few inches shorter than her sister, Sophie had curly auburn hair and eyes so blue they seemed to reflect a summer sky. Releasing Beth, Sophie added, "And it smells wonderful."

Beth had done her best to make the house as festive and bright as possible for her daughters. She'd spent long hours draping fresh evergreen boughs on the staircase leading to the second-floor bedrooms. Two of the three Christmas trees were loaded with ornaments. The main tree in the family room was still bare, awaiting their arrival so they could decorate it together, which was a family tradition.

A trio of four-foot-tall snowmen stood guard in the hallway near the family room where the Nativity scene was displayed on the fireplace mantel. Decorating had helped take Beth's mind off the fact that her ex-husband would be joining them for Christmas. This would be the first time she'd seen him in three years. Oh, they'd spoken often enough, but every conversation had revolved around their daughters. Nothing else. No questions asked. No comments of a personal nature. Just the girls and only the girls. It'd been strictly business. Until now.

Until Christmas.

They both loved the holidays. It was Kent who'd first suggested they have several Christmas trees. Always fresh ones, which was one reason Beth had been attracted to the Christmas tree farm when she started her new life.

"I've got lunch ready," Beth said, trying to turn her attention away from her ex-husband. He still lived in California, as did the girls. He'd stayed in their hometown of Sacramento, while Bailey and Sophie both attended university in San Diego. According to their daughters, Kent had asked to come for Christmas. She'd known for almost two weeks that he'd made reservations at the Thyme and Tide B and B in Cedar Cove. The news that he'd be in town had initially come as a shock to Beth. He hadn't discussed it with her at all. Instead, he'd had their daughters do his talking for him. That made everything more awkward, because it wasn't as if she could refuse, not with Bailey and Sophie so excited about spending Christmas together as a family. But Kent's plans had left her with a host of unanswered questions. Was this his way of telling Beth he missed her? Was he looking for a reconciliation? Was she? The questions swarmed in her head, but the answers wouldn't be clear until he arrived. At least she'd be better able to judge his reasons. His intentions. And her own...

"Just like it used to be," Bailey finished. Beth had missed whatever she'd said before that, although it wasn't hard to guess.

Just like it used to be. These were magic words, but Beth had recognized long ago that the clock only moved forward. Yet the girls' eagerness, Kent's apparent insistence and her nostalgia for what they'd once shared swept aside her customary reserve.

"Mom?" Bailey said when she didn't respond. "We're talking.... Where are you?"

Beth gave a quick shake of her head. "Woolgathering. Sorry. I haven't had much sleep lately." Exhausted as she was, managing the tree farm and getting ready for Christmas with her daughters—and Kent—she'd hardly slept. She couldn't. Every time she closed her eyes, Kent was there. Kent with his boyish smile and his eyes twinkling with mischief and fun. They'd been happy once and somehow they'd lost that and so much more. Beth had never been able to put her finger on what exactly had gone wrong; she only knew that it had. In the end they'd lived separate lives, going their own ways. Their daughters had kept them together—and then they were off at college, and suddenly it was just Kent and Beth. That was when they discovered they no longer had anything in common.

"You're not sleeping?" Bailey's eyes widened with concern.

Sophie elbowed her sister. "Bailey, think about it. This is the busiest time of year for a Christmas tree farm. Then there's all this decorating. And, if we're really lucky—"

"Mom made date candy?" Bailey cut in.

"And caramel corn?" Sophie asked hopefully, hands folded in prayer.

"Yes to you both. It wouldn't be Christmas without our special treats."

"You're the best mom in the world."

Beth smiled. She'd had less than three hours' sleep, thanks to all the Christmas preparations, her dogs and…her incessant memories of Kent. Traffic at the tree farm had thinned out now that Christmas was only three days away. But families were still stopping by and there was quite a bit to do, including cleanup. Her ten-man crew was down to four and they'd coped just fine without either her or Jeff this morning. While he drove out to the airport, she'd been getting ready for her daughters' arrival. However, as soon as lunch was over, she needed to head back outside.

Beth and the girls had booked a skiing trip between Christmas and New Year's, and after the hectic schedule of the past two months, she was counting on a few relaxing days with her daughters. Their reservations were made and she was eager to go. Ted Reynolds, good friend that he was, had offered to take care of her animals, which reminded her of the one hitch in her perfectly planned holiday escape.

"Before we sit down to eat, I need to tell you we have special guests this Christmas."

"You mean Dad, right?" Bailey led the way into the other room, where there was more greenery and a beautifully arranged table with three place settings.

"Well, yes, your father. But he's not the only one...."

"Mom." Bailey tensed as she spoke. "Don't tell me you have a boyfriend. It's that vet, isn't it?"

"Ten guests, actually," she said, ignoring the comment about Ted, "and they aren't all boys."

"Puppies?" Sophie guessed.

"Puppies," Beth confirmed, not surprised that her daughter had figured it out. "Ten of them."

"Ten?" Sophie cried, aghast.

Without asking, Bailey went straight to the laundry room off the kitchen. "Where did you get ten puppies?" The instant she opened the door, all ten black puppies scampered into the kitchen, scrambling about, skidding across the polished hardwood floor.

"They're adorable." Sharing Beth's love for animals, both girls were immediately down on the floor, scooping the puppies into their arms. Before long, each held at least two of the Lab-mix puppies, the little creatures intent on licking their faces.

Unable to resist, Beth joined her daughters and gathered the remaining puppies onto her lap. One curled into a tight ball. Another climbed onto her shoulder and began licking her ear. The others squirmed until one wriggled free and chased his tail with determined vigor, completely preoccupied. They really were adorable, which was good because in every other way they were a nuisance.

Sophie held a puppy to her cheek. "Where'd you get them, Mom?"

"They were...a gift," she explained, turning her face away to avoid more wet, slurpy kisses.

"A gift?"

"But why'd you take all ten?" Bailey asked, astonished.

"I didn't have any choice. They showed up on my porch in a basket a week ago." Beth didn't say that discovering these puppies had been the proverbial last straw. They'd literally appeared on her doorstep the same day she'd learned Kent was coming here for Christmas. For an insane moment she'd considered running away, grabbing a plane to Fiji or Bora-Bora. Instead, she'd run over to the Hardings' and ended up spilling her heart out to Grace. Under normal conditions, Beth wasn't one to share her burdens with others. However, this was simply too much—an ex-husband's unexpected visit and the arrival of ten abandoned puppies, all during the busiest season of the year. The Hardings had given her tea and sympathy; Ted had been wonderful, too. Beth was grateful for his willingness to watch her animals but she refused to leave him with these ten additional dogs. So she'd made it her goal to find homes for all of them before Christmas. Which didn't give her a lot of time...

"How could someone just drop off ten puppies?" Bailey asked as she lifted one intrepid little guy off her shoulder and settled him in her lap.

"Who could do that and not be seen?" Sophie added. "I mean, you have people working all over this place."

Beth had certainly asked around. "Jeff saw a woman with a huge basket at my door. He thought he recognized her from his church, but when he asked her, she denied it. Then later, Pete, one of the drivers, claimed he saw a man on my porch with a basket. I talked to five different people and got five different stories. All I know is that I've got to find homes for these puppies before we leave for Whistler." And preferably before Kent arrived, although that was highly unlikely.

"Have you found any yet?" Bailey asked.

"No...but I've put out the word."

"You'll do it, Mom," Sophie said confidently. "I know you will."

"How old are they?" Bailey stroked a soft, floppy ear.

"Ted thinks about two months. Between six and eight weeks, anyway."

"They're irresistible. You won't have trouble finding homes," Sophie said.

Beth wished she had even a fraction of her daughter's faith. In October, she'd found homes for four part-golden-retriever puppies. Coming up with those homes had been hard enough—and now ten more. She hoped the season would help.

She'd offer assistance with training if the new owners wanted it—and she'd push the all-important spay-and-neuter message. Ted had promised to give the owners a break on the price, too.

Working together, Beth and the girls corralled the puppies and got them back inside the laundry room. Then they washed up for lunch. Thankfully, the girls' favorites didn't require much effort; the tomato basil soup and toasted cheese sandwiches were on the table within minutes.

"Now I truly feel like we're home," Bailey said, spooning up the thick soup.

Sophie sighed contentedly. "This place is starting to feel more like home all the time."

Beth had moved to Washington State following her divorce. For fifteen years she'd taught business and management classes at an agricultural college outside Sacramento. After she and Kent had split up, Beth felt she needed a change. A big one. An escape. She'd read about this Christmas tree farm for sale while browsing on the internet and had become intrigued. As soon as she'd visited the property and toured the house, she was sold.

Her general knowledge of farm life and crop cultivation had come in handy. She knew just enough about trees not to be intimidated. Besides, Wes Klein, the previous owners' son, had helped the first couple of years. She'd soon picked up everything else she needed to know. She hired the same crew each season and was pleasantly surprised by how smoothly things had gone this year, the first year she was on her own.

In addition to Christmas trees, she sold wreaths and garlands, which were created by three members of her staff who devoted all their time to this endeavor. The Kleins used to have only a handful of orders for holiday wreaths. Beth had turned that into a thriving aspect of the business. Plus, overseas sales of Christmas trees had doubled in the past three years. Beth had always enjoyed the season, but never more than now. She felt she was actively contributing to a lot of families' happiness this Christmas.

The girls cleared the table and put their plates and bowls in the dishwasher.

"I've got to get back outside, but before I go, I need you to tell me what's going on with your father." From the girls' startled expressions Beth realized she should have led into the conversation with a bit more finesse. But subtlety wasn't exactly her strong suit and she was short on time.

"Dad wanted to come for Christmas," Bailey answered, as if that was all the explanation required.

"Did he give you any particular reason?" she asked suspiciously.

Sophie shook her head. "None that he mentioned."

That wasn't too helpful; still, Beth persisted. "But why this year?"

Bailey shrugged. "Don't know. All I can tell you is that he said he missed us and asked if he could join us for Christmas. We couldn't say no. You wouldn't want us to, would you, Mom?"

"Of course not." Beth looked from one daughter to the other. "He didn't say anything more than that? You're sure?"

"Positive." Both girls widened their eyes, expressions innocent as could be.

Convinced there was more to this sudden desire to be with them—and remembering Grace's suggestion that the girls might be more involved than they were letting on—Beth hesitated. She wanted to probe deeper but really needed to get to work. As it was, she'd lingered with her daughters well into Jeff's lunch hour.

"You'll be okay without me?" Beth asked, abandoning all inquiries for the moment.

"Mom, it isn't like we're six years old!"

"I know, I know, it's just that I hate leaving you so soon after you got here."

"Go," Bailey said, ushering her toward the door. "We'll be fine. We'll unpack our suitcases and put *It's a Wonderful Life* in the DVD player."

"I want to watch it, too," Beth protested. It was their favorite Christmas movie.

"Okay, we'll hold off until tonight. Now go."

Walking out the door, Beth blew them a kiss, the same way she had every time she left for work when they were youngsters.

The second the door closed, Bailey turned to her sister. "Do you think Mom suspects anything?"

"I'm not sure…."

"I told you we needed to get our story straight before we saw her!"

"I didn't think she'd drill us with questions the instant we walked in the door. Just remember, this whole idea was yours," Sophie reminded her.

"But you agreed! Dad's miserable without Mom, and Mom needs Dad whether she's willing to admit it or not."

"Well, she's *not* willing to admit it, not yet," Sophie said. She rinsed out the soup pan and placed it in the dishwasher. "I never really understood why they got divorced," she mused.

"Yeah." Bailey was wiping off the kitchen counter. "It didn't make any sense."

"When they told us I thought they were joking. Some joke, huh?"

"Could there be anyone else involved?" Bailey asked, growing introspective. "Mom mentioned that vet again. Ted something."

"Ted Reynolds. She hasn't dated in ages, but she seems to like him. He could be trouble."

Bailey frowned. "The problem with Mom is that she's living inside an…an emotional cocoon." She nodded, pleased with that description. "She's consumed by this tree farm so she doesn't have to think about Dad or the divorce or anything else."

"Who made you the expert?" Sophie muttered.

Bailey ignored the sarcasm. "I took this really great psychology class, and I recognized what Mom's been doing for the past few years. We've got to shake her up, make her realize the divorce was a terrible mistake."

"It's not just the tree farm, it's those darn puppies," Sophie lamented. "With puppies constantly showing up on Mom's porch, she can focus all her attention on them. She spends a lot of time training her dogs for those canine therapy programs—"

"And being the unofficial rescue facility," Bailey threw in.

Sophie nodded. "And now there's this Ted guy. Getting Mom and Dad together isn't going to be as easy as you think."

"What did you tell Dad?" Bailey asked.

Sophie slouched into a chair and stared at her sister. "Just that it's important to Mom that we all spend Christmas together."

"Did he ask why?"

"Not really. He said he didn't have any fixed plans for Christmas, and if Mom wanted him to come he would."

"What are we going to tell them when they discover we arranged this?"

"What we should've said when they told us they were getting divorced. This is stupid. They should've tried harder."

"They just grew apart, that's all, but if they'd made an effort they could've gotten close again, right?"

"Right."

"Marriage takes work," Bailey said, feeling wise. The research for her recent psych essay on "Family in the New Millennium" had made that very clear to her.

"I just don't want them to be upset with us," Sophie said, worried.

"They can't. It's Christmas. We brought them together… okay, under false pretenses, but they can't be mad because we're only doing what's best for them."

"Amen. Sing it, sister."

"We'll sing it in two-part harmony."

"Dad gets here when?"

"Tomorrow afternoon."

"Perfect." Sophie held up two crossed fingers. "I believe. I believe."

"So do I," Bailey echoed. This was going to be the most wonderful Christmas of their lives and it didn't have a single thing to do with the wrapped packages under the tree. It was because of the gift they intended to give their parents.

And each other.

The snow had stopped falling, and the grounds were so pristine and lovely, they could've been on a book cover. Or a Christmas card. The evergreens were daubed with snow, giving them a flocked look that was more beautiful than anything Beth could reproduce with the sticky artificial stuff her crew applied to the more elaborately decorated trees in the shop.

"We're back," Bruce Peyton said as he approached Beth. "And this time, we're definitely going home with a tree."

His pregnant wife, Rachel, looked so much better than she had two weeks ago. Beth had learned later that Rachel was hospitalized with food poisoning that same evening. Bruce's teenage daughter, Jolene, was with them today, as she'd been before.

"Are all the best trees taken?" the girl asked, her eyes wide with concern.

She had a point. The trees closer to the house had been thinned out, but there were still a number of excellent spruces and firs in the far lot. "Not to worry," she assured Jolene. "I always save the best for last." She handed the girl a cup of warm cocoa. "If you'd like, I'll have my foreman take you to the back twenty in the ATV and you can see for yourself."

"Really?"

"Really," Beth confirmed. She led them over to Jeff, made introductions and gave him Jolene's request.

The ATVs were built for two, so Jeff took one and Jolene climbed on behind him. Bruce took the second vehicle. Rachel looked at the hard seat, then eyed the dirt road speculatively.

"I think I'll stay here and visit with Beth while you two choose the tree."

"You can't," Jolene said loudly. "You *have* to help pick out the tree. That's the most fun part."

"I'm just not sure I'm up to this."

"Let me take you for a test run," Bruce suggested.

Rachel remained hesitant, then nodded. "Okay, but don't be upset if I decide to stay back."

"I won't," Bruce said.

"I really want you to come with us," Jolene insisted.

"I know, honey. I will next year. I'll come with you and your little sister. Don't forget, it'll be her very first Christmas."

Jolene hugged her quickly. "Okay."

Ten minutes later, Rachel was sitting in the office, drinking a bottle of apple juice as Beth finished her paperwork.

"I doubt they'll be long," Beth told her. "The trees there are gorgeous, especially with this afternoon's snow."

"I hope Bruce and Jolene don't go overboard and choose the biggest tree on the farm."

Beth chuckled. "Jeff knows that people look at a tree and have no idea how large it is until they try to get it in the house. He'll keep them realistic."

"Oh, good. Jolene loves Christmas." Rachel leaned back in her chair. "I consider this our first real Christmas as a family. We were married last year but I was so busy cleaning and moving that it didn't feel very Christmassy."

"There seem to be a lot of firsts for your family," Beth said gently.

"I agree. It hasn't been a smooth transition for us, but everything's come together in the past couple of weeks."

"I'm glad," Beth said. She wasn't entirely sure what Rachel meant. Busy though she'd been, when the Peytons originally came for their tree, Beth couldn't help noticing the tension between Rachel and Jolene. The change in attitude, particularly on Jolene's part, was encouraging.

Twenty minutes later, the two ATVs roared into the yard. As soon as the engine was shut off, Jolene leaped off the back of her father's vehicle and raced toward Rachel.

"We found the most beautiful tree," she said excitedly. "It's just *perfect*."

"Where is it?" Rachel asked, laughing at Jolene's unabashed enthusiasm.

"You should've seen her," Bruce said, joining them. "Jolene was like a rabbit, hopping from one tree to the next."

"Dad, you're embarrassing me," the girl protested, but not too vigorously. In fact, it looked as if a smile was permanently affixed to her face.

"Exactly where is this wonderful, perfect Christmas tree?" Rachel asked again.

"Jeff's going back in the pickup for it now," Bruce explained. He reached into his pocket for his wallet. "While he's doing that, I'll pay for the tree and get out the rope so we can tie it to the top of the car."

"When we take it home, we're all going to decorate it together," Jolene said happily.

"My girls and I do that," Beth told her. "I always decorate several trees, but I leave one undecorated so the four…three of us can do it together once they're home from college."

Jolene looked at her father and Rachel. "Will you wait for me when I'm in college, too?"

"You bet," Rachel said, raising one thumb.

That seemed to satisfy the teenager. "It won't be that long, you know."

"No need to rush it," Bruce commented.

The phone rang, and since Jeff was busy, Beth grabbed it. "Cedar Cove Tree Farm," she said. "Beth speaking."

"Oh, Beth, I'm so glad I caught you."

It was her friend, Grace Harding, the head librarian who'd adopted a golden-retriever mix from the previous batch of puppies. She sounded harried.

"What can I do for you, Grace?" Beth asked.

"We need a small tree."

"How small?"

"One that'll fit in a hotel room. It's for a family who just arrived in town. Friends of ours."

"Sure. I can have Jeff cut one for you and deliver it myself."

"Oh, would you? I know this is last-minute, but these are two special friends who once rented our house on Rosewood Lane. That was years ago—but Ian's in the navy and it looks like they're moving back. They have two children. They're only here for a few days, but I can't bear the thought of them spending Christmas in Cedar Cove without a tree."

"I'm on it," Beth said. "Don't worry, I'll see to everything, including lights and decorations. Shall I bring it to your place?"

"Yes, please. I don't know how to thank you."

"You already have," Beth said. Replacing the phone she looked at Bruce. "Now, I don't suppose I could interest you in adopting a puppy?"

"A puppy?" Jolene perked right up. "Could we, Dad? Rachel? *Could* we?"

Bruce shrugged uncomfortably. "I don't think so, sweetheart. With the baby coming and everything…"

"What kind of puppy?" Rachel asked, reaching for Bruce's hand.

"They're a Labrador mix. They're all black and extremely cute. You could have the pick of the litter."

Jolene clasped her hands and turned pleading eyes to her father.

Bruce held Rachel's gaze and after a moment nodded. "But remember, Jolene, you're responsible for training and taking care of the puppy."

"I will, Dad, I promise. I've always wanted a dog! I want a girl and I'm going to name her Poppy."

"Poppy's a good name," Rachel said.

"I can help with the training," Beth offered, leading all three of them to the laundry room. It didn't take Jolene long to choose the puppy she wanted.

One down, nine to go.

2

Earlier in the month, Grace had been pleasantly surprised to get a phone call from Cecilia and Ian Randall, who were stationed in San Diego. They phoned again once they got into town.

"Would it be possible for Ian and me to stop by and visit?" Cecilia asked.

"Cecilia, of course! How are you? I hoped I'd get a chance to see you and Ian and the kids." Grace had a hundred questions. The young couple had always been close to her heart, and she was thrilled at the prospect of having them back in the area.

"Remember I told you the navy transferred Ian back to Bremerton?" Cecilia said. "He's going to be working in the shipyard instead of on the aircraft carrier. Cedar Cove feels like home to us, so we're really happy about coming back."

"That's wonderful!" The Randalls reminded Grace of when she and her first husband, Dan, had purchased their house almost forty years ago. They'd been young, too, with a child and another on the way. Maryellen was a toddler and Grace had been pregnant with Kelly, and 204 Rosewood Lane had been their first real home. In fact, Grace had lived in that house most of her adult life. She'd raised her children there, buried her husband and learned to deal with life as a widow all on Rosewood Lane. The place held a great deal of sentimental value for her and she hadn't been able to let it go, even after marrying Cliff Harding. So she'd decided to rent it out.

The Randalls had been ideal tenants, but the navy had transferred them all too soon. Over the years, Grace had seen a number of renters come and go. Faith Beckwith had resided there for a while; she'd had a difficult time with break-ins perpetrated by the tenants preceding her. That was long past now and the culprits were behind bars, thanks to Sheriff Davis. The most recent renters had left, and the house was sitting empty.

"I think I mentioned that Ian has leave over Christmas. We flew out here yesterday. We came to see my dad and look for housing." She paused. "Dad lives in a small apartment, so we're staying at the Comfort Inn."

Grace had assumed as much, based on their previous conversation. And other than the Beldons' B and B, the Comfort Inn was the only hotel in downtown Cedar Cove.

"Do you have a car?" she asked.

"A rental."

"Come over today if you can and we'll chat."

"What time?"

"Two," she suggested. "Olivia is planning to stop by around then, and I know she'd love to see you."

"Judge Lockhart... I mean, Judge Griffin?"

"Yes."

"I'd love to see her, too. Ian and I owe her so much."

Indeed they did owe a debt of gratitude to Olivia, as did many others in the community. Despite her decades as an attorney and then a family court judge, Olivia had never become jaded or cynical. She looked at each case individually. Over the years she'd made some controversial judgments. In

Ian and Cecilia's case, she'd denied their divorce. That decision had caused quite a stir in the courtroom and around town. She'd used a technicality, urging the couple to try harder and not to give up on each other so soon.

As it happened, Jack Griffin, the new *Chronicle* editor, had been visiting the court that day and had written an article about her decision, which had greatly embarrassed poor Olivia. Nevertheless, his inflammatory piece had been the start of their relationship. And look where that had led! Grace couldn't hold back a smile.

"We'll be there at two," Cecilia said.

"Be sure to bring the kids," Grace told her. "Cliff is boarding a pony over the holidays. She's very gentle, and the owner said we can give rides to anyone we want."

"Oh! Aaron and Mia will love it. See you at two."

Grace finished addressing the last of her Christmas cards and walked down to the mailbox to send them off, knowing they'd be late this year. She wondered how she'd gotten so far behind.

Cliff helped her prepare by setting out a plate of cookies, although Grace suspected he ate as many as he put on the plate. The cocoa was warming on the stove when a car rolled into the driveway.

Beau, her puppy and guard dog, barked, warning them of impending visitors. "Is it the Randalls or Olivia?" Grace asked.

Cliff peered out the kitchen window. "Looks like Olivia." He reached for his coat. "I'll be outside with Pixie, saddling her up for the Randall kids."

"Thanks." Grace dried her hands and hurried to the door. Olivia immediately handed her a fruitcake wrapped in aluminum foil.

"From Mom," she announced, stooping to pet Beau. "She

baked them while she was living with Jack and me, and wanted to be sure you got one."

Grace wasn't a fruitcake fan—except for Charlotte's, which included green tomato mincemeat and pecans. She put it on the counter next to an evergreen spray in a narrow vase.

"That's so thoughtful. How's Charlotte doing?" Grace was well aware that Charlotte and Ben's recent move into the assisted-living complex hadn't been easy.

"She has good days and bad days." Olivia removed her gloves, stuffing them in her pocket, then slipped off her coat and draped it across the back of a kitchen chair. "On Tuesday, Mom phoned and told me she'd made a big mistake and wanted to return to the house."

"But Will's living there now."

"I didn't remind Mom of that. I figured out what was wrong. It's Christmas and she misses all the things that represent the holidays to her. She associates them with the house."

"Poor Charlotte."

"It *is* hard to make such a huge move at this point in her life."

As Beau settled on the rug by the kitchen door, Grace poured them each a cup of coffee. She carried the mugs to the table, then pulled out a chair. "So what did you do?"

"I found the crèche she'd tucked away in the basement and brought it over to their apartment, along with a small Christmas tree and a few other decorations. Then we sat and chatted over tea for a while. After about an hour, Mom said she'd had a change of heart and the assisted-living complex would suit her just fine."

"That's a relief." Grace knew this had been as difficult for Will and Olivia as it was for their mother and Ben. On the whole, though, the new arrangement seemed to be working out.

"I had a call earlier today," Grace said.

"Oh?" Olivia sipped her coffee.

"Remember I mentioned that Ian and Cecilia Randall were coming to town? In fact, Beth was by just a short while ago to drop off a tree for them."

"So they're here?"

"Yes. Since Ian's been transferred to the Bremerton shipyard, they came to spend Christmas with Cecilia's father, and look for a place to live. They're staying at the Comfort Inn."

"When did they get in?"

"Yesterday. Cecilia phoned and they'll be stopping by—" She paused to glance at the kitchen clock. "Anytime now," she finished.

"Why the Christmas tree?" Olivia asked.

"You know as well as I do that Bobby Merrick isn't going to have a Christmas tree for those kids. I explained the situation to Beth and she brought over the cutest tree you can imagine. It's in a pot and won't take up much space. They should be able to set it in a corner of the hotel room without a problem. She even threw in lights and a few ornaments." Grace appreciated all the effort Beth had put into this spur-of-the-moment idea.

"She owes you big-time after you decided to keep Beau," Olivia said.

On hearing his name, Beau scampered from his place by the door to Grace's feet. When she picked him up and held him in her lap, Beau licked her hand, then settled down to snooze, content to be close to his mistress.

"I'm the one who owes Beth," Grace said, brushing her hand along Beau's soft fur. She'd resisted her affection for Beau as long as she could, but his sweet temperament had eventually won her over.

"I heard Beth has ten more puppies to find homes for now."

"Nine," Grace was pleased to tell her. "Beth is elated. Bruce and Rachel Peyton let Jolene have a puppy for Christmas. She's named her Poppy."

"I hope everything's okay," Olivia said, frowning slightly. "I don't want to see them in my courtroom."

"The situation seems to have resolved itself. When I spoke to Rachel, she said all three of them were in counseling and making great strides." Then Grace added, "I'll be grateful when Rachel returns to the salon. My nails are a mess without her."

"Grace!"

"Well, it's true."

They heard a car door slam in the distance. Beau's head came up and he leaped down from his resting place on Grace's lap. Barking, he ran to the front door, tail wagging furiously.

She followed him and opened the door to Cecilia Randall.

"Merry Christmas," Cecilia said, giving her a bright red poinsettia.

Cecilia didn't seem to have changed since the last time Grace had seen her. True, her dark hair was shorter now, stylishly cut, but she was as slim and elegant as ever.

Cecilia broke into a big grin. "You look exactly the same as I remember."

"I was just thinking the same thing about you." Grace set the plant on a small table near the entry. As she closed the door she glanced over at the barn. Ian and the two children were already talking to Cliff, who'd led the pony into the yard. Cliff had Pixie saddled and was introducing her to the children. Grace would serve them cookies and hot chocolate later when they came in. "Olivia's here."

"Oh, good! I was hoping for a chance to see her." As Cecilia moved into the kitchen, Grace hung up her scarf and wool coat.

"Hello, hello," Olivia said. Standing, the two women exchanged hugs.

"Sit, please," Grace said. She took out another mug and filled it with coffee.

There was a lot of laughter and smiling as they caught up with one another, but then Cecilia grew serious. She turned toward Olivia. "I was out to see Allison this morning." She bowed her head slightly. "Do...do you ever visit your son's grave?" she asked in a small voice.

"Yes," Olivia admitted softly. "On Jordan's birthday, Justine and I put flowers by his headstone."

"Ian and I went this morning and cleaned off her grave. The kids brought her a poinsettia."

"It's still difficult, isn't it?" Olivia said, reaching across the table to squeeze Cecilia's hand.

Grace leaned over to grab a tissue and passed it to the young woman.

"Do you still cry?" Cecilia asked, unmistakable pain in her voice. The loss of her infant daughter was an anguish that might fade but would never disappear. Grace knew that from her own experience, losing Dan.

"Yes," Olivia said. "We don't forget our children. Ever. We can't. There's been a gaping hole in my heart—in my life—ever since we lost Jordan. He was only thirteen...." She cleared her throat. "I've chosen to fill that hole with love."

"I have, too," Cecilia whispered. "Love for Ian and our other children. Both Aaron and Mia know they had an older sister. On Allison's birthday last year, Aaron wanted to bake her a cake."

"Did you?"

Cecilia nodded. "It never felt right to leave Allison when Ian was transferred. I'm so glad we're moving back."

"We're glad, too," Grace told her. Then because she was afraid they'd all end up weeping, she changed the subject. "So, you're looking for a house...."

"Oh, yes." Cecilia wiped the tears from her eyes and

straightened. "Ian and I want to talk to you about the house on Rosewood Lane."

Grace smiled happily. "Well, as I said, my last renters left when their lease expired, and the house is empty. Cliff and I would be delighted to rent it to you."

Olivia checked her watch. "Sorry to rush off, but Justine needs me to baby-sit this afternoon."

"Of course." Grace stood, too, and hugged her friend. "If I don't see Charlotte, make sure you thank her for the fruitcake."

"Will do."

"See you Christmas Eve at Noelle's birthday party, right after church." She briefly explained, for Cecilia's benefit, who Noelle was and that she'd been born here at the ranch a year earlier.

"Yes, see you then," Olivia confirmed. She put on her coat and gloves and wished Cecilia a merry Christmas. Grace walked her out, returning to find Cecilia by the back door, looking at her children, who were taking turns on the pony. "About the house," Cecilia began, moving back to the kitchen table. "Ian and I—"

A polite knock sounded at the door, but before Grace could reach it, Ian Randall came inside. "Hello, Grace," he said warmly. "Cliff said I should go on in. He's taking the kids into the barn to feed the horses." Giving an obligatory bark, Beau trotted over to him and Ian crouched down to stroke the sleek, soft head.

"They're going to love that," Cecilia said. "Aaron is such an animal person." She might as well have said, *And so is Ian.*

"Would he like a puppy for Christmas?" Grace rushed to ask, knowing how desperate Beth was to find good homes.

"He'd love one," Cecilia replied, "but with the move, a puppy—"

"He can pick one out. They're at a tree farm owned by Beth

Morehouse, a friend of ours. If you get a puppy, Cliff and I can keep him here with Beau until you're back in Cedar Cove."

Cecilia and Ian exchanged a glance. "That's too much to ask."

"Not at all. And it would be a huge help to Beth. Someone abandoned ten puppies on her porch and she needs good homes for them before Christmas."

"Aaron's responsible, and he'd love it," Cecilia prompted. "Besides, we'd be rescuing a puppy. What do you think?" She looked at her husband, obviously attracted to the idea.

Ian shrugged. "A puppy for Aaron would be a great gift...if you're positive you don't mind keeping him for a few weeks."

"We wouldn't mind in the least," Grace assured him.

"Okay, that's settled. We'll go and see your friend, pick out a puppy." Ian pulled out a chair and sat down next to his wife. "Did Cecilia mention the house on Rosewood Lane?"

"We'd just started to talk about it," Grace said. "I told her it's available and we'd love to rent it to you again."

Ian shook his head.

"You don't want it?" This surprised Grace because she remembered how fond Cecilia had been of the place and all the small homey changes she'd made. "My mistake. I'm sorry," she said with some embarrassment.

"Actually, Cecilia and I were wondering," Ian said, clasping his wife's hand, "if you and Cliff would consider selling us the house."

"Selling," Grace repeated. "Oh... I hadn't thought of that."

"I brought it up to Cliff," Ian continued, "and he said the decision was yours."

"Well...yes, I suppose it is," Grace murmured. Her immediate reaction was not to sell. Her emotional attachment to the house on Rosewood Lane remained strong. "Can I think about it and get back to you sometime in the next couple of days?"

"Of course," Ian said.

The back door opened again and Cliff came in with the two children. Aaron was instantly on the floor, playing with Beau, and Mia ran to tell her mother all about riding Pixie.

The rest of the visit passed in a blur for Grace, preoccupied as she was with Ian's request. She served cocoa and cookies and presented the Randalls with the small Christmas tree, which thrilled the kids, but she was hardly aware of anything that was said. The young family left soon afterward.

Grace and Cliff waved them off and returned to the house.

"From the look on your face, Ian must have said something about wanting to buy the house." Cliff walked over to the coffeepot and refilled his mug. He leaned against the counter as he waited for her reply.

"He did."

"And?"

"I…don't know if I can give it up."

"Then tell them it's only available to rent," he said matter-of-factly.

"But…this is exactly the type of family I'd want to sell the house to." Grace found she couldn't keep still. She walked over to the refrigerator and opened it for no reason. Closing it, she circled the kitchen table.

"I understand." Cliff came up behind her, placing his hands on her shoulders. "It's a big decision."

Grace exhaled slowly. "It is…but I think it's time," she said with sudden resolve. "My old life was on Rosewood Lane. My new life is here with you—and Beau."

Lying on the braided carpet beneath the kitchen table, Beau raised his head and barked once. Apparently, he was in full agreement.

3

Two down and eight puppies to go.

Saturday morning, the day before Christmas Eve, Aaron Randall—as well as his parents and little sister—had stopped by and picked out a puppy. Grace, bless her, had agreed to keep tiny Poko until the Randalls returned to Cedar Cove in the second week of January. He was with her now, as it would've been too difficult to look after the puppy in the hotel room.

The Randalls' rental car pulled out of the driveway just as another vehicle turned in.

Kent. Obviously driving a rental, too. It was a bright blue sedan, not his usual style at all.

It couldn't be anyone else. He'd phoned shortly after he'd arrived at Thyme and Tide, and said he was on his way over.

Despite herself, Beth felt another wave of excitement. She hadn't slept all night, trying to make sense of his unexpected need to connect as a family again. Granted, he saw their daughters more often than she did, since both attended college in California. But all four of them together at Christmas... It had been a long time. Even if, as she suspected, Bailey and

Sophie were involved in this, Kent didn't have to go along with it. But he had....

Still, she wondered if she was reading more into the situation than it warranted; all the same, she considered scenarios of what this Christmas would be like. Then there was Ted. He was a close friend, and while they'd shared little more than a few chaste kisses, the relationship looked promising. She felt it and thought he did, too.

Beth remembered Christmases when the girls were young. She remembered laughing with Kent, the two of them shushing each other as they stayed up half the night assembling tricycles and later bicycles and then fell into bed exhausted. In an hour or two, Bailey and Sophie would be jumping up and down on the mattress, shrieking that Santa had come.

One Christmas Eve they'd gone for a sleigh ride in freshly fallen snow, snuggling under a blanket, keeping one another warm. Kent had stolen a few hot kisses while the girls giggled and hid their eyes, complaining that it was "yucky" to see their parents kiss.

Beth smiled. They'd had some really good years together. Somewhere along the way, though, their lives had changed. No, their marriage had. They'd grown apart. It wasn't any big disagreement, no betrayal or unforeseen revelation. Instead, an accumulation of small slights and annoyances had eventually grown from a small distance into a huge crevasse. One that had deepened and widened over the years until they'd been unable to reach across it....

Was it possible? Did Kent regret the divorce? Beth had more than a few regrets herself. They'd both been so stubborn, so unreasonable, so eager to prove they didn't need each other anymore.

Perhaps if they'd been the kind of people who yelled and stomped around the house, everything might have gone differently. Instead, once the subject of divorce had been broached, they'd been so darned polite. Attorneys said there was no such thing as a "friendly" divorce, but that hadn't been Beth's experience. Theirs had been not only friendly but accommodating and fair. But maybe that was just on the surface. Maybe going ahead with the divorce was *unfair*—to both of them.

She'd gotten busy at the college and Kent had his engineering company. They'd been like those ships in the old cliché, passing in the night, each drifting in a different direction. She had her life and he had his.

Kent claimed he found her friends stuffy and boring, and stopped attending social functions with her. Beth decided *his* friends were snobs. He didn't seem to mind that she stayed home when he had an event, and after a while she wondered if he'd met someone else. It wouldn't have surprised her. Although he'd never admitted it… They were so remote at that point, spending almost no time together. Oh, they slept in the same bed but rarely touched, rarely communicated about anything other than routine or functional things. Like who was picking up milk or paying the electricity bill.

She was the one who'd suggested divorce. At first Kent had seemed shocked. But he'd recovered quickly enough. He'd simply said that if she wanted a divorce, he wouldn't stop her…and he hadn't.

They'd divided everything as equitably as possible, sold the house and parted ways. It'd all been so civilized, so straightforward, as if twenty-three years as husband and wife meant nothing.

When the final decree came through, Beth decided to leave the academic world. She'd been seeking a geographical cure, she supposed, considering it now. The Christmas tree farm had been the solution she'd been looking for. She had her dogs and a menagerie of other pets, including two canaries, a guinea pig and now the puppies. Eight puppies. She also fed a number of feral cats. And she'd made new friends and found new purpose....

Kent—and, yes, it was Kent, as she'd expected—parked the car and turned off the engine. Beth pretended she was busy. Too busy to even glance in his direction. But despite herself, she was excited. Happy.

All she'd ever wanted from him was some indication that he still loved her, that he still cared. His insistence on spending Christmas with her and the girls, no matter how it had come about, was the first time either of them had made a move toward the other. Could this be the start of a reconciliation?

Her heart rate accelerated and she brushed her hair behind both ears. She wished now that she'd worn something other than her ever-present jeans. Dressing up a bit would've been a subtle way of letting Kent know how pleased she was that he'd extended an olive branch. She had on a long-sleeved shirt beneath her red V-neck sweater, which would have gone nicely with her black wool pants. Oh, how she wished she'd put on her black wool pants.

The car door closed, and Kent stood there, looking at her.

"Hello," she said, surprised by how shaky her voice sounded. "Welcome to Christmas Tree Lane—and Cedar Cove Tree Farm."

He zipped up his jacket and grinned. "The house is fabulous. The girls were right."

"Thank you." The porch railing was covered with swags of evergreen and twinkling white lights. More lights hung from the roofline, glittering brightly in the dull gray winter morning.

The passenger car door opened and Beth saw that Kent hadn't come alone. A lovely, young—much younger than Beth—woman climbed out. She was tall, lithe and stylishly dressed in a full-length black coat and long, high-heeled black boots. She towered an inch or two above Kent, who stood at nearly six feet. Her blond, shoulder-length hair was perfect.... Actually, everything about her seemed perfect in an urban, sophisticated way that contrasted painfully with Beth's farm clothes, disheveled hair and work-roughened hands.

Beth blinked and her heart almost stopped as reality hit her. *Kent had brought another woman.* They were together. A couple. He was seeing someone else now. This little fantasy she'd built around a reconciliation was only that—wishful thinking.

It took her a moment to recover and realize that every assumption she'd made was completely and totally off-base. Kent hadn't come to spend Christmas with her and the girls. His sole purpose was to show off this...this model.

Nothing had changed. Nothing ever would.

"Hello." Beth greeted the other woman with a forced smile and an extended hand. "I'm Beth Morehouse. The ex-wife."

"I know," the woman said in a sultry voice that was sweet enough to caramelize sugar. "I'm Danielle."

Just Danielle? No last name? Like Cher or Madonna or Beyoncé?

"Welcome to *my* Christmas tree farm," she said, placing emphasis on her ownership.

The screen door flew open and Bailey raced onto the porch. "Dad!"

Sophie was directly behind her sister. They darted down the stairs like young fawns in their rush to hug Kent.

Her ex-husband opened his arms, and his daughters launched themselves into his wide embrace.

"How are my girls?" he asked, his voice warm with affection.

"Missing you, Daddy," Sophie murmured.

"Who's that?" Bailey asked starkly, frowning at Danielle. Apparently, she was as shocked as Beth.

"This is Danielle Martin," he said, sliding his arms around each of their waists.

Oh, so there was a last name.

"What's *she* doing here?" Sophie demanded.

"Sophie," Beth snapped, appalled at her daughter's lack of manners.

"Danielle's a friend from work who traveled with me," he said by way of introduction.

"Why don't we all step inside, out of the cold," Beth suggested, and marched into the house, assuming everyone else would follow.

The girls had obviously been playing with the puppies when Kent arrived because the second the door opened they swarmed onto the porch, eager as jailbirds to make an escape. Four were already out the door and racing down the porch steps.

"Don't just stand there," Beth cried to her daughters. "Help me."

Laughing, Sophie and Bailey hurried in one direction while Beth went in the other. Even Kent got involved in the chase. The only one who didn't move was Danielle. With her arms crossed, she remained immobile, as if moving a single inch would have dire consequences.

Once the puppies were all inside the house, Beth brought Kent and Danielle in. Danielle perched on the arm of a recliner with her feet off the carpet. She seemed to fear that all the puppies would rush toward her at one time.

Beth called out instructions. "Get the puppies into the laundry room," she told the girls. "I'll give them some treats." This was not the way she'd planned to greet Kent, with puppies creating havoc.

In the momentary quiet of the laundry room, Beth pressed one hand to her chest, which felt as though it was knotted with pain. She would not, *could* not, yield to the icy tide of disappointment or to the surprising burst of white-hot anger. Not now. Not here. She'd rather be dipped in Christmas-tree sap and rolled in holly leaves before she made a fool of herself in front of the girls.

With a deep breath, Beth squared her shoulders and opened a bag of canine treats just as the girls herded in the last three pups. Whether it was the rustle of the bag or the distinctive aroma, Beth didn't care, only that they all came on the run. On another calming breath, she promised to deal with her emotions later as she distributed the miniature bone-shaped biscuits.

She slowly and deliberately wiped her hands on her jeans while arranging her features in her best hostess smile. Returning to the living room, she motioned Sophie and Bailey to the couch and nodded at her guests. "Now, where were we?"

The girls exchanged a puzzled look and obeyed. At Beth's question, they fixed their gazes on their father.

"Are all those dogs…yours?" Danielle asked incredulously.

"No, no. I'm finding homes for them."

"Where are *your* dogs?" Kent asked. "Do you still have Lucy and Bixby?"

"Of course. They're in the heated kennel in the back."

"It's huge. You should see it, Dad," Sophie said, growing more animated as she spoke. "Mom's got six dogs of her own, and she helps with the Reading with Rover program at the library and…and she trains dogs and she just got a puppy herself." She was out of breath by the time she completed her list.

"He's been sickly so she keeps him upstairs," Bailey added.

"In your *bedroom?*" Danielle's eyes widened with what appeared to be horror.

"You started to tell us about Danielle," Bailey reminded her father, turning away from the other woman.

"Well, yes." Kent looked at Danielle. "She's a…friend."

"A good friend," Danielle murmured. "A *very* good friend."

"I can't believe this." Bailey paced their bedroom with her hands locked behind her back. "This is all wrong! Nothing is working out like we planned."

"When did Dad meet Danielle?" Sophie, the practical one, asked. "And where?"

"Why are you asking me? I don't know any more than you do."

Sitting on the edge of the bed with her hands in her hair—as if trying to pull out an answer—Sophie said, "Well, she wasn't there when we visited him at Thanksgiving. And he didn't say a word about her to me, but I thought he might've mentioned it to you."

"I wish." Bailey threw a scowl at her sister. "If he had, we never would've invited him for Christmas. That's for sure. Besides, I'd have told you. What's Dad thinking? Or *is* he thinking? Anyone with half a brain can see she's all wrong for him."

"She can't be much older than we are."

"Did you see how she reacted to the puppies?" Bailey cried. "Like they were diseased or something. Sitting with her feet in the air, as if they'd mistake her leg for a tree trunk. Too bad they didn't."

Sophie groaned. "And did you hear how she talked to me? Like I'm ten years old. For a minute I thought she was going to pinch my cheek and tell me how cute I was."

"Dad and Danielle? It's a joke," Bailey muttered. "A terrible joke."

"That's what you said about the divorce—until it happened."

"I know. I just don't want to believe this…whatever it is." But she'd seen the way Danielle had looked at their father.

Clearly, he didn't have a clue. This woman was set on getting a big diamond ring from him. Bailey was bound and determined that wasn't going to happen. Not on her watch. If ever their father had needed help, it was now. They had to do something before he made the second-biggest mistake of his life. The first had been going through with the divorce.

"Well, you'd better come up with an idea fast, or you'll be spending next Thanksgiving with Dad and your new step-mother. Just you and Danielle and Dad. 'Cause I'm not going. I'll be here with Mom."

"Don't say that," Bailey moaned. "Besides, you'll *have* to come."

"Nope. I don't like Danielle."

"Me, neither."

"There's got to be something we can do," Sophie said.

"What?" Bailey asked in frustration, which was immediately followed by discouragement. "We can't let this happen. We just can't."

"I agree. Think, Bailey. You always come up with good plans."

"I'm trying, I'm trying."

Sophie kicked off her shoes and sat cross-legged on the bed. "First, we have to figure out what Danielle wants. No woman that young and perfect-looking would ever date our dad."

Bailey nodded. As harsh as it sounded, Sophie wasn't saying anything she hadn't already considered.

"We could introduce her to a younger man."

"Who?" Bailey asked.

"Jeff is cute."

"Mom's foreman? He's married. I don't want to be responsible for breaking up a marriage in order to get our parents back together."

"Yeah, that's bad," Sophie agreed. "Okay, who else is there? It's got to be somebody young. I mean, Dad's way over forty."

"So is Mom."

"Oh, Mom," Sophie said miserably, flopping back onto the bed. "She knew. She was so stoic when she introduced herself to Danielle, I wanted to scream."

Bailey had been too shocked to tear her eyes from her father. When she did look at her mother, she couldn't bear the return of the polite frozen smile. From the moment she and Sophie had mentioned that their father would be coming for Christmas, they'd both noticed a change in her.

In the beginning, when she'd heard the news, Beth had seemed confused and a bit panicky. Over dinner the night before, she'd peppered them with questions about their father. She was interested, all right. Interested and intrigued and, after a while, Bailey had sensed a definite excitement. She'd seemed happy, and for the first time since the divorce, they'd seen a brightness in her eyes.

It was exactly the reaction Bailey and Sophie had been looking for. Over the past three years, Mom had put on a great act. To all outward appearances, she was content; she certainly claimed to be. Her new life suited her just fine, she said. What had frightened the girls into taking action was the fact that their mother had started to casually drop Ted Reynolds's name into their conversations.

Beth's eagerness about seeing their dad convinced both Bailey and Sophie that all this talk about contentment was false. They'd been up half the night whispering in the dark, so sure they were right—and now this.

"Have you got any ideas yet?" Sophie sounded worried.

"Where's Mom?"

"Where she always goes when she's upset. She's with her dogs."

"With her dogs," Bailey echoed. The kennel was a place of comfort for Beth, a place of solace. The thought of her mom sitting on the ground with her precious animals gathered around her made Bailey want to weep.

"Where did Dad and Danielle go for lunch?"

"I don't know...."

He'd invited Bailey and Sophie to join them, but of course they'd declined.

"We should've gone with him," Bailey said.

"No way." Sophie shook her head. "I am not socializing with *her.*"

Bailey reviewed various options that began occurring to her. Yes, it would work. She hopped onto the bed and tucked her legs underneath her.

Sophie stared at her. "What are you thinking?"

"We need to show Dad that Danielle's completely wrong for him."

"Well, duh. Just how are we going to do that?"

"There *are* ways." Bailey gave a conspiratorial smile.

Immediately, Sophie straightened. "You think we can do it?"

"I don't just think, I know. Watch out, Danielle. You're in for it now."

4

Judge Olivia Griffin pulled into the parking lot at the Pancake Palace. She'd ordered two coconut cream pies for their Christmas Eve dinner at Justine's. After the meal, they'd attend church services, then head over to Noelle's birthday party. Picking up the pies was on the list of errands she needed to run before collecting Mom and Ben that evening.

The restaurant was packed, which surprised her. She hadn't expected it to be this busy on Christmas Eve Day. But she should have, she mused, as she hunted for a parking space at the back of the lot. Based on last year's experience, her daughter had warned her. With a firm conviction that family came first, Justine had decided to close the Tea Room for Christmas Eve as well as Christmas Day. Her staff was thrilled with the unexpected gift of this extra time off.

Inside the restaurant, Olivia stood in line at the counter waiting her turn. Wave upon wave of happy voices washed through the room. Looking around, she noticed the painted windows, decorated with a variety of holiday scenes. Holly on one window, a snowman on another. She gazed across the room and saw the Randall family in a booth with Cecilia's father, Bobby Merrick. Holding fistfuls of crayons, the two Randall children were bent over their place mats, solving puzzles, connecting the dots or just coloring.

Remembering her conversation with Cecilia the day before, Olivia couldn't help releasing a sigh. The young mother had asked about Jordan, Olivia's son and Justine's twin brother.

It seemed to Olivia that her entire life was divided by that summer. Life before Jordan died and life afterward. Her world had imploded that summer afternoon. No sooner had they buried their son than Stan, her husband, announced that he wanted a divorce. Within a matter of months, she'd lost her son *and* her marriage.

Watching Cecilia and Ian Randall now, sitting close together, so attuned to each other, so much in love, she didn't regret denying their divorce. How could she? She would've given anything if someone had done the same for her and Stan. The pain of losing their son had been so horrific that, instead of bringing them together, it had driven a wedge between them.

When Stan remarried only months after their divorce, Olivia's friends had speculated that he'd been involved with Marge long before Jordan's death. It'd been easy to believe, especially then. Her mother, who was reluctant to say anything bad about anyone, felt Stan had acted irrationally in leaving his family.

Irrationally? Their son was dead. How could either of them remain rational? The grief had killed them, too.

It was all a moot point. Stan had married Marge, and some years later they'd divorced, as well. For a time it seemed that he wanted to get back together with Olivia and had done his best to thwart her budding romance with Jack Griffin. By then, however, Olivia had fallen for Jack, and her sights were set on the future instead of resurrecting the past. It was far too late for her and Stan. When it became apparent that she wasn't interested, he'd found someone else. Justine had told her that Susan, the new woman in his life, was living with him now. Olivia assumed he wasn't willing to try marriage a third time.

Yesterday, Cecilia had asked if she still cried over Jordan. Did a mother ever stop weeping over a lost child? Olivia doubted it. While going through cancer treatments a couple of years ago, Olivia had become desperately ill with an infection. From what others told her later, she knew she'd been close to death. It was while her fever raged that Jordan had come to her. For the briefest of moments she'd seen him as he was that summer, a skinny thirteen-year-old, full of life, eager to prove himself. He'd been a happy boy, smart and witty. Even now when she heard his favorite song by the group Air Supply, tears would prick her eyes. When she thought of her son, she remembered his ready smile, his ease with people, a natural charm that never failed to endear him to others.

Once again, Olivia wondered what would have become of her son had he lived. He had a variety of interests. He'd been good at math and loved to take things apart, then put them back together. He might have been an engineer. Then, too, he was often the go-between when Justine and James argued, helping his siblings settle their differences. Perhaps he would've followed in her footsteps and become an attorney.

Olivia felt a thickening in her throat and blinked back tears. This was silly. Christmas was supposed to be joyous, festive. Now wasn't the time to reminisce about Jordan.

Cecilia glanced up and, seeing Olivia, she smiled. Their eyes connected—mother to mother. Heart to heart. Cecilia knew Olivia was remembering Jordan. And Olivia knew Cecilia was remembering the infant daughter she'd held so briefly in her arms.

Cecilia nodded and rested her head against Ian's shoulder.

For an instant Ian looked surprised, and then Olivia saw him reach for his wife's hand and give it a gentle squeeze.

Tammy, the hostess, touched Olivia's arm. "I have your pies, Judge Griffin."

"Oh…oh, sorry, I got distracted." Olivia pulled out her wallet, paid for the pies and carried them out to the car without looking back.

Olivia had just opened the driver's-side door when her cell phone chirped. She dug it out of her purse, saw it was her husband and pushed the talk button.

"Hello, sweetheart," she said.

"Where are you?" he asked, sounding rushed.

"The Pancake Palace, why?"

"Eric and Shelly arrived with the boys."

"I didn't think they were due until five." Her stepson and his family were hours early. They'd driven from Reno to spend Christmas Eve with Jack and Olivia at Justine's, and Christmas Day with Shelly's family. "Can you feed them lunch or do you want me to come home?" she asked.

"Lunch isn't a problem. I'm calling because I need to know if Beth Morehouse has any of those puppies left."

"I'm sure she does."

"Great. Eric was saying he wanted to get Tedd and Todd each a dog after the first of the year, and he was hoping to find a couple of Labs. I told him about Beth's situation and he's interested."

"Oh, Jack, Beth would be so grateful!"

"That's what I thought. I'll give her a call and take Eric and the boys out to her place later this afternoon. Do you want to meet us there?"

"If I have time…"

"Okay. Love you."

"Love you, too." She ended the call and dropped her cell

back in her purse. Beth would be thrilled to find homes for two more puppies.

Olivia's next stop was the Sanford assisted-living complex, where her mother and stepfather had recently moved. The snow had been cleared from the parking lot and the sidewalk swept and salted. Hugging her coat around her, she hunched her shoulders against the wind and hurried inside.

A large, beautifully decorated Christmas tree sparkling with lights and classic ornaments graced the entry. Red bows were attached to a set of twin chandeliers. Six fresh wreaths festooned the second-floor railing and left a lingering scent of pine. The complex had a homey, welcoming appeal.

Olivia saw Ben first. He was in the card room set off to the side of the main room. He was apparently playing either pinochle or bridge, his two favorite games. Olivia knew Charlotte was waiting for her upstairs. Her mother insisted on reviewing their Christmas-dinner menu, although Olivia had already prepared most of the dishes in advance. Tonight and tomorrow were for family. She had no intention of spending Christmas Day in the kitchen, although she planned to put the turkey in the oven sometime Christmas morning.

The menu was the same one they had almost every year, many of the recipes directly from the cookbook Charlotte had compiled for Justine. Last Christmas, Justine had made copies of her grandmother Charlotte's favorites for the extended family and it was a much-loved treasure.

Olivia headed for the elevator without interrupting Ben's game and went up to the third floor. Charlotte and Ben's small apartment was at the end of the hall. The door was propped open, a sign to all who came that they were welcome.

"Come in, come in," Charlotte said, putting aside her knitting and getting up. She was definitely moving more slowly, struggling a bit. Harry had arranged himself on the back of the recliner, his tail hanging straight down.

Olivia kissed her mother's cheek and urged her to sit again. She herself sat down in Ben's recliner. An end table served as a catchall between the two chairs, and Olivia saw not only Charlotte's knitting but Ben's current crossword. Dutifully, she took out a pad and pen. "You wanted to talk about Christmas dinner."

"Oh, yes. I do hope you intend to serve that wonderful artichoke appetizer."

"Got it," Olivia assured her. It was done and ready to go in the oven. The artichoke and caramelized onion filling was baked in a flaky dough. Everyone loved it. In fact, Olivia had made two because they were sure to disappear quickly.

"The potato casserole?"

"Wouldn't be Christmas without it," Olivia told her.

"Ben likes it with bacon crumbled on top."

"I can do that." Olivia made a notation on her pad to add bacon to please Ben.

"Did Jack make his special cookies?"

Generally speaking, Jack in the kitchen was a laughing matter but he had managed to prepare his favorite cookies—chocolate-dipped crackers sandwiched with peanut butter. They were a hit every Christmas. The cookie had been his own invention, and considering Jack's pride in the recipe, anyone would think it had won him a Cooking Channel top-chef award.

"The cookies are ready, as well."

"And what did the kitchen look like afterward?" Charlotte asked with a knowing gleam in her eye.

"A disaster. I helped with the cleanup."

"You're a good wife."

Her mother had set a good example.

"Justine wanted to serve beef Wellington, so I thought we'd do a turkey tomorrow."

"You can't go wrong with that," Charlotte said.

"No, you can't," Olivia agreed. There'd be stuffing and plenty of gravy, too. Her mother would work with her and add her personal assortment of herbs and spices to create the distinct taste everyone loved. Although Olivia had watched carefully and taken notes, hers never turned out quite the same.

"Anything else?"

Olivia hesitated. With her mother, everything was homemade, from the dinner rolls to the desserts, of which there was always a wide variety. Pecan pie, fruitcake, rum cake, apple strudel and more.

"I bought a couple of coconut cream pies from the Pancake Palace." Half expecting her mother to berate her for taking the easy road, Olivia held her breath.

"Oh, that's wonderful."

Wonderful? Olivia could hardly believe it. Her tensed shoulders sagged with relief.

"Everyone knows the Pancake Palace makes the best pies in town."

Olivia understood how difficult it was for her mother to deal with change. It wasn't easy for anyone, but the older people got, the harder it was. In her eighties now, Charlotte had coped with the transition from home to the assisted-living complex pretty well. She'd given up the house where she'd lived so many years of her life and surrendered much of her independence. Olivia was exceptionally proud of Charlotte and Ben. Naturally, there'd been doubts along the way, but all in all, the move had been a success.

"Anything else you'd like on the menu?" Olivia asked.

"My homemade applesauce."

"Of course, with the sweet pickles from last summer."

Charlotte rested her hands in her lap. "Those will be the last sweet pickles I put up," she said and, after a short pause, resumed her knitting.

Olivia opened her mouth to reassure her mother that there'd be more pickles and more summers, then realized this was Charlotte's way of telling her she was willing to give up that part of her life. No longer would she maintain a large garden or make applesauce and sauerkraut. The time had come to set all those endeavors aside.

A sharp pang of loss stabbed Olivia, but then she brightened. None of those activities, those special times, were really lost. With a little planning and foresight, they could continue into the next generation, and the one after that, too.

"Justine was talking about your pickle recipe a little while ago," Olivia said, and gently patted her mother's knee. "It wouldn't surprise me if she decided to put up sweet pickles next summer."

Her mother nodded approvingly. "I'll help if she needs advice."

"I know you will." A shift had taken place in their family. It hadn't been apparent at first and the irony of it was that Charlotte had recognized it before anyone else. Olivia felt a burst of joy. The recipes, the special family times, the laughter and the pleasures of being together would remain intact. Each generation would take what was produced and what was passed on by the one before, and then share it with the next. Eventually other traditions would be added, too.

"I'll be by to pick you and Ben up at five," she said. Reaching for her purse, Olivia stood.

"When are James and his family coming?" her mother asked as her fingers expertly wove the yarn around the needle. Socks again. Charlotte must have knit more than a hundred pairs over the years. These, no doubt, were for one of the great-grandchildren.

"James, Selina and the children will be there in plenty of time, don't worry." Olivia didn't have the heart to explain that they'd arrived the night before. Charlotte had spoken to her grandson on the phone but she'd obviously forgotten.

Unfortunately, these lapses happened more and more often. Her mother could recall the recipe for sweet pickles from memory, but a brief conversation the day before completely eluded her. They'd have a more definitive answer to Charlotte's memory problems when they met with the specialist in January. Until then, all they could do was wait.

"I love you, Olivia," her mother said softly as Olivia started out the door.

The comment struck her as odd. Her mother rarely said those words. She smiled. "I know, Mom, and I love you, too." She came back and bent over to kiss her mother's cheek. "I'll see you in a few hours."

For an instant Charlotte regarded her blankly and Olivia knew that her mother had no idea why her daughter would be returning so soon.

5

Five puppies now had homes. Five to go.

It'd been love at first sight. Jack Griffin had come by with his son, Eric, and Eric's family. The grandsons had each chosen a puppy. They'd fallen to their knees and eight puppies had raced into their arms. It had taken quite a long time for the boys to make their decisions. In the end, they'd selected two males; in fact, they'd already given their puppies names, albeit not very original ones: Baron and Duke. Five were left, since Eddie Cox had picked one up for his parents—three females and two males. Ted had volunteered to watch over whatever puppies didn't have homes when Beth and the girls drove to Whistler, but she hated to burden him with extra animals.

Instead of returning to the house after she'd seen off the Griffins and their puppies, Beth wandered into the back of the yard where she had the heated kennel. She opened the gate and let her dogs run in among the trees. They were happy to exercise and she enjoyed playing with them, enjoyed their boundless energy.

Her whole family had been pet lovers. From her earliest memories, they'd always had a dog. Kent loved animals, too, which was one of the reasons she'd been attracted to him all those years ago...and now. At one time he'd considered entering veterinary college, but the application process was complex and difficult, with only a few candidates accepted each year. He'd tried two years running and was declined both times. Although bitterly disappointed, he'd decided to change his course of study to engineering. In the end, that career choice had suited him well.

Thinking of Kent, Beth was forced to confront his news head-on. He was involved with someone else. Danielle had made a point of telling everyone what "good" friends they were. Although Kent had called her merely a friend, it was obvious that Danielle intended it to be so much more.

After three years, this shouldn't come as such a shock—only it did. Her heart felt weighted down by grief and disappointment. Yet she was the one who'd set him free. Not once had she made an effort to turn the tide of the divorce proceedings. Perhaps this was one of those classic scenarios; she didn't want him but she didn't want anyone else to have him, either.

Still, she had to ask herself: Did she want her ex-husband back? She couldn't answer that, not with certainty, and in any event the decision had been taken out of her hands. This sense of loss and confusion was probably typical of ex-wives, she reasoned. It must be.

"Mom?" Bailey was calling her.

Pulling herself out of her musing, she shouted and waved. "Over here."

"I saw the Griffins leave and you didn't come back in the house."

Beth didn't feel much like company at the moment. "I thought I'd let the dogs run a bit first," she said.

Sophie joined her sister. It'd started to snow again, thick flakes that drifted lazily down. The wind chilled her through her thick jacket. Because she spent so much time outdoors, she'd learned to ignore the cold. But this particular chill seemed to come from the inside out....

"Are you upset about Dad and Danielle?" Sophie asked, still putting on her gloves. She didn't look at Beth, as though she wanted to hide her own reaction to Kent's "friend."

"You mean because your father has someone else in his life? Oh, heavens, no." She wondered how effective her lie had been.

"We don't like Danielle," Bailey announced for the two of them.

"You have to admit she's beautiful."

Both girls rolled their eyes. "Mom, she's plastic. I can't imagine what Dad sees in her. Besides, she treats us like we're still in diapers."

"Give her a chance," Beth urged. She didn't know why she was championing the other woman when she agreed with everything her daughters said.

"Tell us again, how did you and Dad meet?" Bailey asked.

Instead of answering their question, she asked one of her own. "Did you know that at one time your father wanted to be a veterinarian?"

"Dad?"

"Get out of here!"

"We met in college," Beth said. "You remember that." They'd heard the story a hundred times. It didn't make sense to repeat it now. "Are you sure you want to hear this?"

Their response was immediate and enthusiastic. "Yes!"

"Okay. We met on campus. A friend-of-a-friend situation. My roommate was dating your father, and I was dating another guy named Steve. I liked your father a whole lot more than Steve, but he was with Melanie and I couldn't very well make a play for him. We dated as a foursome quite a bit and then one day Melanie told me she liked Steve better than Kent and I confessed that I liked Kent better than Steve."

"And the two of you wanted to switch dates," Sophie finished for her.

"That is so cool," Bailey said.

"Well, it would've been if the guys felt the same way about us, but they didn't. Steve claimed he wanted to marry me, but I wasn't interested. Kent, on the other hand, only had eyes for Melanie."

"Oh, brother. Clearly, Dad's needed direction in the girlfriend department for a long time."

"We worked it out. Melanie broke up with Kent and I took the initiative and phoned to console him. What he wanted was for me to convince Melanie to take him back...." She paused and kicked at a pile of snow. "I guess I was always the second choice with your father."

"Oh, Mom, that isn't true!"

Beth smiled, letting her daughters know she wasn't serious. Well, maybe she was, not that it mattered.

"Whatever happened to Melanie? Did she marry Steve?"

"No. She left college in our junior year and dated a guy from France. Eventually she followed him there. We lost contact after a while. I haven't heard from her in years."

Princess raced to Beth's side. Panting, the collie dropped a stick at her feet. "You want to play fetch, do you?" she asked, and bent to pet her thick fur. Princess was a rescue someone had brought her. Her friend had found the collie on the side of the road near the freeway. With some effort she was able to get the large dog into the car. Rather than take her to the animal shelter, Beth's friend had brought her to Beth. Half-starved, Princess was in bad shape, and Beth had nourished her back to health. She'd tried to find her owner, but the dog had no identification. Now Princess was deeply attached to Beth and was one of the dogs in the Reading with Rover program Grace had instigated at the library.

"Dad still loves you," Bailey insisted.

"Of course he does," Beth said, and meant it. "We were married for twenty-three years. I'm the mother of his children. While we might have opposing opinions on certain issues, when it comes to you girls, we're in total agreement."

"Bailey means he *really* loves you."

Beth threw her arms around her daughters and brought them close. "Listen, you two. I know this is difficult. Maybe you believed that your father's visit to Cedar Cove meant more than he intended it to mean. Maybe you believed he was making a statement about reconciliation." Well, he'd made a statement, all right. He wanted to introduce their daughters to his "friend." "The reason your father's here is because he wanted us all to meet Danielle. He wants us to welcome her into the family."

"I can't do it." Sophie's chin rose defiantly.

"Me, neither."

For that matter, it wasn't going to be any easier for Beth. Nevertheless, she was determined to do her best.

"They'll be coming back here, and I want us all to make an effort, okay?"

Bailey sighed expressively and, after a moment, said, "I'll try... I guess."

"Will Dad be here when we decorate the tree?"

Beth had assumed not. He was with Danielle and it would be awkward to include the other woman. "I... I don't know, but I don't think so."

"Dad used to enjoy that," Sophie said.

Beth had, too. It was their special family tradition. They'd always waited until Christmas Eve to decorate the tree, which went back to her German roots. Her grandparents hadn't put up a tree until the night before Christmas, a tradition that had come from the old country.

"Shouldn't we at least ask Dad about decorating the tree with us?"

"I suppose…" Beth said without much enthusiasm. He would probably assume the invitation included Danielle.

The girls returned to the house, and Beth stayed outside, letting the dogs run until they were tired. She gave them each a healthy snack, then they retreated to their kennel and she went back inside.

Beth had never intended to own six dogs—make that seven with the puppy upstairs. But then she'd never intended to have her children barely a year apart, either. Kent was still in his last year of engineering school and she was working as a teaching assistant to help support them when she discovered she was pregnant with Bailey. Sophie hadn't been a planned pregnancy, either, and she'd arrived a mere fourteen months after her sister.

Beth had gotten pregnant with Bailey at Christmastime. Christmas Eve, to be exact. Hard to prove, perhaps, but she was sure of it. She'd *felt* it, felt they'd made a baby that night. Beth wondered if Kent remembered and suspected that, after all these years, he'd put it out of his mind.

They could only afford a small tree that year and had waited until Christmas Eve to decorate it. Beth had said it was tradition, and while it hadn't been *his* family's tradition, he'd been a good sport about it. With little money for ornaments, Beth had made their own. Kent had done his part, stringing popcorn and cranberries while she sewed gingerbread men from pieces of felt, decorating them with eyes and a row of tiny buttons down the front. Each was unique, individual. She still had several of the original ones and others, too, that she'd crafted through the years. She kept them carefully packed away in boxes.

It'd snowed that Christmas Eve, too, but their tiny basement apartment was warm and cozy. As a surprise, Kent had purchased two miniature bottles of rum to make hot drinks. After decorating the tree, they sat in front of the woodstove, their only source of heat, and with Beth on Kent's lap and the cat curled up on the ottoman, they'd toasted the holidays. They'd started kissing and then one thing led to another and three weeks later the stick was blue.

That was Bailey.

How excited Kent had been to have a daughter. When they learned Beth was pregnant a second time, he'd hoped for another girl and had gotten his wish.

The early years of their marriage were financially tight. They'd met every crisis, refusing to let their money problems come between them. They were a unit, a couple, determined to beat the odds. And when it was smooth sailing financially, her marriage had fallen apart.

Somewhere, while the girls were in their early teen years, they'd lost the glue that held them together.

Well, good grief, there was no need to analyze the past at this late date. What was done was done. She smiled despite her mood. If ever there was a profound statement, that was it. *What's done is done. Accept it.* Beth found herself humming a Christmas carol as she headed back to the house.

Bailey was on her cell phone in the kitchen. When she saw Beth, she abruptly ended the conversation.

"That was Dad," she explained. "He said he wants to be here when we decorate the tree."

Beth's chest tightened. "Is he… Did he say he was bringing Danielle?"

"I don't know. I didn't ask."

"Where did he take her to lunch yesterday?" she asked conversationally as she considered the situation. Danielle didn't appear to be the sensitive sort who'd recognize that her presence might be uncomfortable for Beth and the girls. Beth decided she needed to brace herself for the inevitable.

"The Lighthouse restaurant, I think."

"Oh." Of course Kent would take Danielle to one of the most expensive places in town.

"What are you making for dinner, Mom?" Bailey asked.

Sophie sent her a pleading look. "*Please* let it be your lasagna."

Beth laughed. "Of course." She'd better add two extra settings to the table.

"With Grandma Carlucci's marinara sauce?"

"Would I use anything else?" The recipe came from Kent's maternal grandmother, who was Italian. Because the dish demanded a lot of time and effort she only served it on special occasions. It was one of Kent's favorites, too. She'd actually made it for him, thinking...well, what she'd thought was irrelevant.

"Did your father tell you when he plans to come over?" she asked, trying to hide how anxious this news made her.

"He's on his way now."

"Okay," she said, rubbing her palms together. "Why don't you girls help me carry down the ornaments and we can have everything ready for when your dad gets here."

"Can we bring Roscoe downstairs?" Bailey pleaded.

"Sure, but you'll need to keep a careful eye on him. He's still a bit weak."

Roscoe was Beau's—the Hardings' puppy's—brother, and the sickliest of the litter. Ted hadn't held out much hope for his survival, but Beth had given the undernourished puppy plenty of love and attention, bottle-feeding him and carefully administering his medication. At three months he seemed to have turned the corner and she thought he'd survive.

"Can we bring Princess in the house, too?" Sophie asked.

"Of course." Her dogs spent more time inside than out.

For the next few minutes Beth and her daughters carried down boxes from the storage area upstairs. Princess watched from her place by the sofa. Roscoe was in his bed with his chin resting on his paws, still too weak to move about much, although he seemed to enjoy the activity around him. "Did you and Dad ever have birds?" Bailey asked, standing near the canaries' cage.

Beth unsuccessfully hid a smile.

"What's so funny?"

"I did have a canary named Tweetie shortly after we were married, but we had to give her away."

"But why? Dad loves animals, too!"

"Yes, I know, but both your father and I were gone during the day. We had to keep the apartment heated for Tweetie, and after the first heating bill, your father insisted I find her a wealthier owner."

"Did you hate giving her up?"

"A little. She went to an aunt of mine, who had her for years." She smiled again. "Your father promised me there'd be other birds when we could afford them."

"But you never got another canary until you came to Cedar Cove."

"And now you've got two."

"So they could keep each other company," Beth said. Kent had long ago forgotten his promise and, frankly, so had she. Then one day last year she saw the canaries in a feed store and impulsively purchased them.

They heard a car drive up to the house.

"Dad's back," Bailey said, looking out the living room window.

"Is... Did Danielle come with him?" Beth asked, trying to make the best of this.

Sophie joined her sister and glared out the window.

"Yup. Danielle's with Dad," Bailey said in a stark voice.

Beth didn't know why she'd expected anything else.

6

"Is that Allison?" Rosie Cox called from the kitchen.

Zach glanced out the window and, sure enough, his daughter's car had just pulled into the drive. "Yes," he called back. She'd gone to pick up her boyfriend, Anson Butler, at the airport, since he'd be spending the holidays with them. Rosie had been cooking and decorating for days in preparation for Christmas. Zach had gotten roped into helping, not that he minded.

Eddie, their son, who was home from college, came out of his bedroom. He'd spent most of the afternoon there, which was unusual. Eddie was tall and lanky, and he'd shot past Zach's six feet by two or three inches. Eddie must be working on some project in his room, but when he heard the commotion in the hallway, he hurried out, earbuds plugged into his ears and his iPod playing. He yanked one plug free. "What did you say?"

"Your sister and Anson are here."

"Cool."

Zach already had the front door open. The decorative lights on the roof flashed on and off, their colors reflecting in the layer of fresh snow. Anson waved. He'd flown in from Washington, D.C., that afternoon.

Anson had entered the army at eighteen and currently worked in Military Intelligence at the Pentagon. Zach was proud of Anson's achievements, although there'd been a time he was convinced the young man was a felon. Zach had done everything he could to keep his daughter away from Anson.

Fortunately, as Zach had discovered, he'd been wrong about his daughter's boyfriend. Anson hadn't been born with many advantages, but he'd risen above those difficulties, thanks in part, Zach believed, to his daughter. The two of them had met in high school, and they'd maintained their relationship all these years.

At this stage, Zach would welcome Anson as his son-in-law. Rosie cautioned him not to rush their daughter into an engagement, and she was right. Allison and Anson were still young and, as Rosie said, these things had to develop on their own. Parents shouldn't involve themselves one way or the other.

Zach opened the screen door for his daughter and Anson, who set down his bag as he stepped inside and extended his hand. "Mr. Cox, thank you for having me." His handshake was firm and solid.

"My pleasure."

Rosie came forward and hugged Anson. "Merry Christmas!"

"You're bedding down with me," Eddie said, leading Anson down the hallway to his room. "You can have the top bunk."

While Eddie showed Anson where he'd be sleeping, Allison followed her mother into the kitchen. "The traffic was a nightmare," she said. "I can't believe this many people are out on the roads on Christmas Eve."

"Everyone has places to go," Zach said, tagging behind his wife and daughter. "Hey, it smells good in here. What's cooking?"

"Honestly, Zach, I've baked ham every Christmas Eve since we were married. You'd think after twenty-four years you'd remember that."

"Right. Ham." Now that he thought about it, they did seem to have ham every year. Rosie used the bone for a black bean soup she served on New Year's Day, which was some Southern tradition she'd read about and adopted. It was supposed to guarantee good luck for the upcoming year. He doubted anyone believed that, but he liked black bean soup and so did Rosie.

By New Year's, the kids would be heading back to school, and he and Rosie would be alone again. Zach had to admit he missed his children. Without them, the house seemed too quiet.

"What can I do?" Allison asked, reaching for an apron.

Zach smiled at his daughter's eagerness to help. She was an intelligent, considerate young woman, and one day she'd make a fine attorney. In her first year of law school, Allison had gotten top grades. Zach was proud of her.

"Dinner won't be ready for a while, but if you want to make the salad you can."

"Sure." She went over to the refrigerator, collecting the lettuce, tomatoes and other vegetables.

Normally, Zach would've sat down in front of the television at this point. He and Rosie both enjoyed football and had spent many a lazy Sunday afternoon watching the Seattle Seahawks. At first she hadn't understood much about football, but she was a fast learner. Before long, she knew the players' names and positions and understood the game. Spending Sunday afternoons with his wife was *fun*.

Anson joined him at the breakfast bar, pulling out a stool and sitting down.

"So how does it feel to be back home?" Zach asked him. Anson wore jeans and an army sweatshirt, and his hair was shorn. Very different from his high school days when his hair straggled to his shoulders and he wore a long black raincoat. The difference between then and now was striking.

"I talked to my mother," Anson said. He looked down as if to hide his reaction.

"You're welcome to invite her for dinner, if you'd like," Rosie offered.

Zach wasn't keen to spend Christmas Eve with Cherry Butler, but he certainly wouldn't refuse to entertain her.

"Thanks, Mrs. Cox, but Mom has other plans. She's got a new...friend." Anson's tongue seemed to trip over the word. "She's sure it's love this time and wants to be with him."

"You'll have a chance to see her while you're on leave," Rosie said reassuringly.

"I probably will."

Zach noticed that Anson didn't sound all that confident.

Rosie started into the dining room and paused in the doorway—underneath the mistletoe. Zach couldn't have planned this better had he tried. He'd hung it there earlier and now, taking advantage of the opportunity, he slipped out of his chair and hurried toward his wife.

Rosie gave him an odd look as if she didn't understand what he was doing.

"You're standing under the mistletoe," he told her.

Surprised, Rosie immediately looked up.

Taking her in his arms, he kissed her deeply, and with an exaggerated flourish bent her backward over his arm. He might be middle-aged, but he wasn't dead yet and he loved his wife.

Anson and Allison hooted and cheered, but he didn't need any encouragement.

"Zach." Rosie was breathless by the time he released her.

So was he.

She planted her hand over her heart as though to slow its beat.

Zach winked at his son, who'd just joined them.

"I remember when we never used to see you and Mom kiss," Eddie reminded them.

Disbelief on his face, Anson looked from Allison to Eddie.

"My parents were divorced for a while," Allison explained. "I'm sure I told you."

"You did, but…it's hard to believe, seeing them now."

Eddie pulled out a stool on Anson's other side and propped his elbows on the counter. "It wasn't a good year for our family, but it all turned out okay in the end."

Anson shook his head incredulously.

"It was a long time ago," Eddie said.

"Not *that* long," Rosie countered.

"What happened?" Anson asked. "I mean, if you don't mind talking about it."

"Basically the divorce just didn't work out for us," Zach teased, his eyes meeting Rosie's. That had been a difficult period in their marriage, but, as Eddie had said, it'd all turned out in the end, due in large part to…

"The judge… Well, she…" Rosie looked at her husband. "You tell them."

"It was Judge Lockhart. That was her name back then. She's Judge Griffin now. I think she could see that the divorce was a mistake for us, but she didn't have any grounds for denying it the way she did with another couple we heard about."

"Actually, I don't think either of us would have accepted a denial. At the time, we were pretty much at loggerheads."

That was putting it mildly, Zach thought, but kept quiet. No point in mentioning it.

"Mom and Dad wanted joint custody of Allison and me," Eddie said. "If Judge Olivia okayed their parenting plan, it meant Allison and I would've had to change houses every few days. Three days with Dad, four days with Mom—that sort of thing."

"They would've stayed in the same school district," Rosie added. She leaned against the kitchen counter, facing the three of them, all now sitting at the breakfast bar. "Zach got an apartment a few miles from the house."

"Judge Olivia told Mom and Dad they weren't the ones who needed a stable life," Allison went on to tell him. "Eddie and I were. The judge didn't want us changing residences every few days, so she gave us the family home. Mom and Dad had to move in and out."

"In other words," Eddie said, "when Dad was with us, Mom stayed at his apartment, and vice versa."

"Zach and I weren't too keen on this plan," Rosie inserted.

Anson grinned. "But apparently it worked."

Zach had to agree. "I remember the night Allison and Eddie brought us together, arranging for us to have a romantic dinner here at the house."

"Our parents needed our help," Eddie said, smiling at his sister. "Actually, that was Allison's idea and it was a good one."

"It was indeed." Zach reached across the counter to take Rosie's hand. He raised it to his lips and kissed her fingers. "And I'm very grateful."

"I am, too," Rosie whispered.

"We owe the judge a big debt of thanks," Allison said.

"And I owe *you* one," Anson said in a low voice, his gaze connecting with hers. "You always had faith in me."

"Oh, Anson, I had my moments. I so badly wanted to believe you didn't have anything to do with the fire that burned down the Lighthouse restaurant."

"The evidence *was* damning," he said, frowning slightly. "I couldn't blame you for doubting me."

"When I learned you'd been at the restaurant that night, and then later, when your mother told me you'd started a number of small fires when you were a kid, my faith wavered."

"Mine would have, too." Again Anson came to her defense. "I looked guilty as sin. I can't blame you, Allie."

"Luckily you saw the man who really started the fire and were able to identify him."

Zach had played a role in determining that Warren Saget, a local builder, was the arsonist. Teaming up with Sheriff Troy Davis, Zach had convinced Anson to come forward and speak to the authorities.

"If it wasn't for your dad, I might still be on the run," Anson said. "Your family's been a lifeline to me," he continued. "Mrs. Cox, Rosie, you've been more of a mother to me than my own. I know Cherry loves me in her way. She never counted on being a single mother, and she didn't have the greatest role model herself. She does the best she can."

Zach admired Anson for defending his mother. He didn't question that she loved her son. Unfortunately, Cherry's life had been a long series of low-paying jobs and living with ne'er-do-wells who used and abused her. Anson had been instructed to refer to these men as "uncle," none of them ever being a father figure of any kind. His father had left Cherry as soon as he discovered she was pregnant. Turned out he already had a wife and family.

"Are we going to play bingo?" Eddie asked, straightening. "It's tradition, you know." He nudged Anson as he said that, and Anson elbowed him back.

"Why don't we set it up while Allison and your mother finish getting dinner ready," Zach suggested. He slid off the stool and headed into the living room. He didn't recall how Christmas Eve bingo had begun, but the kids couldn't have been more than eight and ten. He thought Rosie's parents might've started it and that Rosie had carried it on, since she was big on traditions.

In the living room, Zach took out the game. He handed the cards to Anson to arrange, while Eddie gathered up the small prizes and placed them on the coffee table.

"If you have a few minutes I'd like to speak to you privately," Anson said, sitting next to Zach on the sofa.

Eddie picked up on the "private" part right away and excused himself, mumbling that he needed to make a phone call.

Anson waited until Eddie had left the room. "What I said earlier about you and Mrs. Cox being more of a family to me than my own? I meant that."

"We feel the same way about you, Anson. I'm proud of what you've accomplished."

Anson smiled, as if Zach's words had pleased him. "I never applied myself in school. I didn't really have to. Everything came easily to me, so I got through without trying. I had no real plans, no aspirations. Then I met Allison and she encouraged me to do better—to *be* better. I would've done anything to make her happy."

Zach remembered how he'd separated the two as teenagers. Anson had given his word and broken it, and as a result Zach had refused to allow Anson and Allison to date or even talk to each other. On Valentine's Day, Anson had come to the door and handed Zach a card for Allison. At that moment Zach had begun to see a real sense of honor in the boy.

"I loved Allison when I was seventeen, and I love her now," Anson went on. "It hasn't been easy to maintain a long-distance relationship with me living in D.C. and her going to school here in Seattle."

Zach nodded; he understood the challenges of such a relationship.

"I want you to know I've dated other women, but it's Allison I love."

His daughter had gone out with other young men through the years, but she felt the same way about Anson.

"I believe this conversation is leading up to something," Zach said.

"I'd like to ask your permission to marry Allison," Anson said quickly.

Zach leaned back on the sofa. He'd known this was coming, but hadn't thought it would be so soon. "Allison still has a year of law school left."

"I know. We've talked about that and she's applied to law schools in the Washington, D.C., area."

Zach arched his brows. "She has, has she?" Apparently, this had been an ongoing discussion between them. "So Allison's already accepted your proposal?"

"No, sir," Anson said. Then he nodded. "Well, yes. I realize speaking to you about this is just formality, but it's important to me."

Zach sent him an encouraging smile.

"Allison wanted me to give her the ring when she picked me up at the airport. I told her I wanted to talk to you and Mrs. Cox first."

Zach could bet his daughter hadn't been keen on that. He approved, though. He liked Anson's old-fashioned sense of protocol and his respect for both Allison and her family.

"Rosie!" Zach called his wife. "Could you come here for a minute? Allison, you, too."

"Sure."

Allison came into the other room, holding her mother's hand.

"It seems that Anson here would like our permission to marry our daughter."

Rosie turned to look at Allison. "But you haven't finished school yet and...you're both so young."

"They've taken both matters into account and still want to get married. Allison will continue her schooling in D.C."

"Oh."

"What do you think?" Zach asked Rosie.

"Well...yes, of course. I would welcome Anson into the family with open arms."

"Oh, thank you, Mom." Allison kissed her mother's cheek and then hurried across the room to her father.

"Hold on a minute," Zach said, stopping her. "I haven't given my consent."

"Daddy!"

Wearing a huge grin, Zach stood and hugged his daughter, and then Anson. "I couldn't imagine a son-in-law I'd rather have. You both have our blessing." Zach was confident in the strength of this relationship, despite their age. They'd proven their commitment to each other. He'd miss his daughter, but the family was close and they'd see her frequently.

"What's going on in here?" Eddie asked, returning to the living room.

"Anson and I are engaged."

"Cool," Eddie said.

"We'd like a June wedding, and then I'll move to Washington, D.C., to be with Anson."

Eddie shook his head. "I don't know about Mom and Dad having an empty nest."

"Hey, it hasn't been a problem so far," Zach told him.

"But it could be." Eddie seemed intent on making his case. "Allison's going to be on the other side of the country, and I'll be away at school."

Rosie frowned and looked at Zach. He shrugged, unsure what his son was getting at.

"Mom," Eddie said. "You need someone to mother. And, Dad, who are you going to boss around? Everyone knows Mom won't put up with that for long."

Allison laughed, but Zach was less amused.

"Now, just a minute, young man—"

Eddie interrupted him. "I've come up with the perfect solution."

"You have?"

Eddie nodded. He turned away for a moment and stepped into the hallway, then came back carrying a basket—with a puppy curled up inside, fast asleep.

"Merry Christmas, Mom and Dad."

"A puppy!" Rosie said, lifting the sleeping pup from his warm bed and holding him close. "He's adorable!"

"What a great idea." Zach grinned, delighted at the prospect of taking a dog for long country rambles. He could already picture the three of them—Rosie, the puppy and him—sitting by the fire….

"Actually, you gave me the idea, Dad. A while back you said you missed having a dog around the house. I'm a starving college student and I couldn't afford to buy you guys a big gift. When we went to get the Christmas tree I heard one of the workers say that Beth Morehouse had a houseful of puppies she needed to find good homes for. So…voilà."

"Now, we'll need to come up with a name," he said.

"I've already named him, okay? I had to call him something. I know you like 1940s and '50s movies, so…meet Bogart. Or Humphrey if you prefer."

"Bogie!" Allison said. "That's it."

"Bogie." Rosie smiled. "This is quite the Christmas," she said, cradling the puppy in her arms. "Not only do we gain a son, but we add a dog to the family, as well."

7

"I'll start making the hot chocolate," Beth said, turning away from her daughters. A few minutes in the kitchen would help her prepare to deal with her ex and his…friend. Kent kept insisting Danielle was "just a friend," but Beth felt there was more to it. Really, why would he bring "just a friend" to a traditional family occasion?

Although she had no idea what Kent was thinking, Beth couldn't imagine him actually spending the rest of his life with this woman. It was a mistake. Even her daughters could see that. Kent wouldn't appreciate hearing her opinion, so Beth was determined to keep it to herself—although that was a struggle.

From inside the kitchen Beth heard Sophie greeting Kent and Danielle at the front door and ushering them into the family room. The Christmas tree was still bare, surrounded by the boxes they'd carried down.

"Mom's in the kitchen."

This came from Bailey. Kent must have asked where she was. A moment later, he joined her. "Listen, I'd appreciate it if we—"

"Is there anything I can do?" Danielle asked in the sweetest of voices.

"No, thanks. I've got everything under control," she told the other woman. Her eyes connected with Kent's. She wanted to berate him for bringing Danielle to a family function; instead, she bit her tongue and tried to disguise her feelings, although she suspected she'd failed.

She realized she'd need to get used to the fact that Kent was his own man now and made his own decisions. Beth forced a smile and continued stirring the chocolate.

"Dad," Bailey called. "Come and help."

Kent hesitated and it looked as if there was something else he wanted to say. With obvious reluctance, he returned to the family room, Danielle on his heels.

Beth took as long as she dared in the kitchen. Fortunately, Grace phoned while she was there, which kept her occupied for another five minutes. Beth peered into the family room when she'd hung up. From her vantage point, she could see that the girls had opened the boxes of old ornaments and were reminiscing with their father. Danielle sat on the sofa, her expression bored. Eventually she reached for her cell phone and started texting.

"Mom!" Sophie shouted. "Where are you?"

"Coming!" Beth loaded the serving tray with pretty holiday mugs. She'd decorated the top of each mug of cocoa with whipped topping and chocolate sprinkles, which was how Kent and the girls had always liked it. "Here we go," she said, hoping she sounded cheerful. Surely there was a reward in heaven for first wives who were nice to their exes' new girlfriends.

"Remember this one?" Sophie said, and held up a snowman she'd made with a wood-burning kit when she was around ten.

"What I remember is the blister you got on your finger because you weren't careful," Kent teased his daughter.

"I was so proud of this silly snowman. I was sure I'd make a career out of wood-burning."

Danielle gave a saccharine smile. "It's…lovely." The words rang empty as her phone chirped and she returned to texting.

"It's terrible," Sophie said. "In fact, it's downright ugly."

"Well, maybe," Danielle agreed, putting her cell back in her sweater pocket, "but you were just a kid. I'm surprised you kept it, though. If it was me I would've tossed it years ago."

Beth opened her mouth to defend her daughter, then closed it. No need to get into a useless argument.

"If you think it's ugly, why would you put it on the tree?" Danielle asked. "I mean, you're right, it really isn't very attractive." She stood and retrieved an ornament from the box. "There are some darling ones here." She held up one of the felt gingerbread men Beth had sewn the first Christmas she and Kent were married. "Now this is kind of amateurish, but it's…nice. By comparison."

"We put up the wooden snowman," Beth said, carefully handing Danielle her cocoa, "because Sophie made it herself. The decorated tree in the living room is for show. This one is for family, for memories of Christmases past."

"Sort of like that Charles Dickens book," Danielle said. "The one with the ghosts. And Tiny Tim."

"Something like that," Beth murmured as she brought Kent his hot cocoa.

"Do you have one without any chocolate sprinkles?" Danielle asked.

"Sure." Beth retrieved the cup and went back to the kitchen. She dumped the whipped cream in the sink and added a fresh dollop minus the chocolate sprinkles.

"Mom sewed those for her and Dad's first Christmas," Bailey was telling Danielle when Beth came back.

"The hot chocolate is even better than I remember." Kent spoke quickly, breaking into his daughter's reminiscence.

"I make good hot chocolate, too," Danielle said. "I'm an excellent cook. I want you to try my macaroni and cheese."

"Uh, sure." Kent looked decidedly uncomfortable.

Danielle beamed. "I have a special cooking trick. You start with the boxed kind and then you just add stuff. My secret is to put ketchup in the water when I cook the noodles."

"I'll have to try that myself," Beth said politely, trying not to cringe. Difficult as it was, she turned her mind away from Kent and his…friend. She hated to admit this, but she was jealous of Danielle.

Danielle sneezed once, loudly. So loudly, in fact, that it startled Beth and Princess, too. The sneeze sounded like a moose in heat—or what Beth imagined that would sound like.

"Oh, sorry," Danielle said, clearly embarrassed.

"Bless you," Sophie said.

Bailey handed Danielle a tissue.

"Thank you." She noisily blew her nose. "It's that dog," she said, pointing an accusing finger at Princess. "I'm allergic to dogs."

"Oh, you should've said something earlier." Beth immediately collected Princess and took her to the kennel outside. Even with Princess out of the room, there was still Roscoe, sleeping beside the fireplace. While Beth kept a tidy house, there was bound to be dog hair everywhere. It was the perfect excuse to send Kent and Danielle on their merry way.

"Beth."

Kent met her on the back porch as she returned from the kennel. He kept his hands in his pockets, his arms held close to his body to ward off the cold. He followed Beth inside, to the laundry room. One of the five remaining puppies jumped up, balancing his paws against her calf. Beth automatically reached down and brought him into her arms, resting her cheek against his soft head.

"Listen," Kent said. "I hadn't planned to bring Danielle with me. It's just that—"

"Don't worry about it."

She carefully put the puppy back on the floor. She attempted to brush off his apology because her heart was doing crazy things. With the two of them in such a small space, the atmosphere was intimate, and with both doors closed it was private. All she needed to do was lean forward ever so slightly and their lips would meet…

Where did *that* idea come from? She couldn't give in to the impulse. But it seemed so natural to kiss Kent, to press her mouth to his. Beth immediately opened the door leading into the house.

Unfortunately, she forgot about the puppies. An open door was an opportunity and they took it. They shot out of the room as though fleeing a burning building.

Beth rushed after them and Kent did, too. He trapped one by falling to his knees and had him back inside the laundry room seconds later. Beth wasn't nearly as lucky. Seizing their opportunity, the other four dashed in different directions.

Beth knew the instant one of the puppies made it into the family room because Danielle let out a squeal. "Get that dog," she cried, apparently to one or both of the girls. Her command was followed by another moose-in-heat sneeze.

Beth hurried into the room. "I'm so sorry," she said, and she was. She'd had no intention of freeing the puppies when she'd opened the door. The truth was she'd completely forgotten they were there.

Bailey grabbed one puppy and Sophie another. Beth scooped up the third. The last one made a beeline for the Christmas tree and got tangled in the bottom garland.

"Get those dogs out of here," Danielle shouted between sneezes. "Oh, good grief, there's another one. What is this place—a puppy mill?"

"My mother would *never*—"

"It's all right," Beth said, cutting Bailey off. "Danielle is understandably upset. I apologize, Danielle. I opened the door without realizing—"

"You did that on purpose!"

"Danielle," Kent said, his voice calm and reasonable, unlike hers. "It was an honest mistake."

The other woman sank down on the sofa and held a wad of tissues to her nose before she sneezed three times in quick succession.

"I'm afraid there's dog hair all over the house," Beth said. "Maybe it would be best if—"

Danielle held up one hand, stopping her. The other clasped a tissue to her face. "I have allergy medication. We will not be leaving on my account." This last part was said in a muffled voice that nonetheless conveyed steadfast determination.

Kent sat next to Danielle, who sneezed again.

It wasn't funny; still, Beth couldn't help it—she had to smother a giggle. Kent caught her eye and knew instantly that she was having trouble hiding her amusement, and that was when Beth lost it. She started laughing and tried desperately to hide her laughter by coughing.

"What's so funny?" Danielle demanded.

"Nothing," Kent said promptly, getting to his feet. "I think, uh, Beth might have swallowed wrong."

"This…isn't funny."

"No, it isn't," Kent said. He bent down and untangled the last puppy from the garland on the tree and brought him back to the laundry room.

In the meantime Beth carried Roscoe upstairs and out

of harm's way. Making it through tonight would require a Christmas miracle.

The phone rang as she came down the stairs. Call display told her it was Bob Beldon. They exchanged Christmas greetings, then he said, "I heard you're looking for homes for some puppies."

"Yes, I am."

"Great. Well, I'm interested in taking one."

They chatted for a few more minutes and she'd just replaced the receiver when the phone rang a second time.

"Your mother gets more phone calls than a bookie," Beth heard Danielle comment.

Teri Polgar was inquiring about a puppy for her sister, Christie.

A moment later, another call. This time it was Ted. "How's it going?" he asked.

"About as well as could be expected." She'd mentioned casually that her ex-husband was coming to Cedar Cove for Christmas. Lowering her voice, she said, "Except that Kent arrived with a…friend."

"A friend?" Ted sounded perplexed. "I was asking about the puppies."

"Oh…the puppies." She wanted to roll her eyes. Of course he'd be phoning about the puppies. "Five down and five to go, although I just heard from someone who's a possibility. And if Bob Beldon takes one, too, that'll leave three."

"Listen, I know someone else who could be interested. Gloria Ashton—for her parents," he said. "Would it be all right if I stopped by later to say merry Christmas?"

"Sure. That would be nice." Ted was exactly the balm she needed. And, if he came over, Kent would see that she hadn't been twiddling her thumbs for the past three years.

She missed Kent. She missed their life together and it was

killing her that he'd found someone else. The divorce wasn't the end, she realized now; his remarriage would be. If he married Danielle—and the other woman had certainly staked her claim on him—it would mean their life together was over. Really over.

"Who just called?" Bailey asked.

"Bob Beldon. And then Teri Polgar. And Ted."

"Bob from the B and B?" Kent looked up at her. "Did he want to speak to me?"

"No, no, he was inquiring about a puppy."

"Oh, dear," Danielle murmured and, for good measure, sneezed again.

Beth had assumed she would've taken one of her allergy pills by now.

"What did Ted want?" Sophie asked.

"He'll be visiting later."

Bailey and Sophie seemed gratified by this bit of news. "That's wonderful," Sophie said as Bailey nodded. "He's a real sweetheart."

"Oh?" Kent asked, turning to his daughters for an explanation.

"Yeah, he reminds me of the vet in those James Herriot books you read us when we were little," Bailey told her father.

Ted? James Herriot? What were her girls up to? Beth sent Bailey a disapproving frown, which her daughter chose to ignore.

They resumed trimming the tree, and when they'd finished, it didn't look half-bad. With its mismatched ornaments collected over the years, it had its own homespun charm. There was the wooden snowman Sophie had made at the age of ten. And a photo of Bailey in the first grade, framed in Popsicle sticks. Another that resembled a pincushion, which Sophie had made when she was in the third grade. Beth's gingerbread men. And a few that she and the girls had constructed through the years with varying degrees of artistic skill.

They stepped back and, hardly aware she was doing it, Beth stood next to Kent. Delighted with their tree, she glanced up at him and smiled. He smiled back and their eyes met. Beth had to force herself to look away; when she did, she saw Danielle watching them both.

The other woman's eyes narrowed, and Beth could tell that Danielle wasn't pleased. Without making an issue of it, Beth moved away from Kent.

Searching for something to do, Beth picked up the empty cocoa mugs and carried them into the kitchen. She was busy placing them in the dishwasher when Danielle joined her.

"I know what you're doing," Danielle said without preamble. She rested her hip against the kitchen counter, crossed her arms and glared at Beth.

"Putting dirty dishes in the dishwasher?" Beth asked.

"You don't like it that Kent brought me here."

Beth straightened and leaned against the counter, too, crossing her own arms. "And what gives you that impression?"

"I saw the way you looked at him just now."

"Really? And how was that?"

"You're jealous."

"Am I?" Beth asked, striving to sound anything but jealous.

"You want him back."

Beth laughed. "In case you've forgotten, I had him for twenty-three years."

"And you miss him."

Beth faked a short laugh. "I don't know what you think you saw, but let me assure you, you're mistaken."

"No, I'm not," Danielle insisted.

Beth looked into the other room to make sure Kent and the girls couldn't overhear this rather unpleasant conversation.

"Well, then, let's agree to disagree," she suggested in a low voice, hoping to avoid a pointless exchange.

"You want him."

Beth disregarded the comment, turned her back on Danielle and continued loading the dishwasher.

"You can deny you're jealous all you want, but if you listen to only one thing, listen to this," Danielle said tightly. "He told me about the divorce and how you wanted out of the marriage. You blew it and now you regret it."

This was too much. If Danielle thought she was helping... Well, she wasn't. "Listen," Beth said, pronouncing each word distinctly. "If you want Kent, he's all yours. You're welcome to him." With that she slammed the dishwasher closed and turned to see Kent standing in the doorway.

8

The scent of cinnamon and allspice filled Peggy Beldon's kitchen as she arranged the decorated sugar cookies on colorful plates lining the counter.

The plates of cookies, toffee and hand-rolled chocolates were her and Bob's gift to their friends each year. Peggy enjoyed baking and never more than at Christmas. She began wrapping the plates in red cellophane and tying the ends with a ribbon. She and Bob delivered the plates on Christmas Eve, usually late in the afternoon.

Thyme and Tide, their bed-and-breakfast, did fairly well this time of year and she was grateful that despite a weak economy they continued to be busy. They already had several reservations for the winter months and the summer looked promising.

Currently, they had two guests, who seemed to be a couple, although they had their own rooms. Beth Morehouse's ex and… Diana? No, Danielle. It wasn't unusual to have guests over the Christmas holidays, although Peggy would've preferred to close, but as Bob said, they couldn't turn down business. Christmas or not, they had rooms to rent. She could guarantee that the Christmas morning buffet would be something Kent Morehouse and his friend would long remember.

Humming a Christmas carol to herself, Peggy glanced out the kitchen window and saw her husband pull into the driveway. He'd run a few errands for her. A couple of minutes later, she glanced outside again, wondering why he hadn't come in.

Just then the door opened. Bob knocked the snow off his boots as he entered the house, a big grin on his face. By nature her husband was an upbeat, happy person, always sociable, which was one reason their B and B was successful. Peggy tended to remain in the background, creating the meals, while Bob provided the warm welcome and the entertainment.

"What took so long?" she asked, pausing to kiss him and take the bags out of his hands.

"You should see the grocery store. There wasn't a cart to be had."

"Christmas Eve…what did you expect?"

"Everyone seems to leave the shopping until the last minute—even my wife." He kissed her cheek but not before Peggy saw him swipe a cookie.

Bob reached for a date bar and she returned his sheepish smile with an approving grin. She had plenty to spare and, after his trek to the store, Bob deserved a reward.

"Do you have one for Roy and Corrie?" Bob asked, surveying the kitchen counter and the row of finished plates.

"Of course."

"Troy and Faith Davis?"

"Bob, you know I do. What makes you ask?"

"Just wanted to be sure. I saw Faith shopping and Corrie was coming into the store as I was leaving." Bob poured himself a cup of coffee and sat on the kitchen stool, watching as Peggy put the final touches on the gifts, adding small handmade cards. These cards were another gift. Each included a personal note thanking the recipients for their friendship.

"I'm so thankful to Roy," she said fervently. "Who knows what would've happened if he hadn't been willing to take us on as clients." The private investigator had stepped in at a crucial time in their lives.

"Troy Davis, too," Bob reminded her.

"Oh, yes."

The memory of those painful days took over her thoughts for a moment. A stranger had arrived late one night in the middle of a storm, rain-drenched and seeking a room. Bob hadn't recognized the man but had sensed…something. He'd had a bad feeling about him. Peggy, however, couldn't turn someone away in the middle of a downpour. In retrospect, she wished she'd listened to her husband, because the next morning the man was dead.

"I know what you're thinking," Bob said, sipping his coffee.

"So now you're a mind reader, too?" she asked with a smile. Her husband did possess multiple talents—including acting and singing—but she had serious doubts regarding his psychic abilities.

"After all these years I can read you like a *People* magazine," he joked right back. "It's about Max Russell, isn't it?"

She could pretend otherwise but didn't. "Yes. I was remembering the night he showed up and how you didn't want to give him a room."

"That night was a turning point for me," Bob admitted. "The start of healing. I was finally able to lay what happened in 'Nam to rest."

Bob and his best friend from high school, Dan Sherman—who'd married Grace—had enlisted in the army together under the buddy program. Following basic training they'd been sent to Vietnam. Max had been part of their unit.

The war changed all three men. An incident involving the deaths of innocent civilians had haunted them.

For years Dan Sherman had struggled with depression. When he was in that state of mind, he'd block out family and friends, isolating himself from the world.

After the war Bob had turned to alcohol for solace. Their marriage suffered, and more than once Peggy decided to leave him, taking their son and daughter. Each time Bob convinced her he'd give up drinking and be the husband she deserved. He'd tried, but with limited success. After a few weeks of sobriety Bob would return to the bottle. He hit bottom after losing a promising job, and that was when he went into rehab. Thankfully, he came out a different person. He hadn't had a drink since that day more than twenty years ago. Or was it twenty-five? She no longer kept count of the years. Each day was a victory, each day a blessing.

"I mailed Hannah a Christmas card," Peggy confessed. Even now, knowing what she did about the young woman, Peggy had a soft spot for her despite the grief she'd caused them both.

Hannah was the dead man's daughter and, in fact, had been responsible for his murder.

"Did she write back?"

"No." Peggy knew it was highly unlikely that Hannah would acknowledge the card. That was fine. Perhaps it was for the best.

"You really came to care for her, didn't you?"

"Well, yes, but…" Peggy had mixed feelings about the woman. Hannah had attempted to steer blame for the murder toward Bob, and that was unforgivable in Peggy's eyes. Still, the poor girl had lived a hard life with a father tortured by the past. Max took his self-hatred out on Hannah and her mother. Hannah's mind became as twisted as her father's, and as far as she was concerned, he deserved to die.

She'd tried to kill him once before and, to Hannah's horror, her beloved mother had died instead. Her father had survived the car accident, which made Hannah's hatred of him even greater. She had deeply loved her mother and to lose her when she'd so carefully planned to kill Max had nearly destroyed her. Hannah redoubled her efforts to make her father pay.

Again Bob's instincts had been on target. From the first he hadn't trusted Max's daughter, who'd shown up at their home after her father's death. Although he wasn't able to identify exactly what he disliked about Hannah, he'd made his feelings clear. Hannah had avoided him as much as possible. It wasn't until much later that they understood why.

"I'll be forever grateful those days are gone," Bob murmured, still sipping his coffee.

"Me, too," Peggy agreed. "You're free now. The past is over and the future is bright."

"I'm a lucky man," Bob said.

Nevertheless, those memories were all too vivid, all too real.

"Hey, why so melancholy?" Bob said, tipping up her chin with his index finger. "We have a lot to celebrate. Hollie and Marc will be here this afternoon and we'll have a real family Christmas."

Peggy instantly brightened. Their children were coming for the holidays and spending a few days. To have both of them there was a rare treat. Their family had healed in the past few years.

Hollie and Marc had grown up in the volatile atmosphere created by their father's problems with alcohol. As much as possible, Peggy had shielded them. It'd taken her years of Al Anon meetings to straighten out her own thinking. Without realizing what she was doing, Peggy had enabled Bob in his drinking. Once she'd stepped aside and allowed him to deal with the consequences of his actions, he was forced to admit that he had a problem.

Those years of struggle had taken a heavy toll. It was only since the move to Cedar Cove that Hollie and Marc were willing to have a relationship with their father. Both were professionals, married but without children. Peggy envied her friends their grandchildren but, so far, her own kids had shown no interest in starting families. Peggy had accepted the situation and was content to lavish affection on her friends' grandchildren, especially those of her best friend, Corrie McAfee.

"We'd better head out with those gift plates soon, don't you think?" Peggy said. She wanted to be home when the children arrived with their spouses.

"Anytime now."

"Everything's just about ready," she said, and finished the last of the gift cards with a flourish.

Bob put his cup in the sink and walked into the large family room, where they'd set up the Christmas tree. "I have an early present for you."

"Oh?" she asked, her curiosity piqued.

He looked pleased with himself. "Actually, your gift's in the garage."

"Bob," Peggy breathed. They'd discussed buying her a new vehicle, but she'd assumed she'd be making the choice. "You bought me a car?"

Bob laughed. "Sorry. That's a natural assumption but no, it isn't a car. I hope you aren't disappointed."

"Of course not, but I am somewhat curious as to why this can't wait until morning."

"Well… This is the type of gift we'd generally talk about in advance."

She couldn't imagine what he was talking about. "Give me a clue."

"Remember the other day when we were at the library?"

"Of course…but what's that got to do with anything?" Peggy couldn't recall anything special taking place. They'd dropped off books and picked up others. Both were big readers and loyal library patrons.

"Remember the children reading to the dogs?"

"Well, yes, Grace told me about the program. It seems to be doing well."

"Largely thanks to Beth Morehouse, the woman who owns the Christmas tree farm."

"Where we bought our tree," she said, certain Bob would clarify everything in a moment. Her husband had a flair for drama, which was one reason he volunteered at the local theater. Over the years Bob had appeared in a number of productions, everything from musicals to *Death of a Salesman.* It was his creative outlet the same way gardening and cooking were hers.

"I'm sure there's a point to all this," she said, urging him to explain.

"There is."

"Wonderful. Might I suggest you get back to my Christmas gift that's currently being stored in the garage?"

"You'll see."

"I'm waiting with bated breath," she returned, smiling.

"Stay here."

"Okay," Peggy said. "Do you want me to close my eyes?"

Bob paused at the back door and nodded. "Good idea. Close your eyes."

Peggy sat at the kitchen table with one hand on her coffee mug and the other in her lap and squeezed her eyes shut. She wondered if her gift was what had kept Bob in the garage so long after he'd driven home. After a couple of minutes she heard him come in.

"Can I open my eyes yet?"

"Just a second."

Her husband's footsteps echoed as he moved toward the Christmas tree. "All right," he called out. "You can open your eyes now."

Peggy did, and then blinked. Beneath the tree, surrounded by wrapped gifts, sat a basket, one she kept in the garage and often took into the garden. Bedded down inside was...a puppy. A small black puppy.

Peggy didn't know if she should laugh or cry. "You got me a *puppy?*"

"I was thinking we could use a dog," Bob said.

"But a puppy?" she said, unsure of her feelings.

"Look at her, Peggy, she's so cute. I couldn't resist. We need a dog, and Beth Morehouse has a litter of ten she needs to find homes for."

"So *that* was the connection with Beth and the library. You volunteered," she said. "Obviously."

"Well, yes..."

"You'll train her?"

"If you want, but she's your dog. You're happy about this, aren't you?"

The puppy raised her head and regarded Peggy with large doleful eyes.

"What do you want to name her?" Bob asked, lifting the tiny squirming creature out of the basket and bringing her to Peggy.

The puppy immediately made herself at home in Peggy's arms. "Let's name her... Millie."

"Millie, it is," Bob said. "Merry Christmas, sweetheart."

"Merry Christmas, darling. And Merry Christmas, Millie."

Millie barked, adding her own greetings.

9

"Let's go for a sleigh ride," Bailey said excitedly, as if this was the most brilliant idea of the century. "Can we, Mom?" She clasped both hands. "I mean, now that Gloria and Chad have picked up the puppy…"

"Ah…" Beth hesitated as a sense of dread filled her. Every minute with Kent and Danielle felt more awkward than the one before.

"Mom, we should. Dad's never seen the Christmas tree farm." Sophie was as animated as her sister.

"You want to, don't you, Dad?" Bailey asked, hurrying to her father's side and slipping her arm through his.

"That way Danielle can breathe some fresh air and not have to worry about sneezing," Sophie said in a solicitous voice.

Beth didn't dare look at her ex-husband. She had to believe he was as miserable as she was. This entire family Christmas was a disaster. She'd seen the expression on his face when she'd so vehemently declared Danielle was welcome to him. Shock and pain had flashed in his eyes so quickly she wasn't even sure she'd read his feelings correctly. Everything inside her cried out to take the words back, swear that none of it was true. But she couldn't do that. Not with Danielle standing right there.

"Danielle probably isn't up to this," Kent said with an unmistakable lack of enthusiasm.

Beth figured the other woman would willingly return to the Thyme and Tide. She couldn't be enjoying the afternoon any more than Beth was. The only ones who seemed to derive any pleasure from this fiasco were Bailey and Sophie, who were apparently oblivious to the tension in the room.

"A sleigh ride *might* be fun," Danielle said with a half-hearted shrug.

Bailey and Sophie leaped up and down and clapped their hands. Their behavior reminded Beth of when they were youngsters and were told they could stay up past their bedtime.

"I didn't know you had a sleigh," Kent said as he reached for his coat and gloves. His scarf, Beth noticed, was one she'd knit him years earlier for Christmas. It warmed her to know that he still wore it. Did he think of her every time he put it on?

"The sleigh, which is pretty old, is in one of the outbuildings," she said. "It came with the property. We don't use it much."

"A sleigh ride is perfect after a snowfall, though. Right, Mom?" Sophie asked.

Perfect wasn't exactly the word she'd use.

"You don't have any horses." Kent seemed to be looking for excuses to get out of this. Beth didn't blame him; she'd rather avoid a cozy ride herself. She'd had about all the togetherness she could handle.

"Mom's neighbors. The Nelsons," Bailey explained. "They have horses and said we can borrow them anytime we want." Without waiting for the go-ahead, Bailey picked up the phone and grabbed the personal directory Beth kept in a kitchen drawer.

"We'll have a great time," Sophie told Kent.

"The Nelsons said no problem." Bailey replaced the receiver, her eyes shining with glee.

"I'll go get a few blankets," Beth muttered, eager to make an escape. She rushed up the stairs and into her bedroom. Slumping on the edge of her bed, she brought her hands to her heated face. She wasn't sure how much longer she'd be able to pull this off.

"Get a grip," she ordered herself. She walked into the master bath and splashed cold water on her cheeks. Her reflection in the mirror revealed that her face was flushed. She looked feverish. This wasn't due to illness, though, but acute embarrassment.

"Mom," Sophie called her from the foot of the stairs. "The Nelsons said they'd bring over the horses."

Beth came out of her bedroom. "Okay," she called down. "I'll be there in a minute." Collecting warm blankets from the hall closet, she returned to the main floor.

By the time she got her hat, coat and gloves, Kent and the girls had opened the doors to the storage shed where the sleigh was kept. The large white uncovered sleigh had two red velvet benches, one of them for the driver.

John Nelson, who lived next door, walked over, leading two large geldings. Kent introduced himself. Danielle was still in the house, refreshing her makeup or so Beth assumed.

"When you're finished, would you mind if we took the sleigh out for a ride?" John asked.

"Of course not," Beth told him. She glanced up at the sky. "I can't imagine we'll be out long. When we're finished, I'll take the sleigh over to your place."

"I appreciate it, Beth. You're a good neighbor."

"So are you."

The harnesses were in the storage shed, and John helped Beth hitch the two horses to the sleigh.

Danielle had come out of the house but remained on the porch until that was done. John left, and the girls climbed on board the sleigh to arrange the blankets.

Danielle looked uncertain, as if she wasn't sure a sleigh ride was something she wanted, after all. "It's cold out here." She squinted at the sky. "And it looks like it's going to snow. Plus, I'm expecting a phone call."

"Snow! Isn't that *wonderful?*" Bailey sounded as if snow was the most magical thing that could possibly happen.

"I'm not used to the cold."

"Then you need to sit between us," Sophie said. "Bailey and I will keep you snug and warm."

Kent helped Danielle into the sleigh, and Bailey and Sophie immediately covered her lap with blankets and wrapped an extra one about her shoulders. By the time they'd finished, all that showed was Danielle's pinched face.

Not until Beth climbed into the worn front seat did she realize that the only place left for Kent to sit was next to her. He seemed to realize that at the same time she did. They stared at each other until Kent got into the sleigh. They sat as far apart on the bench as humanly possible.

"Would you like me to take the reins?" he asked, refusing to look at her.

"If you'd like." She handed them over, knowing he was capable of managing the horses and sleigh.

They started off with a jolt and Danielle let out a cry of alarm. After the initial jerk, the ride went smoothly. The horses' hooves made muted clopping sounds as the sleigh glided over the snowy road.

"You going to be my navigator?" Kent asked.

"Sure."

Kent had moved toward the middle of the seat and she did, too, for fear of falling off if the sleigh hit bumpy ground.

Kent seemed willing to overlook her earlier comment. She was grateful and wished she could take back the lie. "Go left at the fork in the road," she told him, pointing in that direction.

"How many acres do you have here?" he asked, sounding genuinely interested. The trees had been trimmed and shaped until they were the perfect size for Christmas. Now they glistened with bright, fresh snow.

"Forty acres in total, but only twenty are planted in trees. I'm planting another five acres each year and replacing the ones we've cut."

Kent held the reins loosely. "I assumed most families bought artificial trees these days."

"Certainly that's the trend, but there are still plenty of people who prefer a fresh tree, especially if they can chop it down themselves. It makes for wonderful memories. And after Christmas, people cut them up for compost, so ecologically speaking, you could argue that they're superior."

"That's good."

"In addition, a lot of my trees are shipped overseas."

"Really."

She chatted easily, explaining what she'd learned in the past three seasons and her hopes for the future. After a while, she paused, embarrassed that she'd talked for so long. "I apologize. I didn't mean to drone on like that."

He gave her a quick smile. "You really love it here, don't you?"

"It's a very different lifestyle from California, but I needed a change. I was in a horrible rut." The instant the words were out, she regretted being so honest. "I didn't mean that the way it sounded. What I said earlier, it…isn't— I wish…"

"Don't worry about it," he murmured.

Kent had always been ready to forgive and forget; she admired that about him. She was the one who held on to hurts far longer than she should.

"We should sing Christmas carols," Bailey suggested, and then broke into "Silent Night." Sophie joined in and so did Kent. Beth added her own voice. The last one to sing was Danielle. Unfortunately, she was off-key and sounded terrible.

Beth chanced a look at Kent and found him glancing at her at the same time. They broke into giggles, which they did their best to hide.

The group's enthusiasm faded after two or three songs, and their voices gradually dwindled away.

"Remember our first Christmas?" Kent asked, keeping his voice low.

"I thought about it…recently. It was a magical time for us, wasn't it?" He met her eyes for several seconds until she forced herself to look down. The intensity of the attraction she felt confused her. Disconcerted her. Oh, dear. It was happening again and this time Danielle was with them.

As the sleigh glided through the snow, she pointed to another turn in the road, one that cut through the property.

"Right or left?"

"Left." She was so caught up in the moment that she'd said *left* when she meant *right*.

Kent turned right. "Sorry," he said, sounding flustered. "You said left, didn't you?"

"No, this is fine," she told him. She clenched her gloved hands in her lap, grateful that the wind and cold were a convenient excuse for the color splotching her face.

"Oh, look," Sophie cried. "It's snowing again."

Thick, fat flakes drifted lazily from a slate-gray sky.

"It'll probably melt by morning," Danielle said, "and everything will be mud and slush."

"But for now it's beautiful," Beth countered. This was the coldest winter on record in the Pacific Northwest. The weatherperson broadcasting from the Seattle TV station had been effusive about the unusual amount of snow in the area, especially this early in the winter.

"I'm cold," Danielle complained. "And I can't move my arms."

"Let me help you," Bailey said.

"Ouch! You're pulling the blankets tighter. I feel like a sausage."

"I thought you said you were cold."

"I am, but I want to breathe, too," Danielle snapped. "Take this ridiculous thing off me."

"Girls," Beth said, twisting around. Danielle was right; she did resemble a sausage. "Make her comfortable."

"Can we go back to the house soon?" Danielle pleaded.

"I'll head over there now," Kent told her. He glanced at Beth and grinned boyishly. "Okay, navigator, which way?"

"Recalculating, recalculating," she said, using the tinny voice of her car's navigational system.

Kent laughed and turned the sleigh around when he came to a place where that was possible.

"Do you ever think back to those early years?" he asked with his attention focused on the road ahead. "When we were first married…"

The snow was coming down thicker and faster, making for limited visibility.

"I…try not to, but yes, I do." She hadn't wanted to admit that, but it seemed senseless to deny the truth. "You?"

"Sometimes." He paused. "What happened to us, Beth?"

"I…wish I knew."

"Me, too."

"Are we there yet?" Danielle asked plaintively.

A question hovered on the end of Beth's tongue but she refused to ask it. If Kent was looking for a second wife who was completely her opposite, he'd found that woman in Danielle.

She and Beth were about as dissimilar as any two women could be. Perhaps that was what he wanted. The thought depressed her… Unless he was telling the truth and Danielle really *was* just a friend. But in that case, why did she stick to Kent like glue? Why had he even brought her to Cedar Cove?

"Mom?" Bailey asked. "My birthday's in September—when did you get pregnant with me?"

"Bailey!" Beth was shocked that her daughter would ask such a question, especially in front of Danielle.

"Christmas Eve," Kent answered.

"Really? Wow. You're sure?"

"Yup."

"So tonight's more of a celebration than I realized."

"What about me?" Sophie wanted to know.

"Easter," Beth said. "It was an early Easter that year. We were at your parents'. Remember, Kent?"

His eyes widened as the memory drifted back. He caught her eye and they both struggled to contain their amusement. They'd slept in the guest bedroom, which was just down the hall from his parents' room. Their bed squeaked…so they'd rolled onto the floor and Kent's foot had become tangled in the lamp cord and the lamp came crashing down on him. On hearing the crash, his mother had knocked on the door to make sure everything was all right. It'd been a comedy of errors.

"What's so funny?" Danielle demanded.

Beth felt guilty for being so rude as to exclude everyone else from their private conversation. "I apologize, Danielle," she said, turning around. "Kent and I were…just remembering something that happened years ago."

"I was the result," Sophie announced proudly.

"Can we talk about something different?" Danielle said, clearly not amused.

"Of course," Beth assured her.

"I always wanted a brother," Bailey said. "An older brother."

"You got your sister instead."

"Yeah. And not only that, she's younger."

"I never had a sister," Danielle said. "And *my* brother was younger and a real nuisance. He used to spy on me and my friends."

"Sophie used to spy on me."

"Did not."

"Did, too."

"Girls," Beth said, annoyed by their behavior. "You're out of grade school. Please act like it."

They broke into peals of laughter.

"What?" Beth turned again to see what her daughters were laughing about now.

"Mom, you're so predictable. That's exactly what we told Danielle you'd say."

Kent pulled the sleigh over to the shed and handed the reins to Beth while he jumped down. He helped Sophie out first, then Danielle and Bailey.

"I'll take the sled over to the Nelsons'," Beth said, but before she could set off, Kent leaped back into place beside her.

"I'll go with you."

"That isn't necessary," she told him, thinking he'd want to be inside with the others.

"Yes, it is. You aren't going to argue with me, are you?"

"I…no."

"Good, because it would be very tempting to stop you the way I used to once upon a time."

Beth swallowed hard. She'd forgotten. In the early days of their marriage, anytime she disagreed with him, Kent would take her in his arms and kiss her.

10

"Honey, can you get the door?" Corrie called from the back bedroom. She swore that if Roy didn't get his hearing checked soon, she'd start ignoring every word he said. That would give him a little demonstration of what she put up with every day.

"Okay," he yelled from the living room.

With an exasperated sigh Corrie went back to her wrapping paper and ribbon. She was almost finished with Noelle's birthday gift, the one they'd take to Grace Harding's party. She still needed to arrange the last of the Christmas presents under the tree before their children arrived for dinner, which would be followed by Christmas Eve church services. After that, they'd go to Noelle's first-birthday celebration at the Hardings'. Gloria, Roy and Corrie's eldest daughter, would be coming tonight. Corrie hoped Gloria would bring Chad Timmons.

She couldn't help worrying about Gloria, who was single, pregnant and determined to manage on her own. What disturbed Corrie most was the fact that there was no reason for Gloria to be so stubborn. Chad loved her; Corrie was convinced of that. She'd invited him to dinner and hoped Gloria wouldn't be upset with her. Oh, she hadn't made a secret of it, but she hadn't talked it over with Gloria, either.

Mack and Mary Jo would be with them and of course little Noelle, too. She'd been born on Christmas Eve one year ago, at the Harding ranch; Mack had delivered her. Corrie had a lovely birthday cake ready for her adopted granddaughter, not to mention a pile of gifts. Corrie couldn't wait to watch Noelle open them. There was nothing like a baby to bring excitement and joy back to Christmas.

"Corrie," Roy shouted. "It's the Beldons."

"I'll be right there," she shouted back as she finished tying the ribbon on the gift she'd just wrapped.

Corrie had been expecting Peggy and Bob to stop by at some point that afternoon. It was tradition. Every Christmas Eve the Beldons came over with a plate of Peggy's homemade cookies and specialty candies.

"Merry Christmas," Corrie said, hurrying into the room and opening her arms. She hugged Bob and then, after taking the plate from Peggy, embraced her, too.

"I hope we aren't interrupting your day."

"Nonsense," Corrie told her. "You know you're welcome anytime."

"Especially when you come bearing gifts," Roy joked.

"Sit down, please. I've got eggnog and coffee, whichever you prefer."

"We can only stay a few minutes," Bob said, claiming the corner of the sofa. "Hollie and Marc are driving over from Spokane."

"Wonderful! I'm glad they can make it." Corrie hadn't met the Beldons' daughter and son, but she'd heard lots about them. She and Peggy often met for lunch and had a strong friendship.

"It'll be good to have them here for Christmas."

"We'll have a full house ourselves," Roy said. "Mack and

Mary Jo are coming for dinner tonight and they'll be here on Christmas Day, as well."

"Gloria will be here tonight, too, and she'll attend church services with us," Corrie added.

"And Christmas Day?" Peggy asked.

Corrie shrugged. "She didn't say. I imagine she'll come for dinner, unless…"

"Unless?"

"Unless she plans to spend it with Chad."

"Ah, yes. How are things going between her and Chad?"

"Fine, I think. Gloria hasn't said much, but she seems happier these days, less…confused. I know they're seeing each other regularly. If they have any wedding plans, however, they haven't shared them with us."

"Chad put the crib together," Roy said. "I volunteered and so did Mack, but Gloria said Chad would do it."

"That sounds positive," Peggy murmured.

"I just wish those two would get married," Corrie responded. "I know the world's different these days. So many young women choose to be single mothers, but it's hard work."

"A baby needs a father," Roy inserted. "I wanted to tell Gloria that, but Corrie wouldn't let me."

"When has that stopped you in the past?" Corrie retorted as she headed into the kitchen to get their drinks. It still annoyed her that her husband had gone against her wishes and informed Chad of Gloria's pregnancy. After she and Chad had broken up, Gloria had wanted to keep the information from him.

The irony of her daughter's situation astonished her. This was history repeating itself. Well, almost…

Years ago, in college, Corrie had discovered she was pregnant after Roy had ended their relationship. Instead of letting him know, she'd returned home and given her daughter up for adoption. Not until they'd reunited a couple of years later did Roy learn about his baby. And not for more than three decades did they actually meet her. Her husband had been determined that the same thing not happen to Chad Timmons.

Peggy helped her prepare the coffee. Roy and Bob had both requested eggnog, which Corrie poured into festive glasses decorated with green holly leaves and red berries. They'd once belonged to her mother and Corrie reserved them for this special season and for special friends.

"What have you heard from Linnette?" Peggy asked when they were all seated again.

"She and Pete will be in North Dakota over Christmas."

"Was it just a year ago that Pete drove her to Cedar Cove for Christmas?" Roy asked, shaking his head.

Corrie felt the same way. So much had taken place this past year…. During the holidays, Linnette, their younger daughter, had brought home a man she'd met, a farmer named Pete Mason. They'd liked him, but at the time Peggy hadn't thought the relationship was going anywhere. Pete farmed with his brothers near Buffalo Valley, where Linnette had recently accepted a position as a physician assistant. Although Linnette hadn't been in Buffalo Valley long, she seemed genuinely happy for the first time since Cal Washburn had broken her heart. Soon after that, she'd packed up her car and set off with no destination in mind. Peggy had worried endlessly, sure this was a formula for disaster. Then Linnette had phoned from this small prairie town where she'd ended up and sounded…content. She'd sounded more like herself than she had in a very long while.

Corrie hated that her younger daughter lived so far from the family. But she loved Linnette enough to realize she had to make her own decisions. Pete had fallen in love with her first and initially Corrie feared Linnette might have married on the rebound. Those concerns had been laid to rest. On Corrie's recent trip to Buffalo Valley, after the birth of Linnette and Pete's son, she had all the reassurance she'd ever need. It was abundantly clear that Linnette loved her husband and the life she'd created in this small North Dakota community.

"We had quite a Christmas last year," Roy commented, chuckling. "Mack had just been hired by the fire department and he was at the Hardings' to deliver Mary Jo's baby."

Bob grinned. "What I remember was Mary Jo's three brothers racing around town looking for her."

"And not a one of them had any sense of direction."

"Hey, be fair. They'd never been on this side of the sound before."

"And now Linc lives here, too."

"And married to the Bellamy girl."

"They are the sweetest couple," Peggy said with the hint of a sigh. "I saw them in the grocery store the other day. It was positively romantic just seeing the two of them together. We spoke for a few minutes and apparently Linc and Lori are spending Christmas with her family."

"Well," Bob said, "that's an improvement. Bellamy was trying to ruin Linc's business. Until you and Troy intervened..."

Roy shrugged off Bob's comment. "I'm glad they reconciled with Lori's family, but I don't know why Bellamy couldn't just accept the fact that they're married. End of story."

"It wasn't the only wedding this past year, either," Bob said. "Faith and Troy tied the knot, and of course so did Mack and Mary Jo."

"I do love a wedding," Corrie said. To her way of thinking, there should be one more, and preferably soon. She'd feel so much better about Gloria's situation if she was married to Chad.

"Well..." Bob lowered his empty glass. "I hate to cut this short, but we've got a few other stops to make."

Corrie and Roy walked their friends to the front door and thanked them again.

"This is one small way of repaying you for all you've done for us," Peggy said.

"How can you say that?" Corrie asked. Their friendship had been one of her biggest blessings since moving to Cedar Cove. "You've done so much for *us*."

"You kept me out of prison," Bob reminded them, referring to the death at the B and B. "Believe me, I'll be forever grateful for that."

"Ancient history," Roy insisted, standing on the front porch. He wrapped his arm around Corrie's shoulders.

"Ancient history to you, perhaps," Bob said, "but it's something I'll never forget."

They got into their vehicle, and Corrie and Roy returned to the warmth of the house.

"I really didn't do that much," Roy protested. "Bob was so obviously innocent...."

"Are you complaining about the cookies and candy they brought?" she asked, half-joking.

"No way!"

"Then enjoy and quit your muttering."

He laughed. "You're right. Have you tasted that English toffee yet? It's good stuff."

"Don't tell me how good it is, I'm resisting."

"Why?"

Corrie rolled her eyes. "Because it's hard enough not to overindulge during the holidays without you telling me how good everything tastes."

"Fine. Leaves more for me."

Sighing, Corrie brought the tray into the kitchen and covered it with a towel. Out of sight, out of mind. She returned to the back bedroom and resumed wrapping gifts.

Fifteen minutes later, Roy poked his head in. "You about done?"

"Yup. I'm putting the final touches on the last package. Why?"

"Anything here for Gloria?"

"Of course."

"Well, she just parked outside the house."

"Oh." Corrie felt a bit flustered.

"She isn't alone."

"Did Chad come with her?" Corrie couldn't hide the excitement in her voice.

Roy nodded. "Only they don't seem to be in any big hurry to come inside. They've been sitting in the car chatting for the past ten minutes."

Corrie arched her eyebrows. "Can you tell if they're arguing?" She certainly hoped not!

"I didn't want it to be obvious that I saw them."

"Good point." Still, one might think that Roy, a private investigator, would know how to watch without being seen.

"Besides, this is *their* business."

Another good point, although that hadn't troubled him earlier when he'd gone to see Chad, which she restrained herself from mentioning.

The doorbell chimed.

"I'll get it," Roy said.

Corrie made her way into the kitchen and brewed a fresh pot of coffee. She heard Roy greet their daughter and Chad, and she quickly joined them.

"I know we're early," Gloria said. She held hands with Chad—a positive sign. "Chad thought we should all talk before everyone came for dinner tonight."

"Sure," Roy said, sitting down in his recliner.

Gloria and Chad took the sofa, huddled close to each other.

Corrie slid onto her favorite chair, her heart in her throat.

A tense silence pervaded the room as both she and Roy waited for whatever announcement was about to be made.

Gloria looked at Chad as if she wanted him to do the talking.

"Gloria and I wanted you to know we decided to get married," he blurted out. "She agreed to marry me a couple of weeks ago but we wanted to keep it to ourselves until Christmas, and—"

Corrie was instantly on her feet. "That's wonderful news!" she said, interrupting him and clasping her hands together. Her mind was whirling. While she hoped it would be soon, for the baby's sake, she'd love a June wedding. That would give her enough time to plan. She'd get started first thing after Christmas. They'd need someplace special for the reception and, of course, there were the invitations, which they'd want to send out immediately. They'd have to find a dress; at this stage of her pregnancy, Gloria probably wouldn't fit into Corrie's wedding gown, which was a shame.

"When's the happy date?" Roy asked.

"Actually…we're already married," Chad said.

Corrie blinked, assuming she'd misunderstood. "Already married?" she repeated. That wasn't possible!

"When?" Roy asked, following the first question with a second. "Where?"

Again it was Chad who explained. "I'm afraid I'm responsible. Gloria said she'd marry me but we couldn't agree on a date."

"I wanted to wait until after the baby's born and have a summer wedding," she told them.

Corrie nodded, understanding.

"And I wanted us to be married *before* the baby's born," Chad said.

Ah, yes, Corrie thought, seeing the problem.

"So we decided to simply go ahead and get married right

away and then, this summer, have another ceremony and a reception."

"Makes sense to me," Roy said, obviously pleased by this unexpected turn of events.

"Why didn't you let us know?" Corrie asked, feeling a twinge of hurt despite her happiness. Even if it was a quick affair, she would've liked to be there.

"I agree we should have asked you to attend," Gloria said. "But if you were there and Chad's parents weren't, they would've felt cheated. So we just did it. We applied for the license and were married a couple of days later."

"By whom?"

"Judge Griffin," Chad said. "At the courthouse. Mack and Mary Jo stood up with us." He paused. "I don't blame you for being upset."

"We're not upset," Roy told him, and Corrie nodded.

"As Gloria mentioned, we plan to have another ceremony later, with friends and family from both sides."

"This way we *all* get what we want," Corrie said happily. A marriage and a baby—another grandchild for her and Roy—and a wedding.

Roy stood, extending his hand to Chad. "Welcome to the family."

"Thank you." The two men shook hands.

Corrie hugged her daughter and Chad. She'd spend the next few months getting ready for the wedding and reception, and the thought filled her with anticipation.

"Mom and Dad, there's another reason we stopped by early."

"Oh?" Corrie murmured.

"You're not pregnant with twins, are you?" Roy asked, half-joking.

"No. We wanted to get your okay before we had one of your gifts delivered."

"All right...." Roy glanced at Corrie, clearly wondering if she knew what this was about; she shook her head, as confused as he was.

"Did you hear someone left ten puppies on Beth Morehouse's porch?"

"We did," Corrie confirmed. "In fact, Bob was just telling us he got one of those pups for Peggy."

"And we chose one for you," Gloria said.

Their daughter had gotten them a puppy?

Corrie stared at her.

"Not long ago, Dad talked about a Labrador he had while he was growing up and he got a nostalgic look in his eyes. I heard about these puppies from Ted Reynolds, and Chad and I went to Beth's house today to pick one up."

"If you don't want the dog," Chad said, moving toward the edge of the sofa, "Gloria and I will take her. She's cute as a bug and has personality to boot."

"Where is she now?" Corrie asked.

"At my place," Gloria replied. "We thought we'd bring her over tomorrow."

"A puppy." Roy wore a silly grin, as if the prospect delighted him. "What about a name?" he asked.

"I know—Asta. That's the dog in the *Thin Man* movies, remember?" Corrie suggested.

"Perfect for a detective's dog." Roy smiled. "Even if the original Asta was a boy."

"Asta it is," Corrie said, adding, "We need a puppy in the house again."

This was going to be the most wonderful Christmas in recent memory. Weddings, grandchildren—and now a puppy.

11

"Come in out of the cold," Danielle said as Kent and Beth returned to the house after delivering the sleigh to the Nelsons'. It might have been Beth's imagination, but she suspected Danielle had been standing by the door waiting for them. She had her cell phone in her hand again.

She immediately ran up to Kent and spoke urgently in his ear. Kent looked decidedly uncomfortable as she hugged him, but put his arms lightly around her. Beth saw Danielle's hug as a claim of ownership. Unable to watch, she stepped around the embracing couple and hurried into the kitchen, grateful for the escape.

Bailey and Sophie were standing in a corner of the family room, whispering heatedly.

"Girls?" Beth said, wondering what they were up to. They didn't seem to be arguing, but clearly had different opinions on something or other. "Is everything all right?" she asked.

Bailey turned around so quickly, she nearly stumbled. "Ah…sure. Why wouldn't it be?"

Sophie narrowed her eyes as Danielle and Kent stepped into the room.

"It was a…lovely afternoon, but it's time I…we left," Dani-elle said, and then inclined her head as if to say the decision was final.

"You're *leaving?*" Bailey cried in apparent shock.

"You're not staying for dinner?" Sophie sounded equally shocked.

"I thought you came to Cedar Cove so you could spend Christmas with us," Bailey reminded her father.

Frankly, Beth was just as glad to see them go. She didn't understand exactly what had happened between her and Kent in the sleigh, but whatever it was had made her feel confused and a bit panicky. She'd actually *wanted* him to kiss her. Her ex-husband had brought another woman to spend Christmas with the family, and yet Beth could hardly stop herself from leaning into him….

"Kent will be back on Christmas Day," Danielle said to the girls, as if they were small children in need of reassurance. "Christmas Eve is a time for family and—"

"Our father *is* family," Bailey protested as she curled her hands into tight fists. She seemed to be on the verge of tears.

Sophie cast a pleading glance at her father. "Daddy?" she implored.

Kent hesitated.

Danielle tugged him over to the door. "I need to go. Don't worry, your father will be back in the morning." She turned to him, hissing, "The girls need to spend time with their mother, too."

"I'll stay," Kent said decisively. "That is, if you're sure it's what you want." The question was directed at Beth.

Holding her breath, she realized she didn't have a choice. Which meant that her Christmas Eve dinner would be shared with Kent and… Danielle. What she wouldn't give for a peaceful evening alone with her daughters. Instead, she was forced to watch her husband—er, *ex*-husband—with another woman.

"Mom?" Bailey whispered.

"Of course you should stay," Beth said, just a little too brightly.

"Mom's making lasagna," Sophie said, and then added, apparently to enlighten Danielle, "It's a family tradition. The recipe comes from Grandma Carlucci."

Danielle pursed her lips in a pout, then squared her shoulders, coming to some decision. "In that case, I insist on helping."

The last thing Beth wanted was this woman in *her* kitchen. "All I need to do is get the lasagna in the oven," she said. "It's already put together—just needs to bake."

"Well, then, I'll make a salad," Danielle said.

"Mom always makes Caesar salad and garlic bread," Bailey told her.

"I can make a Caesar salad." Danielle pushed up the sleeves of her sweater and grabbed an apron off the countertop, staking out her territory.

Beth felt as though the other woman had declared war. Fine. In that case, she was prepared to surrender without a fight. This was Christmas, and if Danielle wanted to plant her flag in Beth's kitchen, she was welcome to it. Only Beth wouldn't be there.

"Are you sure you don't mind making the salad?" she asked.

"I offered, didn't I?" Danielle placed one hand on her hip.

"Okay, then, there's no reason for me to stay. I'll use the time to deliver one of the puppies." She'd drive the Randalls' puppy over to Grace Harding's place.

Danielle cast her a triumphant look, as if to say she'd taken great satisfaction in maneuvering Beth out of her own kitchen.

Sophie smiled; Beth could tell this was precisely what she'd hoped would happen. "Dad, you should go with Mom."

"Kent!" Danielle said sharply. "I might...you know, need you."

"Dad," Bailey challenged, "do you want Mom driving on treacherous roads *alone*? What if she had an accident?"

Beth tried to remember whether her daughter had ever taken drama. If so, she'd had a good teacher. The kid was ready for Broadway.

"It's fine, Kent," Beth assured him, trying to hide her laughter and not quite succeeding. "I've driven these roads alone any number of times."

"But not when there's *snow* on the ground," Sophie wailed, as if she'd attended the same drama class.

"Your mother knows what she's doing," Danielle tossed in casually. "She'll be perfectly fine *by herself*." The last two words were given heavy emphasis.

Again Bailey and Sophie turned to their father with wide eyes even Scrooge couldn't have ignored.

"Dad? Are you really going to let Mom go out all on her own?"

"Would you ever forgive yourself if anything happened to the mother of your children?" Sophie wailed.

Unwilling to be part of this ridiculous conversation any longer, Beth grabbed her coat, gloves and scarf and headed for the back door. She was outside and halfway to the car with the puppy in its carrier when Kent jogged up behind her.

"Hey, wait up," he called.

"Kent, really, this isn't necessary."

"According to our daughters, it is."

Beth rolled her eyes. "I don't remember you being manipulated quite this easily when we were married." She opened the rear passenger door and placed the puppy's carrier inside.

Kent climbed into the front passenger seat and waited until Beth joined him before he responded. "Did you ever stop to think I might actually *want* to accompany you?"

She hadn't. For the life of her, Beth couldn't manage a single word. In fact, it was all she could do to breathe. All at once the interior of her SUV seemed to shrink until it felt as if the two of them were trapped inside a box the size of a milk crate. Her mouth went dry and she concentrated on driving rather than the man she'd loved and married and…left. Oh, how she wished she could turn back the clock.

Risking a look at Kent, she wondered if he was thinking the same thing.

The silence that stretched between them threatened to snap.

"I…" She started to say something—although what, she wasn't sure.

"I was—"

They both spoke at the same time.

"You first," she said.

"No, you."

She laughed. "Please, you go first."

"Well," he murmured after a few awkward seconds, "I was just thinking back to all the animals you rescued while we were married. Remember Ugly Arnie?"

Like she'd ever forget the injured raccoon she'd found at their back door. "How could I forget him?"

"Vicious, ungrateful—"

"Kent, he was in pain! As I recall, you aren't exactly Prince Charming when you aren't feeling well."

"Prince Charming? So is that how you remember me when… I was feeling good?"

She doubted that he expected an answer, but she gave him one, anyway. "You had your moments."

"So did you."

"Thank you." They could play nice, she realized. It hadn't always been this silent battle of wills.

"I kind of thought you'd remarry," he said, frowning as he spoke.

"Really?" She, on the other hand, hadn't even considered the possibility that Kent might marry someone else—well, other than in some vague, abstract way. Certainly not some-one like Danielle. Beth was astonished that Kent would find this hard, brusque woman appealing. Yes, superficially Dani-elle was attractive—okay, gorgeous—but she seemed to lack all the qualities Beth had expected him to value.

"If you did remarry, I assumed you'd choose a vet."

"Oh, my goodness…" Without thinking, Beth eased her foot off the brake and the car swerved on the icy road and went sideways. "Hold on," she cried.

Kent braced his arms against the dashboard until the car came to a complete stop on the side of the road. "You okay?" he demanded.

"I'm fine…what about you?"

"My heart is somewhere in my throat," he said, "but other than that I'll survive. What just happened? I didn't see any-thing in the road."

"It's Ted."

"Ted? Who's Ted?"

"The local vet… He said he'd stop by this afternoon and I need to be there."

"Give him a call," Kent muttered, as if it was of little con-cern.

"I will." She reached across for her handbag and grabbed her cell, pushing the button that would connect her with him.

"You have him on speed dial?" Kent asked with raised eyebrows.

Beth ignored the question and waited impatiently for Ted to

answer. After four long rings, the phone went to voice mail. She exhaled loudly, then carefully put the car in Reverse and turned around.

"Where are you going now?" Kent asked.

She would've thought the answer was obvious. "To Ted's place. He's probably with an animal, so he couldn't get the phone."

"You could've left a message."

He was right, she could have, but that seemed rather unfriendly. Besides, she wanted to explain. "His place isn't far from here," she said, instead of responding to his comment.

The silence returned.

Again it was Kent who broke it. "Do you see a lot of this Tim fellow?"

"Ted," she corrected. "About once or twice a week, I guess." She downplayed the veterinarian's role in her life, which had taken on more significance in the past three or four months. There'd been a shift in their relationship, beginning in late September, when he'd come over after caring for a sick goat nearby. He'd stayed for a glass of wine, followed by a leisurely dinner.

A week later they'd met in town, and Ted had insisted he owed her dinner. That was how it had started, almost innocently. Recently, however, it'd become more. Ted had kissed her, and that had been a turning point. Lately, Ted had taken to dropping in during the evenings, and Beth looked forward to his visits.

"Any particular reason Ted was coming to the house?" Kent asked nonchalantly.

"Nothing formal, if that's what you mean. To wish us a merry Christmas. And I want him to meet the girls. He has a line on someone who wants a puppy, too."

"So it's serious? Between you and him?"

"We have a lot in common," she said, well aware that she hadn't really answered the question.

Ted's driveway came into view, and she signaled, then drove down the long gravel road that led to his home and his veterinary clinic.

Ted was in the yard clearing snow. When he saw her car, he smiled and waved, then leaned his shovel against a tree.

Beth parked and turned off the engine, slipping out of the car.

Walking over to meet her, Ted grinned from ear to ear. "Good to see you, Beth," he said. He didn't kiss her, no doubt because he'd noticed there was a man with her.

Beth tried to see the veterinarian as Kent might. Ted was a few years older, a big man with large, strong hands and an easy smile. He had a receding hairline, visible despite his wool hat. His gentle nature comforted animals—and people.

"Kent Morehouse," Kent said, stepping forward, his hand extended.

Ted pulled off his glove to shake hands but his gaze immediately shot to Beth.

"Kent is my ex-husband. He's here to spend Christmas with the girls," Beth said, feeling uncomfortable saying anything more.

"Oh, yes. You mentioned that Kent was planning to visit," Ted commented.

"I was just driving to the Hardings' to drop off a puppy when I recalled that you were coming over today," she said quickly.

"Well, seeing that you've got visitors, perhaps I shouldn't—"

"No, please, I want you to," Beth said, eager to reassure him. "In fact, I was hoping you'd stay for dinner."

"Dinner?" Kent repeated, frowning.

"Yes, dinner," she said pointedly. "I'm making lasagna. A family recipe."

"My grandmother was Italian," Kent added in a meaningful voice, essentially explaining that this was *his* family's recipe.

"Kent's, uh, friend is with the girls, preparing a Caesar salad and garlic bread."

"That sounds wonderful."

"It will be," Beth said. "*Please* say you'll join us."

Ignoring Kent, Ted stared at her for a long moment. "You're sure?"

"I'm positive."

Ted nodded decisively. "Then I accept. Thank you. What time would you like me there?"

Beth was about to suggest as soon as possible, but before she could, Kent spoke.

"I believe Beth mentioned something about dinner being ready around five."

"Yes, five. We're eating early so we won't be late for church," she murmured.

"Can I bring anything? Wine? Dessert?"

"I've got everything covered, but thanks." She wanted to visit longer, but Kent had already walked back to the car and stood with the door open, waiting for her.

"I'll see you soon," Ted promised. "And I've got a couple bottles of a nice red. To go with the lasagna."

"Thank you," she whispered, and hoped Ted understood how much she appreciated his willingness to show, once again, what a good friend he was. As good a friend as Danielle....

12

Justine Gunderson busied herself in the kitchen, enjoying an afternoon free from the responsibility of managing the Victorian Tea Room. She'd given the staff an extra day off so they could celebrate Christmas Eve with their own families.

The holiday season at the tearoom had been hectic, with a number of special high teas. Her favorite had been Tea with Santa. The children had been so excited, and Santa, a theater friend of Bob Beldon's, had played the role with verve and charm.

In a few years Livvy would be able to go, but for now the toddler, at nearly eighteen months, was too young for Santa in his frightening red suit.

The back door opened, and her husband entered the house. Seth was a blond Swede who towered well over six feet. Just seeing him made Justine's heart react with a surge of love. She'd never expected to marry, let alone have a family of her own. In fact, she'd gone out of her way to avoid serious relationships...until she'd worked on her ten-year high school reunion. That was when she'd run into Seth Gunderson, who was also on the reunion committee.

She'd known Seth nearly her entire life. He'd been her twin brother's best friend. As irrational as it sounded, after the accident that claimed Jordan's life, Justine had wanted to blame Seth. If he'd been with her brother at the lake that day, Jordan might not have died. Seth would have noticed that her brother hadn't surfaced after diving off the floating dock. He would've gone after him. If only Seth had been there....

But he hadn't. It'd been Justine who'd held her brother's lifeless body on the dock until the paramedics showed up.

That fateful summer afternoon had forever changed her world.

Seth smiled at her as he stripped off his coat.

She smiled back and felt, as she so often had in the past, that Jordan would have approved of her marrying Seth Gunderson. Through the years, at various times, Justine had sensed her twin's presence. During those indescribable moments of connection, she hadn't felt the horrific loss of her brother; instead, she'd felt his blessing. Jordan seemed to be standing right beside her, smiling and happy, teasing her the way he'd once done, full of life and boyish humor.

The first time it'd happened was shortly after she'd given birth to Leif. Still in the hospital, exhausted and woozy from the drugs, she'd closed her eyes. Suddenly, Jordan was there before her, and he wore the biggest, goofiest grin she'd ever seen. He was telling her how happy he was for her and Seth; she was sure of it. She could almost hear him saying how excited he was that they'd decided to name their son after him: Leif Jordan Gunderson.

"Daddy, Daddy." Leif shot across the room, dropping his handheld computer game on the way, with Penny barking at his heels. "Santa's coming tonight!"

"He sure is." Lifting the boy high above his head, Seth nuzzled Leif's tummy while the little boy squealed in delight.

Hearing her brother, Livvy toddled out, clutching her teddy bear under her left arm, pressing its face against her side. Livvy and that silly bear were inseparable. She'd be getting her first doll from Santa this Christmas. Justine sincerely hoped Livvy would enjoy the doll as much as she did her teddy bear.

"How's my girl?" Seth asked, setting Leif down and reaching for his daughter. He planted a noisy kiss on her cheek. She, too, squealed with delight.

"Hey, don't I get one of those kisses?" Justine teased.

"You bet." He came to her in the kitchen and slipped his arms around her from behind, planting his hands over her still-flat stomach. "How long have you been working in here?"

"A while." The family cookbook her grandmother, Charlotte Jefferson Rhodes, had compiled, lay open in front of her. Various ingredients, organized according to the recipes, were spread along the counter.

"Seems to me you were in the kitchen when I left for work this morning. Are you sure you're up to this?"

"Stop worrying, okay?" Hosting the family for Christmas Eve dinner required a lot of extra preparation, but Justine never turned away from a challenge.

"Did you bake those homemade rolls I like so much?" Seth asked, eyeing the covered breadbasket.

"I did that first thing this morning."

Seth grinned. "I hope you doubled the batch."

"I did."

"That's my girl."

Justine reached up and kissed him. "I promise you can have as many as you want."

"How are you feeling?" Seth asked.

"I feel wonderful. I always do when I'm pregnant."

Seth closed his eyes. "I don't know how we let this happen," he said as he feathered kisses down the side of her neck.

Justine giggled and put her arms around her husband's neck. "You'd think by now we'd know how babies are made."

"If it was up to you, we'd live in a shoe and have a dozen children."

"Three suits me just fine," she assured him, although she'd be the first to admit she loved being a mother. She could hardly believe that at one time she'd been willing to give all of this up without even knowing what she'd be missing.

The pregnancy would be this year's Christmas surprise for her family. Keeping it secret had been far more difficult than she'd expected. At least a dozen times she'd been tempted to tell her mother and her grandmother. Both would be thrilled.

"Can I help with anything?" Seth asked.

"You could check Livvy's diaper," she said.

Seth swept his daughter into his arms and carried her to her room. When he returned a few minutes later, Livvy's head lolled against his shoulder.

"Did you have a chance to get the mail?" he asked.

"Not yet."

"I'll do it." Seth set Livvy down on the carpet. She leaned her head against the sofa cushion. She'd woken late that morning and hadn't been interested in a nap. Now her eyes drooped as her thumb found its way into her mouth.

Justine had sucked her thumb, too; so had Jordan. After washing her hands, Justine picked up her sweet baby girl and brought her back to her crib. She gently placed her inside and covered her with the blanket Charlotte had knit for her.

Seth came into their daughter's bedroom as she sat beside the crib, watching Livvy's deep, even breaths.

He stood beside her. "It's difficult to fathom how much love we can have for children, isn't it?" he whispered.

"Impossible to believe until we become parents ourselves," she whispered back.

They left the bedroom and Seth closed the door.

"Anything interesting in the mail?" Justine asked as he sat down, flipping through the envelopes. She poured her husband a cup of tea and joined him at the kitchen table.

"The usual Christmas cards—and one rather interesting letter."

"Oh? Who from?"

Seth leafed through the holiday cards until he came across a plain, business-size white envelope. He glanced at it again, then handed it to her.

Justine saw that the envelope held her name—and only hers. The return address made her catch her breath. After taking a moment to compose herself, she raised her eyes to meet Seth's. "It's stamped prison mail. The postmark is Shelton, Washington—that's where the state prison is. One of them, anyway."

"I noticed that, too."

"There's only one person who could be writing me from there." The paper seemed to grow hot in her hands.

"Warren Saget," Seth muttered.

Justine dropped the letter on the table and avoided looking at it.

"Aren't you going to open it?" her husband asked.

"I... I don't know." She'd once had a deep affection for Warren, a successful local builder, although he was old enough to be her father. They'd dated for a while. He'd liked having a tall, beautiful woman on his arm, and she'd liked the fact that he was rich and powerful and made no physical demands on her.

He couldn't. That was their little secret. With Warren she was safe from emotional—and physical—entanglements. Safe, until she'd agreed to work on the class reunion project and Seth had shown up. Justine hadn't wanted to become involved with Seth, yet he was all she thought about. Warren had offered her a huge diamond engagement ring. He was willing to do anything not to lose her. But even that diamond hadn't enticed her. All she wanted, all she *needed,* was Seth.

"I wonder if Warren has any idea of everything he did for us," Seth commented.

Her husband's words jarred Justine from her reverie. "You mean what he did *to* us, don't you?" Warren had tried to destroy them.

"But in the end that's what saved our marriage."

"You're right," she said slowly. "Ironic, isn't it?"

"We were killing ourselves with the restaurant, working all hours of the day and night…."

"You don't need to remind me," Justine said, shaking her head at the memory. It'd been a difficult period in their marriage. They'd been working impossibly long hours with no time as a couple or a family.

The restaurant had been Seth's dream. For nearly ten years he'd saved his money from fishing the crab-rich Alaskan waters. He'd lived on a sailboat in the marina while in town, and spent every waking moment studying restaurant management. He'd dreamed of one day opening an elegant seafood restaurant in Cedar Cove. Together they'd made his dream come true, and the Lighthouse had been the success he'd always planned.

But Seth had worked far too hard. Justine shared his dream, and they'd redoubled their efforts until it all became too much. By then Leif had been born, which meant Justine was torn between being with her son and working at the restaurant.

Their marriage had started to show the stress of too many demands and too few hours. For the first time Seth and Justine had been at odds.

Then, one night, the restaurant had burned down. All their

dreams, all their hard work, their blood, sweat and tears, had gone up in smoke.

Even now, memories of that night were surreal. After being contacted by the authorities, they'd rushed to the scene and walked around in a stupor, shocked and bereft. It wasn't long before the fire inspector declared it'd been arson.

Someone had purposely set their restaurant on fire. The police had what they called "a person of interest," a high school kid who'd worked there briefly before Seth let him go. Anson Butler had a history of being in trouble and had started fires when he was younger. Someone had seen him inside the restaurant that night. Then Anson disappeared.... Meanwhile, Justine and Seth were left to pick up the charred remains of their life. The stress on their marriage brought them close to the breaking point.

It didn't help that Warren took every opportunity to talk about how good things had been between them. Justine didn't believe it, not for a minute; still, it was comforting to have someone pay her that kind of attention.

Not working and depressed, Seth had struggled emotionally. He'd given up fishing in Alaska, and she was grateful. She wanted her husband with her. Leif needed him. So did she.

It was during this time that she'd come up with the idea of building a tearoom and giving it the ambience of England's Victorian era. The plans were already in motion when Seth was approached by a family friend who owned a boatyard and offered him a job in sales. Seth took it and turned out to be a natural.

Later, thanks to Sheriff Troy Davis, Warren Saget was arrested, tried and convicted of arson. Currently, he was serving time in prison.

Justine poked at the envelope with her finger. She expected to feel *something*. Some emotion. Regret. Anger. Something.

Instead, she felt nothing. Only a sadness that Warren could have been this vindictive, this desperate. He'd never forgiven her for leaving him and he'd wanted to punish Seth for stealing away the one woman who understood him, understood his needs.

"Are you going to read it?" Seth asked.

"Do you want me to?"

He thought about it, then nodded.

Personally, Justine would be content to toss the letter. Yet a part of her wanted to know what Warren had to say. Taking a deep breath, she opened the envelope and pulled out a single sheet of paper. She read it, then crumpled it in one hand.

"What did he say?"

"Just that he'll be up for parole in a few years and wondered if I'd be waiting for him when he's released."

"You're joking!"

"The man is delusional," she groaned. Even now, Warren seemed to be living in a dreamworld. He'd convinced himself that she was pining for him, anticipating his release. Needless to say, she had no interest in the man who'd done his best to ruin her and Seth's lives.

Taking the letter, she threw it inside the recycling bin, among the unwanted flyers and empty cereal boxes.

Seth grinned, and she grinned in reply. "Merry Christmas, my dear husband."

"Merry Christmas, my darling wife."

13

"What are we going to do?" Sophie whispered to her older sister. "Nothing's turning out like we planned."

"You're telling me?" Bailey muttered back. Dinner was on the table. The lasagna, with the salad next to it, sat in the center. Wooden serving utensils leaned against the side of the large salad bowl. The bread was out of the oven, and the warm pungent scent of butter and garlic wafted through the house.

Peering out the swinging kitchen door into the formal dining room, Bailey saw that the situation was even worse than she'd realized. Mom was in one corner of the room, deep in conversation with Ted Reynolds. Danielle and Dad stood on the opposite side. Danielle appeared to be talking Kent's ears off, no doubt regaling him with horror stories of the time she'd spent alone with his daughters. She was clutching her cell phone—again. While Kent and Beth were away, she'd made repeated calls but hadn't connected, growing more and more frustrated. Her impatience with Bailey and Sophie had increased just as quickly.

Okay, so that part of their plan had worked perfectly. Danielle had been stuck with the two of them, and she hadn't liked it one bit. She'd been outsmarted by Beth and wasn't in any mood to be friendly with Bailey and Sophie. Besides, she was distracted, frequently calling and texting some unknown person.

Not long after their parents left, Bailey and Sophie had learned that Danielle knew next to nothing about making a Caesar salad. She assumed all salad dressing came out of a bottle. When Bailey informed her their mother made her own, Danielle snarled that she could make her own, too, only she needed a recipe. Tearing through Beth's cookbooks, she finally came up with one but was disgusted by half the ingredients. No way was she using anchovies! In the end, she'd opted for the bottled Italian dressing she'd found in the fridge.

"Your mother makes her own dressing. Oh, yeah, I can tell!" Danielle had brandished the half-full bottle. "That's the most ridiculous thing I've ever heard," she'd raged. "You're just saying that so I'll feel inferior." Danielle fumed until Kent returned. Her cell phone was in her hands constantly, and her thumbs worked at sending text messages. Bailey and Sophie had several whispered conversations about it, wondering who she was trying so hard to reach.

Danielle had cornered Kent in the dining room, her mouth moving at warp speed. It didn't look as if Dad had an opportunity to say much of anything.

Bailey refused to believe he was dumb enough to actually fall for Danielle. It contradicted everything she knew about her father.

The instant their parents had walked in the house, Bailey sensed something was wrong. She'd quickly discovered the cause. Mom had invited Ted Reynolds to dinner. Oh, great. Based on what she'd heard from Beth, Bailey had suspected for a month or two that Ted was interested in their mother. The invitation had probably been a defensive move on Beth's part; unfortunately, it'd sent the wrong message to Dad.

Now Bailey and Sophie were battling on two fronts. They certainly could've done without this additional complication.

"Look at them," Sophie muttered as the sisters peeked out the door. Mom was still talking to Ted, with her back to Dad, who also had his back to her. If that wasn't bad enough, Danielle chattered at their father like a noisy crow. Her parents couldn't even look at each other. Communication, what little there was of it, had come to a complete standstill.

"This isn't going to work." Bailey felt like dumping the so-called Caesar salad over her parents' heads. "We need to figure out what to do next."

Sophie nodded. "We've got to think of something fast."

"This divorce should never have happened," Bailey moaned—not for the first time. If she or Sophie had guessed their parents were planning to split up, the girls would've stepped in much earlier. Now the situation was much more difficult, and there were other people involved. Now she and her sister were stuck cleaning up the mess.

Bailey shrugged. She brought the salad plates into the dining room and said, "Dinner's ready if you'd like to sit down." She did her best to sound cheerful and festive.

They took the chairs closest to where they stood. That put Danielle beside their father, and Ted and their mother across from them, leaving the two end chairs for Bailey and Sophie.

"Mom made the lasagna," Bailey said, although everyone already knew that. Before she could mention Danielle's role in their dinner, the other woman broke in.

"And I made the salad and the bread, which I'm sure you'll find delicious."

Both men smiled, apparently impressed with the woman who'd managed to spread garlic butter on a sliced baguette. From their admiring gazes, one would think Danielle was qualified to open her own restaurant.

Bailey wanted to point out that the lasagna had required a great deal more expertise than buttering bread. She opened her mouth, but before she could utter a word, she caught her mother's look. Funny how much Mom could communicate in a single glance. Bailey snapped her mouth shut.

Beth served generous slices of lasagna. The salad and bread were passed around the table to sighs of appreciation. Ted poured the wine he'd brought with him. After filling the glasses, he looked around the table. "A toast?"

They all raised their goblets, but before Ted could speak, their father beat him to it. "To a wonderful meal shared with family and friends."

"Hear, hear," Ted added. They all touched the rims of their glasses, then tasted the wine.

"This is excellent," Beth said, praising Ted's choice.

"Very good," Kent agreed.

Wine, Bailey mused. That was it. A common link—her parents were both interested in wine. Well, so was Ted, but she was going to ignore that.

"It's a pinot noir," Ted was saying, "from Oregon."

"Ted and I discovered it a couple of weeks ago at a fund-raising event," Beth said. "I generally prefer the rich, deep reds, so this one took me by surprise."

Oh, yes, life was full of surprises, Bailey thought. Some of them weren't pleasant, either—her mother and father being a prime example.

Dinner became less awkward as they enjoyed the wine and the meal. Conversation revolved around the holidays. Beth talked about the ski trip to Whistler, and the girls chimed in, excited at the prospect of an entire week on the slopes. In the past it had been a family trip, with their father included.

As soon as everyone had finished, Bailey and Sophie jumped up, eager for an excuse to leave.

Bailey carried two dinner plates into the kitchen and set them in the sink. Sophie followed with two more.

"Why didn't you *do* something?" her sister hissed. "Getting Mom and Dad back together was your idea."

"That doesn't mean I have to do everything, does it?" she returned in a heated whisper. A few suggestions from her younger sister certainly would've helped.

Back in the dining room, Bailey could see that Danielle was texting on her cell phone again, keeping it hidden below the table, although everyone knew what she was doing.

"I'm afraid we'll have to leave early," Kent said reluctantly. "Unfortunately, Danielle isn't feeling well."

"Can I get you anything?" Beth asked, sounding concerned.

Bailey wanted to suggest a broom, but her little joke was unlikely to be appreciated, so she said nothing.

"I apologize," Danielle murmured, pressing her fingertips to her temple. "I have a terrible headache that won't go away."

A headache? That was the weakest excuse in the book. A regular ol' headache? Couldn't she be a bit more imaginative? Perhaps a sprained thumb from all that texting?

"So you won't be able to come to church services with us?" Sophie asked with such a lack of sincerity it was embarrassing.

"I think I should get Danielle back to the bed-and-breakfast," their father said.

Mom didn't waste any time retrieving their coats. Standing at the front door, their dad loitered a moment, as if he wanted to say something else. "It was a lovely day," he finally said.

"Thank you," Beth said simply.

"Kent?" Danielle insisted.

"When will I see you again?" Kent asked, directing the question to Beth. His eyes held hers.

"Ah…"

"Mom." Bailey jabbed her elbow into her mother's side.

"Tomorrow?" Beth suggested, poking her right back. "Christmas morning. You and Danielle are welcome to join us."

Danielle shook her head. "I doubt—"

Kent cut her off. "What time?"

"Anytime you want, Dad," Bailey threw in. "Early, though. You should be here when we open gifts."

"I have a *really* bad headache," Danielle reminded him.

"Why don't we wait until morning and see how Danielle feels," Beth said.

Their mother was being far too congenial. In fact, she was ruining everything. Bailey had hoped it would be just the four of them. If her parents could be together, remember Christmases past and enjoy each other's company, then maybe they'd finally figure things out....

Their father shook Ted's hand. Why did everyone have to be so darned polite? The two men locked eyes for an instant. Bailey hoped her father was staking claim to Beth, but she couldn't read his expression.

"Bailey and I'll do dishes," Sophie offered.

Bailey stared at Sophie. What was her sister doing? The last thing they needed was to give their mother time alone with the local vet. She was half-smitten with him already. *Smitten.* That was an old-fashioned word, one their grandmother might have used, but Bailey had always been fond of it.

She followed her sister into the kitchen. "Why'd you do that?" she cried.

"I thought you wanted to discuss ideas about getting Mom and Dad together."

"By leaving her alone with *Ted?*"

"Oh...yeah. I guess I didn't think about that."

"No kidding! Well, you keep an eye on them," commanded Bailey. "If they get too close, tell me." Sophie obediently pushed the door open a crack and looked out. Bailey started loading the dishwasher. Thankfully, their mother had emptied it earlier, so all Bailey had to do was put the rinsed dishes inside.

"You ready to go back out?" she asked five minutes later.

Sophie shook her head. "No," she said flatly. "Go ahead without me."

"No." It was important to Bailey that they present a united front.

Her sister took her time transferring the leftover salad to another bowl and wrapping up the bread, which Bailey noticed had barely been touched. She didn't want to be catty but Danielle had been a little too generous with the garlic. Their father hadn't tasted more than a bite or two. And Bailey was convinced he'd only eaten that to be polite.

To her credit, Danielle had created a halfway decent salad using the bottled dressing. But then who could go wrong with store-bought dressing?

"What are Mom and Ted doing now?" Sophie asked.

Bailey peeked out the swinging door, stepping around her sister. She saw that her mother and Ted had returned to the dining room table and were finishing their coffee. The atmosphere was almost…intimate, vastly different from what it'd been earlier. His arm across the back of an empty chair, Ted was leaning back, speaking animatedly about one thing or another. Whatever he was saying obviously amused Beth, who laughed more than once. She looked relaxed and at ease.

This wasn't how it was supposed to be! It should be Dad in that chair. It should be Kent laughing with Mom. Not Ted Reynolds. Bailey didn't have anything against him; he was a decent guy. But he wasn't their father.

"Well?" Sophie said from behind her.

"They're getting along just fine," Bailey muttered.

"We should break it up," Sophie said, drying her hands on a kitchen towel. Everything was inside the refrigerator and the counters were wiped clean.

Bailey swung open the door. "Okay if we join you?" she asked, feigning cheerfulness.

"By all means." Ted removed his arm from the back of the chair, straightened and set his cup on the table.

"How long have you two known each other?" Sophie asked.

"A while." Beth was the one who answered. "I've brought more than one dog to Ted. He helps me with the rescues, too."

"You must like animals," Sophie went on.

Bailey thought that was a dumb remark. The guy was a vet; obviously he liked animals.

"I do." Ted hesitated. He must've thought it was a dumb remark, too. But then he added, "And I like your mother."

His announcement fell like bricks from the sky.

"What about my dad?" Bailey asked.

"Yeah, our dad," Sophie echoed plaintively.

"Oh, dear," Beth whispered. "If you two have any hopes that your father and I are getting back together, you need to forget them. It's much too late for that."

14

"Who'd be calling on Christmas Eve?" Bobby Polgar asked when Teri hung up the phone. It was after dinner, and the children were—finally—all snug in their beds.

"Beth Morehouse," Teri said. "She wants to know if it would be all right if she dropped the puppy off tonight instead of in the morning." Actually, it sounded as though Beth needed to get out of the house.

"What did you tell her?"

"I said come on over."

Bobby glanced into the family room, where he had three scooter-riders out of the boxes ready for assembling. The triplets were eight months old now and crawling. Robbie, the firstborn, was already standing on his own. Teri figured he'd be walking soon; the boy was fearless. Little Jimmy, the middle child and the smallest, was content to continue crawling, and Christopher, the youngest by a couple of minutes, loved sitting on the floor, banging pots and pans. Bobby felt sure their son was destined to be a drummer.

"I asked James to give me a hand assembling these," Bobby admitted a bit sheepishly.

"You'll do fine." Her husband might be a chess genius, but he didn't excel in certain other areas—like household repairs. Or "assembly required" toys.

"Are the boys down for the night?" Bobby asked.

Teri nodded, too exhausted for a detailed description of what it took to get all three to fall asleep at roughly the same time. Their nanny had the next two days off to spend the holidays with her family, and it felt like she'd been gone for a month. Teri's sister, Christie, had agreed to help make Christmas dinner and look after the triplets.

"Come and sit with me," Bobby said, holding his arm out to Teri.

She sat beside him on the sofa and laid her head on his shoulder. Bobby was semi-retired these days, following the birth of his sons, and Teri was grateful. Bobby and his best friend, James, had developed a chess-based computer game that consumed a great deal of their time, since they were now working on the second version. Still, Teri was glad to have her husband at home instead of on the road.

Closing her eyes, she remembered how she'd met Bobby Polgar. It had definitely been an unusual introduction…. He was in a championship chess match in Seattle and to everyone's shock he was losing. The chess world was aghast that the great Bobby Polgar could be toppled. One look at the chess player on the TV screen told Teri what his problem was. Bobby was distracted by his hair, which was too long and kept flopping in his eyes. He needed a cut.

In retrospect she was astonished that Security had let her through to see him. When she explained why she'd come, Bobby had stared at her as if she was some kind of lunatic, but he'd allowed her to trim his hair. Then she'd quietly left. Bobby had gone on to win the match and afterward he'd sought her out. Crazy as it sounded, that was how it all began.

She wasn't quite sure when she fell in love with him. In the beginning, she'd fought against having any feelings for this man. Really, what could come of it? She was a hairdresser from a little backwater town and Bobby Polgar was a champion chess player admired by the whole world. He might be infatuated with her for a while, but his affection would quickly wane. She'd bore him, and Bobby would soon grow tired of her.

Talk about an odd couple! But fall in love with him she did, despite her efforts not to. And when she fell, she fell hard.

She'd questioned why an intellectual like him—a celebrity to boot—would love someone like her. He'd said that she brought emotion into his life, that he liked her practical and intuitive approach, that she'd taught him how to *feel.*

Before that tournament in Seattle, every minute of Bobby's life had been involved with chess. He lived, breathed and slept chess. It was all he thought about, all he cared about…until he fell in love with her.

"You're smiling," Bobby said now, brushing the hair off her forehead almost as if she were a child.

"I was remembering our honeymoon." They got married in Las Vegas. Bobby had been in a chess competition there, and they were given the most luxurious penthouse suite in the hotel. The morning after their wedding night, Bobby had to leave for a chess match. Teri had stayed in bed and turned on the television to watch her husband play.

She knew from the first move he made that his mind wasn't on the game. He was thinking about *her,* thinking about coming back to the room and making love to her again. Then something happened; she could almost see the transformation taking place… His expression changed. Even his posture changed. Bobby had realized that the sooner he won, the sooner he could return to their room. His focus, his attention, went straight into the game. His opponent didn't stand a chance. The poor man lost in record time. A second later, Bobby popped out of his seat and raced for the elevator, the camera crew on his heels.

Teri had been waiting for him…

The doorbell chimed and Teri sighed, not wanting to leave the comfort of her husband's arms and the warm memories that had wrapped themselves around her. She started to get up, but Bobby stopped her.

"I'll get it."

As Bobby was rising to his feet she slipped her hand around his neck and brought his mouth down to hers for a lengthy kiss. They broke it off when the doorbell chimed again.

Bobby's glasses were askew and his face flushed by the time he moved away from her. He cleared his throat. "You need to warn me before you do that," he muttered.

"Okay, I will," she said, smiling up at him. "That was just to say how much I love you."

Bobby cleared his throat again and gave her a small, crooked smile. He never quite knew how to respond when she mentioned love. "Thank you," he whispered, then hurried to the door.

In a minute he was back with Christie and James. They were another odd couple, Teri mused. When she'd first met James Wilbur, she hadn't known what to think of the tall, exceptionally thin man who served as Bobby's driver. It wasn't until much later that she discovered James was Bobby's dearest friend. He'd been a chess prodigy like Bobby, but James had suffered a breakdown caused by all the pressure. He'd disappeared from the public eye and been forgotten by everyone except Bobby. Her husband refused to abandon his friend, so he'd hired James as his driver. For years no one had recognized

Bobby's chauffeur as the teenager who'd made chess history along with Bobby Polgar.

As soon as James met Christie, he fell for her. Teri hated to be the one to tell him, but her younger sister came with plenty of baggage, just like she had. To her complete surprise, Christie had fallen in love with James. Their relationship had been a series of stops and starts, had taken a number of unexpected turns. But in the end Christie had dumped the losers who'd taken advantage of her, gone back to school and straightened out her life.

A year ago, over Christmas, she'd split up with James. A story in the press had identified him as James Gardner, the prodigy who'd disappeared. It might not have been such a big news item if not for the fact that he'd still been part of the chess world all that time. He hadn't played in years, not since his collapse, but he enjoyed belonging to that world. Christie hadn't been able to tolerate his deception, his inability to trust her with his secret. Eventually, however, they'd reconciled and their estrangement had led them to a greater understanding of each other.

Teri realized James was like Bobby, in that chess was all he knew. He'd acknowledged he no longer wanted to play high-pressure big-money chess, but liked being close to the game—and close to the one friend he could count on, Bobby Polgar.

"We're here to help with the kids' Christmas gifts," Christie announced.

"Wonderful." Teri patted the empty space next to her on the sofa. "We'll let the men put together these toys while you and I visit."

"Sounds like a great idea to me," Christie said. "By the way, the house looks gorgeous." She gestured at the candles arranged on the fireplace mantel and at the Christmas tree, its lights reflected in the picture window overlooking Puget Sound.

Falling in love had changed Christie, just as it'd changed Teri. The hard edges of her personality had softened. She'd proven to herself she could get whatever she wanted as long as she worked hard and persevered. Christie had recently graduated from Olympic Community College, and she planned to start her own business, photographing the contents of houses for insurance purposes. Teri was proud of her little sister.

"I heard from Johnny this afternoon," she told Christie. Johnny was their younger brother. He was in school, attending the University of Washington. "He'll come over for dinner tomorrow. With his new girlfriend." Johnny never lacked for girlfriends, but he hadn't met anyone who was going to change *his* life. Not yet.

Teri had been more of a mother to him than their own. Another memory floated into Teri's mind. Soon after she'd married Bobby, Teri had made a huge dinner and invited her family to the house to meet her husband.

Sadly, her mother had arrived half-drunk, and from the moment Ruth stepped through the door, she did nothing but find fault with Teri.

Bobby wasn't about to let his mother-in-law insult his wife and had handled the situation in a firm, yet subtle way. He'd wordlessly picked up Ruth's purse and set it by the front door, indicating it was time for her to leave. Ruth had immediately taken offense and, dragging her fourth—or was it fifth?—husband, she'd stomped out.

"James, what do they mean by a flat-head screwdriver?" Bobby and James sat on the family room floor with the pieces of one scooter scattered about the room. Bobby held out the instruction sheet, frowning at the diagrams. Then he turned it upside down before turning it right side up again.

"I didn't know there was more than one kind of screw-driver," James confessed.

"You learn something new every day, right?"

"Right," James agreed.

"I'll get a flat-head screwdriver for you," Teri said, sliding off the sofa.

Bobby gazed up at her as if she were the most brilliant woman who'd ever lived. "You have one?"

"That and a Phillips and a square tip…" She went to the kitchen drawer and returned with the required screwdriver.

"Do you need anything else?" she asked, handing it to him.

"Uh…" He showed her the instruction sheet. "Can you tell me what I'm supposed to do with that?" He pointed to the drawing of a part.

"Teri," Christie said, getting up from the sofa. "It looks like these two are going to need a bit of assistance."

"Looks that way," she concurred.

"We can do this," Bobby insisted.

"Yeah," James echoed, but without much conviction.

"Do you want them to help us?" Bobby asked his friend.

James regarded Christie, and then Teri. "I don't think it would hurt. What about you?"

"I don't need help," Bobby said, "but if Teri wants to volunteer I won't stop her."

Teri and Christie exchanged an eye-rolling glance.

All of them were on the floor when the doorbell chimed yet again.

"That'll be Beth Morehouse," Teri said.

"Oh, were you expecting her?" Christie asked. "Why's she here?"

"Delivering a puppy," she said on her way to the door.

"Teri, don't tell me you and Bobby are getting a puppy!" Christie called after her.

"No," James answered on her behalf. "We are."

"James!" Christie yelped. "Isn't this something you should've discussed with me first?"

"Well…"

Before he could respond, Teri walked into the living room, followed by her guest. Beth held a basket—with a small black puppy staring out. The little creature wore a pink bow that contrasted with its glossy fur.

"Oh, she's adorable."

"Yes, and she's all yours," James told her. "Merry Christmas, darling."

"Merry Christmas," Christie said, her voice choked.

"Why are you crying?" James asked, drawing his wife into his arms.

"I… I always wanted a…dog."

"I know."

Christie threw her arms around James's neck.

Teri took the basket out of Beth's arms. "Thank you so much for bringing over the puppy."

"I was happy to," Beth said. "I know this little girl will have a wonderful home, so thank *you*."

"Our pleasure," Christie murmured.

James kissed her forehead. "Merry Christmas, my love," he said again. "I thought we could name her Chessie."

"Chessie! Of course." Christie laughed.

"You'll get your gift later," she promised in a husky voice.

James turned three shades of red. "I'll hold you to that," he said. "Now come and meet your dog."

15

After dropping off the puppy at the Polgars', Beth headed back to her house on Christmas Tree Lane. She'd enjoyed her brief visit with Bobby and Teri and James and Christie. The two couples were obviously devoted to one another. Watching them all working together, assembling toys for the triplets, reminded Beth of those early years with Kent. Finances had been tight back then, but they'd managed; their happiness had more than compensated for the luxuries they'd done without. She missed those times, and yes, she missed Kent, too.

On the way home Beth felt empty inside. For three years she'd pretended she was happy. Pretended she'd rather live her life without Kent. It'd all been a lie.

And now it was too late.

The girls would be getting ready for evening services at the church and the three of them would arrive together. Kent had said he might attend, as well, but she knew he'd sit with Danielle, not with Beth and the girls. That made sense, but it was another blow she wasn't ready to deal with.

While waiting at a red light, she saw the open sign at Mocha Mama's. Because she didn't want to return home until she'd regained control of her emotions, she decided to go in. Stopping for a quick cup of coffee would give her a chance to sort through her feelings, to better understand what was happening and accept the reality that she had lost Kent for good. The life they'd once had was truly over.

She pulled into a parking space and turned off the engine. Sitting in the car, she pressed her hand over her eyes as unfamiliar and unwelcome emotions swirled through her. This Christmas was nothing like she'd anticipated. For weeks she'd looked forward to her children's visit. She'd carefully planned events, shopped, wrapped gifts, cooked their favorite meals. What she realized now was that she'd done it for Kent, too. Since he was coming to Cedar Cove for the holiday, she'd wanted to remind him of what they'd had. Of everything that was gone now, but could…perhaps…be recovered. She hadn't even acknowledged this to herself. Not really.

What made it all so impossible was Danielle. Facing the ghosts of Christmas past, back when she and Kent were so much in love, only depressed her now.

When Beth entered the coffee shop, she saw that it was nearly deserted. A teenager stood behind the counter, playing a handheld game. He didn't seem to notice he had a customer.

"Hello! I'd like a decaf Americano," she said briskly.

Startled, the kid glanced up. He blinked and reluctantly set aside his game. "Anything else?"

"No, thanks." She paid, adding a nice Christmas tip, and waited for her coffee.

A couple of minutes later he delivered it in a to-go cup, which was fine, although she wasn't in any rush to leave. Carrying it with her, she chose a table by the window, one that overlooked Harbor Street.

She gazed out at the serene and yet festive view of the town's main street. Garlands were strung across it. Silver bells dangled from the lampposts, and the town had never seemed more inviting. A light dusting of snow glistened on the large Christmas tree, which blinked red and green lights, outside city hall, while Christmas carols were broadcast from the bell tower.

"I wondered if that was your car outside."

Stunned by the familiar voice, Beth turned. Kent stood next to her small table, although she hadn't seen him come in.

"What are you doing here?" she asked breathlessly.

"I decided to take a drive—"

"Where's your friend? Danielle?" she interrupted.

"At the Thyme and Tide. Resting. And, Beth, she really is a friend."

Sure she was. Ex-husbands usually traveled with *friends*. But apparently the headache was real.

"She took a couple of aspirin and is lying down."

Beth cupped her hands around the paper cup, the heat of the coffee stinging her palms. "I hope she feels better soon."

"She'll be fine." Without waiting for an invitation, Kent pulled out a chair and sat down across from her.

"You want a coffee, sir?" the kid behind the counter called out.

"Sure. I'll have whatever she's having," he said.

"You got it," Mr. Game Boy said with a promptness he hadn't demonstrated earlier. Maybe her generous tip had something to do with it.

"You looked deep in thought when I walked in," Kent said, relaxing against the back of the chair. He extended his legs into the aisle, crossing them at the ankles. He seemed so comfortable, so calm, as if he hadn't a care in the world.

Beth stared at her ex-husband, unable to grasp how he could remain so unaffected by what had happened between them.

Perhaps Beth was the only one who had regrets, who

wanted to examine the reasons their marriage had failed. What did it matter, anyway? she reflected darkly. Kent was with Danielle. He'd moved on, and she should, too.

"Beth?" he said, breaking into her thoughts.

She looked over at him, wondering what he'd just said.

"You worried about something?"

"Of course not," she said, forcing a brightness into her voice. "Why would you think that?"

"You never were much of a liar."

Beth shrugged, knowing it was true.

"Why are you out here, anyway?"

"I dropped off a puppy. A Christmas gift."

He seemed to be waiting for her to explain why she hadn't gone directly home. If she knew the answer to that question, she wouldn't be sipping blistering hot coffee and feeling as if the entire world was against her.

"So, how long have you and Ted been...friends?"

"Oh, for some time now."

"Is it serious?"

"No." She managed a nonchalant smile. "Perhaps I should've clarified that. I routinely see Ted on a professional basis—and yes, we've been out socially." She didn't mention the few kisses they'd shared because, frankly, it wasn't any of his business. When it came to *his* friend, she'd rather not know.

"But it could develop into something serious?" he asked.

This was even more difficult to answer. "I suppose. If we both wanted it to."

"And do you?"

She stared down into her coffee to avoid looking at him.

"No." Then she quickly shook her head. "Well, maybe."

"Maybe," he repeated slowly.

"It depends."

"On what?" he prodded.

Beth straightened. "I'd rather not talk about Ted and me. I didn't ask you about Danielle."

"True." He nodded. "All right, what *do* you want to talk about?"

"Do we need to talk about anything?"

He hesitated. "I guess not."

The kid brought over Kent's coffee and he paid for it. He was about to take his first sip when Beth warned him, "Careful, it's hot."

Kent sipped his coffee guardedly and grimaced. "You're right."

Beth took another sip of her own coffee, which had cooled slightly. "The puppy I delivered—it was to the Polgars."

"Polgar. That's an unusual name. As in Bobby Polgar, the chess champion?"

"Yes, he lives in Cedar Cove."

"Bobby Polgar lives here?" Kent arched his brows, clearly impressed.

"His wife is, or rather was, a local hairdresser. She's a wonderful, wonderful person."

"You mean to tell me Bobby Polgar married a beautician?" Kent grinned, as if the idea amused him.

"Don't say it like that. Teri's perfect for Bobby and now they have triplet sons...."

"And they took a puppy?"

"Actually, no. The puppy was for Teri's sister."

"What did you want to say about the Polgars?" Kent asked.

"I... I was remembering how it was with us when the girls were little."

"We talked about that earlier."

"We did," she agreed. "Those early Christmases, the basement apartment, those silly gingerbread decorations I sewed."

"What you're really saying is that you wonder what happened to us."

So Kent was the one brave enough to lay it on the table, the subject neither of them had been willing to broach until now.

Beth suppressed the urge to say it was too late. All of a sudden, she didn't want to dig up the past anymore, a past that was full of hurts and slights committed on both sides. If they dug too deep, she didn't know what they might uncover. Anyway, what was the point? They weren't together anymore. He had a new life and so did she.

Another part of her, the more rational part, recognized that unless she knew why her relationship with Kent had dissolved, history might repeat itself. If she did fall in love with Ted, she could revert to the same pattern that had destroyed her marriage to Kent.

"I don't think we can or should assign blame," Kent said, sitting up. He leaned forward and extended his arms, cupping his coffee between his hands. "So… I guess we should figure out what went wrong."

Beth swallowed hard, unsure where to start. She couldn't.

"Do you want to go first?" he asked. Kent, too, apparently found it difficult.

"No. You go."

"All right." He took a breath. "Once the girls got their driver's licenses, they didn't seem to need me anymore. They had their own lives. And that's the way it should be."

"A father's more than a chauffeur," she said with the glimmer of a smile. "But I know what you mean. They were becoming adults, so our role as parents changed."

He nodded. "And you had your career, while I had mine."

"At some point, without even being aware of it, we lost sight of what's important," Beth said. "And then it became a matter of pride, as if the most vital thing was proving how little we needed each other."

He nodded again.

"You stopped attending college social functions with me, and I retaliated by not attending your business dinners."

He lowered his gaze. "I'm sorry, but I found them boring."

"They were." She'd be the first to admit it.

"You always made them fun, though—in a slightly scandalous way," he said, grinning. "I got all the gossip. We'd stand in a corner and you'd tell me the most inappropriate stories."

"And you'd embarrass me by laughing at the most inappropriate times," she reminded him, and had trouble not breaking into giggles right then.

They looked at each other in silence.

"We both got absorbed in our lives, apart from each other," he finally said.

"We became strangers who happened to be married."

"I can't think of a single defining incident, an event that triggered the end of our marriage. Can you?"

"Not really." It was more an accumulation of grudges, of minor slights and careless acts. Oh, there were plenty of small decisions Beth had made through the years. Decisions that seemed inconsequential, insignificant. For some reason she thought of the morning Kent had asked her to drop off a letter at the post office. It was on her way to the college, while he was driving in the opposite direction. She told him she couldn't because she was running late. Really, how much time would it have taken? A minute? Two? Kent hadn't complained. He'd dropped off the letter himself.

Then there was the night she'd phoned and asked Kent to pick up bread and milk on his way home from work and he forgot. Such a little thing, but it had annoyed her no end.

At some stage she must have decided to ask nothing more of

Kent. Was that when the pettiness began? When they turned to a silent battle of wills? How ridiculous they'd been. How silly and selfish and juvenile. No wonder their marriage had crumbled into pieces....

Beth visualized the slights, the put-downs, the irritations on both sides as pebbles, each a small stone in the growing pile that eventually crushed their marriage. Kent was right; it hadn't been any one thing. Nothing big. No infidelity. No drugs or alcohol abuse. No money problems.

"Folks," the teenager said. He stood in front of their table with a tray and a white rag. "We're closing now."

"Oh." Feeling disjointed, Beth looked up.

"Normally, I wouldn't mind staying while you finished your coffee, but it's Christmas Eve and my grandma's at the house."

"No problem," Kent said. He took one last drink of his coffee and left the cup on the table. "Thanks, and merry Christmas."

"Merry Christmas," Beth echoed. She left her cup behind, too.

Kent walked her to her car. He seemed to have more he wanted to say. Beth knew she did. Perhaps later...

"I'll see you at the church in twenty minutes," Kent said. He tucked his hands inside his pockets. "Bob at the B and B told me where it is."

"I'm going to pick up Bailey and Sophie. We'll see you there."

He started to turn away, but Beth stopped him.

"Kent..."

"Yes?"

"Would you mind sitting with the girls and me?"

He smiled. "I'd be happy to," he said.

Beth smiled back. Even if that meant Danielle joined

them—well, she could tolerate that. It was the season of good-will, after all. The important thing was for their family to be together.

16

Emily Flemming blew out the last candle after the seven o'clock Christmas Eve service at the Methodist church where her husband, Dave, was pastor. Every pew had been filled and the choir had sounded glorious. Both of their sons had gone back to the house with her parents. Emily appreciated the fact that the service was relatively early. Some churches waited until after nine, and the Catholic church always had a midnight mass.

Dave finished greeting the last of his parishioners, Bible in hand, as Emily joined him in the vestibule.

"That was lovely, sweetheart," she told her husband. Dave worked hard on his sermons, heading over to the church two hours before the first service in order to practice and pray. He took his responsibilities seriously and looked after his flock.

"Thank you." Dave slipped his arm around Emily's waist. "Did you see the man with Beth Morehouse?"

Emily had noticed him, and it wasn't the local veterinarian. Emily had suspected for some time that a romance between Beth and Ted Reynolds was in the offing. But when she'd seen Beth with this other man, she'd changed her mind. Judging by the electricity that sizzled between them, they were more than acquaintances or even friends. "I saw him."

"That's her ex-husband. His name is Kent."

"Her ex-husband?" They sure didn't act like exes, Emily thought. They'd exchanged frequent looks throughout the service and seemed keenly aware of each other. At first, Beth's glances had been shy, but as the service progressed, she'd grown bolder. Several times their eyes had met, and neither seemed inclined to look away.

The two girls had been sitting on one side of Beth, with Kent on the other, closest to the aisle. The girls hadn't exactly hidden their delight.

"On her way out of church, Beth mentioned a litter of part-Labrador puppies that were left on her doorstep. Ten in all."

"Ten? But I thought she was leaving for a short vacation with her daughters."

"She is, so she needs to find homes for these puppies quickly. She's only got two left and wanted to know if we're interested."

"Are we?" Emily asked, almost afraid of the answer.

"I was thinking a couple of puppies would help teach Mark and Matthew a sense of responsibility."

"Mark's been asking for a dog," Emily added with some reluctance. Her fear was that her son would lose interest and she'd be the one taking care of his dog. She had no concerns about Matthew; he was the dependable one.

"I was thinking—"

"Dave, before you say anything, we need to consider this very carefully. A puppy, let alone two, is a lot of work and—"

"Mark's old enough to understand that. Besides, Beth sounded desperate to find a good home for these dogs. Especially at this late date."

Emily could feel herself weakening. Especially when her husband was regarding her with a puppy-dog look of his own....

"I had a Lab while I was growing up," Dave said.

Emily nodded, remembering his fond stories about the family pet.

"We named him Blackie," David went on. "Not very original, but, oh, how I loved that dog."

"In other words, you'd like our sons to have the same wonderful experience with a dog that you did?"

Dave smiled sheepishly. "But only if you agree."

While she wasn't one hundred percent sold, Emily was willing to take a chance.

"Can we at least look at them?" Dave asked, his eyes alight with excitement.

"Tonight?"

"Well, yes. It would be perfect. The boys are with your parents and we can drive out to Beth's place. By the time we get back, Matthew and Mark will be asleep. When they wake up in the morning, the puppies will be there—the best Christmas gift ever."

Clearly, her husband had worked this all out.

"All right," she said, holding back a smile. "We can go see the puppies, but there are no guarantees. Understand?"

"Definitely," he assured her. "We'll go to Beth's and look at them, and if you don't think it'll work, or you take an instant dislike to either dog or whatever, then we'll leave."

She raised her eyebrows. Dave knew her far too well. The minute she laid eyes on those puppies she'd be lost. She couldn't possibly say no. Especially since he wanted to provide his sons with the same childhood experience that he'd enjoyed.

During a quick phone call to the house, Emily told her mother that she and Dave had an errand to run. She explained what it was, and her mother promised that the boys would be in bed when Emily and Dave returned.

While Emily was talking to her mother, Dave contacted Beth, who said it would be fine to stop by the house that evening. In fact, she wished he would, because she planned to leave with the girls early on the morning of the twenty-sixth, so the sooner these last two puppies found homes, the better.

In the car on the way to Beth's house, Emily gazed out at the sky. The night was clear, with a million stars twinkling like jewels, but far more precious than any stone she'd ever seen. Her eyes fell to the wedding ring on her left hand. She'd almost removed it when she believed Dave was having an affair. Those had been dark days in their marriage and she'd been so sure, so completely convinced, that her husband was seeing another woman. It wasn't as if pastors were exempt from temptation.

In retrospect, she felt embarrassed that she'd suspected Dave of anything so underhanded. Yet what else was she to believe? He was gone almost every night and, well…thankfully those days were over. Probably every marriage went through at least one rocky period.

"Dave?"

"Yes, love?"

"I think Beth and her ex-husband still have feelings for each other."

Dave didn't speak for several minutes. "I had the same impression," he finally said.

"What do you suppose went wrong between them?" Emily asked.

"Probably the same thing that went wrong with us."

"Lack of communication," she murmured. "I guess it almost always comes down to that."

They pulled into Beth's yard and saw another vehicle parked next to hers.

"Maybe Kent's still with her," Dave commented.

Emily had heard Kent was staying at the Beldons' B and B. Rumor had it that he hadn't arrived alone, but if so, whoever he'd brought hadn't been at the church.

The front door opened and Beth stepped onto the porch to greet them. "Welcome, welcome! Please, come inside."

Dave held Emily's hand as they walked into the gaily decorated house.

"The girls have hot cocoa on the stove. I hope we'll be able to interest you in a mug."

"With whipped cream," Kent added, joining Beth.

He extended his hand to Dave. "We met in church earlier. Kent Morehouse."

"Dave Flemming, and my wife, Emily."

"Hi, Emily. Good to see you again, Dave."

Beth led the way into the kitchen. She opened the door leading to the laundry room and returned a moment later with two beautiful black puppies. They wore the saddest, most forlorn looks Emily could imagine.

"These two are the last of the litter, both males." Beth handed one to Emily.

"They're gorgeous," Emily said, falling hard and fast. All it had taken was one look, and she was convinced these puppies needed to be part of their family.

She sat on one of the kitchen chairs, holding the puppy on her lap. The little creature licked her hand, then immediately curled up and went to sleep. Yup, Emily was lost. Mark would love this dog and she felt confident he'd do a good job of feeding, training and caring for this puppy. Matthew, too, would love and train his dog.

When Emily glanced up she saw that Dave was holding

the other puppy, all the while engaged in conversation with Kent Morehouse.

"The sermon tonight really touched me," Beth said. "I've heard the Christmas story all my life. But I'd never really considered the role Joseph played. How he must have loved Mary."

Emily agreed. "It's a beautiful love story and one that's often overlooked." This was Dave's gift. He looked at Biblical stories in ways that stirred people's hearts and brought them closer to God. He could take familiar passages and study them from a different point of view, bringing contemporary relevance and new insight.

Beth returned to the stove, and removed the pan from the burner. Bailey and Sophie, who'd poked their heads in to say hello, were playing a computer game in the family room.

"Girls! Cocoa," Beth called out.

Neither seemed to hear her, too engrossed in their game. Shaking her head, Beth finished filling the mugs and brought two of them to Emily and Dave, both sitting at the kitchen table.

Kent picked up the other two, then he and Beth sat down with her guests.

"I see they've taken a liking to us," Dave said, motioning to the puppy on his lap. The second one was asleep, too, chin now resting on Emily's arm.

"You know what a soft touch I am," she complained laughingly.

"Yeah, I guess we're a two-dog family now."

"Dave was telling me he likes to golf," Kent said to Beth a moment later.

"It's a prerequisite for pastors," Dave joked. "A lot of men bond over the sport."

"There was a time not so long ago when Dave gave it up, though," Emily said. "We were going through a difficult financial period and he didn't want me to know how bad things were. The idiot let me think he was out golfing when he was actually working at a second job." Emily wasn't sure about confiding anything so personal, but she felt this was something Beth and Kent might benefit from hearing.

"How did you find out?" Beth asked.

"Peggy Beldon casually mentioned that Bob missed seeing Dave on the golf course."

"Of course, Emily didn't say anything at the time. She just waited for me to come back to the house. She was cool as a cucumber—until I walked in the front door."

"Was that before or after I dyed my hair blond?"

Beth stared at her. "You went blond?"

"It was stupid, but we do stupid things when we're desperate."

"We do," Kent agreed far too quickly.

"In the end we worked everything out, thank God," Dave said. "I made such a mess of my marriage. I nearly destroyed my wife's faith in me."

"And then there were those missing jewels," Emily added. There was far more to the story.

"Oh, yes, the jewels." Dave sighed, lifting his mug of cocoa.

"Missing jewels?" Kent asked, looking from one to the other.

"It's a long story, so allow me to condense it. One of the older ladies in the church, Martha Evans, died and several pieces of her jewelry turned up missing."

"Dave was the last person to see her alive," Emily said. "Which immediately threw suspicion on him."

"So everyone assumed I was the one who took the jewelry—even my wife," Dave said, grinning at Emily.

She smiled back. "What else was I supposed to believe?" she murmured. "Besides, I found Martha's earring in his suit pocket. Only I didn't know it belonged to Martha or that someone had purposely placed it there. At the time, I imagined my husband was having an affair."

"My goodness, you two had quite a few troubles, didn't you?" Kent glanced at Beth.

"What saved your marriage?" she asked.

"Prayer," Emily said, "and the two of us talking honestly. Dave finally admitted we had more bills at the end of the month than money, and that he was doing two jobs."

"And Sheriff Davis was instrumental in capturing the man responsible for the theft of Martha's jewelry," Dave explained, "with Roy McAfee's help."

"What an incredible story!"

"It really is, and I'll fill in the missing pieces the next time we see you," Emily promised. She took a last swallow of her cocoa and stood, the puppy in her arms. "We need to head home. My parents are looking after the boys."

"Wait," Kent said. "I want to know who actually took the jewelry?"

"Someone who worked on Martha's will, a paralegal," Dave explained. "His name is Geoff Duncan. He's serving prison time now. He was trying to impress his fiancée's family, so he stole the jewelry, pawned it all and spent the money."

"Lori Bellamy, the fiancée, didn't have a clue what Geoff had done," Emily said. "She's Lori Wyse now. She got married not long ago to Lincoln Wyse, who opened a body shop in town earlier this year. They seem to be a good match, although they had a few problems with Lori's family. But apparently that's all settled now."

"This Geoff guy. Did he have a grudge against you?" Kent asked.

"Not that I know of. I was just the perfect candidate for him to frame because, as Martha's pastor, I spent a lot of time with her. Like I said, I seemed to be the last person to see her alive, and I was also the one who found the body. The obvious suspect." He shook his head. "Thank goodness Sheriff Davis and Roy McAfee looked beyond the obvious."

"It must've been a terrible time for you," Beth said sympathetically.

"The worst, but we made it through and I'm so grateful we did."

"I can imagine."

"Some people are far too willing to give up on…" She let the rest fade once she realized what she was about to say. Emily didn't want to embarrass the divorced couple.

Kent moved closer to Beth. "I agree."

"So do I," Beth said, almost before the words had left Kent's mouth.

They looked at each other, but the moment was broken by the sharp peal of Kent's cell phone.

He answered it on the second ring, and although Emily couldn't make out what was being said, the person calling him was clearly female—and clearly upset.

"Yes, of course," he said. "Yes, I know." He closed his cell with a snap. "I apologize, but I need to leave."

He reached for his coat and, after a few words of farewell, was out the door.

"I know it's none of my business, but who was that?" Dave asked Beth.

"His…friend," Beth said.

Emily looked at Dave just as he turned to look at her. So the rumors of a female companion had been correct, and for some reason this woman had stayed back at the B and B. There were more obstacles to a reconciliation between Beth and her ex-husband than either of them had guessed.

17

"Did you see the way Dad looked at Mom during the service?" Bailey whispered to her sister in the darkened bedroom. Sophie was in the twin bed next to hers. Although she'd turned out the lights several minutes ago, Bailey was too excited to sleep.

"Yes, I know but—"

"They're falling in love all over again," Bailey broke in. "I can *feel* it."

"Well, maybe, but…"

"But what?" Bailey muttered. Sometimes her sister could be so…negative. Well, she refused to allow Sophie's skeptical remarks to dampen her good feelings. For a time it seemed that everything they'd planned was about to fall apart. Then, at the very last minute, their father had shown up at the church… alone. It'd been perfect. Just perfect.

Bailey hadn't asked about Danielle and neither had Sophie. Their dad had slipped into the pew next to Beth, and their mother had smiled over at him and…

Oh, it'd been sheer bliss. Love radiated between them. If this were a movie, a crescendo of music would have burst forth, and there would've been joyful singing in the background. Actually, there *was* music, but it had come from the church choir. Still, the effect was pretty satisfying.

"Can I talk now?" Sophie asked impatiently.

"Oh, all right."

"I have a question."

"Ask away." Bailey sighed, suspecting that Sophie was going to ruin Bailey's Christmas Eve by casting doubt on the likelihood of their parents reuniting. Her father had introduced Danielle as a "friend." *They* were the ones who'd made the assumption that she was more than that.

"What about when Danielle phoned? Dad left in a mighty big hurry after that."

"Yeah, I know," Bailey admitted with more than a little reluctance.

"He's still at Danielle's beck and call."

"But we can't be sure of all the circumstances and—"

"There are no *buts* here," Sophie fumed. "I don't know what Dad sees in Danielle, but there's obviously something."

"Whatever it is, I trust Dad to do the right thing." Bailey rolled onto her back and stared up at the ceiling. Leave it to Sophie…. Now she was worried again. Their father was smart—she hoped. Deep down, she couldn't believe he was involved with Danielle. In fact, the more she thought about it, the more certain she was. He might have brought Danielle with him, but from the moment he arrived Kent only seemed interested in Beth. Danielle was far more attached to her cell phone than she was to their father.

"Mark my words, Dad doesn't care about Danielle," Bailey insisted in a confident voice.

Sophie sighed loudly. "I wish I could believe that."

"Maybe we should help him along."

"Bailey, no!"

"No?"

"No," she repeated. "If we step in now, it'll just complicate everything. Dad has to do this on his own. Otherwise, we'll sabotage the whole reconciliation."

Bailey slowly absorbed her sister's words. Although Sophie was younger—and not studying psychology—she could occasionally be really smart. "Have you ever thought of going into diplomacy? You'd be great."

"You think so?" Sophie loved getting compliments.

Well, everyone did, but her sister was so transparent. She made no effort to hide how much she enjoyed hearing nice things about herself. Bailey could almost see Sophie's self-congratulatory little smile.

"Trust me," Bailey said, returning to the subject at hand. "Mom and Dad are going to remarry. I can feel it."

"Well...we can wish."

"Oh, come on," Bailey urged. "*Believe* it."

"You really buy into that positive thinking idea, don't you?"

"Yes," Bailey concurred. "And you should, too." In her opinion, it would go a long way toward raising Sophie's spirits.

"I'll consider it," Sophie said.

Pulling the sheet and blanket up over her shoulder, Bailey shifted onto her right side, her back to her sister. Despite Sophie's pessimism, Bailey believed with all her heart. She remembered the look her parents had exchanged in church that night. The look of love, of regret and the promise of reconciliation.

Tomorrow morning, when it was Christmas, the biggest and best present wouldn't be under the tree. It would be the fact that her parents still loved each other and wanted to remarry.

On Christmas Day, they'd finally acknowledge their feelings, and the rest of their lives would begin.

Bailey was sure of it.

18

"Merry Christmas," Bruce Peyton whispered as he drew Rachel into his arms.

Smiling, Rachel arched her back and yawned. "Is it morning already?"

"It sure is. I've got coffee brewing and Jolene's up."

Rachel turned her head to look at the clock. "Bruce, it isn't even eight." She could easily have slept another hour. Or two.

"I know, but Jolene's anxious to get to the presents."

With some effort, Rachel sat up. She was noticeably pregnant now and the baby was more active every day. Thankfully, the worst of the morning sickness had passed.

The pregnancy had been unplanned and Jolene, her thirteen-year-old stepdaughter, hadn't yet adjusted to her father's remarriage when she was forced to deal with the news about the baby. The marriage itself had resulted in a difficult transition for the girl, but the pregnancy complicated everything that much more.

Her relationship with Jolene had grown tense. The stress became too much for Rachel and eventually she felt she had no choice but to move out of the family home. Only recently—just weeks ago—had she returned.

The counseling sessions had helped a great deal and they were learning to coexist and work together as a family. Rachel was excited about spending Christmas with her husband and stepdaughter. She and Jolene had planned the dinner menu together and they'd spent most of yesterday in the kitchen, preparing vegetables and side dishes and dessert.

During the afternoon they'd also made a breakfast casserole to put in the oven Christmas morning while they opened gifts. And Jolene had baked her first cinnamon rolls from scratch. Rachel hadn't told her, but this was her first experience, too. The rolls had turned out well, if Bruce's lavish praise was any-thing to go by.

All the while, Poppy, their new dog, had lounged in the warm kitchen, with occasional bursts of activity and escorted trips to the backyard.

"Would you like tea in bed?" her husband asked her.

"I'd love some."

"And I'd love to bring you some," he said, grinning. "In fact, I'll do anything. I'd stand on my head in the middle of the street in a snowstorm if it meant you'd be with me every Christmas morning for the rest of my life." Leaning forward, he pressed his lips to hers. "Merry Christmas, my beautiful wife."

"Merry Christmas, my silly husband."

"I'll be back in a minute with your tea." Bruce kissed her again, and then he was gone.

Rachel sat up in bed and rearranged her pillows. She held one hand over her stomach, letting her unborn daughter know how much she was loved. Next Christmas, this little one would be crawling around, eager to tear open packages. Ra-chel closed her eyes, savoring the vision of all the wonderful things the next year would hold.

Bruce returned with a steaming cup of tea, which he

handed her just as Jolene burst into the master bedroom, carrying Poppy.

"Rachel, you're awake, aren't you?"

"I'm getting there."

"Hurry up," the girl said, holding the puppy close to Rachel. "There are gifts out there just waiting to be opened."

"Okay, okay," Rachel said, squinting as Poppy licked her face. "Give me five minutes."

"That long?" Jolene whined, and then laughed out loud, sounding young and carefree.

"You're certainly in a good mood," Bruce teased, hugging his daughter.

"Daddy, it's Christmas. Everyone's in a good mood on Christmas Day."

If only that was true. Memories of her childhood drifted into Rachel's mind. After her mother's death, she'd gone to live with an unmarried aunt who'd seen Christmas as a commercial wasteland and refused to partake in anything so frivolous. There'd been no tree, no presents. It was just like every other day, except that Rachel didn't have to go to school.

She'd listened attentively as her friends told of their wonderful holidays and longed for the time when she'd celebrate Christmas with a family of her own. And here it was, unfolding right before her eyes.

Setting her mug aside, she tossed back the covers and slid out of bed. "Did someone say something about presents?" she asked.

Jolene placed Poppy on the floor, grabbed Rachel's hand and led her into the living room. "I put the casserole in the oven."

"Great. Did you preheat it to three hundred and fifty degrees first?"

"Yes, I did."

"You're going to be a terrific cook."

"I already am," Jolene said. "I made dinner the whole time you were gone and I did a good job, didn't I, Dad?"

"Yup." Bruce joined Rachel on the sofa. "Unfortunately, I didn't have much of an appetite."

Jolene sighed. "All he could think about was you and the baby."

"But Rachel's with us now, and that's what matters."

"Hey," Rachel said, "are we going to sit around all morning discussing the past or are we going to open gifts?"

Her question got the desired results. "Open gifts!" Jolene said with renewed energy.

Rachel went back to the bedroom for her robe and tied it loosely about her waist as she slipped her feet into fuzzy slippers.

Bruce had a nice fire going in the fireplace, and Poppy lay stretched out in front of it, snuffling in her sleep. The radio was tuned to a station that played Christmas music without any commercial interruptions. The casserole was baking in the oven, and the scent of bacon and cheese wafted into the room. This was as idyllic a picture as Rachel could ever have conjured up in some blissful fantasy.

"Who gets to open a gift first?" she asked, settling onto the sofa with her husband.

"I have to sort through them all before we open any," Jolene said. "I'll hand everything out and *then* we open them. One at a time," she ordered.

"Then get to it, girl," Bruce said with a laugh, reaching for Rachel's hand.

Jolene walked over to the lighted tree, which they'd just finished decorating yesterday, and got down on all fours, rooting through the gifts. She pulled one out and sat back, checking the name tag.

"This one's for Dad," she said and, stretching forward, passed it to Bruce.

He held the rectangular package close to his ear and shook it. "Who's it from?"

"Rachel," Jolene said. "Looks like a shirt to me."

"Don't spoil the surprise."

"Dad, it's obvious." Jolene grinned from ear to ear.

She disappeared again, foraging under the tree.

"What are you looking for now?" Bruce asked, setting the box at his feet.

"A special gift," Jolene said, her voice muffled.

"Who's it for?"

"Rachel, from me."

"Oh, I love getting gifts." Rachel smiled at Bruce. Considering the months of tension between her and Jolene, she was pleased that her stepdaughter was so eager to give her presents. She leaned her head against her husband's shoulder. This was what she'd always hoped Christmas would be like, surrounded by people she loved and who loved her.

"Here it is," Jolene announced, scooting out backward from beneath the huge tree.

Rachel took the package from her. It was the size and shape of a shoe box.

"Can Rachel open it now?" Jolene asked her father. "Even though that's not the rules."

"That's up to Rachel."

Jolene looked at her, eyes dark and serious. "Will you, Rach?"

"If you want me to."

"I do." She sat on the floor as she waited for Rachel to unwrap her gift.

"I made it myself," Jolene said, her eyes bright as she bit her lower lip. "I hope you like it."

"I'm sure I will." Rachel carefully slid the ribbon off and

peeled back the decorative paper. The box had, indeed, held Jolene's new gym shoes. Rachel lifted the lid and stared down at a white hand-knit baby blanket, enfolded in pink tissue. Rachel hardly knew what to say. "You…you knit this yourself?" She drew it out, marveling at the complexity of the design.

Jolene nodded. "We learned how to knit in an after-school class. I bought the pattern and the yarn at that craft shop downtown, the one where Mrs. Flemming works. I worked on it every day. I made a lot of mistakes," she admitted. She hurried to Rachel's side, kneeling in front of her. "See? Here's one."

It was so small Rachel had to squint to see it.

"There are other mistakes, too."

"Oh, Jolene, it's *perfect*." Rachel struggled to hold back tears. "I'll bring your sister home from the hospital in it."

"You will?"

Rachel leaned forward and brought Jolene toward her, kissing her hair. "I'll always treasure it, because you made it for me and the baby."

"Don't tell me you're both going to get all weepy on me," Bruce groaned.

"I might," she said, struggling to hold back the tears.

Jolene raised her arms and wrapped Rachel in a big hug.

"I love you, Jolene," Rachel whispered.

"I love you, too… You're going to be a great mother."

Bruce put his arms around them both. "She already *is* a great mom," he said.

Jolene nodded and met Rachel's eyes. "Yes, she is."

19

This was Sheriff Troy Davis's first Christmas with his wife, Faith. It was a second marriage for both. Each of them had been blessed with a long and happy first marriage and each had suffered the loss of their beloved partner. Recently, they'd found a renewed sense of purpose and love with each other.

As it was their first major holiday together, they'd divided the time between his daughter, Megan, and her family and Faith's son, Scott. Christmas Eve had been spent with Megan, her husband, Craig, and their infant daughter, Cassandra.

Today, Troy and Faith were headed for Scott's home. Late Christmas morning, Troy loaded up the car with the Christmas gifts and treats Faith had prepared for her son's family. They'd delivered a carload of presents and homemade sweets to Megan the night before, as well. Faith had been baking for weeks, not that Troy was complaining. He hadn't enjoyed the holidays this much in a very long while. During the last years of her life, Sandy had been in a nursing home, and Troy hadn't bothered with decorating their house or putting up a tree. For the first time since Sandy went into the care facility, it actually felt like Christmas to him. He hadn't realized how much he'd missed all the fuss and bother.

"Can we make one stop?" Faith asked as she climbed into the front seat beside him.

"Sure," he said. "Where?"

"The Beldons'. Peggy and Bob were so kind to bring us that plate of goodies. I'd like to reciprocate."

"The Beldons probably have more than their fair share of candy and cookies."

"This is a peach-and-raspberry cobbler. They can eat it now or put it in the freezer. Peggy's always thinking of others, and I wanted to do something nice for her."

"Then of course we'll drop by."

"It'll just take a moment," Faith promised. "In fact, you don't even need to get out of the car."

Troy reached for his wife's hand and gave it a gentle squeeze. He loved Faith. He'd loved her when they were in high school, and he loved her now. After Sandy died, Troy had never expected to marry again. And then… Faith came back into his life. Their courtship had had its ups and downs, but despite some confused and difficult times, Troy wouldn't change a thing. Faith was with him now. Nothing else mattered.

The Beldons' Thyme and Tide Bed-and-Breakfast on Cranberry Point was en route to Scott's house, so it really wasn't out of their way. Troy entered the long driveway and noticed three vehicles parked in the area reserved for guests. He remembered that Bob had mentioned that their children would be visiting from Spokane, which accounted for two cars. The other must be a guest.

"I'll be right back," Faith assured him as he eased to a stop.

She got out of the car, opened the rear passenger door and took out the cobbler in its lidded plastic container. She'd put a bow on top, giving it a festive look. He hoped she'd tucked one in their freezer for him—and he didn't need the bow!

Bob Beldon answered the door and Faith went inside. Troy listened to Christmas music and sang along with Burl Ives on the car radio. Two or three minutes later, Faith reappeared and motioned for him.

Troy turned off the engine and started toward the house. Something was definitely wrong. He could see it in Faith's stance as she stood in the doorway, waiting for him.

When he approached, Faith said, "Oh, Troy, I'm afraid there's a bit of a…situation here. I think you might be able to help."

"What kind of situation?"

She moved aside and he walked into the house. The instant he did, he heard a woman shrieking and crying uncontrollably in the background. She seemed to be having some sort of temper tantrum. Troy heard things being thrown against the walls.

"It's one of our guests," Bob said, coming toward him. "She arrived with Kent Morehouse, Beth's ex-husband. We thought they were a couple—but apparently not. Seems she was supposed to meet up with a sailor from the navy base, but something happened. She hasn't been able to tell us what."

"So what's her relationship with Kent?"

"Friends, I guess. She works for him."

Kent wandered into the foyer with his hands in his pockets. He looked completely baffled. "I'm sorry," he said. "I tried talking to Danielle, but she's too upset to make much sense. As far as I can tell, the young man she came to see has decided to dump her."

"On Christmas Day?" Troy wasn't impressed with the sailor's timing.

"She hasn't stopped crying…"

"For hours," Peggy inserted. "And throwing stuff. I don't know if she's broken anything but…"

"She refuses to answer the door," Bob added. "She must have blocked it with a chair or something, because we can't get in."

Troy could well imagine what this was doing to the family's celebration.

"I think all Danielle wants to do now is get back to California. I went on the internet to find a flight, but talking to her is impossible." Kent shook his head.

Troy moved down the hallway to the guest bedrooms and knocked on the door. It wasn't hard to tell which room was Danielle's.

"Sheriff Troy Davis," he announced authoritatively.

Silence followed, which was a blessing after the racket of the past several minutes. Then they heard the unmistakable sound of furniture being moved.

"What seems to be the problem here?" he asked when Danielle slowly opened the bedroom door.

"I have to get out of here," Danielle said, dabbing her eyes with a wadded tissue. "I *hate* this place."

"I found a flight that can get you to LAX, leaving Sea-Tac in a few hours," Kent rushed to say. This was obviously the information he'd been wanting to tell her for some time.

"Fine," she said, slamming her suitcase shut. It was on her bed, although little else was. In fact, the room looked as if it'd been hit by a hurricane. Bedding lay on the floor. So did a potted poinsettia, with dirt scattered everywhere, and a framed picture, its glass now broken. And that wasn't all…

"I'm really sorry about this," Kent said, apologizing to the Beldons.

Danielle seemed to think he was talking to her. "Why didn't Hunter tell me sooner?" she wailed. "It worked out so well that I could come here for Christmas… He said he'd be tied up, but I said that was fine because my boss invited me to visit his family until Christmas Day and then…then…" She broke into a fresh bout of tears. Angrily, she grabbed the tissue box from the floor and jerked out three. "Then Hunter waited until this morning to tell me…. He didn't even do it to my face. Instead, he sent me a text message and said he was seeing someone else. He let me come all this way and make a fool of myself." She dabbed at her eyes again. "Now all I want is to get away from this horrible town…."

"We'll need to get her to the airport."

Kent shifted uncomfortably. "I had plans with my family but I feel responsible for her. I'll drive her to the airport."

"I want to go home!" Danielle screamed. "I don't care who takes me to the airport. Isn't there a taxi or something?"

"I have a friend who owns a car service," Troy offered. "He can drive you to the airport."

"Fine!" Danielle shouted. "I want to leave *now.*"

"Please call your friend," Kent said. "And I'll pay whatever it costs."

The small group watched as Danielle finished gathering up the last of her things, stuffing them in her carry-on. Kent seemed relieved not to be taking her to the airport. She swung the suitcase off the bed, and it landed on the floor with a loud thump. Straightening her shoulders, she wheeled her bag out of the room, ignoring everyone.

As soon as she'd left, Kent slumped on the edge of the bed and heaved a sigh. He lowered his head and plowed his fingers through his hair.

"You all right?" Troy asked.

Kent nodded. "I've made a big mess of things."

"It's not your fault the sailor broke it off."

"No," Kent said. "My mistake was taking her out to meet

Beth and the girls. I let them assume Danielle and I were romantically involved. It was a stupid thing to do and I regretted it almost immediately." He looked disgusted with himself. "Danielle went along with it, since she knows I still love my ex-wife and she wanted to do me a favor. But she totally overplayed her role." He sighed again. "I wanted to tell Beth last night, but before I had a chance Danielle phoned in hysterics because she couldn't get hold of her boyfriend. After that, the situation went from bad to worse." He gestured around him. "I've botched everything."

"Don't be so sure," Faith said, coming to stand next to Troy.

"Do you think there's a way to salvage this?" Kent asked hopefully.

"Troy and I were in the pew behind you and Beth at the service last night. I believe if you speak to Beth honestly, you'll discover she feels the same way."

Kent's eyes brightened. "Really?"

Faith nodded.

"First let me see if I can arrange this airport ride," Troy said, reaching for his cell. He punched in the appropriate number and waited. Logan, the son of a friend, had recently started a car service, focusing on airport transportation. He was hungry enough to take the fare, even if it was Christmas Day.

After a short conversation, Troy closed his cell. "He'll be here within thirty minutes."

"Have you ever done anything so stupid you wonder what you could possibly have been thinking?" Kent asked Troy.

The sheriff wasn't sure whether this was a real question or a rhetorical one. He decided to answer it, anyway. "We all have, at one time or other. All you can do is learn from it—and you've certainly done that. And like Faith says, things will probably turn out okay."

Kent looked up and gave a slight nod. "I appreciate the encouraging words."

After a few minutes, Troy returned to the kitchen. The Beldons had gathered there. Danielle sat in the living room next to her suitcase, crying quietly. He did feel sorry for her. This couldn't be easy; no broken relationship was.

Kent wanted to pay for the damages, but the Beldons refused. And at their insistence, no charges would be laid. They, too, sympathized with Danielle, despite their exasperation with her out-of-control behavior.

To be on the safe side Troy and Faith remained at the B and B until Logan arrived and Danielle departed.

They left a few minutes later. Faith sighed as Troy turned out of the driveway.

"Well, that was an unexpected interlude," she said in a good-humored voice. "I don't know what would've happened to that poor girl—and Kent—if we hadn't got there when we did. You're my hero, Troy Davis."

"And you're my sweetheart," he returned, smiling in her direction.

20

"Now what?" Will Jefferson asked. He held his gloved hands upright like a surgeon about to enter the operating theater.

"It's a turkey," Miranda Sullivan teased, "not an appendectomy."

Will lowered his arms.

"We're going to stuff it," Miranda said.

"You mean I'm actually going to put my hands *inside* that bird?" His look was incredulous.

"Yes." It was difficult to keep a straight face when Will took everything so seriously.

"I've never done this before."

Miranda rolled her eyes. "Really? You could've fooled me."

"Are you making fun of me?" he asked, eyebrows raised.

"I'm doing my best not to."

Will grinned. "Well, this is hard work. First time in my life that I've cooked a turkey."

"We'll do fine."

"I'm glad you're with me," he said, "and not just because of the turkey."

"I'm happy to be here."

Quite unexpectedly, Will had invited Miranda to spend Christmas Day with him. They'd worked together at the Harbor Street Art Gallery for the past several months. She'd started as part-time help, working a couple of days a week. Gradually, Will had increased her hours.

In the beginning they hadn't gotten along. He thought she was too opinionated; she thought he was stubborn and dictatorial. But as the weeks progressed they'd formed a strong friendship. She'd taken a step toward compromise and he'd taken one, too, and they'd met in the middle.

Recently...well, *very* recently, that friendship took another turn. Miranda wasn't ready to put a name to it; she wasn't sure it was safe for her heart to define it. Not yet. But...there was definitely a sense of excitement that sizzled between them.

They'd kissed. She'd kissed him once, shocking herself far more than she'd shocked Will. And he'd kissed her. More than once.

Will had moved into his childhood home a few weeks earlier, purchasing the residence on Eagle Crest Avenue from his mother. This made it possible for Charlotte and Ben to move into the Sanford assisted-living complex without the additional worry of what would happen to their home.

Will and his sister, Olivia, had come up with the idea and coincidentally the move had benefited Miranda, too. She lived near Gig Harbor, a twenty-minute drive from Cedar Cove. The lease on her apartment was up, and she'd been hoping to move closer to the art gallery when Will approached her about living in his apartment on the premises. He'd had it remodeled and she could move in whenever she wished.

It was an offer too good to refuse. Her best friend, Shirley Bliss, had urged her to accept. Miranda grew a bit sad as she thought about Shirley. They'd become close after they'd both lost their husbands. Miranda had been married to an artist and Shirley was one herself. They'd helped each other adjust to widowhood.

Shirley had remarried a couple of months ago, and as soon as Tanni, her daughter, graduated from high school, Shirley planned to move to California with her new husband, Larry Knight, who was a nationally known and highly respected artist.

It would be hard to see Shirley leave the area and yet Miranda couldn't begrudge her friend this happiness. They'd stay in touch, of course, but...it wasn't the same.

Will had been attracted to Shirley. His ego had taken a beating when she chose Larry Knight over him. The fact that he'd introduced Shirley to Larry had made the whole situation especially galling for Will; Miranda understood that. When he'd first started paying attention to *her,* Miranda had reason to think he was trying to make Shirley jealous. She wouldn't stand for that and made sure Will knew it.

Lately, however, there'd been a shift in the way he treated her. But his first tentative attempts to deepen their relationship didn't work, mainly because Miranda didn't trust him. He'd invited her to dinner and she'd refused. Later, she felt bad about that and she'd taken him a store-bought chicken. So they'd ended up having dinner together, after all. That was the night he'd invited her to spend Christmas Day with him.

"Now what?" Will asked. He was pushing the homemade stuffing into the cavity.

"Keep going until you can't get any more inside."

"Okay. Although this is kind of a revolting activity."

She laughed. "Will, why did you buy a twenty-three-pound bird for just the two of us?" she asked.

"I don't know... At least there'll be plenty of leftovers."

"Enough to feed an army," she muttered.

"And a navy," he added.

He finished with the stuffing, and washed his hands while Miranda basted the turkey and placed an aluminum-foil tent over top. "Okay, it's ready for the oven," she said.

She held open the oven door and Will slid the turkey inside. "How long will it take?" he asked.

"Twenty minutes a pound, so do the math."

"Seven and a half *hours?*"

"You'll build up an appetite," she said. "And we can have some crackers and cheese while we wait."

"And a nice glass of wine…" Will pulled off his oven mitts. "Any other suggestions?"

"As a matter of fact, yes." She left the kitchen and went into the living room to collect her bag. Reaching inside, she took out a wrapped gift. "For you," she said playfully, handing him the large square box.

Will looked a bit uneasy, which told her what she already suspected. He hadn't purchased her a gift. She hadn't really expected him to. Besides, this was more of a thank-you for having her over.

"It's small, just a token," she said. She didn't want to embarrass him or make him feel guilty for not reciprocating.

"Go ahead and open it," she urged.

"You shouldn't have," he said theatrically. He sat down on the sofa and tore away the paper. When he saw the jigsaw puzzle, he grinned. The picture was a seascape, with dolphins and tropical fish swimming in a blue, blue ocean. "Hey, good idea! We can put it together this afternoon."

Miranda stood and started to clear off the table. "I used to enjoy doing puzzles," she told him. "This table's big enough to lay out all the pieces."

"Here. Now you open my gift," Will said.

Miranda turned around, leaning against the table's edge. She frowned as Will gave her the small, beautifully wrapped gift. The shape and size hinted that it'd come from a jewelry store.

"Is this a marriage proposal?" she joked, and then laughed nervously, wondering how she could have asked something so idiotic.

"Not yet," he returned quite seriously.

Miranda stared at the package, almost afraid to remove the wrapping.

"Open it," he said.

Reluctantly, she untied the ribbon. "You didn't wrap this yourself."

"You're right, the store did." He stood next to her and nudged her to continue unwrapping.

"I...wasn't expecting anything like this," she said. "All I got you is a puzzle."

"I know you'll be surprised, which makes it all the more special."

Her hand trembled as she carefully slipped off the paper. Holding her breath, Miranda lifted the lid of the small blue box. Inside was a gold coin, a very old one, she guessed, framed by a gold bezel.

"It's from a sunken treasure ship found off the Florida coast," Will explained.

Taking it from the box, she saw that the coin was attached to a fine gold chain. Will took it out of her fingers, placed it around her neck and secured the clasp. She could feel the coin resting at the base of her throat, the metal smooth and cool. Automatically, she pressed her hand over it.

"It's treasure, Miranda," Will whispered. "Just like you are to me."

She blinked a couple of times, hardly able to fathom that Will Jefferson would do this for her. Or that he'd say such a thing.

"I…" Speaking seemed impossible, and whatever she said, whatever words of appreciation she managed to form, would never be enough. "I don't know how to…thank you."

"You're kidding. You, speechless? I don't believe it."

"Don't joke, Will. I mean it. I don't think anyone's ever done anything like this for me."

Will kissed her then. Really kissed her. He was gentle and loving, and when he raised his head, his eyes were filled with promise.

21

"Mom, what time will Dad get here?" Sophie asked, as she and Bailey hurried into the kitchen. "Is Danielle coming, too?"

Beth had expected them long before now. She was clearing away the last of their brunch dishes, irritated that she hadn't heard from Kent. She was determined not to contact him, although she considered it bad manners to keep his family waiting on Christmas Day. "I don't think your father actually gave us a time," she said with more generosity than she felt. He'd certainly implied it would be that morning.

"Oh," Sophie murmured.

"It's already afternoon," Bailey said. "We've never opened our gifts this late."

That seemed like a minor complaint to Beth. The thought of spending Christmas Day with Kent's…friend was enough to make her feel like going back to bed. Playing hostess to Danielle was above and beyond the call of duty.

It hadn't bothered her nearly as much until she'd realized how deeply she still loved Kent. For the past three years, she'd been able to live with a degree of contentment, refusing to acknowledge how lonely she was.

"Mom, call Dad and ask when he's going to be here," Bailey said.

"Why don't *you* phone him?" Beth suggested. She purposely banished the picture of Kent and Danielle cuddled together while their daughters impatiently awaited his arrival.

"Okay."

Cell phone in hand, Bailey sat down, propping her elbows on the kitchen table.

Beth tuned out her daughter's conversation as she silently prayed for the strength to get through the day. Depression weighed heavily on her. If she managed to survive this Christmas, she'd tell Kent she'd made a mistake. She loved him and wanted him back in her life. Only she couldn't tell him that in Danielle's presence.

No, she might as well forget any hope of a reconciliation, she told herself. Danielle was young and beautiful and competitive. She wouldn't give Kent up easily. Beth had made the mistake, and now she had to live with the consequences.

"Mom? Mom?"

"Yes," Beth said, turning her thoughts away from her ex-husband.

"Did you hear what I said?"

"Sorry, no."

"Are you feeling all right?" Sophie asked, joining her sister at the table.

"I...don't know." What Beth really wanted was to escape to her room with a fake flu bug and leave the girls to celebrate Christmas with Kent and Danielle. But she couldn't do that to her daughters. She'd muddle through and somehow find the strength to pretend all was well.

"Dad's on his way," Bailey told her.

"Good." She forced a smile. Turning from the sink, she

grabbed a dish towel and wiped her hands dry. Needing fortification, she went to freshen her makeup.

Upstairs in her bathroom, she stared at her reflection in the mirror. Sad. Sad. Sad. She straightened her shoulders, saying, "You can do this. You can do this."

When she walked down the stairs she found Kent standing by the front door. She stopped abruptly before she reached the bottom. He looked up at her; their eyes met, and her heart immediately reacted. She gave him a tentative smile.

Kent smiled back.

He spoke first. "Merry Christmas," he said.

"Thank you." Her voice sounded wispy. "Merry Christmas."

"Dad," Bailey said excitedly, rushing over to him. She paused and looked around. "Where's Danielle?"

Kent broke eye contact with her. "She isn't here."

"Isn't here? Did she stay at the B and B?"

"Not…exactly." He bent down to take off his boots.

"Then where is she?"

Kent glanced at his watch. "I imagine she's at the airport about now."

"The airport?" Sophie repeated. "I thought she was spending Christmas in Cedar Cove."

"That was her original plan. She came with me, hoping to meet up with a sailor she'd met when he was on leave in California. Apparently, she read more into the relationship than she should have."

"*What?*" Beth asked in shock. "She came to meet up with a sailor? But…"

"Danielle was hoping to see this guy, Hunter. She and I were talking about that, and I told her I still had feelings for you, but wasn't sure what to do when you asked me to come here for Christmas. She offered to come with me and—"

"Wait." Beth's hand flew to her chest. "I asked *you?* I think there's been some misunderstanding." Beth noticed that the girls had skittered off as she spoke.

Kent frowned. "You mean you didn't?"

Beth frowned, too. "Are you saying you *weren't* the one who wanted to spend Christmas as a family?"

"Bailey! Sophie!" Beth and Kent shouted at the same time.

"Bailey Madison. Sophie Lynn," Beth threw in for good measure.

Their two daughters reappeared, looking sheepish.

"Okay, we admit it," Bailey said, hands in her back hip pockets. "The thing is, Sophie and I think this whole divorce is wrong. We thought if the two of you were together at Christmas, you'd realize what a terrible mistake you made. Then Dad had to go and ruin everything by bringing Danielle."

"I didn't exactly bring her," he clarified. "Danielle told me she intended to visit the area at the same time, and we discovered we'd be on the same flight and had booked rooms at the same bed-and-breakfast."

"Just a minute," Beth said in confusion. "But she works with you, right? That's all true?"

"Yes. She works in the accounting department."

"Are…are you… Have you ever been involved?"

"Good heavens, no."

"But…"

Kent broke eye contact. "While we were at the airport waiting for the plane, we started talking. Just like I already told you, I explained that I wasn't sure how I felt about being here this Christmas. I missed my wife, but the girls had hinted that you were seeing the local vet and I didn't want to be a fifth wheel. So Danielle said what you needed was some competition and I…agreed. I felt it was worth a shot, anyway. So she put on this ridiculous act and—" He shrugged, glancing up the staircase at Beth. "I regretted the entire charade immediately, but by then it seemed too late. The whole thing had taken on a momentum of its own...." He shrugged. "I just hope you can forgive me."

The girls sent each other a triumphant smile, as if they were personally responsible for this turn of events.

Kent continued to hold Beth's look.

She bit her lip and started down the remaining steps.

"Problem is," he told his daughters, "I don't know how your mother feels about me. It's been three years."

"Mom's crazy about you," Bailey said.

"Of *course* Mom loves you," Sophie added her voice to her sister's. "She'd be a fool not to."

"What about Ted Reynolds?" Kent asked.

"What about him?" Bailey returned. "Mom loves you, not Ted."

"I'd rather have your mother tell me so herself." Kent stood with one foot braced against the bottom step. He stretched out his arm to Beth.

She placed her hand in his. "Oh, Kent, I've never stopped loving you. I never will."

He grabbed her by the waist and lifted her down the last two stairs, setting her feet on the ground.

As Beth slipped her arms around his neck, she buried her face in his shoulder. "We've both been so foolish."

He kissed her again and then again, as if he couldn't get enough of her.

Cradling his face with her hands, Beth gazed into his eyes, aware of their daughters grinning from the sidelines.

"These girls have a lot of 'splainin' to do," Kent said in a stage whisper.

"It was Bailey's idea," Sophie maintained.

"Both of you were being ridiculous about this stupid di-

vorce," Bailey said quickly. "We felt we had to do something."
She obviously intended to share the blame—or the praise.

"So you conspired to bring us together," Kent muttered.

"You aren't mad, are you?" Bailey asked, moving closer
to her sister.

Kent brought his attention back to Beth and kissed the tip
of her nose. "Are *you* upset?" he asked.

With her husband's arms around her and the Christmas tree
lights shining in the background, Beth had to admit she wasn't.
"Not in the least. Actually, I think it was a brilliant idea."

"Okay, if you must know," Sophie said, "I did help Bailey a little."

"Isn't this the best Christmas ever?" Bailey exclaimed, hugging her sister. "And we haven't even opened our gifts yet."

Beth had to agree. This was the best Christmas of her life.

Epilogue

Valentine's Day

"This is so romantic," Bailey said to her sister. "I'm so happy, I want to cry." They left the kitchen, ready to set out the plates and forks to serve cake to their parents' guests.

"We did it," Sophie said, almost giddy with happiness. "I don't know *how,* but it worked. Mom and Dad are back together."

"Just like they were meant to be."

Their parents were remarried and their dad was now living at 1225 Christmas Tree Lane, where he planned to take on the business aspects of the farm.

Beth came down the stairs and into the living room, with Kent directly behind her. "Oh, girls, the table looks lovely."

"Thanks, Mom."

The coffee- and teapots were filled and the cake sliced. This wasn't a wedding reception, Beth had explained to her daughters. It was an opportunity to introduce Kent to her friends and neighbors in Cedar Cove.

Bailey thought her father had never looked handsomer or her mother more beautiful. They were constantly together now. It had started while they were all in Whistler during

Christmas break. Bailey couldn't remember a time they'd had more fun as a family. After their short vacation, Kent had returned to California. Before he could move north to Washington State, he needed to make some decisions and changes.

Within six weeks he'd sold his engineering company to his partner, packed up his house and found responsible tenants. In between all those negotiations and all that packing, Kent flew up to Cedar Cove practically every weekend to be with their mother. It was the most romantic thing.

They'd remarried in a private ceremony on January twenty-eighth. Only the girls and Kent's brother Michael, who'd come in from California to act as best man, had been in attendance. Afterward, their parents had sent out announcements to family and friends. From the comments Bailey heard, everyone seemed to think this remarriage was wonderful. To Bailey and Sophie it was just plain…right.

"We have our first guests," Sophie called out, standing by the living room window. "It's Grace, the lady who has Beau."

"Grace Harding," Beth said. "And her husband, Cliff." She headed for the door.

"There are four of them," Sophie added.

"The other two are Olivia and Jack Griffin."

Their mother ushered their guests in out of the rain. Grace and Olivia stepped inside the house and were warmly greeted by Beth and Kent.

"I think we might have met earlier," Kent said, shaking hands with the two men. "Didn't I see you at the Christmas Eve service?"

Both men nodded.

"Would you like some coffee and cake?" Bailey asked politely.

"Sure! Thanks." The two men eagerly accepted her offer while the women raised their hands to decline. "We're driving to Seattle for a Valentine's treat," Grace said. "I'm saving my calories for that."

"Me, too," Olivia chimed in. "By the way," she told Beth, "my mother sent you a small gift. The ladies in her knitting group made you several cotton dishrags. Not very romantic, perhaps, but Mom says everyone can use extras."

Beth took the package gratefully. "Charlotte is always so thoughtful."

"Oh, Ben and Mom both send their very best wishes. She wanted me to tell you that bringing the dogs to Sanford Suites has been a real blessing to everyone. They all just love working with those dogs."

"It's a help to me, too."

Bailey smiled. Apparently, her mother was using the senior citizens to help her with dog training. Beth claimed this provided two benefits in one: not only did the older people get a form of therapy spending time with the dogs, they also got a sense of purpose from it. The Reading with Rover program at the library was another of her successes.

Beth slipped an arm around Kent's waist. "I have to admit that getting those dogs to Sanford Suites can be a bit of an ordeal."

"You won't need to do it alone anymore," Kent told her and, leaning over, gave her a quick kiss.

Seeing her parents like this, so openly in love, Bailey almost forgot her job.

"Since Olivia isn't having cake, you can give me a bigger slice," Jack whispered. Bailey threw him a conspirator's smile and willingly complied.

"I heard that, Jack Griffin," the judge said from the other side of the room.

"How's Beau?" Sophie asked.

"I believe he's the smartest dog I've ever owned," Grace

said, beaming with pride. She entertained them all for several minutes with stories of the puppy's antics.

The sound of another car pulling into the driveway attracted everyone's attention. "Oh, good," Sophie said, peering out the window. "It's the couple who owns the bed-and-breakfast where Dad stayed during Christmas," she announced. "Oh, and look! They brought their dog."

"They named her Millie," Beth said. "I've been doing dog obedience classes with her and four of her siblings over the past two months."

Bob and Peggy Beldon sat down for cake and coffee just as the Griffins and Hardings left. Millie lay contentedly at Peggy's feet.

Bailey hurried into the kitchen for a doggie treat, returning just in time to hear Bob Beldon say to her father, "Welcome back to Cedar Cove." Bob dug into the white cake with raspberry filling.

"You'll never guess who we heard from," Peggy said conversationally and then, before anyone could guess, she answered her own question. "Danielle!"

Bailey was all ears. Sophie, too. Her sister set down the coffeepot and waited for the punch line.

"And?" Their dad frowned; clearly, Danielle wasn't a good memory.

"She sent a check to pay for the damage she did and wrote a letter of apology."

"I'm glad she apologized," Kent said. "She caused quite a scene."

"I'll say," Bob muttered between bites of cake. "I've been in theater for twenty years, and I've never seen more of a drama queen than that woman."

"But she had a broken heart," Sophie said, looking at Bailey. "Right?"

Her younger sister was far more charitable than Bailey was inclined to be. She had a point, though. They could afford to be generous. Their parents were together again, and, after all, Danielle's plan to make their mother jealous had started out as a misguided favor to their dad.

"In my opinion, the sailor who dumped her made a lucky escape."

"Bob," Peggy said pointedly. "Be kind."

"Okay, okay. At least she was responsible enough to pay for the damages and send us a note of apology."

"I still feel bad about all of that," Kent said. "I had no idea she'd react the way she did."

"It wasn't your fault," Bob told him. "We appreciated your offer to pay for the damages, but you weren't the one who created the mess. We mailed Danielle a letter after the first of the year, and three weeks later the check arrived." They chatted for another twenty minutes, and then the Beldons went home, with Millie heeling very nicely.

The Flemmings and their two sons stopped by next, passing the Beldons in the driveway. The dogs were at home, but Matthew and Mark spoke animatedly about their puppies whom they'd named Charlie and Sam. It was obvious that the boys had taken very successfully to dog ownership. Bailey remembered when she and Sophie had become dog owners for the first time. Watching the two brothers reminded her of the summer their parents had allowed them each to choose a puppy at the local animal shelter. Bailey got a beagle and Sophie had an Australian shepherd. They'd named them Barney and Fi Fi, and those dogs had been their companions for more than ten years.

Over the course of the next two hours, more people than Bailey could keep track of came and went. Bruce and Rachel Peyton arrived with their newborn daughter, Corinna. Jolene had gotten one of the puppies for Christmas, too, and bragged equally about Corinna and Poppy, her dog.

Troy and Faith Davis came by for cake and to chat with their parents. So did the McAfees, who were full of compliments about *their* puppy, Asta—as smart and charming as the dog in those movies, Roy bragged. Everyone was so friendly. Bailey was in charge of serving cake and Sophie busied herself with coffee and tea.

Soon after, Teri and Bobby Polgar, plus Christie and James Wilbur—proud owners of Chessie—dropped over with a bottle of champagne. Then Will Jefferson and Miranda Sullivan, sporting an engagement ring, brought *another* bottle.

By the end of the afternoon it seemed as if everyone their mother knew in town had made the effort to welcome Kent to Cedar Cove.

Everyone, that is, except Ted Reynolds, the veterinarian.

Briefly, Bailey had wondered if her mother's friend would stop by. No one said anything, but Sophie noticed and so did Bailey. That saddened her a little because she knew that Ted and her mother were fond of each other.

"Well, that looks like everyone," Beth said, carrying the leftover cake into the kitchen.

"You girls did a great job."

"Wait!" Sophie cried out. "I see a car coming down the driveway."

"It's Ted," Bailey said excitedly.

"Ted?" Beth pushed open the kitchen door and stuck her head out. "Oh, I was hoping he'd have a chance to come." She brought out a piece of cake and set it on the table, as if it'd been there all along just waiting for Ted's arrival.

Kent opened the front door and extended his hand. "Good to see you, Ted."

"You, too. I'd like you to meet my friend Lana."

Ted had a female friend? Bailey met her sister's eyes.

"Ted," Beth said, holding out her hand to him. "I'm so glad you brought Lana. I've been wanting to meet her."

Mom knew about this? Bailey thought that was a good sign. Lana was a petite attractive blonde who seemed as effervescent as Ted was low-key.

Ted stood with his hand protectively around Lana's waist. "Everyone, this is Lana Carr."

Bailey and Sophie introduced themselves after their parents did.

"Sit down, please," Beth said and gestured Ted and Lana toward the chairs. While they took their seats, Bailey and Sophie handed them plates with cake and took drink orders.

"You know, your mother and I haven't had any cake yet," their father said. "I don't suppose we could get a slice, too?"

"Sure thing, Dad."

Bailey cut two additional slices and brought them in while Sophie prepared coffee for their guests.

Bailey went back to the kitchen to start cleaning up, and Sophie joined her there a couple of minutes later. When she opened the kitchen door, the sound of their parents' laughter drifted toward her.

"Everyone seems to be getting along," Bailey commented.

"They are. I think Mom and Dad and Ted and Lana are going to be good friends. Did you hear how they met?"

"Mom and Dad?"

"No, Ted and Lana, silly."

"Tell me."

"She brought in a dog who'd been hit by a car. She used to work for a vet in Tacoma, a friend of Ted's, until she moved to Cedar Cove. His friend had mentioned Lana was single and wanted to introduce them, but Ted said the timing was bad."

"Yeah, he had his eye on our mother," Bailey murmured.

"Lana saw his picture and thought he looked like a nice guy, but let it go. She figured he'd contact her if he was interested."

"But he didn't."

"No. And then Lana found the injured dog and brought him to the nearest vet, not even knowing it was Ted until she got there. She helped him operate on the dog and did such a good job that he offered her a job at the animal hospital."

"And she accepted."

"That's such a romantic story," Sophie said.

Bailey nodded. "This is a romantic town."

Her sister gave a contented sigh.

"You know, I like Cedar Cove," Bailey said. "I like it a lot."

"I do, too."

It was the kind of town anyone would love to call home.

★ ★ ★ ★ ★